The Hooligan Navy

◆

CGC Roger B. Taney (1947)

The Hooligan Navy

A True Story About the Old Coast Guard

◆

Wesley E. Hall

Writers Club Press
San Jose New York Lincoln Shanghai

The Hooligan Navy
A True Story About the Old Coast Guard

Writers Club Press
an imprint of iUniverse.com, Inc.

For information address:
iUniverse.com, Inc.
5220 S 16th, Ste. 200
Lincoln, NE 68512
www.iuniverse.com

ISBN: 0-595-19017-0

Printed in the United States of America

Dedication

◆

To Sturgis Hiller, a first class hooligan, and all the swabs and officers of the Old Coast Guard, especially the ones who served aboard the CGC *Alert*, the CGC *Bramble*, the CGC *Chautauqua*, the CGC *Escanaba*, the CGC *Storis*, and the CGC *Taney* back in the old days.

Sturgis Hiller and Wesley Hall (Baltimore, 1948)

Epigraph

———————◆———————

BEER SWILLING PIGS
by Dolly Juhlin, ©1997

[A poetic glimpse of the "Old Guard"..."I wrote [this] with memories of my dear husband, MKC Lowell E Juhlin...best darn Coastie in the world."]

Best in the service, those old Coasties are
Ever the heroes, ever the stars

Everyone was tough, strong, smart and courageous
Real men they were, though sometimes outrageous
Sweet are the memories they hold in their hearts
Wine, women and song and a couple of false starts
In or out of trouble, honest or shady
Long live the Coasties in Hooligan's Navy

Loveable sorts, a most likable lot
Into deep water they sailed, like it or not

Now they get flack from the likes of you and me
Gone are the days when things weren't quite so P.C.
Perhaps new folks are jealous, and some women too

Inside these old Coasties are more than true blue
Give 'em some slack and loosen the line
Semper Paratus they are, their stars will always shine

[Reproduced with permission of author]

Contents

◆

Preface

———————————————◆———————————————

This is a true story of life in the U. S. Coast Guard in the late 1940's. More specifically, it is the story of an enlisted man, a sparks, who entered the Service at the end of World War II, after considerable action in the Pacific fighting the Japanese, and served aboard the cutters Alert, Bramble, Chautauqua, Escanaba, Storis, and the Taney.

It is also a brief excursion into the world of the Old Coast Guard, an outfit that measured the worth of a man by what he could do and how well he could do it. In the late 'Forties (from a distance) this "holligan navy" looked like the U. S. Navy. The uniforms were almost identical. Commissioned and enlisted alike wore small "shields" on the lower right sleeves of their uniforms, and the eagles on the officers' dress and undress caps were not quite the same. Aside from these almost invisible differences, the Navy was far more spit-and-polish, by the book.

This story began with a multitude of misunderstandings—on my part. Some of which were costly and counter productive, as the saying goes. I was a veteran of the war in the Pacific, ex-U. S. Navy, a sailor fresh out of the world's saltiest deep-sea fighting force. And here I was shipping over into a small coastal service run by the U. S. Treasury Department, an outfit that spent most of its time chasing rum runners and dope smugglers. I was certain I had signed up for a lot of fun and frolic.

To begin with, I was under the impression that Coasties were "shallow-water sailors." End of story. After all, it was their job to guard our coasts, and their ships were hardly more than *boats*. I had no illusions about how rough sea duty could be aboard small ships, because I had spent the last year and a half of WW2 aboard a one-hundred-and-ten-foot wooden subchaser battling the Japs. Despite its embarrassingly diminutive size (by Navy standards), the USS *SC-995* had faced the mighty Japanese Navy at Peleliu and in the Philippines and was doing air/sea rescue service at Saipan/Tinian at the end of the war.

At any rate, since I had served as second radio on a Navy "communications" ship (The *Subchaser 995* had been converted to a landing craft, communications (LCC) and turned over to "MacArthur's Navy" just after I went aboard), had had the responsibility of sixteen U. S. Army transceivers, in addition to the regular ship's radio, had learned how to copy press at thirty words a minute, and been subjected to every kind of emergency imaginable (including *kamikaze* attacks, meeting the enemy head-on in island invasions, typhoons, and running aground twice)—was it not reasonable to assume that I would be able to handle any radio problem the Coast Guard could hand me?

One hitch in the Coasties cleared up all of these misunderstandings for me.

Acknowledgements

◆

I want to thank Sturgis Hiller for insisting that I write about our experiences in the Coast Guard of the late 1940's. He began insisting while we were still in the Coast Guard, based in Juneau, Alaska, and calling the CGC *Storis* our home; and he continued insisting for at least twenty years, right up to the time I completed the first draft and gave him a copy.

Of course, I have to give my wife, Sharon, a great deal of credit for her unwavering support during the writing and re-writing of this *picaresque* about beer-drinking swabs and former girlfriends.

Thanks also go to Jack Eckert (of *Jack's Joint* on the Web) and Fred Siegel (of *Fred's Place* on the Web) for their help in getting the word out to former and present Coast Guardsmen that *The Hooligan Navy* was close to publication. Jack graciously placed my Chapter Twelve ("Weather Station Fox") in one corner of his fabulous web site (www.jacksjoint.com/default.htm), set it to music and inserted a picture of the fantail of the CGC *Taney* (after toning down some of my Anglo-Saxon). Fred provided me with some very good photos of the cutters on which I served (I especially appreciated the one of the CGC *Storis* breaking ice (from his Photo Album) (cf. www.fred@fredsplace.org) and gave me an opportunity (in his Reunion Hall) to let the visitors to his web site know about the eminent publication of my book.

I want to thank Dolly Juhlin for allowing me to borrow her rollicking (and accurate) poem about the hooligan navy ("Beer Drinking Pigs"), which she wrote in memory of her late husband, MKC Lowell E Juhlin.

Finally, I would like to mention that Scott Price, Deputy Branch Chief, Coast Guard Historian's Office (G-IPA-4), U. S. Coast Guard

Headquarters, 2100 Second Street, SW, Washington, D. C., gave me the go ahead to use photographs from the official U. S. Coast Guard web site.

Introduction

◆

The year was 1947 and the three of us, all recently discharged from the wartime Naval Reserve, were holed up in the basement of the men's dormitory at East Central State College, Ada, Oklahoma, like three unhappy wharf rats. We had fared poorly when the first semester's grades had come out, so poorly we had been placed on academic probation and notified by the college registrar that our G. I. Bill of Rights money would be cut off at the end of the spring semester unless we shaped up considerably.

Another serious setback, perhaps even more damaging to our morale than the loss of the free ride with Uncle Sam, had occurred one early morning at the municipal airport. Only moments after Bill Archer had mowed down half an acre of cornstalks alongside the runway, damaging the Cessna trainer in which he had just soloed, we had been informed by our instructor that Scott Milfay, ace WW2 fighter pilot, had just plunged to his death at the St. Louis International Airport. He was flying a Cessna, same model as ours, without a parachute.

E. T. Goodrich was stretched out on a bottom bunk in that basement dormitory with his hands behind his head, and it was his turn to say something. I had summarized our situation as I saw it, and Archer had suggested that we ought to get into *Kilroy* (my 1935 V-8 Ford) and drive to Garner's Pool Hall (in our hometown) and shoot some snooker. But Goodrich's position, which we knew only too well, was that we hitchhike to California and look for work. He generally prefaced his hitchhiking scenarios with, "Mostly, I just want to get out of this godforsaken, dried up, frozen wasteland."

This time he began to list the reasons he wanted to leave cold, barren Oklahoma. There were no jobs for someone with his background, there were no girls with a free spirit, there was no ocean to sail. And now that there was no war, we could hitchhike anyplace we wanted to go with none of the restrictions our relatives had had to tolerate..

"Heck, I bet we could hitchhike overseas, see the world. And there would be no Japs waiting just over the horizon."

I got up from the table where I had been writing a letter and poured myself a cup of coffee. Archer shoved his cup toward me and I filled it. Then both of us started talking at the same time. Archer reminded Goodrich that he had never gone to sea, and he sure as heck had never had to worry about the Japs, since he had sat out the war in the States. I admitted that I liked the idea of going to California, that I had done it that past summer and had found a job with Pacific Gas and Electric in the Sierra-Nevadas.

During the silence that followed, Red Foley suddenly stopped howling on the radio and a cheerful voice sang out, "Hey, all you Navy vets out there! How would you like to take a ride with the United States Coast Guard? Right now, for a very short time, the oldest of the Armed Services is offering ex-Navy sailors a two-year enlistment. And, hear this, you can keep your Navy rating!"

Archer was the first to speak. "Shallow Water Navy. I vote No."

Goodrich, without opening his eyes, said, "That outfit never leaves the States. I think I'd like to travel some before I settle down, see the world."

"I like the part about the two-year hitch," I said. "We could take anything that long. I think I would like to reenlist in the Navy.

That's the way the conversation wound down. At the time I thought it was a total stalemate. Archer quite frankly did not want to go anyplace, Goodrich wanted to hitchhike to anyplace, and I was about ready to go back to the Navy. The Maritime Service also sounded good to me. As a ship's radio operator, I would have no trouble finding a ship.

One thing for sure, it was our last day at East Central State. That much we had agreed upon. College life was not for us. And Archer's argument that we could survive forever on the twenty dollars a week we received from the *Fifty-two Twenty Club* (another handout from Uncle Sam) was sounding more ridiculous by the minute.

"Who needs a ride?" I asked, finally, getting up and going to my bunk. "I'm heading for Konawa and the River Bend."

"I'm heading for California," said Goodrich. "I've had it with this place. Anybody goin' with me?"

Archer turned and stared at me. I nodded and he nodded.

"Tell you what," I said. "Let's go have a talk with our folks and then head for Okie City and check out the Armed Services, see what each of them has to offer."

"I'm not joinin' anything," said Archer, "but I'll go to the City with you."

Goodrich laughed and we exchanged glances. "Old Arch just can't resist a party, but when it comes down to something serious he heads for Garner's."

Shipping Over Fever

———————◆———————

The decision, which had not been an easy one, had been made, the papers had been signed, and, on that crisp, cold day in February, 1947, my two friends and I raised our right hands and swore an oath to uphold the Constitution of the United States and to obey our superior officers in the U. S. Coast Guard.

Semper paratus!

And although the three of us were ex-Navy sailors, veterans of World War Two, and natives of Seminole County, Oklahoma, we were about as different in temperament and inclination as three young men could possibly be.

In February of 1947 I was twenty-one, six-three in height, attractive to the girls (mostly because of my flaming red hair and green eyes), and ready for anything. As the sixth son of Horace Greely Hall, a dirt farmer and itinerant Baptist preacher, I had received an excellent education in Matthew, Mark, Luke, and John, as well as the Arts and Crafts of Fisticuffs. Looking back, I was perhaps a bit arrogant and chauvinistic. I had, after all, grown up in the fabled River Bend Country of Seminole County, Oklahoma, where male chauvinism was in full bloom. To cover up any shortcomings I might have in the social graces, repartee, and such I had developed a volatile temper that was cocked and ready at any given moment.

Just prior to this and for a period of three years I had operated sixteen
U. S. Army transceivers and a twenty millimeter anti-aircraft gun aboard
a 110-foot wooden subchaser in the central and western Pacifics. Hence,
the life of a Ruptured Duck, which at first had seemed so delightful and
challenging, had rapidly become a bit too tame for me.

My two friends, so like me in terms of circumstances but so different
in every other way, were as ready for an adventure as I was.Eugene
Tuney "Gooch" Goodrich was, like me, twenty-one and unattached. In
his brighter and happier moments, he resembled an aging Bogart down
on his luck. However, I knew him to be a calm, happy-go-lucky fellow
without a mean bone in his body. He was the calm, level-headed member of our trio in the clinches, the one who finally said, "Come on, let's
go home."

Billie Don "Curly Bill" Archer, unattached and irresponsible, came
from a family of musicians, good-time Charlies, and moonshiners, a
matriarchy whose roots were smalltown but definitely not back country. He had never done a lick of physical labor in his life at the time I
knew him, but he was an adventurer and a good sport, and, a thing that
I admired a great deal, fearless in the face of imminent danger. Some of
his detractors accused him of being too dumb to know fear.

The three of us had arrived in Konawa, Oklahoma, on that February
morning, our day of departure for Oklahoma City and the world, with
no expectations of a local or national turnout. And we were not disappointed. We did, however, anticipate and receive the attentions of a very
pretty soda jerk by the name of Patsy Huddleston, who was present at
the Temple Pharmacy Drug Store, where the Trailways bus paused once
each weekday morning to pick up the mail and a passenger or two.

We had spent the night at my parents' farm in the River Bend, talking and drinking strong black coffee until daylight.

Jamie Lee, the prettiest face and body in that part of the country, had
contrived to spend the night with Jessica, my kid sister; and in the heavy
darkness just following a false dawn, on the bitterly cold front porch,

she threw her arms around my neck and clung there until I finally laughed and said, "Okay, okay, I give up! I won't go!"

"Rusty, you fibber! You would die and fraternize with the Devil before you'd give up this crazy scheme of yours!" She pulled herself off the floor, snuggling beneath my left ear. "All I ask is that you write to me and let me know what you're doin'. No, there's one more thing I'm askin' of you, and you already know what it is."

"I don't have a clue."

"You know! Don't fall in love with any of them West Coast bathing beauties."

At that point Goodrich and Archer emerged from the kitchen, closely followed by my whole family. The three of us, having said our says, jumped into the family's old Buick truck and, with my old ex-mule skinner dad at the steering wheel, left quickly. In Konawa I offered to treat everyone to breakfast at the Pigg Stand, my excuse being that I might as well splurge because the U. S. Coast Guard was about to start picking up the tab for everything.

"Don't mind if I do," said my father, nosing the old flatbed truck in at an angle to the curb. He was in extremely good spirits because the evening before I had given him the ignition key to my beloved *Kilroy*, a '35 Ford V-8 sedan in excellent condition. "Look's like Ima's about ready to open up."

The four of us watched as fat little Ima Pigg, an identical triplet and co-owner, waddled through the lighted cafe and unlocked the front door.

Ima and her sisters took after both sides of their family. The Piggs were all short and fat and mean-tempered, while the maternal side, the Shorts, were without exception tall and skinny and full of pranks and practical jokes. The three girls, looking like peas from the same Pigg pod, had turned out to be short, fat, good-natured pranksters.

"Believe it or not," sighed Archer, "that roly-poly gal was once trim and quite pretty. Can you believe that?"

"I cannot believe that," said Goodrich.

"I've known them only about ten years," I exaggerated, "but it seems to me they started out fat and got fatter."

"Well, boys," said my old man, ignoring what had gone before and getting noisily out of the truck, "I guess it'll be awhile before you'll be back in these parts."

"He hopes," I kidded. "Don't you think he ought to be the one to pick up the tab, fellas?"

Instantly, my father, who was not nearly as deaf as most people thought, pretended to be getting back inside the car.

"Aw, take pity on him," said Gooch, his face still deadpan. "I understand all that money he buried in his backyard was dug up by the hogs and eaten a long time ago."

"Don't joke about a thing like that," said Dad. "Let's git inside and try some of Ima's coffee."

"Can I just go inside and sit?" asked Archer. "I think I've had enough of that stuff to last me all the way to California!" Before anybody could say anything, he added, "All I want is eggs and hashbrowns and, of course, bacon and biscuits and gravy."

*   *   *

At nine o'clock sharp, anxious to get things moving, the three of us pushed back our plates and got up, leaving Dad to finish his coffee alone. He pretended not to watch as we went to the back of the truck and gathered up our duffel bags, which we had packed in close to the cab. We waved and moved back around to the sidewalk, where he joined us, already busy with a toothpick.

"I'd drive you down to the drug store, boys," he commented off-handedly, "but I guess the exercise'll do you good."

We laughed, tossing our stuff in a pile at his feet. He ignored our teasing and stuck out his hand to Gooch.

"Eugene, you have no business foolin' around with the likes of these two juveniles," he said with great seriousness. "You're a clean, decent boy, and I for one hate to see you go off with them."

"I know, Mr. Hall. They're not a good influence on me."

Dad nodded, looking quite pleased, and turned to Archer. "Curly, your poor old uncle needs you out at the still. Why don't you git on out there and let these two boys go to the West Coast by themselves?"

"That's exactly what my uncle said!" laughed Archer. "But I reckon I'll go along to keep them out of trouble."

"Well, see that you do." Dad pumped his hand and nodded. Then, after pretending he had forgot all about me and was actually turning toward the truck, he stuck out his hand to me, without looking in my direction.

"Rusty, my boy, I told your mother when you was just a babe-in-arms you'd never turn out to be a cowboy or a farmer. Told her you'd end up ridin' the rails like your brother Cliff, or maybe somethin' even worse. I don't have the least idee why you want to go an' join up with the Navy ag'in. Looks like you'd of got enough travelin' durin' the war."

I put my left arm around his neck, feeling him stiffen in embarrassment.

"Oh, git on! There comes your bus!"

"Take care of *Kilroy*, Dad."

"Don't you worry none at all about that car." By the tone of his voice I could tell he was glad to have the hugging over. "You don't plan to come back an' claim it someday, do you?"

"Hey!" I protested. "I'm not *giving* it to you!"

"Ever'body heard you do just that. I don't hold with Indi'n givers."

"They're the worst kind," agreed Goodrich, who was one thirty-second Seminole.

Dad nodded once, tossed his hand into the air as a farewell gesture, and headed for the driver's side of the truck.

"Don't take no wooden nickels, boys."

We stood there hunched down inside the collars of our topcoats, watching as he backed out and headed down Main Street. Our breathing had created a great white cloud that was hanging about our heads.

I punched Archer, "Now, there goes a fine old tight-wadded cow-puncher."

Archer nodded thoughtfully. "Yeah, and I can tell by the look on your face you're wonderin' if you'll ever see him again. Nobody has a handle on the future, Rusty. Who knows from one moment to the next what's going to happen, to any of us?"

"You know," I laughed, "I think you're turning into some kind of philosopher." I removed a tear from my right eye and slung the old canvas duffel bag over my shoulder. "Come on, let's go down and say hi to Patsy."

                    *   *   *

It was to be a remembered day, as the Seminoles used to say, that February 14, 1947, one year almost to the day since I had returned home from the U. S. Navy and World War Two.

We made it into the Temple Pharmacy just ahead of the bus driver and purchased our tickets from Patsy. Then, silently, I went out and climbed into the bus and took a seat next to a window. Gooch beat Archer to the seat next to me. Then for the tenth time, while the driver settled in, I glanced into the packet I had received through the mail a week before. It contained the travel orders for all three of us. And since I was going in as Radioman Second Class, I was in charge of the *draft*.

Also inside the envelope were twelve chow chits, good at all leading Oklahoma City restaurants, along with three hotel chits, which would be honored at the Skirven Tower the night of February 14, and three first class, one-way tickets on the Atchison-Topeka and Santa Fe Railroad.

Our E. T. D. for the West Coast and the U. S. Coast Guard was eight hundred hours the next morning, and the orders said simply that the three of us would report at once to the Commanding Officer, Twelfth Coast Guard District, San Francisco, California.

As the bus pulled away from the curb, I glanced about at my old party buddies. The endless and unflagging conversation that had begun two days before had finally ceased. Archer was already asleep, with his mouth open and his eyes closed. He was grinning stupidly.

"Did you ever see anything as pitiful as that?" I asked, punching Gooch. "Maybe we should have left him at Garner's."

Archer, as we knew only too well, had not intended to join the Coast Guard. But at the last minute, his excuse for not joining removed and in an attempt to save face, he had signed the papers and held up his right hand.

"He'll thank us for shanghaiing him once we get him well away from hearth and home, and that little blonde over in Ada."

I nodded, adjusting my chair and stretching my feet out beneath the seat in front. "You know, he really can't see worth ten cents. Maybe I did wrong telling the doctor what I did. What if the Coasties—?"

Gooch glanced at me, frowning. "The Coasties will make a deckhand out of him, and for that you don't need to see very much. Don't worry about it. He deserved what he got for carrying on that charade, and for eating up all the attention he was getting for going off on a great adventure."

For a long time I sat with my face close to the befogged window on my left, occasionally wiping a spot and studying the dead, frozen world outside. It was both sad and exciting to me, to be leaving this desolate Oklahoma countryside behind. It was a shucking off of exterior things and, at the same time, a purging from within. I was leaving family and friends behind, perhaps never to return, and heading into a brand-new and very different way of life. I was going back to the sea and ships, and this time there would be no Japs lurking just over the horizon.

I could not remember a more exciting prospect than what lay ahead for me and my buddies.

Suddenly, I became aware that the bus had stopped. The driver stood up, turned, and called out, "Ok City, folks! Ever'body off!"

*   *   *

Just after daylight the next morning, following twelve hours of dreamless sleep, the three of us put on our civilian suits and topcoats, looking like very young and very prosperous businessmen. I led the way to the elevators and did the talking downstairs in the big reception room. To a uniformed attendant I nodded and asked if he would get us a cab. Archer, tearing badly but grinning happily, had not a word to say. Goodrich's normally deadpan kisser had taken on a tragic look, which said louder than words that he was quite happy.

In no time at all, it seemed, we were across town and getting out of a tired-looking taxicab onto the windswept and slippery street at the big train depot. Without a word, having gotten a delicious whiff of fresh, strong coffee, I raised one finger and headed inside. My fellow musketeers fell in behind me without protest. In the long, narrow cafe at one end of the waiting room I spotted an empty booth and headed for it.

"You're in charge," said Gooch, looking across the booth at me. "So it's up to you to get our tickets."

I knew it rankled my two friends that I had been put in charge of the draft, their complaint being that, technically, we were all three just third class petty officers and that I was therefore not the ranking member of our group.

"Never mind the tickets," I said. "Let's get some coffee. You're not in a hurry, are you?"

Archer was studying a menu. "I think I'll order breakfast, Red. Don't we still have some chow chits?"

"Better not," I advised. "You'll be sorry."

Archer asked, suspiciously, "Why will I be sorry? Because you know something about the food here? I don't think so." Before I could say anything, he added, "Them chow chits won't be worth a nickel in Frisco."

"Go ahead, order a big plateful of something. I want you to."

A waitress showed up and stood looking down at us, her notepad ready.

"Three coffees," I said, "and my friend here wants—"

"Nothin' right now," said Archer. "Give me a minute."

Goodrich was staring at Archer's menu, disapproval written all over his face.

"Go ahead and order," I said, "both of you."

"He's tryin' to pull somethin'," said Archer, batting his eyes and smiling. His big baby-blue eyes were bloodshot and tearing badly. "But I for one aint going to fall for it."

"Aw, hell," said Goodrich, "don't pay any attention to him. I'm orderin'. Get out the chits, Red."

I opened the big manila envelope and pulled out some chow chits inside a rubber band and began tapping them on the table, looking toward the waitress. She was chewing something and appeared to be fascinated with the three of us. I peeled two of the tickets off the top and tossed them like playing cards to my two friends. To the girl I said, "How about three cups of coffee, to begin with?"

The waitress seemed to shift into gear and off she went, writing on her pad. While Archer and Goodrich were still studying the menu, she returned with the coffees. "Fifteen cents, please."

"Are you eating, Red?" asked Archer, without looking up.

Glancing at my watch, I said, "I wish we had time for you two to fill up at this greasy spoon, but we're running short on time. There will be a dining car on the train, and in case you don't know it our tickets are First Class. Linen, China, and silverware, fellows."

*   *   *

The train was two miles long, as sluggish as a hippopotamus, and the color of soiled girene fatigues; but we were ushered into a very clean and comfortable coach that was located between the dining car and a club car. That, I informed my friends, was an ominous sign of extremely good luck. We would be able to party all the way to the West Coast.

"We have died and gone to heaven," nodded Goodrich, looking glum. "Don't it make you wonder?"

"About what?" asked Archer, trying to be serious for a change. "All I got to say is that I hope to hell we know what we're doin'."

"This is just the Coasties' way of welcoming us aboard," I said. "Stop bein' paranoid and enjoy. Somebody ring for room service."

At this moment, I would not have changed places with Saint Peter at the Golden Gates. And even Archer, who soon discovered that the train was occupied by a large number of liberal civilians with bottles, was fast forgetting home and loved ones. Before the day was out he was glassy-eyed with good cheer.

Gooch was maintaining a sad exterior, which, as I said, was a good sign. For most of that first day he carried on at length to me about the terrible mistake we were probably making, eventually convincing me that he was happier than at any time in our mutual past. When he came up for air, I reminded him that at least we were going somewhere, doing something. Anything, I assured him, had to be better than running back and forth between Hickville and Howtown chasing skirts. We had practically flunked out of college, and I for one was tired of all the partying and drinking.

At times during that first night we sailed along so fast the clicking was merely a high-pitched zinging to contend with; at other times the train would creep along for what seemed like hours. Eventually, Goodrich and I went looking for Archer and found him in a poker game with three roughnecks from a Texas oil field. Naturally, they had a bottle.

Returning to our car around midnight, we found that a porter had turned our day coach into a *sleeper*, with individual compartments for each of us! Goodrich and I stuffed the unresisting Archer into one of them. My final comment of the night was, "Wait till he wakes up in the morning and finds himself inside a tent that's hurtling toward Mexico at fifty miles an hour!"

I woke up the very early next morning with a start. Always an early riser, I opened my eyes in complete darkness, my senses bombarded by the acrid smell of combusted coal, which had evidently built up in the compartment during the four hours I had slept, and the clickety-clicking of the iron wheels striking the section breaks in the railings. With a grunt of pleasure at the realization of where I was, I wrestled into my salty old Navy dungaree trousers and hopped out into the tunnel-like hallway in my barefeet. My two friends were still sound asleep. But to be certain, I pulled the canvas flaps of their compartments back and peeked inside. Archer was lying on his back with his mouth wide open and snoring loudly.

No sign of life greeted me in the compartment as I worked my way to the restroom and back. There, in the darkness, I searched about until I found my shoes, put them on, and went out to the little platform between the cars. The stars were bright against the strip of blackness above my head, and occasionally in the distance I caught a fleeting glimpse of a light from some ranch house. I thought about the dining car. It would not be open for a good three hours.

All that day and night we worked our way down across west Texas and southeastern New Mexico. Lubbock, Alamogordo and Carlsbad, a land even more treeless than the one from which we had come. Eventually, we made it to El Paso, where we were derailed for six hours in a twenty-acre railroad junkyard. Sometime during the night the train inched its way northwestward out of town and began to pick up speed across the Arizona desert to Phoenix.

In Yuma our train found another siding. Opening a window and looking out, sure, enough, some distance down the tracks, I saw a familiar little shanty covered with big signs. I told Goodrich and Archer about the time a train had run off and left me in this place. I was on my way to San Diego at the end of Christmas leave, 1945, and I had fallen in with a dozen or so sailors who had not stopped drinking since Okie City. On that occasion, since I was the only one still wearing shoes, I was talked into getting off and running back down the tracks for a new supply of bourbon, pogey bait, and cigarettes. Besides the shoes, I was wearing only a pair of undress blue trousers and a white Navy T-shirt. The porter had shouted that we would stop for fifteen minutes, which would be more than enough time for me to dash down to the little shack, which we could plainly see from our windows.

"And the train ran off and left you," nodded Goodrich.

"Yeah, and it took my seabag, the rest of my uniform, my orders—"

"So, you hitchhiked to Dago."

Archer laughed, poking me. "You told us about that at least six times. You beat the train there and was about to be hanged, drawn, and quartered when your papers showed up."

"Red," said Gooch, looking almost happy, "you are always getting yourself in trouble. Right now, you're headed for big trouble with the Coast Guard brass." A glance in Archer's direction caused him to add, "Aren't you aware that old Red here wrote something naughty on his enlistment papers? He's not an RM2."

"What is he then?" cried Archer. "That's what I thought he was. Aint that the reason he's in charge?"

"He's a Third Class Radioman," said Goodrich, not looking at me. "And just you wait till the Coasties wakes up to that fact." To me he said, "Oh, I know, you think you deserved to be a Second Class."

"Yeah, I do," I said. "I passed the test for Second Class, and that ensign was supposed to apply for the rate change."

"But he was busy with the war and forgot it," nodded Goodrich. "Well, you'd better have a better story than that for the brass."

"What happened?" demanded Archer, whacking me on the arm. "You just wrote down the wrong rate and got it?" Astonishment was written all over his face.

"Well, you see, Archer, my boy, I passed all the requirements for Second Class. But at that time our attention was being diverted by such things as *kamikazes* and typhoons and island landings, and so the Third Officer on my subchaser just never got around to filling out the necessary paperwork. It was on my mustering-out papers that I had completed all the requirements."

"Then what's the bitch?" asked Archer.

"Well, none, as far as I'm concerned. I did it as a prank. I never thought they would make me a Second Class!"

"The dude back in that recruiting office is going to get the shaft for that," said Gooch. "Shit, Curly, you outrank old Red Dog here."

"Nobody is going to get the shaft," I insisted. Leaning toward a dirty window and looking at the forlorn landscape outside, I said, poking Archer, "How about running down to that little shanty and buying us a bottle?"

Gooch nodded, "Yeah, an' take your time."

"Hey," said Archer, "this train's loaded down with that stuff." He got to his feet, "I'll be right back—"

"I was just kidding," I said, erasing in the air above my head.

From Yuma, just as the Southern Pacific had done a year earlier, our train angled northward toward Los Angeles, going considerably faster than at anytime before. For three days we had inched along across an empty desert, but now we slashed through congested areas with absolutely no regard for anything that might pull out in front of us. And the whistle never let up!

On the morning of February 19 we were awakened by a porter who made it sound like a priority matter that we get dressed and prepare to disembark immediately. The way he put it was, "Yall sailor boys gettin' off riet soon now! Bettah git yo' thangs an' git ready!"

"Hey!" complained Archer. "No breakfast?"

"No, Suh! No breakfas' todeh. Gottah git off riet away!"

"Well, this is it," I said, sitting up in my compartment. "Now, we'll find out what the Coast Guard has in mind for us."

Government Island

◆

I said, trying to sound calm, "Anybody seen the orders?"

From the baggage compartment the porter had brought our three duffel bags; and after a thorough search of mine, I turned and stared at my two friends. To Goodrich, who was looking at me suspiciously, I said, "Search Archer. He's probably misplaced them."

And, sure enough, despite his protests that he had not seen them, they turned up on the deck beneath where he had been sleeping.

It was still not fully daylight when we disembarked from the train and entered the great bedlam of the Terminal Building in San Francisco, a place all three of us had visited on our way home from the war. Indeed, no sailor, soldier, or marine who has ever returned to the States from the Pacific and landed in San Francisco, has escaped this melting pot of the Armed Services. Our first stop was the small but rather autonomous world of the Terminal restrooms. Although perhaps a bit less chaotic than when I had last seen the place at Christmastime, 1945, the barbershops and shoeshine parlors still had waiting lines. And the row upon row of urinals and pay-toilets and lavatories where men of all ranks and skin colors were relieving themselves and shaving and washing themselves were doing a lively business.

"This is enough to turn a person against taking a piss," said Goodrich. "And there's no way in hell my bowels will function in this den of inequity."

Later, having refreshed ourselves somewhat, we walked up Market Street, feeling the excitement of a great city finishing out another big night. There were already hordes of pedestrians hurrying along, although it was beyond me where so many people could be going at that hour.

"What do our orders say?" asked Gooch. "What next?"

"Ask Archer," I said lightly. "Far as I know he's still looking after them."

"I couldn't make heads or tails of them," complained Archer, grinning. "Proceed at once to someplace and report to somebody is about all I got out of them."

"Let's get some breakfast and look at them," I suggested. "We've got about four hours to kill, if I'm remembering correctly."

*   *   *

One thing that had been bothering me ever since I had received my orders in Oklahoma City, with *RM2* behind my name, was just what the Coast Guard was going to expect of me. Even though I had never actually been a Radioman Second Class in the Navy, I was not worried about the technical aspects of holding down a radio watch. I had had a great of experience sending and receiving messages by voice, brass key, and semiautomatic *bug*. It was, I decided, the fear of the unknown, which would leave me as soon as I was assigned to a ship.

Archer, as if he had read my mind, said that he had no doubt we could teach the Coasties a few lessons about seamanship. We were, after all, ex-Navy. "We've been through the real thing," he bragged. "Like old Goodrich says, this outfit is a *shallow-water navy!*"

I admitted that I had had similar thoughts, especially about holding down a radio watch. What did the Coast Guard have that could compare to what I had already been through?

"I'll bet they'll ask our advice on all kinds of stuff," said Archer.

Goodrich shook his head doubtfully. "I think we better not take that attitude, Curly. We don't know a damned thing about this outfit."

We found a small, noisy cafe at the bottom of Market and ordered short stacks, bacon, and coffee and reassured ourselves we had done the right thing.

"I hope we all get sent to the same place," said Archer.

"That won't happen," I assured him. "But, if we're lucky, maybe we'll all be stationed here in the Bay someplace. Come on, clean up your plates and let's go. I feel a strong urge to bring the U. S. Coast Guard up to date on marine technology."

"There you go!" laughed Archer. "We'll show 'em how to run their pretty little ships up and down the West Coast."

An hour later, having been carried all over the city by a taxi driver who knew out-of-towners when he saw them, we finally made it to the Twelfth District Coast Guard Building, not far from Fisherman's Wharf. There we had to sit in an immaculate reception room while our papers were being processed. Finally, a girl in a white, close-fitting uniform with little blue anchors on her collars, appeared with a manila envelope with my name on it.

"I wish somebody'd tell me why you get to be head honcho," complained Archer. "I think I ought to be in charge, since I've got the right-arm rating."

"Here," I said, handing him the envelope.

"Is that okay?" asked Archer, looking at the girl.

"I'm afraid not," she said with a smile. "But if you like you could take it up with Personnel out at Government Island."

"What in the world is that?" said Goodrich with a frown.

"You'll find out on your own," she said, looking amused. Up close she was quite pretty, I thought. To me she said, "Know how to get there?" I quickly shook my head. "Take the electric across the Bridge, get off at the fifteen hundred block of Fifteenth Street, in Oakland, and either walk the six or so blocks to G. I. or hire a taxi. Just follow the signs, and when you come to a bridge, you'll know you're there."

"Since when is the Coast Guard hiring civilians to do their paper-work?" asked Archer. "My friends and I feel threatened."

"Sorry about that," said the girl, flashing Archer a smile.

*   *   *

When we were zipping across the San Francisco Bay, Goodrich admitted that he had never heard of a place called Government Island and did not like the sound of it. "Doesn't it remind you of Mare Island?" he worried.

"Aw, the Coast Guard don't use that place," argued Archer.

"Don't worry about it," I put in.

"Do we know where this place is?" complained Goodrich. "Did she say it was in Oakland?"

"Wasn't she just about the snazziest thing you ever did see?" said Archer. "These West Coast girls all look different from—"

"Who?" I demanded, looking around quickly. "Watch what you say."

"Remove that tight-fitting dress and them false eyelashes and she'd be just another naked female," said Goodrich, looking tragic.

"Take that uniform off and you'd have riots in the street," Archer bragged. "I swear she was the most beautiful thing I ever saw! When we get settled at this Government Island, I'm lookin' her up!"

"Oh, how absence makes the heart grow fonder," said Goodrich. "What would your little honey in Ada think if she could hear you talk like that?"

By one o'clock, having missed noon chow entirely, we emerged from the chaos and devastation of downtown Oakland (We had momentar-ily forgotten part of our travel instructions) to find ourselves facing a small beer joint in east Oakland. An old sorry-looking sign proclaimed *Ted and Roy's Hooligan Bar*, which seemed amusing at the time. The door was as dilapidated as the one on Garner's Pool Hall, and Archer had to wrestle with it to get it open. We went inside and straddled plastic-covered stools at the bar.

After two beers, we began debating the pros and cons of going directly to Government Island. One of the pros was that this just might be our last glimpse of freedom for quite a spell. Archer was for remaining until close to evening chow time.

In the end reason prevailed and we forced ourselves back out onto the street. My one concern, I said, was that I did not wish to begin my Coastie career with a Captain's Mast, and if we did not cross that bridge and get ourselves checked in we would automatically be AOL.

When we found the bridge the girl had mentioned, Goodrich wanted to know, "What kind of a cap do Coast Guardsmen wear?"

"Why?" squinted Archer, shading his eyes and staring down the bridge.

"They wear the same old cap we wore in the Navy," I said. "Golfball."

"Then we're there." Goodrich pointed down the bridge. "That's got to be the sucker on watch."

"I believe you're right," I said. "Do you fellows realize that up until this moment we have been free men. Once we hand that swab our orders, we'll be the property of Uncle Sam for two long years."

At this Archer stopped dead in his tracks and glared at me. "Well, look who's making noises! If it wasn't for you, Red Dog, we'd probably be shooting snooker at Garner's!"

"Or sipping beer back there at *Ted and Roy's*," chimed in Goodrich.

I attempted an imitation of a tour guide addressing blind visitors from out of state. "And, now, ladies and gentlemen, we are at the Main Gate at Government Island. This once great receiving, training, and distribution center of the mighty United States Coast Guard had no equal on the West Coast back during the war; but today it's just another small, flat, man-made island, like T. I. out there in the Bay. You can see—I'm sorry, you can't see—it's an almost-deserted city of two-story frame buildings arranged in rows, widely-spaced and running north and south. On our left, as we pass through the gate, we see—that is, I see—two large white cutters moored at a long dock. They appear to be somewhat smaller than Navy destroyers."

"Cut out the shit, Red," said Archer. "You're givin' me a headache."

By this time we were standing in front of the gate watch, who had heard some of what I was saying. He was not amused.

I handed him the manila envelope and saluted.

"You boys shipping over?" He was paying me no attention.

"From the U. S. Navy," said Archer, proudly.

"Big-ship men, huh?" scoffed the watch. "Well, I think you'll find things quite different in this outfit. Maybe not much easier, but very different."

"I understand the Coast Guard sticks around close to the coasts all the time," teased Archer. "I like that."

"We stick around a lot of places, mate. Okay, take these to that building over there. The first one with the sign. They'll process them and get you settled. Welcome to the Service."

At the Personnel Office we were issued a number of chits and a duty schedule and told to go directly to the Ship's Store for our clothing allowance.

"It's the fuckin' Navy all over again," Archer complained, his hands full of skivvies. "Except for that doll over at district H Q."

"Will you shut up about her?" growled Goodrich. "She can do better than you on Skid Row."

At evening chow, dressed in smelly new dungarees and carrying a heavy steel tray loaded with food, I led my two buddies to an empty table under a row of large windows. Before sitting down, I took a long look about at the fifty or so sailors scattered around the large messhall. It was indeed a lot like being back in boot camp.

"Man, this food smells good," said Archer.

"I didn't get this kind of chow in the Navy," I agreed, looking at my tray.

"Yeah, but you gotta remember this is peacetime and you spent all of your Navy time overseas," said Goodrich. "I stayed here in the States and the chow was always pretty damned good."

As the tables filled up, we were joined by several Coasties, most of whom were Ship's Company, judging by their faded dungarees and that certain air of superiority I had encountered on a number of occasions in the Navy. Some of them nodded briefly, and one, after studying my face for a moment, said,

"Haven't seen you around before."

"Just got in."

"Name's Layton. What district did you come from?"

"No district," said Archer, trying to sound mysterious. "We're all three from the U. S. Navy."

Goodrich and I exchanged frowns at this remark. Looking down at my food the whole time, I said, "We shipped over back in Oklahoma City a few days ago."

For a time nobody said anything. I tried a time or two to smooth over what Archer had said, but there was suddenly a pronounced chill in the air. Layton stared from one to the other of us and then got up and moved to the other end of the table.

"I reckon you come in to give us boys a few lessons on how it's all done," said a Coastie sitting next to Layton.

"Nope," I hastened, "we expect to learn a few things."

There was a low chuckle at this, but nobody said anything for a time.

"Shit," said Archer, "let's face it. This is a shallow water outfit."

"Will you shut up!" hissed Goodrich, glaring at our friend.

Layton's face had darkened and now he was glaring at Archer. "Quite obviously you boys don't know from shit what this outfit's all about. I'll give you about a week, once you ship aboard one of our cutters."

"Give us a week for what?" laughed Archer. "I aint seen nothin' yet but some little ole boats painted a very pretty white and tied up at the dock. How far do you fellows venture out, anyway, a quarter of a mile max? Don't tell me you sometimes go all the way to the horizon. Shit, you ought to spend some time on a Navy cruiser or maybe a wagon— out in the Pacific!"

All of the Coasties at our table were by this time looking at Archer, their food forgotten Two of them had half-risen from their seats, with their forks still in their hands!

"Listen, fellows," said Goodrich, solemnly, "my friend here and I barely know this kinky-haired joker beside us. All we know about him is that he's a moron with an extremely big mouth."

Archer was grinning happily at this, evidently pleased by the attention he was getting. "Aw, come on, Gooch, you know what I'm sayin' is the truth. This aint a real sea-goin' outfit."

Looking at Layton, I said, "This fellow and I happen to believe that the Coast Guard is a salty outfit." I bent my head toward Archer, "He, on the other hand, is trying to be funny. He thinks he's a real jokester."

"Just how I had him figured," said Layton, relaxing. "Who'd you say this asshole is?" Without waiting for an answer, he continued, "I'd recommend that you two stop fraternizing with him." After letting that soak in, he added, "Especially when you're on liberty down in East Oakland. It might not be healthy for you."

"And I shore as heck wouldn't be seen with him at *Ted and Roy's*," added the Coastie next to Layton.

Quite suddenly my face had begun heating up. I glanced hastily at Goodrich, who was looking at me and shaking his head.

"I wish you hadn't said that," he told Layton.

I had, of course, stopped eating and now slowly I laid my fork on the table.

To Layton Goodrich said, calmly, "Why did you have to put it that way, *recommending, for our sake?*"

"That was good advice. I said it because with a mouth like Asshole's, he's gonna git you two in real trouble. And I wouldn't want to see that happen to two nice guys like you and Red there."

"Well, I'm sure glad you tipped me off to this danger," I said lightly. "My friend and I hate trouble more than anything else in the world, don't we?" I was now looking at Goodrich.

"But do we ever," he said, rolling his eyes. "Red, let it go."

"Yeah," I said, "let it go." I let my eyes focus for a moment on the Coasties around the table, including Layton. "Any of you boys planning to go to this *Ted and Roy's* this evening?"

Layton straightened up, looked about at his friends. "Some of us drop in there just about every evening. Right fellows? Anybody going ashore tonight?"

The pug ugly beside Layton was nodding.

"Pretty rough duty you've got here," I said. "Liberty every night, an eight-to-five job, good chow—Maybe there's something to what Archer said about the Coasties. Maybe you boys don't know about the real world."

"We've all put in time aboard the weather cutters and buoy tenders and ice-breakers," said Layton, "and let me tell you it's ten times rougher than anything the Navy's got."

At this I rose, tray in hand, "We'll look forward to libertying with you boys tonight. *Ted and Roy's*, okay?"

*　　　　　*　　　　　*

Later, in the barracks, Goodrich had this to say, "Sometimes I wish I'd never laid eyes on either one of you two lunkheads. Archer, all you do is get something going and, Red, despite all your show of being a peaceful guy, you fall right into it every time and end up getting us all three in a brawl. I'm sick and tired of getting knots and bruises for you two, and I for one am not going to show up at that Coastie hangout in East Oakland tonight. In fact, I am going to make certain I never show up at that place *anytime*."

"Hey," chuckled Archer, "you don't think I'm crazy enough to show up there tonight, do you? That's Red Dog's baby, not mine." He looked from one of us to the other and whined, faking it, "I'm a lover, not a fighter, for Christ's sake!"

"I had no intention of dragging you two along," I said. "Besides, you'd just get in the way."

With that I left the barracks building and walked down the broad avenue of frame buildings and entered the Personnel Office. There I asked the first yeoman that looked my way for a liberty chit. The yeoman stared at me distastefully for a moment.

"You just got in today?"

I nodded, "So what?"

"You're restricted to the base for twenty-four hours."

"Why?"

"Not that I have to tell you, but it's because you have to be confined for that length of time before and after your shots."

Dumfounded at this, I demanded to know what shots. I hadn't had any shots. The yeoman, sounding bored, informed me that the three of us were due at the dispensary at zero-eight-hundred hours the next morning. Disgusted, I wheeled, mumbling under my breath that I had already had a thorough physical. Then as I charged toward the door, I found myself facing Layton.

"Do you have any pull around here?" I blasted into his startled face.

"Why?"

"I need a liberty chit for tonight. And his pencil-pusher tells me I'm quarantined."

Layton was suddenly grinning, "Leave it to me, Red. I'll git one down to you at the barracks right away. How about your buddies?"

"Yeah, get them chits, too."

*   *   *

"I'm not goin," said Goodrich. "It's about time I made it clear to you two I'm not goin' to fight every time one of you gets into trouble."

"Yeah, I know," agreed Archer. "But that crazy bunch of hooligans might kill ole Red."

"Shit. Haven't you seen him in a brawl?"

"Well," nodded Archer, "now that you mention it, that time at Garner's, he brought old Big Boy Cravins down a notch. And, let's see, twice at *Bit of Bavaria*—in Ada."

"Did you ever see him *lose* a fight? And do I need to remind you that he grew up with five of the best fistfighters in the River Bend?"

"Yeah, I hear you, but in a bar and all them guys goin' at him from different directions. Somebody ought to watch his back."

"Well, you go then. I'm not putting my neck on the line just because he's mad at somebody."

"Hah! If you're not goin', I'm sure as heck not!"

At that point I walked in, having overheard the last statement and guessed at all the rest. I went to my newly-assigned bunk and began to put on undress blues. On the right lower sleeve of the blouse was a brilliant white shield.

About the time I reached for my shoes, a slender kid with a stutter showed up with the three liberty chits and beelined it straight to me. I took them without comment, tossed them on my bunk, and proceeded to lace up the new black regulation Coast Guard shoes. The uniform was smelly and had great creases in it, and the white golfball cap did not want to rest over my right eye. Then, with a few swipes of a sock across my shoes, I picked up one of the chits and left the barracks building without a word and headed for the Main Gate.

Archer and Goodrich, having ignored me all the time I was dressing, finished combing in front of small mirrors attached to their bunks.

"What did that kid give him?" asked Goodrich.

"I'll lay money it was liberty chits."

"Not likely. They would never give us liberty our first night here. In the Navy we'd be quarantined for a couple of days."

Archer walked down the aisle between two rows of bunks, reached down and picked up the chits. "Yep, I was right."

"We'll give him time to get across the bridge," said Goodrich, accepting one of the chits. "Wonder how he managed these?"

"He probably went to the C. O. and threatened him."

*   *   *

East Oakland was cold, damp, and apparently deserted. A recent rain had turned the sidewalks and streets a slippery black, except where puddles mirrored the widely-spaced streetlights and the on-and-off green and red and yellow neon lights advertising Jax and Lucky Lager beer and rooms by the hour or by the night. An occasional Yellow Cab would shoot down the street, bouncing from puddle to puddle and careening off the streetcar rails in the center of the avenue. Except for these, even though it was only nineteen hundred hours, I walked the entire distance from Government Island to *Ted and Roy's* without seeing a soul.

The idea of meeting Layton in a public bar and fighting him was now repugnant to me. He had opened his big mouth, had indeed thrown down the gauntlet; so I had to deal with this tall, rough-looking hooligan Coast Guardsman, whom I did not know and with whom I had no particular quarrel. Archer had done it again, and there was no way out for me. The thought crossed my mind (not for the first time) that my little buddy was a troublemaker and, on this occasion, for the first time since I became acquainted with him, behaving like a coward.

The thought also occurred to me that not only was I risking broken bones and a bloody nose, but I was taking a chance that could land me in the brig and give me a black mark that would go with me throughout my Coast Guard career. I resolved on the spot to avoid at all costs getting into this kind of situation in the future. After settling with Layton, I would stay out of Archer's affairs. I would mind my own business and refuse to let my friend or anybody else put me in such a position again.

Ted and Roy's, apparently impervious to the drabness outside, was alive and noisy and showing signs of a wild evening well launched. The green and red neon lights above the big mirror behind the bar, which were the only lights in the place, did strange things to facial appearances, making it very difficult for me to tell who and how many were in the place; but before I settled at the bar with half a dozen other Coasties, I had to assure myself that Layton was not present.

Perhaps, for one reason or another, Layton and his friends wouldn't show up. Or if they did, perhaps there would be no trouble. I would certainly not be the one to start it. I would have a beer or two and stick around long enough to establish my presence to anybody who might know Layton. But the small hair on my neck began to stand up, as the thought occurred to me that for all I knew the place might be full of this hooligan's friends.

"You must be a stranger in these parts, pilgrim," called out the bartender, imitating John Wayne. "What'll yall have?"

Ignoring his question, I asked, "Do you know a Coastie named Layton?"

"Well," he laughed, putting his big hands on the bar. He was a tall, rawboned man of about fifty, with a very hard face. "I reckon I have seen him around a few times." He slid his hand across the bar. "I saw you this afternoon, didn't I? I remember that red hair. I'm Ted, co-owner of the establishment. Once upon a time I was a Coastie, too; and I guess I know most of the Coasties in these parts."

I took his hand, which was firm and strong, and when he stopped talking and straightened up, I told him I had just come in from the Midwest.

"Well, Red, on behalf of *Ted and Roy's*, the main Coastie hangout of Oakland and San Francisco, I welcome you. First beer's on the house." With that, he turned to a row of glasses, "I'll have one with you, if you don't mind."

As I raised my beer in salute, the door flew back and three men in undress blues entered noisily, boisterously. The leader, I realized at once, was none other than Layton, who had undergone a metamorphosis since evening chow. He was red-faced and excited and quite obviously three-sheets in the wind; and when he spotted me at the bar, he bellowed for all to hear:

"There he is, Big Ship Navy! Came down here, fellows, to show us Coasties a thing or two, said he was a real salt and we was a bunch of namby-pambies!" He advanced toward me, waving his arms and shouting, "Give us a drink, Ted—and put it on this fellow's bill!"

I had turned on the barstool and was observing Layton's antics.

Ted, leaning across the bar, said, "Lower your voice, Layton, if you want a drink in this place. You've probably already had too much."

"Fuck you!" shouted Layton. "Give us a beer—on Red here!"

"I'm warnin' you, Layton," said Ted. "Keep it down. You've got everybody's attention already."

"Well, I'm gonna get this peckerwood's attention in about a second," said Layton. "After I break ever' bone in his body I'm gonna throw him out in the street."

"Give them a beer, on me," I said to the bartender. To Layton I said, "I don't want any trouble with you, mate. If what my friend said is still rankling you, I'll apologize for him."

Layton snorted disgustedly and backed off a step, "Your friend *rankling* me? Shit, I don't give no never mind to that. It's your balls I'm after."

Ted's long arm snaked across the bar suddenly and his big hand clamped onto Layton's left shoulder. "Once more I'm tellin' you to keep it down and go on about your business. If you don't, I'm goin' to call the goddamned police!"

A number of Coasties in the bar had risen from their chairs and were glaring at me. I heard the word *ex-Navy* and *redhead*.

Layton, shaking himself free of Ted, moved in on me and made an awkward attempt to shove me off the barstool.

"Look, Layton, let's forget about what went on at chow today!" I said above the noise. "I don't want any trouble with any of you!"

"Yeah, I guess so!" shouted Layton, ceasing his sparring maneuver and swinging from left field at my face.

I saw Ted disappear behind the bar. Later, I would realize that he had bent down to get a small baseball bat. Still half-sitting on the barstool but with one foot on the floor and my back braced against the bar, I let fly a short, right jab at Layton's chin. Most of my upper body was behind it, and the sound of my knuckles against the unprotected and protruding bony nose was sharp and audible throughout the bar. This this was followed immediately by a loud groaning sound from the audience. Layton's head popped back and he fell into the arms of his two friends.

"Okay!" yelled Ted. "Everybody sit down, go back to your seats! This palooka asked for it and he got it! Any more trouble and I'm callin' the cops, is that clear?"

Layton, apparently out cold, was being helped to his feet.

To my surprise, some of the Coasties nearest me were beginning to grin and nod at each other. One of them hit me on the shoulder and said, "Right on, Navy!" And another called out for all to hear, "Did you see that six-inch punch?"

Ted, wiping furiously and still glaring at those who were taking their time about sitting down, said to me, "Enjoy your beer. You did your best to avoid this swab." He held the bat up for me to see, "I hate to use this thing. It's bad as hell for business."

Layton's two cronies had gotten him straightened up between them and were walsing him about, apparently uncertain what to do. Someone had poured a pitcher of beer over his head, and beads of beer were standing out like blood on his face. The whole upper half of his uniform was soaked.

"Mates, why don't you take him on back to G. I.?" suggested Ted. "And when he wakes up, tell him I don't want to see him in here again the rest of the month!"

Just as the three unhappy friends of Layton departed through the door with their boneless burden, Bill Archer and E. T. Goodrich burst into the room. Archer, looking quickly about and spotting me at the bar, rushed toward me.

"What happened, Red? You and that guy Layton already finished?"

Ted, siphoning a beer, called out, "These your friends, Red? Do they always show up after the fun is over?"

Archer, looking disgusted, blurted out, "I can't believe it! We was right behind them three guys! They didn't have time to get in here and get Red mad enough to cold-cock Layton!"

Ted said, "It took about two seconds."

On the Alert

◆

The first surprise I had coming from the Coast Guard at Government Island was the absolute absence of pressure, spit-and-polish, and shit details. The three of us were there to await assignments. End of story. No mustering at zero-eight-hundred hours, no uniform-of-the-day malarkey, and no Captain's Inspections. Indeed, nothing at all was expected of us.

It made one hell of an impression on me.

Following morning chow our first full day there, we procrastinated around the barracks, expecting some CPO to come along at any moment and assign us to a shit detail. The building, capable of housing fifty men, was all ours; and up and down the wide avenue between the two rows of buildings nobody moved, except at chowtime. So what did we do that day? Nothing at all but worry about when the shit was going to hit the grinder.

"It's weird," said Archer. "This place must've been somethin', once upon a time. But right now it's a graveyard."

"Yeah, well, don't ask for trouble," said Goodrich. "I like this peace and quiet. How about you, Red?"

"Apparently, all we've got to do is eat and sleep till our orders come in," grinned Archer. "You can't beat that kind of routine."

Since there was no reveille or boatswain's whistle to wake us up, we missed morning chow. At noon we sat at a table with half a dozen of the Ship's Company, yeomen for the most part, and tossed out questions about the island, the cutters tied up at the pier, and what was likely to happen to them. We, in turn, were questioned about the evening before at *Ted and Roy's*. The question was, Why had all three of us ganged up on Layton?

"Is that what he told you guys?" Archer bristled. "The fact is he made the mistake of takin' on Red here."

The ranking yeoman at Personnel, Connelly, turned and gave me the eye: "Word is you boys jumped him after he was too likkered up to fight. He's got quite a reputation around here so I don't think you took him down all by yourself."

"Lucky punch," I said. "Where is he?"

"Alameda Coast Guard Air Station Hospital. Are you saying you did that with one punch?"

Goodrich, with Archer pitching in occasionally, then told what had taken place at the little Coastie bar.

"Funny thing," said Connelly, "according to three eye-witnesses Red here caught Layton off-guard, hit him with brass knucks, then you other two jumped in and finished him off."

"What was these three eye-witnesses doing all this time?" asked Archer. "Heck, Goodrich and I weren't even there at the time, but the three witnesses was."

On the second morning, shortly after breakfast, we were standing outside our barracks building when the PA system opened up, "Will Goodrich, Eugene T., report to Personnel?"

"D-Day!" sighed Goodrich, shaking his head. "Keep your fingers crossed this isn't some shit detail."

"Well, it's for sure they don't make up orders that fast," said Archer. "What can it be but a shit detail?"

Goodrich had not stayed around to listen to Archer theorize, and by the time we made it up to Personnel here he was back out on the front stoop looking like the world had fallen in on him. Archer groaned at the sight, but I let out a yelp, followed by:

"What did you get?"

"What?" demanded Archer. "You're going to the North Pole."

"Guess again," said old Goodrich, with just the trace of a smirk on his sad kisser. "I'm Ship's Company. Right here on G. I.!"

"Yeah, come on!" scoffed Archer. "Ship's Company my ass!"

"Right here," nodded Goodrich. "No rolling deck, no remote lighthouse, no friggin' weather station in Outer Mongolia."

I grabbed the orders from Goodrich's outstretched hand and stared at the first page. The thought of calling this place home was not all that jolly, in my thinking. I definitely did not want to hang around this deserted boot camp. But I put on a good front with, "If that's what you want, old buddy! This definitely calls for a celebration at *Ted and Roy's*. Archer and I will pick up the tab."

"Red, you know I'm flat broke," moaned Archer. "You buy the beers this time, and I'll buy them when we get paid."

"Yeah," I nodded, grinning, "but by that time we'll all be out of here."

"I've got to report back here to Personnel in one hour," said Goodrich. "What say we decide what we want to do at noon chow? I'm not sure I want to go back to that bar anytime soon."

But at noon chow that day nobody at our table did any talking except Goodrich, who had crowded us in with the Personnel crew. He was the saddest-looking thing I had ever seen, and I was happy for him.

On Thursday at noon chow at that same table, our Ship's Company buddy, after denying up until the last minute that any orders had come in, asked Archer where he would like to go, if he had his druthers.

"Mind you, I won't have anything at all to do with it when it comes. But let's hear it from you, where would you really like to hang up your hat?"

"Well, not here, that's for sure," said Archer. "Anywhere but this godforsaken island. The seagulls here are drivin' me crazy."

"I thought you liked it," complained Goodrich. "How would you like a loran station on Newfoundland?"

"Hey!" yelped Archer. "Why would you ask a thing like that?" To me he demanded, "Has this ex-buddy of ours got my orders, Red Dog? He's up to somethin'."

I nodded, "It would seem. Now, all you have to do is get them away from him." From Goodrich's behavior I was certain that he was not carrying bad news.

"Well, fellas, I've got to get back to the office," said Goodrich, rising. "Here." He removed a Manila envelope from inside his blouse. "Don't say I never gave you anything." To me he growled, "The lucky dog."

Archer, finally onto Goodrich, was so excited his hands were shaking. He grabbed at the folder, yelling, "Where am I going?"

"To Hades, eventually," said Goodrich. "But as much as I hate to tell you this, you're headin' for the Coast Guard's equivalent of Hog Heaven. Fisherman's Wharf."

"You've got to be kidding," I said, snatching the orders and, with Archer clawing at me, reading aloud, "Proceed without delay to Fisherman's Wharf, Pier Forty-three, San Francisco, and report to the C. O. of the Coast Guard Tug."

As Goodrich left with his tray, he said in a most solemn voice, "It's like my dear old daddy always said, 'The undeservin' git all the breaks.'"

"That certainly applies in your case!" I called out. "Now, go get me my orders!"

*   *   *

With Archer gone and Goodrich working eight-to-five like a civilian, it did not take me long to exhaust the possibilities of Government Island. By the afternoon of my first day there alone I had walked its circumference and measured its breadth and girth. The one thing that kept me going was the hope that my orders would come any minute. Well, during the day that is, while the Personnel Office was open and the yeomen were on the ball. At sixteen hundred hours every day I was free

to go on liberty, but without my old hometown buddies there just was-
n't much enjoyment in hanging over the bar at *Ted and Roy's*.

The week that followed Archer's transfer to Fisherman's Wharf I
made a few acquaintances aboard the two weather ships tied up at the
dock, the CGC *Chautauqua* and its identical twin, or so it seemed to me
at the time, the CGC *Escanaba*. Both ships had quite a history, which I
was to learn later, is true of most Coast Guard cutters. But on the Eskie,
as it was called, I ran onto a quartermaster that had oral diarrhea on the
subject. He told me that this particular two-fifty-five-foot Indian cutter,
the Escanaba II (WPG-64), was built in San Pedro and commissioned
just the year before; but the Eskie I began as a patrol ship on the Great
Lakes, based at Grand Haven, Michigan, back in the early 'Forties. It was
assigned to the Greenland Patrol and convoy duty just before WWII;
and in 1943, while on convoy duty, she was sunk by a Jap sub.

One day it occurred to me that I had not written a single letter or
postcard home. Of course, until the last few days there had been little
opportunity. In the barracks there was a small table on which were
writing materials

I began with a short, silly letter to my little sister, Jessica. Then in a
more somber mood I penned a long letter and made two extra copies
and sent one each to Jody Summers, Alice Chastain and Darleen
Caulfield, girls I had spent the most time with back in Oklahoma. Life
in the U. S. Coast Guard, I told them all, with varying degrees of enthusiasm, was very exciting. After writing these words, I stared around at
the empty barracks. Then I followed that with, "Any day now I will
receive orders to go to a small ship or perhaps a lighthouse or maybe
some distant outpost. It doesn't really matter to me. I'm where I want
to be, doing what I want to do." I finished off each letter with this
remark: "I have no idea when I will get to return home."

I had held off to last the letter I needed to write to Jamie Lee, my girl
in the River Bend. For a long time I sat there thinking about her, but in
the end I laid aside my pen, paper, and envelopes and went for a walk.

Goodrich, more serious than ever now that he was a member of Ship's Company, told me one day that I did not need to pester him non-stop about my orders, that when they came in he would post them on the bulletin board. For that remark I stopped picking up his tab at *Ted and Roy's* and sitting with him and the other yeomen at chow. The truth was that I preferred the conversation of the half-dozen sparks from the Indian cutters.

One day toward the end of that long week (It was at noon chow), I joined him at the Personnel table. Actually, he had caught my attention when I came through the door and waved me over. I took my tray and sat down across from him.

"What do you do all day everyday on those cutters?" he asked. "I see you going to one or the other of them right after morning chow, and I know for a fact you don't have any chores to do here on the base."

"Oh, I shoot the breeze with the dit-dah boys mostly," I replied. "No, that's not exactly right. I vegetate, waiting for you to come up with some orders for me. How about it, old buddy? Quit stalling."

"Hah," he said, looking like a badly beaten dog. "All I do is take them, not dish them out."

Was I seeing on his face what I thought I was seeing? I asked myself. Old Goodrich was happy about something. "You bastard!" I shouted, standing up. "I'll bet you've got my orders on you right now! You do, don't you?"

Without warning I leaned across the table and rammed my right hand down inside his blouse, putting my right knee in a great mound of marmalade as I did so. He grabbed my hand and held on while I struggled to get a good hold of the envelope.

"Back off!" he yelled. "All right, I'll give you the orders! Jesus!"

Two glasses of milk had toppled, filling both of our trays and now a river of white liquid was pouring into his lap.

"I knew it, you buzzard!" I said, bringing the envelope to light.

With his lap now full of milk and marmalade, Goodrich sat observing me through tragic, half-closed eyes. "My God, Red Dog, a body would think you really want to get out of this place. If I had only known a transfer meant that much to you—!"

"What would you have done?" I snarled. "Where am I going?"

I was trying desperately to open the flap, which was not only pinned down but glued. Then, once I had the thing open and the first page out, I couldn't seem to find the punch line in the orders.

"It's your surprise," grunted Goodrich, beginning to swab up some of the milk. "Find out for yourself." He pushed his tray of food to one side, looking disgusted. "We had hoped to be stationed here in the Bay area, remember? But it looks like that aint gonna happen."

"You're right about that," I said. "Where in the world is Humboldt Bay?"

After the laughter and hand-clapping died down, Connelly asked, "Ever hear of Eureka, the Sequoia redwoods? The *Alert's* tied at the docks in Eureka, which is about two hundred and eighty-seven miles north of here, not all that far from the Oregon state line. It's a one-twenty-five footer assigned to air-sea rescue on the northern California coast."

"You've got exactly what you wanted," said Goodrich. "Admit it."

"Maybe," I mused. "I guess I'll find out when I get there."

From the messhall we walked to Goodrich's barracks (He had been moved in with the other yeoman in a barracks building full of Ship's Company); and while he changed I studied my orders. I was, of course, supposed to leave "by the first available transportation"; but I had already decided that there would be nothing available until the next morning.

"How much loot do you have?" I asked. "How about we pick up old Archer and do a little celebrating tonight?"

Goodrich surprised me with: "I believe it is incumbent upon the three of us to do just that, since it will probably a while before we can get together again. Archer and I will foot the bill."

        *   *   *

In the darkness just before dawn I got up and began dressing out of my seabag, having to feel for the undress blue uniform, socks, and neckerchief. Goodrich, who had dropped off to sleep on one of the empty bunks about two o'clock, was lying on his back in the pitch blackness behind me. As it turned out, he was pretending to be asleep because just as I sat down on my bunk to put on my shoes, he began to complain.

"You don't leave for four hours, Red."

"Thought I'd take a last stroll around this sad excuse for an island, maybe drop by one of the cutters for breakfast."

"They allow that?"

"Sure. Want to come along?"

"What the heck. Turn on a light."

As we left the barracks, day was breaking over Government Island, revealing a colorless landscape of long, silent, identical buildings separated by a wide, rain-soaked avenue of black asphalt. We walked with hands deep inside our peacoat pockets down to the water's edge and stopped, facing across the fog-shrouded Bay.

"How does it feel?"

"What?" I asked. "Oh. Pretty darn good, actually. At last I've got something to do, someplace to go. I was beginning to think I might have to sit out my hitch right here on G. I."

"I know what you mean. And it beats hell out of runnin' back an' forth between Konawa and Ada, chasing skirts. Bein' in the Coast Guard, I mean. But I don't envy you this Cutter *Alert*. Chances are you'll find yourself in some pretty rough shit in that air-sea rescue duty."

"Naw, I doubt it. What's important, I'll be getting back into a radio shack. Come on, let's head around the island and see if chow's ready on the *Chautauqua*."

At nine o'clock on the nose a Jeep from the Motor Pool showed up at Personnel. I had stashed my gear, which now included a brand-new seabag and a ditty bag, beside the stoop out front and couldn't have been more ready for the ride to San Francisco. Goodrich, of course, was there to see me off.

In the packet with my orders was a one-way bus ticket from Frisco to Eureka. I would worry about finding Humboldt Bay and the *Alert* when I got there. I stuck out my hand and my old buddy took it, nodding once.

"Drop me a line once in awhile," I teased.

He laughed, looking pained. "You don't even write to Jamie Lee so what're the chances you would write to me?"

"I wrote to her once. Seriously, if you get any mail for me, see that it's transferred to the *Alert*."

"You expect such favors from me, after last night? It's a wonder we both didn't end up in the brig."

I tossed my gear into the backseat of the Jeep and jumped in beside the driver, waving back over my head as we scurried away. After a brief pause at the Main Gate for the man on watch to log us out, the driver floor-boarded the Jeep all the way across the bridge to East Oakland.

When we reached the Terminal Building in San Francisco an hour later, I lost no time checking bus schedules north. I had four choices, the first being a bus that would leave in less than an hour and get me into Eureka about breakfast time. I hoisted my seabag onto my left shoulder, looped the little pull line of the ditty bag over my right shoulder and headed for the restrooms one floor below.

I felt good. Things were finally happening.

From the Terminal Building I sought out the Greyhound Bus Depot, and to my surprise the northbound bus was waiting, with the engine running and the door open. I checked my seabag at the baggage counter inside and got aboard, braced for a very long ride through the Big Trees Country. A lot of it would be after dark, but that was all right because I had a lot to think about. And I needed the sleep, having gotten almost none the previous night.

The bus, finally loaded, was only about half full. For a time I wondered why everyone chose to sit up front, but after we had stopped about two dozen times, letting off and picking up passengers, it became quite clear that I was almost the only through passenger.

Around dark I settled on the long back seat and stretched out, and the next thing I knew it was six o'clock the next morning. We had just popped out of the trees above Eureka, and as the bus turned and twisted downward, I caught glimpses of giant Sequoias outlined against a brilliant blue sky. Shortly, we were on a cobblestone street full of water puddles, ample testimony that we were arriving only minutes after a heavy rain.

I had by this time moved up front and was hanging over the driver.

"Looks like one of those rare days for this part of the country, sailor. Eureka gets more than its share of rain."

"Was that Humboldt Bay I saw awhile back?"

"No doubt about it."

The smell of frying eggs and hashbrowns hit me at the door of the bus terminal, but I had no intention of settling for a civilian breakfast. It was only six o'clock; so I had plenty of time, I figured, to make it to the ship and get a real breakfast.

There was only one taxicab in sight. The driver, a slouchy man with a two-day beard, was leaning against it contemplating me, but making no move to help me with my luggage.

"Just toss it in the back, mate," he said, lifting his spent cigarette and taking a last draw. "You headin' for the docks?"

I nodded, inspecting the backseat of the taxi. The floorboard was covered with trash, and the seat itself was stained in several places.

"You can ride up front with me if that don't suit you."

"Thanks a lot."

I carried my seabag around to the front on the passenger's side and set it in the floor and got in, straddling it. The ditty bag I left strapped over my left shoulder.

Five minutes later the driver pulled in close to a long dock, at which two cutters were tied up, end to end. They appeared to be about the same length; but one was black and old and looked like a pile of rusting steel, while the other was brilliantly white and sleek, reminding me of a wooden yacht.

Ignoring the cabby's open hand, I got out, tossing my gear to the dock.

"You assigned to one of them boats there?"

I looked at him. All the way from the bus depot he had not said a word to me, and now in his voice was a note of condescension.

"That's right. But I don't have the slightest notion which one it is."

"Well, you better hope its the ugly one."

"I was hoping it would be the pretty one."

"That's because you're goin' on appearances. You'll work your ass off on that other'n."

"I took out my wallet and laid two one-dollar bills on the palm. "Keep the change."

"Whup! I get ten dollars for that trip out from Eureka."

I turned and walked to my seabag and picked it up. Then I glanced back. He was still holding out his hand. "You may get ten dollars from some people, but all you're getting from me is in your greedy hands." With that I headed down the dock.

"Hey, mate!" shouted the taxi driver. "Do I have to go to your Old Man for my fare? Fork over eight more bucks!"

"Go to anybody you want to," I called back. "But that's all you're getting."

"Man, you don't need no more enemies than you already got in this here town!"

That brought me to a sudden stop. "What is that supposed to mean? I don't have any enemies around here at all."

"I beg to differ with you. Just by the mere fact that you're a Coastie you have lots of enemies in this Humboldt Bay area. Every fisherman in these parts hates your guts."

"I don't know anything about that," I said, puzzled. "But one thing I do know is that you're not getting any more money out of me."

The taxi driver threw up his hands, incredulous. "You'll be hearin' more about this!" With that he turned and got into the cab. "Next time you want a ride in this town, don't come to me."

I walked slowly past the old bucket, keeping an eye out for some kind of life on board. There was no name or number on its bow, but on the brilliantly white cutter just beyond, I could make out the number *630*, which was no help to me at all. It had to be the *Alert*, however, since the other one was definitely not an air-sea rescue ship.

It wasn't until I stepped upon the two-by-twelve gangplank of the white cutter that something in faded dungarees and a white skivvy shirt popped out of a hatch and greeted me. It had to be the cook, I figured, because a dirty white apron was dangling from his neck.

"I'm looking for the Coast Guard cutter *Alert*," I called out, waving.

The CGC Alert passing beneath the Golden Gate Bridge (1947)

"Well, you found it," chuckled the man, who appeared to be about fifty. He had a small strip of fading and unruly hair above each ear.

"I'm Hall, radioman."

"Come on aboard. I'm Tully, the cook. And I guess you're our new sparks," he said. "Let me give you a hand with that bag."

Maybe I had heard wrong, I thought. Did he mean I was the radioman-in-charge?

Tully had big hands and a big, good-natured face; and it was apparent at once to me that he was a good man to know.

Once the gear was in a pile on the ship, we shook hands.

"You look like somebody that's been on a ship before," he said. "You a ruptured duck from the Navy?"

"How'd you guess?" I laughed.

"Well, I'll tell you. You shore as hell don't look like a recruit, and since you didn't know this was the Cutter *Alert* I figured you wasn't no seasoned Coastie. You walked like a sailor across that plank, though."

"So I had to be a ruptured duck!"

"A Goddamned ruptured duck lookin' for a mud puddle!" He whammed me on the back.

Old Tully's head almost reached my shoulder, but in girth he was considerably larger than me. He carried his pouch proudly, however, I noticed, as if it were some kind of badge of honor.

"On this ship I'm the cook," he said, off-handedly. "Nobody but nobody gives me any crap. Anybody gives you any crap about bein' from the Navy, you just let me know. I'll starve him to death." He tapped me on the shoulder to get my attention. "Come on, I'll show you where to stow that stuff."

Down the starboard side of the little ship we went, with Tully in the lead, waddling like a big contented duck. Without a word, he bounced through a hatchway, banged his way down a steel ladder, and came to a stop finally just inside what had to be the crew's quarters. For a moment, he wheezed and coughed, taking no pains to lessen the noise he was making even though the compartment was occupied by a dozen sleeping men.

"Hey!" somebody yelled. "Can't you keep it down a bit?"

"Stow it, Big Mouth," warned Tully. Then to me he said, "Why don't you find an empty bunk and leave this stuff, then come forward and I'll fix you some breakfast. These lazy assholes in here was up most of the night fishin' a Portygee out of the drink and prob'ly not a one of 'em will make it to the mess deck before noon."

I nodded, feeling just a bit uncomfortable. It was quite clear to me that if anybody else but Tully had made such a disturbance there would undoubtedly have been an altercation of some kind. And who was to say that these disturbed ones would not take out their anger on me later, once the cook was no longer around? I hastily deposited my gear on an unoccupied bunk and left by the same exit Tully had used. I had no idea where the galley and messdeck were; but by following my nose, I discovered it one deck above and just forward of the quarters.

"Listen," said Tully, once I was seated and had a cup of coffee, "you look like a savvy guy, so I'm gonna lay a thing or two on you. Listen or not, makes no never mind to me. All right? This ship's sittin' on a powder keg here in Humboldt Bay, an' one of these days it's gonna go POW! You can depend on it. I've been cook here for a year, an' I know what I'm talkin' 'bout. You mind your P's and Q's an' you might come out of it all right, but if you don't you'll end up either dead or wishin' you was."

I nodded slowly. "What, may I ask—?"

"You hear me, Red?"

"Sure, I hear you," I said. "But what's going on?"

"'Goin' on'? Hell, man, we've got this whole bay mad as hell at us and ready to kill our asses! We go out ever' day an' confiscate and quarantine these fishin' boats, puttin' the Portygees out of business, makin' it impossible for 'em to make a livin'—an' they an' ever'body that's kin to 'em and relies on 'em to buy their wares is after our balls! It's got to where we have to go ashore in pairs when we want to see a movie or buy a bottle of beer!"

"What do they do, lay for Coasties?"

"Hell yes they do! You decide to go ashore you get somebody to go with you. Me, I stay aboard ship most of the time. Even the fuckin' city police is mad at us."

Tully's big round face was flaming red, looking like it might explode any minute. The thought occurred to me that he just might be pulling my leg. Maybe this was some kind of 'initiation' into the Ship's Company.

I accepted the large platter of food he brought out and waved under my nose, acknowledging with raised hands and a startled WOW! just how impressed I was! After forking a mouthful of hashbrowns, I told him it was a Rembrandt, enough to bring tears to a hungry man's eyes. Tall, homebaked biscuits, fresh eggs over-easy, two thick slices of blackened ham, hashbrown potatoes, and thick brown gravy! I was still shaking my head in dismay when I finished; and, looking up, I realized that Tully was as proud as a peacock at the way I was carrying on.

"You didn't see food like that at G. I., I'll bet."

"It is a fact, Cookie."

"Well, you just remember what I told you."

A slender brown kid in dungarees and a brilliant white cap pushed back on his head suddenly appeared. He nodded, smiling, and appeared to be trying to decide what to say. In the face he was as pretty as a young girl; and, in that split second that our eyes met, it seemed to me that there was something almost coquettish about him. He had large brown eyes, raven-black hair, and full, sensitive lips.

"Your name Hall?" he finally asked. "I'm supposed to tell you to report to the bridge on the double." He sounded apologetic. "The Old Man wants to see you."

"Okay by me," I said, nodding.

"Eat your chow," growled Tully. "He'll probably keep you waitin' when you bust your ass to git up there."

"I'm Miranda," said the kid, extending his hand.

I exchanged hands with my fork and took his. "Just call me Red. You a quartermaster?"

Miranda blushed like a girl being invited out on her first date. "Well, not actually. I was just assigned to the bridge because the Boats and I don't get along very well."

I batted my eyes, glancing at Tully.

"Our boatswain's mate likes Tony but the feelin's not mutual."

"I'd like to work on deck, but he's always—!" protested Miranda, stopping in mid-sentence. Suddenly, with his mouth clamped shut, he dashed through the forward hatch.

"He's a good kid," said Tully, "but Larsen's got him antsy."

Then Miranda was back, standing nervously with his back against the forward bulkhead a few feet away from me and Tully. "He wants you on the double, Red," he said. "Sorry."

"He'll git him when Red's finished eatin' his chow," said Tully. "Go tell him I said that."

Miranda smiled thinly, his face very pale, "I can't tell him that."

"Sure you can!" laughed Tully. "Hell, I'm not afraid of that old bastard. He's way more bark than bite."

"I'm finished," I said. "Thanks, Tully."

"Don't mention it."

When I arrived outside the captain's stateroom a short time later, I told Miranda to hold on a moment until I could make himself presentable. "First impressions, you know," I said with a grin. "By the way, what's he like?"

Miranda smiled for the first time, "He's a pussy cat, if you don't do something wrong. Be sure to let him do the talkin'."

"I know the type. Okay, my friend, go ahead, show me in."

We had paused in front of a beautifully polished solid oak door, the kind found on homes in old exclusive neighborhoods. It was outfitted with polished brass fittings, including a nameplate and a knocker.

Miranda raised the knocker and let it drop once. Instantly, from within came a rumbling, growling noise that sent my eyebrows upward. Then we heard a heavy chair being shoved about inside.

"A pussy cat?" I said, nervously.

"His bite," said Miranda, grinning and opening the door.

The instant I looked into the deep-sunken eyes of the Old Man, a tall, hump-shouldered salt with mighty bags beneath his eyes, I decided that if appearances meant anything here was no pussycat. And as for his bite, that remained to be seen.

"Hall?" The sound of the old man's voice actually rattled something in the room.

"Yessir. Hall, Sir."

"Well, git on in here!"

I ducked inside and stood at attention in the center of the small room.

The Old Man, whose name was Lt. Commander Mike Miklokowski, according to the brass nameplate on the door, circled a large mahogany desk and fell heavily into a swivel rocker. He was in full dress blues, with the exception of a cap, which was lying upside down on the desk on a stack of papers. He looked like a man more used to foul weather gear than dress blues and polished black shoes, and I was certain he was no blue-water sailor, but an old salt of the world's great oceans.

"You're a fuck-up, I understand!" he shouted, causing my mouth to drop open. From the desk he lifted what appeared to be a service record. "In the Service two weeks and already you've got a black mark! Why'd they send you to me? I won't stand for no shit on this cutter, you understand. One false move from you and your ass is mud."

For one of the few times in my life I was speechless. With cap in hand, I just stood there at attention, not batting an eye.

"Well, goddamn it?"

"Well, Sir, I don't know what you're talking about. How have I—?"

"Oh, you don't know how you've fucked up? Is that what you're sayin'? Well, I'll add *stupidity* to the list. You actually don't know?"

"No, Sir."

Had the Brass at Government Island found out about that evening at *Ted and Roy's*? The faked pass! Had the Personnel Officer—?

"Well, I'll refreshen your memory, sailor! You lied to the recruiting officer about your petty officer rating at the time of bein' discharged from the Navy! Remember?"

"Sir, I can explain that—"

"Never mind, never mind! What I don't understand—" he stopped and glared at me. His old leathery face seemed to have softened a bit.

"What I don't understand—is how in hell you managed to make 'em believe you! I think that must be a first, by cricket! Just by puttin' down that you was a Second Class Radioman—!"

I glanced at him and saw that his mouth was slightly twisted into what looked like the makings of a grin. "On the one hand, I don't want no maverick sonofabitch giving me trouble by breakin' the rules, but on the other anybody that can outsmart the goddamned white-collared pencil-pushin' bastards in this spit-and-polish outfit *could* make a damned good sailor! Which're you?"

"Yessir."

The Old Man stared at me out of the corners of his eyes, waiting.

"Don't git no wrong ideas, now," he went on. "You behave yourself an' you'll be all right." He scanned a page of my record. "I just hope you can handle the radio stuff. My sparks is retiring in about one week, an' I need someone that can step right in an' take over for him. What I want you to do is learn ever'thing there is to know about that radio shack as soon as possible. If that fuckin' chicken farmer gits off this ship too quick—Well, I just don't want to think about what might happen. Oh, hell, git on out of here and report to the Chief!"

"Yessir."

I lost no time joining Miranda outside the captain's cabin.

"Wha'd I tell you?" the kid grinned.

"All the blood's inside," I said, wiping my brow. "I'm lucky to be alive."

"I heard every word said in there, so don't pretend. Next, I'm supposed to head you in the direction of the radio shack. It's right back there, two doors down."

"You know," I said, "it's taking some getting used to, this *door* and *wall* business. Next thing, somebody'll be saying *floor*, instead of deck! What kind of an outfit is this?"

Miranda, swinging along in front of me like a girl with big hips who knows she's being watched, laughed but said nothing until he reached the second door. "Red, you sound like an old salt, to hear you talk—but you're too young for that," he said, admiringly. "I'll bet you—"

"What's this guy's name?" I asked, ignoring what he had said.

He nodded, making a face. "It's Robinson. By the way, if you thought the Old Man was a character, wait'll you meet this one."

"Thus far all I've seen aboard this ship are characters."

Miranda rapped twice on the brass plate. "You seen me and I'm no character."

From inside came the squeak of a swivel chair and a single garbled word, which Miranda interpreted to mean *enter*. He turned the handle to the door and pushed it inward. "Sparky, here's your replacement!" To me, speaking rapidly, he said, "How about we eat chow together at noon?"

Ignoring him, I ducked into the radio shack, leaving the door wide open. (Like the Captain's this was a solid wooden door.) A man that looked to be in his sixties was seated in front a typewriter that was bolted to a leaf extending out from the operating position. There was a double row of radio receivers and transmitters at his right elbow.

"I've been expectin' you. Find a seat." The old sparks had a thin, long face almost as tragic as Goodrich's. Without bothering to turn around, he took my outstretched hand. Open on the typewriter in front of him was a heavy Sears and Roebuck catalog, and on the glass-covered counter at his right elbow was a penciled list of items and how much they cost.

The radio shack was four small bulkheads of radio equipment, books, and cables. Besides the narrow glass-covered operating position that ran across the forward bulkhead and the old Underwood typewriter strapped to a wooden leaf that extended from the radio position, there was one other piece of furniture, a swivel rocker bolted to the deck in front of the typewriter. The overhead was a chaos of cables, wires, and pipes.

"I saw your papers for about two minutes," said Robinson, his face wrinkled with doubt. The Old Man grabbed them away from me and said some ex-Navy know-it-all was on his way up from Frisco. You reckon he was talkin' 'bout you?"

I straightened up quickly at this. "I'm ex-Navy but—"

"Well, let me tell you somethin' right off the reel," he growled, his eyes focused on a spot about two feet to the left of my face. "This job's no pushover, even for a Coastie with experience. You think because the *Alert's* a cute little white cutter it's gonna be something like a pleasure craft, like a holiday cruiser, don't you? Well, mate, you've got a surprise comin' to you. It don't even go out until the weather's too bad for regular shipping—and sittin' at the dock it bounces and wallows like a cork. And add to that the fact that the radio has to be manned ever' second we're at sea—an' there's just goin' to be you to man it! If we're out a week, which could happen easy, you'll not sleep for a week!"

"I take it you're getting ready to retire."

"Shit. I been tryin' to retire for a month of Sundays. But I can't until a replacement shows up that can cut the mustard. For one damned thing, the Skipper has to approve the swop, an', Sonny, he don't approve of just ever'thing!" After a pause he added, "I doubt seriously we'll find anybody this entire year."

"I'm your replacement."

Robinson swiveled about and studied my face. "Not likely, anytime soon. No fuckin' ex-Navy can just walk aboard and take this headache over. You not only have to handle voice and CW operations in the worst conditions this side of the North Atlantic, but you've got to know how to mend and repair ever' piece of this goddamned worn-out equipment in here! We don't get repair service up this far north, an' we don't go down to Frisco but once a year. An', my boy, you won't be able to afford the luxury of gettin' seasick—because there would be nobody to relieve you."

"I reckon I can do the job," I said, feeling the heat rising toward my hairline. "I've had some experience with rough conditions on a little nothing ship."

Robinson's eyebrows shot up. "Have you now? In the fuckin' Navy? Have you ever been aboard anythin' this small at sea? And if you have, for how long?"

"Yes, Chief, I have. Smaller than this—and for one hell of a long time."

Robinson was shaking his head. "In the Navy? Not likely, mate. You expect me to believe that?"

"Believe what you like."

"What was it, a PT-boat?" sneered Robinson.

I was working hard at controlling myself. I moved to one end of the operating position, facing old Robinson. "Have you ever seen a wooden subchaser, Chief? They're one hundred and ten feet long and thirty-four feet wide athwartships."

"You spent how long on one of them things?"

"The better part of two years."

"You was a radioman then?"

I nodded but said nothing, having decided that this had gone on long enough.

"Ever do any repairin'?"

I walked to the door. Miranda was still out in the passageway. I returned. "Chief, my rating was radio tech before it was radio operator."

"The hell you say." After staring at me for a time, he added, "If you aint lying to me, you just might be the sonofabitch I been waitin' for. Grab a seat."

The Portygees

◆

The side of me that loved the sea, that made me gaze with longing and anticipation through the wide mouth of Humboldt Bay at the Pacific Ocean each time I went out on deck, that prompted me to go with Miranda each evening to the deserted stern and listen to the slap-slap of the tide coming in against the pilings, now began to affirm the rightness of my decision to join the Coast Guard.

Any day, any hour, we would receive an emergency call on the radio that would send us out. What could be better than frequent trips to sea with a beautiful, safe harbor to come home to? I listened patiently, and sometimes attentively, to Miranda's flat, matter-of-fact accounts of rescues up and down the coast, to his kid's version of the on-going feud between the Coasties and the Portuguese fishermen, and to his inevitable digressions into his own personal problems aboard the cutter.

Through all of it I was smelling the salt air of the open sea and visualizing countless hidden coves and small picturesque villages perched on the rocky shores of the Northern California coast just waiting to be explored.

For at least a week the *Alert* sat at her mooring, docile and contented. It was, someone in the bridge gang told me, the longest period of peace and quiet and boredom in the history of the cutter. No messages came in, even from San Francisco, and none went out; and the routine aboard the ship had become so relaxed most of the crew began renting lockers in town and buying new wardrobes of civvies and spending off-duty nights ashore. But, of course, anyone who ventured beyond the sound of the ship's fog horn (or failed for any reason to hear it) was destined to face a Captain's Mast and restriction to the ship.

I did not venture ashore during this whole time. From an hour or so before morning chow each day until my rendezvous with Miranda on the stern in the evening, I stayed busy in the radio shack, familiarizing myself with the transmitters and receivers, the testing devices, and the storeroom of spare parts. Chief Robinson spent his days studying the Sears and Roebuck catalog and agonizing over such things as the sizes and shapes of his chicken coops and the amounts of money to figure for wire and lumber. His orders were being cut, the Old Man had assured him; and just as soon as he gave the word that I could take over he would be sent to San Francisco for discharge.

The weather had behaved itself all week, undoubtedly the principle reason we had had no business. One evening I said to Miranda that if the weather reports could be trusted, we were in for a very big storm that night. I pointed toward the western horizon. "See that thin, dark line? That's the forefront of it. By three o'clock in the morning it'll be right over us."

Miranda groaned. "Yeah, and you can bet we'll have to go out in it. Some Portygee will run out of gas."

"Don't the Portuguese know better than to fish in bad weather? And why don't they take out enough gas for the return trip?"

From the darkness came Miranda's boyish laughter. "One, they don't know any better; two, they don't want to know any better; and, three, they love to force us outside the harbor in such weather."

To me the feud did not make any sense at all. The Coast Guard was there to safeguard the coast and assist any fisherman or sailor in trouble. Why would anybody go out of his way to fight his benefactors?

"Tell me something. Is the feud a result of jealousy, on the part of the fishermen?" I asked. The ones I had observed closely were dressed poorly and looked as if they hadn't seen a bathtub in a month. "Is it maybe because the Coasties steal their girlfriends?"

Again Miranda laughed and this time there was a sarcastic note in his voice. "Have you ever seen one of those Portygese girls? I'd rather rub up against a pig!"

"Then you tell me, why do they hate us so much?"

"Wait till you really get to know our boatswain's mate. You have to go out on an inspection tour to really understand what's goin' on." After a time he added, "We deprive them of their livelihood when we quarantine their boats, and the Chief loves to quarantine boats."

"'We deprive them of their livelihood'?"

"We inspect their boats, which generally fail to pass for one reason or another, and we quarantine them. We put a sticker on their boat that says that such-and-such must be done and another inspection made before they can fish. If they look cross-eyed at Larkin—"

"And this feud has been going on for a long time?"

"Yeah, I guess so. Probably even before Larkin came aboard. But it's got a lot worse here lately, since he took over the inspection tours."

I sat for a time thinking this over, then I said, "What's your trouble with Boats, Tony? Why does he give you a hard time?"

The kid took his time about answering. Finally, he said, "I'll tell you, Red." His voice was as soft as a girl's. "You're different from Boats and the rest so I guess I can tell you. Everybody aboard this boat thinks I'm a—"

"Thinks you're a what?" I asked. It was so dark I could no longer make out his face in the darkness of the stern.

"A guy that's turned onto other guys."

*   *   *

Sometime after midnight I was awakened suddenly from a deep sleep. A hand was clamped onto my shoulder and somebody was saying something to me in a loud whisper.

"What is it?" I said, trying to sit up.

"Keep it down! No need of disturbing the crew just yet, but we're gettin' ready to shake a leg." It was Chief Robinson, wearing only a white T-shirt and a pair of dungaree trousers. "Thought maybe you might want to get the jump on everybody, maybe hit the messdeck for sandwiches and coffee. In about ten minutes you'll have to stand in line."

"How do you know we're goin' out?"

The old chief was already across the room going through my footlocker. When he returned, he whispered, "How do sparkies always know things before anybody else? Better take these along to the shack with you." He shoved a windbreaker and a sock ski cap into my face.

In the empty messdeck we gathered up sandwiches made of thick slices of pressed bologna and cheese and liverwurst and onions and pickles, three apiece, and large mugs filled with steaming black coffee. The Chief, hovering over me like a mother hen, told me what my sandwiches should contain and how many sandwiches I should prepare, explaining that we were no doubt in for a *helluva* night.

I was amused by old Robinson's youthful exuberance and possessiveness, thinking of it as an extension of the week-long coaching I had suffered through. I had decided that it was much simpler to go along with the old codger than to argue with him. He was a man with a single idea, getting out of the Coasties; and if I so much as left off one slice of dill pickle, he would undoubtedly read it as a threat to his own retirement!

In the radio shack, we settled into our first sandwiches. An additional chair had been anchored to the deck at the port end of the long counter, and now I sat in it and watched Robinson as he tried to get his Dagwood down. The dill pickles and the thick slices of onion were distracting me a bit from the liverwurst, finally bringing tears to my eyes. I glanced over at the Chief through bleary eyes and smiled, thinking what an old bastard he was.

"What're you grinnin' at, Red? You got hemorrhoids?"

"I'm sitting here eating this godawful sandwich like an idiot. I wasn't even hungry, Chief."

"What's wrong with that sandwich?" Robinson demanded, trying to grin. "Well, don't eat the sonsabitch if you don't want it! Stow it an' the other one in my drawer here, before the fun starts."

"You didn't tell me how you knew we are goin' out."

"I just know, ole buddy. Any minute now the static in that speaker right over your head is goin' to git worse an' a high-pitched squeal in Portygese is goin' to—"

At this my mouth had dropped open and I just stared at the lunatic. "Are you telling me you got me up out of a warm bed and fed me dill pickles and onions just on a hunch?"

"I'm tellin' you, Red! Any minute now. Trust me!"

"Shit, I'm goin' back to my sack!"

"You won't ever make it."

I tossed the rest of my sandwich into the wastebasket and started to get up. My coffee mug on the glass countertop had commenced to move very slowly to the starboard. "Man, you've got be just about ready for a Section Eight."

"I'm ready for a discharge." Robinson grinned at me, his mouth full of sandwich. "This is gonna be my last friggin' time out. From now on it's dry land for ole Louie Robinson." It was obvious he was enjoying my consternation. "Ever heard the one about the sailor that started walkin' inland with a shovel over one shoulder?"

"He was carrying an oar."

"Yeah, well."

I reached for my coffee mug as it began to move to the starboard. Outside the wind was already whistling through the antenna wires and the halyards. The static in the overhead speaker seemed to be picking up. I slid the mug back in place and turned it loose. Immediately, it headed toward the typewriter.

"The sea seems to be acting up," I observed, refusing to look at the Chief. I could tell he was staring at me and grinning.

"It's already hit the coast north of here," he said, casually. "I figure there'll be at least one Portygee in trouble just about now."

Sure enough, at that moment from one of the speakers came a series of pops and crackles. My belly muscles tightened. This old coot just might be right!

"That's him, warmin' up the final tubes," grinned Robinson. "The sonsabitches never disappoint you. And sometimes I think they draw straws to decide which boat'll be out of gas. Of course, sometimes, I guess, there's a tie, because we have to tow in two of them the same night."

From deep within the layers of static in the speaker, as if from a barrel, came a terrified and unintelligible voice.

"Okay, Red, go wake the Old Man! I'll get this peckerwood's location, once he calms down! Tell the skipper it's a Portygee in trouble."

Without a word I leaped to my feet and rushed out into the passageway. I had not been able to make sense out of a single syllable the fisherman was yelling. Perhaps Robinson was having me wake the Old Man for nothing, but if so he would be the one that would have to face the music later.

I rapped once on the skipper's heavy oak door and instantly the sound of a crash came from inside and a moment later the bellow I was expecting, as the Old Man thrashed about in the darkness. "Goddamnit! What is it? A fisherman in trouble? Git your ass in here!"

I opened the door and said, "Yessir! The Chief—Sparky—!" I stuck my head through the door just as the Captain turned on a light. "Sparky sent me to—!"

"A Portygee? Then git your ass on the double down to the wardroom and wake up the duty officer! I reckon that would be Rhodes! And get Boats up and tell 'im we're gettin' underway! Hold up a minute! The first thing I want you to do is go wake the motormack. Tell 'im we're gettin' underway!"

"Yessir!"

Then, as I rushed away, there came still another blast, "Alert the cook! Goddamnit to hell! Why don't them dadblamed fishermen take enough fuel to git home on?"

Even down in Officer Country, which was practically sound proof, I could still hear the thunder and rumble of the Old Man's voice. Lt. Rhodes, the Supply Officer, and Lt. Bertinelli, who shared a stateroom, were already on their feet, struggling to get dressed.

"We headin' out?" asked Mr. Rhodes, nervously. "Did the Old Man know I was in my quarters?"

"I guess so, Sir," I said with a grin. Then I added, "According to Sparky a Portugese fisherman is in trouble."

"Okay! Go wake Boats and the motormacks!"

"Aye, aye, Sir!"

"We're in the Coast Guard now, Hall!" laughed Bertinelli. "You reverting to your Navy training?"

"I'm unlearning about as fast as I'm learning!" I said with a laugh.

I raced up the ladder to the bridge, my heart giving it hell at the prospect of going out in such a storm. Now, this, I told myself, is the way to go!

When I burst through the door of the radio shack, Robinson was serenely munching on his second sandwich and sipping coffee. In the typewriter before him was a sheet of paper. I pointed toward it and looked at him. He waved me off and kept on chewing. I looked closer and saw that he had identified the fisherman, where he was stranded, and why.

"Is it really an emergency?" I asked.

"I don't have the faintest idea."

"Are we going to have to go out?"

"That's up to the Old Man. I say we will."

I slumped into my chair and reached for my coffee. It had backed up against the port bulkhead, along with a dirty saucer, an opened package of Chesterfield cigarettes, and Robinson's ball-point pen. All of which were beginning to inch back to starboard.

"Well?" I asked, pointing toward the sheet of paper in the typewriter. "What did the fisherman have to say?"

"Same old stuff, Red. He's out of gas. Now, the funny thing is, my friend, he went out fishin' knowin' full well how much gas he had and how far he would be able to go and still git back home. So what does he do? With a storm comin' up he goes till he runs out of gas. Luckily, he just happens to find himself in Moro Cove, a nice, sheltered little place about eighty miles from here and hard as hell to get into in the pitch darkness of a storm." Robinson had lowered what was left of his big sandwich and was, I thought, looking a little pale around the gills. "Oh, I made out enough to know where he's claimin' to be and that he's takin' on sea water—"

"What do you mean 'claiming'?"

"Maybe he's lyin'. They do that sometimes, you know." He glanced at me and burped, frowning. "But I've got a hunch this one's on the level."

"Then it is an emergency!"

"I didn't say that. Here, run this up to the bridge."

At the door he stopped me. "Better round up all this loose stuff and do somethin' with it, before we put out to sea. It's gonna git right active around here soon's we leave the harbor."

Even before we had cleared the Coast Guard Life Boat Station, which was perhaps a mile from the mouth of Humboldt Bay, it was impossible to take a step without hanging onto something. I left the Chief sitting in front of the typewriter and went outside to the little passageway. There I clung to the lifeline and drank in the clean, damp sea breeze we were heading in to. We were still inside the harbor, yet there was no way I could stand without hanging onto something! What would it be like outside the harbor?

Hearing a snapping and popping from one or the other of the two speakers, I returned to the shack and took my place next to the Chief.

"Better strap yourself in," he said, pointing toward the canvas belts at the base of my chair. "Ever ride a buckin' horse?"

"Can this little wooden ship take it?" I asked. "I mean once we got outside the harbor?" I gathered up the strap and buckled it around my waist. "Is it put together tongue-in-groove?"

"Hell, I don't know! I'm surprised that you of all people would worry about something like that. What would your subchaser buddies think?" When I had no reply to this, he added. "I reckon you must've got close to one of them typhoons they have over in the western Pacific, didn't you?"

I nodded. "I always thought it was going to break in the middle every time the wind got up."

Suddenly, the deck became heavy beneath us. It seemed as if we were moving upward in a very fast elevator!

"We are no longer land-locked!" cackled Robinson. "What you're now feelin' is the Pacific, the meanest goddamned ocean in the world! And all the time you thought the Atlantic was the roughest!"

"You're wrong there, Chief. But I am surprised it's this rough along the coast."

"Hell, it's the coast that's makin' it rough! Don't you know that?"

Then we were dropping fast! And when we hit the bottom of the valley, Robinson said, "We're headin' right into it! Better hang on!"

The jolts, which became predictable, were bone-jarring; and each was followed by a sickening wallow to the port and a high, climbing movement to the starboard.

Robinson, hanging on for dear life, yelled, "I once ast you if you could handle yourself at sea. Now, I guess we'll find out. But I was hopin' you'd down more of that onion and limburger sandwich."

"Just remember," I warned the old reprobate, "if I fail this little test you'll never see that chicken farm."

I could feel my entire stomach roll and bounce like a ball each time the ship went through one of its cycles. Glancing around at the old Chief, I was startled at what I saw.

"You all right?" I called out in amazement.

"Yeah," he said. "After we're out awhile, I'll get my shit back together ag'in." He had turned a pale green; and as he spoke his mouth twisted pathetically, as though he were about to lose everything.

"You should not have eaten that liverwurst and all those onions," I said, genuinely sympathetic. "That was enough to make a horse sick."

"It wasn't that. I git this way ever' time we go out. But I'll be all right in a few minutes."

At this point, Lt. Bertinelli popped into the shack with a clipboard in his right hand. He was leaping from one handhold to another and bouncing off the bulkheads. When he saw the Chief's face, he steadied himself and said, "You look a bit peaked, Chief. Think you can get this off pretty soon?" Whereupon he removed a sheet of paper from the clipboard.

"Through all this Q-R-goddamned-Nancy, Sir?" demanded Robinson. "Who the hell do you think I am, Superman?" He took the message and slapped it down on the counter.

"Let Hall wrestle with it," said Bertinelli, glancing quickly toward Robinson. "You don't look good."

"The Chief's right, Sir," I said. "Maybe when we stop pitching so bad we can get it through."

"I think you ought to try," said the lieutenant. "Ole Lewis here is too goofed up to do it."

"Go ahead, Red," said Robinson, with a sickly twist of his lower lip. "It won't make a damned bit of difference to me. I'm gettin' out of this crap shoot."

I looked at the Chief, who was ignoring me; then, turning, I said to the Communications Officer, "I could try CW."

Bertinelli nodded, looking pleased. "That's code, right?"

Against the port bulkhead was my old friend from the Navy, a TDE transmitter, already warmed up. It was monolithic and packed a punch like a two-ton mule. With no intention of using it, Robinson had turned it on sometime earlier, a reflex action.

"CW," mused Bertinelli, bending over me at the transmitter. "What are you doing now?"

"Getting ready to dip the final," I said.

"The Chief here knows you can't work this thing, or he wouldn't even give you the chance! Right, Chief?" To me Bertinelli said, "Nobody has used this since I came aboard. Mainly because nobody has been able to send and receive CW, I guess."

"Why the hell would anybody want to use CW when we're within voice range?" demanded the Chief. "He won't be able to get anybody with it, even if he could get this dinosaur to goin'."

The Hallicrafters receiver was, I knew, tuned to the operating frequency of NMC, base radio at the Twelfth District Coast Guard headquarters. But the speaker attached to it had been muted. Now, as I unmuted and increased the volume with my left hand, I reached across to the transceiver at Robinson's position and backed the volume off, eliminating a lot of noise, what the Chief had called Q R Nancy.

The Chief was watching me like a hawk.

"It's in that drawer in front of you," he said. "Not that it'll do you any good."

From the drawer I pulled out an old brass key. It was exactly like the one I had used on the Navy subchaser at Manus Island when we had run aground and I had sent S O S for three hours nonstop. Experiencing a healthy dose of déjà vu, I plugged it into the socket at the operating position and glanced at the Chief.

"Yeah, that's the one. But you won't be able to zero beat the TDE."

Holding the key down with my right hand, I began to flip knobs on the transmitter. From the speaker came a high-pitched scream, and as I adjusted the final amplifier tubes, this became a thin little squeak that eventually petered out completely.

"My aching back," said the Chief. "I think you did it, Red. See if you can get a rise out of NMC."

I began to tap out in International Morse. *NMC DE NRUP K.*

Instantly, over the speaker came *NRUP DE NMC QSA 5 K.*

I sent the message, a very short one, in no time flat and received a roger. The lieutenant patted me on the back and headed for the bridge.

"Let's see what kind of a lie he's goin' to tell the Old Man," said the Chief, leaning and flipping a switch that I had not noticed up to this time. "I've got a speaker mounted in the pilothouse."

From a speaker on one of the shelves above the operating position we began hearing background noises. And in less than a minute we began hearing footsteps.

"Cap'n, our new radio op sent that message in Morse Code, sent it in two minutes flat without a mistake. No repeats. Slick as a whistle."

Captain Miklokowski mumbled something we couldn't make out. Then, loud and clear, "Oh? In this mess?"

"Very, very professional. I've never seen anything like it. To me it sounded like a string of meaningless dits and dahs, and I couldn't read a bit of it. Chief Robinson said it sounded like a fucking teletype to him, the way Hall sent it."

Chief Robinson flipped the speaker off and turned to me. "Hell, they never would acknowledge me when the fuckin' QRN was this bad." He started to laugh but ended up coughing. I just sat there. "I think we scared the shit out of the boys at NMC. They're not used to havin' CW hurled at them that fast. An' right now they're all probably astin each other who the hell's aboard the *Alert.* They know damned well it wasn't me sendin' that."

Not long after that Lt. Bertinelli was back. "Chief, in your opinion is Hall ready to take over here?"

"Yes, Sir, he is." Robinson straightened up. "I have no doubt about it at all. I guess I'll go pack my bags and head for Arkansas."

The lieutenant laughed, ignoring the last part of what Robinson had said, and slapped me on the back. "Let me be the first to welcome you aboard, Sparks."

Later, Robinson, who had lost most of the pea green from his face, unstrapped himself and said that he was going below to get some shut-eye. He would, he said, be up to relieve me after morning chow.

"I'm goin' to dream of domineckers and Rhode Island reds," he said, bumping me on purpose on the way to the hatch. "An' I don't intend to give a thought to whether you can handle this wasp nest or not."

For a time after Robinson disappeared I stood in the door of the radio shack and stared into the pitch-black storm, keeping an ear cocked for a break in the static from the speakers. Any variation might turn into another emergency. But would I be able to translate the calls for help, the way the old Chief had?

It seemed to me that the ship was in grave danger of crashing into the giant black boulders that were piled helter-skelter along the coast. And the thought that we were proceeding at a lively clip quite close in *without benefit of radar* raised the short hairs on the back of my neck.

Then, still hanging out there looking into the darkness, I experienced something close to an epiphany. It was like a joining of the mind and the body, during which I had no fear or even concern, only an exhilaration that I had not felt for a long time. It came to me that this was the way to go; and feeling more devil-may-care than I had ever felt before, I said into the fine salt spray that was whipping around the bridge, "Do your damnedest!"

Radioman-in-Charge

◆

Chief Robinson, true to his word, showed up right after morning chow call, wanting to know how things were going. I assured him that all was well.

"I'm not gettin' off this damned ship a day too soon," he said, wheezing. This turned into a fit of coughing.

"Are you all right, Chief?"

"Hell no I'm not all right. I've got hemorrhoids so bad I can't set down, an' ever' muscle in my body hurts like hell. All this bouncin' an' rollin' an nose-divin' an' keepin' late hours an' the goddamned dampness an' cold—!"

Lt. Bertinelli's head popped through the door. "Hey, Hall, if you want a look at the cove we've been searching for, it's dead ahead."

"Take off, I'll watch the shack," said Robinson, falling into his swivel chair. I nodded and went out, closing the door.

Visibility was still very poor. High winds and continuous thunder and lightning had left with the night, replaced by heavy sheets of rain and an almost impenetrable blanket of fog. I stood just inside a hatchway on the port side of the main deck, partially protected from the driving rain, and tried to make out something ahead. Great black rocks towered above the ship on that side and seemed to go on forever, up and down the coast.

The mouth of the cove I could not make out, regardless of how hard I tried. My eyelids felt stiff and dry from my all-night vigil, but I knew I would not be able to sleep until the fisherman had been found, the rescue accomplished, and the ship was on its way back to Eureka.

Castleberry, a stocky quartermaster known for his vulgarity and practical jokes, was suddenly beside me. "I just heard the Old Man give the word to board this sonofabitch and check him out if he's still afloat."

"What's he going to do if he finds out the Portugese has no emergency?" I asked.

"I know what I'd do," said Castleberry. "I'd see to it he has one."

The cutter began to nose around to the port, directly toward the rocks! At this point, feeling a bit queasy at the prospect of piling up in such high seas, I threw up my hands in dismay. Then, just when I expected us to hit something, there appeared a small opening dead ahead.

"The Old Man really knows this coast," said Castleberry proudly. "He's a bastard in port but at sea you won't find a better commanding officer."

The opening had widened, revealing a thick wall of mist and, while we watched, the short, stubby mast of a fishing boat. At first the little unpainted single-masted shrimp boat seemed to be sitting in a great pile of black stones, but within minutes it became apparent to me that it was indeed floating free and clear and at anchor in calm waters.

"Look, that S. O. B.'s at anchor!" snorted Castleberry. "He's in no danger at all of going aground! And he's too high in the water to have taken very much on!"

As the *Alert* swooped in upon the tiny fishing boat, a dark figure emerged from the cabin and began to wave his arms and shout in Portugese. I had moved to the port bow and from the Old Man's booming replies to the fisherman, which were sent forth through the ship's PA system, I was able to put together the story, that the boat was out of petrol but that the crew had managed to stop the leak in the hull.

"We're comin' aboard!" I heard the Old Man shout. "Prepare to be boarded!"

The Portugese skipper had raced to the rear of his boat, which was pointed toward the cutter, and was cupping his hand to his ear in obvious consternation.

"You *comprendo* all right!" boomed the Old Man. "But whether you do or not, we're comin' aboard!"

Then out of the tiny cabin other dark figures in rain gear began to file! In disbelief, I counted out loud, "One, two, three, four!" Four men besides the skipper had been below decks all the time!

"What's this?" screamed the Old Man. "What are all of you men doing aboard this miserable derelict?"

The boarding party, led by Chief Boatswain's Mate Larkin, a formidable man in his heavy foul-weather gear, was soon to discover that the five Portugese had consumed a great deal of vino and were indeed in very fine spirits. They would gladly share with the *vetty* fine Coast Guard boys—if they only had any left. The gas tank was also quite empty, the boatswain's mate relayed back to the cutter. When Larkin demanded to know why he had come so far from his home port without a spare tank of gasoline, the skipper shook his head, grinning broadly and saying again and again, "*No comprende, señor!*"

Inside the cove the storm was not so fierce. Indeed, it seemed to be diminishing somewhat. The Old Man, after delivering a vitriolic address to the five happy fishermen, who had been assured that they were going to be towed free of charge back to their home port, ordered the anchor dropped. The *Alert* would sit out the storm there and return to Eureka when he got good and ready, he said, aiming his last words at the fishermen.

Castleberry, trailing along behind me, commented that Larkin should put the fishing boat on a very long towline and cut a few short corners around and among the rocks. Maybe the bastards would take word back home that this old shit had to stop. The fun over, I headed for the radio shack, leaving Castleberry still complaining.

At anchor the cutter bobbed about like a cork, making it difficult to move without support. Robinson was poring over his catalog and did not look up when I entered and sat down.

"Why doesn't somebody do something about this stupid feud?" I asked. "What's the sense to it? What good did that fisherman get out of all this?"

"You want to know about *sense*? And what *good* it did that wino?" snorted Robinson. "Who said there was any sense to it? For that matter, was there ever a feud that made sense? And as for the good it did that fisherman, for one thing he's getting a free ride all the way home. I'll bet he wishes he could pull this stunt everyday."

"I mean why doesn't it stop? Is it going to continue forever?"

"Hey, listen, Mate, it takes two to tango. As long as the Portygese pull this kind of shit I think we'll keep slapping notices on their boats, even when they don't need them."

I settled in at the second operating position and put my head on my hands. In seconds I was sound asleep. Sometime later I awoke with a start, realizing that my face was sliding on the glass counter and my hands were down near the deck. I sat up and looked around. The Chief was writing something on a sheet of paper.

"It looks to me like *everybody* loses," I said, picking up where I had left off. After a pause, I added, "The real problem seems to be that the fishermen think they're being over-protected."

"The real problem is pride," said Robinson, looking wise. "Theirs and ours. Pure dee ole pride."

It was my turn to snort. "All we would have to do is leave them alone. You obviously don't consider the feud a problem.

"Well," said the old Chief, "one thing for sure. If they'd put life-saving equipment and fire extinguishers and two-way radios aboard their boats, we would leave them alone."

"And how about Larkin? Would he leave their women alone?"

"How about him?" He condemns their boats for a variety of reasons, including poor equipment. Who's side you on?"

"I'm not taking their side," I said, "but is it possible our regulations are too strict?"

"Maybe. Who the hell really cares whether they float or sink? I shore as hell don't. Why don't you go back to sleep?"

I nodded, tight-lipped. "And I think that about sums up the thinking of the crew of this little boat."

*   *   *

When the *Alert* made it back to Eureka two days later, the storm having finally given way to a brilliantly clear blue sky and a calm sea, I was summoned to the bridge and informed by Lt. Bertinelli that henceforth I would take Chief Robinson's place on the fishing-boat inspection team. I had not fully recovered from than when, a few minutes later, Larkin's announcement came over the PA system:

"Now hear this! The following people will report to the starboard boat rack in five minutes: Miranda, Hall, and Houston! On the double!"

I had just sat down at a table in the messdeck with a cup of coffee, after six hours on watch; but while Larkin's voice was still bouncing off the bulkheads, I got up and carried it across the room and turned it upside down on the coffee urn grate. Evidently, Robinson had decided at the last minute not to go, probably to get back at me. This way I would learn quickly what we were up against with the fishermen. Apparently, what Larkin was doing did not bother him much.

However, despite the fact that Robinson had been in his sack with Sears and Roebuck all the time I was on watch, I felt no resentment for this little stunt. I wanted to take part in the inspections.

Miranda headed me off as I was preparing to go topside, and it was obvious to me that he was very upset.

"What's wrong?" I asked, slapping his shoulder.

"Larkin's out to get me," he said, pale-faced. "He just told me the next time I go on liberty he's taking me to a room."

"Good lord."

"He's bi-sexual, you know."

At that moment I became aware that the Chief Boatswain's Mate was staring at us from just outside the forward hatchway on the port side of the ship. He was bent slightly at the waist and peering in at us, his massive shoulders almost touching both sides of the hatch opening. He was about the same size and build as my brother Bart, which meant that he weighed in excess of two hundred pounds. He was perhaps an inch shorter than me. Looking at him now, I wondered if this big slob had a steel jaw and fists like my brother.

"What the fuck you two stallin' around for?" bellowed Larkin, angrily. "Git your asses topside on the double!"

"I thought we had five minutes!" I yelled, continuing to dress.

"That was five minutes ago!" And with that the Chief turned and disappeared.

"He's in a good mood, compared to what he's like once he begins to drink," said Miranda. "Man, I wish I didn't have to go on this detail. I wish you didn't, either."

"We'll be okay," I assured him. "Together we can take this dude."

Miranda shook his head sadly but said nothing. He was already in undress blues and wearing a clean white cap, having no doubt been notified earlier that he would be on the team. Despite what the Chief Boats had said, I took my time, while Miranda fidgeted about between me and the hatchway, breathing heavily and rolling his eyes from time to time.

When we finally showed up at the starboard boat rack, Larkin was in a real tizzy, pacing back and forth and shouting something at the coxswain, Houston. His back was to me and Miranda.

"What's your big hurry, Chief?" I asked, trying to sound unconcerned. Larkin wheeled and stared, and for once his mouth was clamped shut. I calmly took my place at one end of the boat hoist. Suddenly, he bellowed, "Well, you goddamned idiot! Don't you know that we've got about four hours of daylight and at least six hours of inspectin' to do? An' ever damn Portygee out there just waitin' to kill our asses?"

His voice boomed across the water, easily reaching the very fishing boats we were preparing to inspect. Glancing at one of the boats, I saw heads straighten up and turn in our direction.

Larkin then proceeded to spell out just how rotten the fishing boats were and how ever' man Jack in the fishing fleet knew the boats were illegal and so tried to bribe and cover up anyway they could!

While Miranda and I lowered the boat, the Chief continued, cataloging not only the shortcomings of the Portugese but of the three men assigned to him on this detail. Finally, as Houston fiddled with the motor, stalling for the Chief's orders to start it up, he quieted down, his face scarlet and the muscles of his lower jaws still working. He had taken the wide seat in the center of the boat, and Miranda and I were relegated to the small bow seat. Then I became aware that the Boats was staring at me.

"Hey, Sparks," called Larkin, "looks like you're gonna get to meet the Portygese up close an' in broad daylight. You sure you're ready for this little sight-seein' tour?" He was obviously enjoying himself at my expense, speaking rhetorically. I said nothing at all, and after a period of scowling and stretching his neck about, he turned about to the coxswain. "Git this shit-barge underway!"

"He puts on a good act before we leave the cutter—to impress the officers!" Miranda said into my ear. I nodded but didn't say anything.

The constant *splat-spat* of water against the bow of the boat and the roar of the motor made it impossible for the Chief to overhear anything we might say to each other.

"He actually loves to go on these trips."

"You've got to be kidding!"
"Wait an' see."

*   *   *

For the second time in so many days I had been called *Sparks*, and I had to admit that it sounded good. Only the head honcho of the radio shack deserved to be called that.

There in the bow our backs were catching a fine salt water spray each time the boat skipped and slapped. Miranda complained about it, but I was enjoying it and the bright, promising morning. The water was a shade darker than the sky; and, surrounded as we were by white boats and buoys, I was in my element. Humboldt Bay, encircled by a lacework of swiftly rising beaches, was on this day busy with the picturesque little fishing fleet, most of which was now at random anchor. For the time, the storm had chased everybody home.

But my euphoria lasted no longer than it took that little dinghy, traveling at full throttle, to travel fifty yards on an almost glassy-smooth surface. Well before I was ready, the boatswain's mate was again barking orders to our coxswain:

"All right, Houston, that one over there! Pull 'er in on the port side!" He was looking at his clipboard. To Miranda he shouted, "Git ready to secure the bow! Don't depend on any of them dumb Portygees to do it!" Of course, by this time we were surrounded by fishermen, all of whom could easily make out what Larkin was bellowing.

While I wondered what I was supposed to do, the dinghy swooped in and settled next to an old black sloop. It was perhaps forty feet long and riding high in the water at the end an anchor line. In the forward end, taking up most of the deck space, was a low cabin with square windows; and even from some distance away, it had been obvious that it was in serious need of scraping and painting. Everywhere were signs of decay and peeling paint, especially around the windows. Leaning casually against the short mast just astern of the cabin was a man dressed in an old black canvas jacket and a dirty white T-shirt. He was grinning, his brilliant white teeth making a slash across his dark, whiskered face.

"Welcome, *amicos!*" he called to us, straightening up, as the Coast Guard dinghy made contact with the port side of his boat. Houston had timed his landing just right, so that the gunwale merely nudged the side of the fishing boat before it became dead in the water. "I b'en 'spectin' you!"

"Yeah, I'll bet you have," growled Larkin, good-naturedly, standing up and making his way onto the larger deck. "How you doin'? Mendariz, aint it?"

"Hey, Chief, you remember! *Si*, Mendariz ees the name, an' you are the Coast Guard big cheese!"

"Right you are," grinned Larkin. "What you got in the locker?"

Miranda led the way up over the gunwale and into the fishing boat. The deck was strewn with garbage, fishing tackle, rolled nets, empty kegs and straw-covered wine jugs. It was impossible to take a step without stumbling over something. Tony headed directly for the cabin, brushing past Larkin and the Portuguese fisherman, and I followed close upon his heels. There was a very strong odor about the boat, a dead-fish smell that was tolerable in the salty breeze coming in from the sea; but the moment I stuck my head inside the cabin I almost gagged at the infinitely worse odor of wine puke mixed with death and decay!

"Hold your nose," said Miranda. "You'll need to check out the two-way radio. If he's got one. I'll look for the other stuff."

My breathing was an act of willpower and coming in short and slow jerks, and I was finding it difficult to concentrate on radio equipment when I was not sure I would make it back to fresh air in time.

"You'll get used to it," said Miranda, coughing and laughing at the same time. "But nobody but a Portygee can stand this shit for very long. Well, I see he has a fire extinguisher. But does *eet* work? Maybe he even has some life-saving gear."

Beneath an old canvas raincoat that had once been painted yellow and was now peeling badly, I found the two-way radio, a Hallicrafters VHF ship-to-shore transceiver, of ancient vintage. After carefully lifting the coat with two fingers and dropping it on a box of empty wine bottles to one side, I brought out the radio. The power switch was already on.

"Found it?" asked Miranda.

"It apparently doesn't work. Unless there's another switch someplace."

"Don't bother," laughed Miranda. "Why would he have another switch?"

"Because, maybe, he thought it might prevent a drain on his battery."

Sure enough, I found a jerry-rigged toggle switch in the DC line near the battery. With some trepidation, I flipped it and instantly there was a humming in the transceiver. Miranda, impressed, stood over me, peering into the mess of wires and cables that I had uncovered beneath the cabin decking.

"I'll give you odds he's never had that radio turned on."

"I'd say that's a safe bet." I picked myself up out of the garbage pile and examined the tuning dial on the transceiver and set it on the CG harbor frequency. Beneath a pile of rags I found the mike; and seeing that it was attached, I pressed the button and spoke into it, "Hello, hello! Testing! Condor, this is Condor One."

"Is it working?" asked Miranda. "I found most of the other stuff."

"Well," I said adjusting the tuning dial and increasing the volume on the receiver, "it appears to be." Into the mike I said, "Condor One, I need a signal check."

Larkin, carrying a green wine bottle, entered the cabin. "What's the poop?"

Miranda said, "Everything's okay, except maybe the radio."

The fisherman, carrying another green bottle, shoved in against me. "The radio works fine! Maybe somebody *ees* asleep on the cutter, no?"

"Nobody sleeps in the Coast Guard," said Larkin, lifting the bottle and swallowing thirstily. "Your damned gear is no good."

"Maybe ze transmitter on jore boat—" began the fisherman.

Suddenly, a voice, definitely not Chief Robinson's, burst from the speaker, "Condor One, I hear you loud and clear!"

"That's a goddamned woman's voice!" snarled Larkin, surprised.

"The point is, I think," I said into Larkin's face, "that this equipment does work." I lifted the mike, "This is Condor One. Please identify yourself and give me your location."

Only a mild ripple of static came back to me.

"She will not talk no more," said the fisherman. "That ees what I think."

"Well, who the hell is she?" demanded Larkin.

"She ees the daughter of a vetty good friend of mine," nodded Mendariz.

Larkin turned the bottle upward and emptied it.

"Well, Mendariz, ole buddy, I'm happy to say you're in fine shape! But why in hell don't you clean up this mess? Toss all this shit over the side!"

"Thank you, thank you! I weel do just that, as soon as thees headache goes away."

The three of us single-filed out to the stern of the boat, where Houston was stretched out on his back in the sun, apparently sound asleep. The Coast Guard boat was at the end of its tether some six or eight feet away.

In short order, Larkin had the coxswain awake and hauling in the boat, while Miranda and I took our seats, this time facing in the other direction. We were ready for a refreshing breeze and maybe even a little salt spray.

"Is this a typical inspection?" I asked the kid.

"No, not quite," grinned Miranda. "This boat got past Larkin. I would say that is definitely not *typical*."

The next boat was smaller and cleaner but Miranda was unable to find a fire extinguisher; and the one following that was even smaller and dirtier than the first, if possible, and minus a two-way radio. Larkin, who was beginning to feel very good, happily stapled official restriction notices on both pilothouses.

On each boat he was handed a green or blue or brown bottle of wine, which he consumed entirely before leaving the boat; and by mid-afternoon he was in a jolly mood and quite witty about the whole process. Uncle Sam, he told the disgruntled fishermen, was their Big Brother, there to protect them from themselves. Then, loud enough for them to hear, he would add that if they had any goddamned sense they'd know that.

"You turds have two things I like," he told a tall, very sober fisherman. "Your wine and your women."

The fisherman, his smile gone, said, "I think you do not know anything about our women, *señor.*"

"You think I don't, eh?" laughed Larkin. "Hell, for ever' boat I don't condemn I lay one of your women."

"I think you lie, *señor.*" The tall fisherman had squared off at Larkin, pale and shaking with anger.

Boats, apparently paying him no mind, ripped a restriction notice from his clipboard and stapled it to the cabin of the boat. "You think so, huh?" Then, without another word, he turned, climbed into the boat, and we left.

At the next boat, a long, clean, white one that looked like a sailing schooner, we were met by a young woman who was wearing a black windbreaker, topped off by a floppy, wide-brimmed hat that shaded her alert, brown eyes. Around her shoulders fell great piles of wavy black hair.

Larkin, chuckling happily, stood up and tried to grab the gunwale of the fishing boat; but the dinghy took a notion to bounce just as he did so, causing him to topple backward. He yelled for Houston to do something, but our coxswain was in the stern of the boat, and Miranda and I were in the bow. As the three of us watched helplessly, he landed across the gunwale of the little motorboat and as he tried to right himself, his massive weight pulled him over, clipboard and all! It happened so quickly he had had no time even to save his official warning signs and book of regulations, the infamous leatherbound *Official Coast Guard Smallboat Inspection Manual.*

Instantly, Houston had him by the hair at the base of his skull and was maneuvering him back toward the oarlock in the center of the boat. Each time his mouth cleared the water, he made a great effort to bellow something; but whether by design or accident, the coxswain would somehow let his head dip beneath the water again, just in time to shut off the words.

"He's a heavy sonofabitch!" yelled Houston. "You guys come up here and help me git him in' the boat!"

"Hous—ton!" Larkin managed finally. Then he began to cough.

"Yeah, I hear you, Chief! Just a minute!" Houston had moved forward in the boat, working his boss to the spot where he wanted him. "I've got you!"

"You've got me in the wrong place, you cocksucker!" screamed Larkin, beginning to thrash. "Turn loose of my hair—!"

"All right, if that's what you want!" Houston released his hold and sat back in the boat to watch, and Larkin disappeared once again beneath the surface of the water.

"Stubborn old coot," observed Houston. "But if he drowns, I'll git the blame. So I guess I'd better try to rescue him, whether he likes it or not."

The boatswain's mate surfaced finally and began to bounce about like a giant balloon, heading no place. His coughing had subsided, but he was continually taking in water and spewing it out in various directions.

"Where's my clipboard, goddamnit?" he finally got out.

"Oh, it's gone, Chief!" called Houston, almost cheerfully. "We tried to save it but—!"

"You sonofabitch you!" snorted the boatswain's mate. "You just wait till I get my hands on you!"

"Hey, all I did was try to help you out of the drink!" said Houston, standing up in the boat. "You lay a hand on me and I'll—"

Finally, with the very pretty but solemn face in the fishing boat peering down upon us, the three of us slid the two-hundred-and-fifty pounds of boatswain's mate onto the center seat of the little dinghy. It all but swamped the boat, but at last we had him stretched out like a felled hog ready for slaughter. At this point I stood up and said to the girl:

"Mind if I come aboard?"

The girl's mouth twisted downward slightly as she replied, "Is there any way I can stop you?"

"You were the one on the radio."

"So? Do I get arrested for that?"

I had made no move to climb onto the deck with the girl.

"If you wish to come aboard, why don't you do it?" she asked, not quite so sharply as before. "Don't you hooligans do about as you please with us *foreigners?* Us *Portygees*, as you call us?"

"My first day on the job here," I said. "I don't exactly know what we do with you people." I put my right leg over the gunwale of the fishing boat and rested my weight there, but as the dinghy rose and fell with the movement of the water, my left foot continued to make contact with it. "Why didn't you laugh when the Chief fell into the water?"

She replied quickly, "I do not laugh at this man for falling into the water—unless he does not come up. He is not a funny man."

I pulled myself over the gunwale and stood up, looking her in the eye. I was certain I had detected something in her voice beyond mere dislike.

"Please go on."

"This man is the enemy here, the troublemaker. He keeps my people from making a decent living—"

"Wait a minute!" I burst out. "Do you mean this one man, alone?"

"He keeps it going. Yes, he is the one."

"Well, I admit he comes down hard on some of the fishermen, but he is carrying out orders."

"He carries out more than the orders."

Below in the motorboat Larkin was beginning to come out of it. His head was hanging over the side, and each time the boat rolled his face made contact with the water. But Houston had regained his nerve and was making certain his boss did not slide into the water again.

"Are you saying that this stupid feud continues because Larkin— keeps it going?"

"That is what I am sayin'. Do you think my people want trouble with the United States Government? We are here to fish."

"Hey!" bawled Larkin. "Git back in the boat! We're goin' back to the cutter!"

"You seem—" the girl began, her voice just above a whisper. "Can anything be done about this man?"

"I don't know," I said, preparing to hop back into the boat. "Maybe."

"*Vaya con dios.*"

When I looked back, the girl was still facing toward the boat. She raised her hand slightly and her pretty face softened into a smile.

The Triangle

———————◆———————

Hatcher stood with his feet wide apart in the center of the crew's quarters and flexed his muscles, while Maze and Castleberry sat on their bunks and argued over cards and waited. He had just taken a shower and the only thing he was wearing was a wet towel around his neck. If and when he gave the word, the three of them were going to 'hit the beach and look for broads'.

Across the quarters on the starboard bulkhead I was sitting on my bunk polishing my shoes with a brush. Miranda watched me and complained about what I was planning to wear on my first liberty in Eureka.

"Don't you have any civvies at all, Red? I know, wear your black leather jacket and some dungarees. While you're in town why don't you buy some slacks and maybe a sweater. You better not wear a Coastie uniform."

"I don't much like civvies," I said casually. "Especially bluejeans. Makes me look like a hooligan."

"I'm comin' with you," he said, standing up. "Remember what old Sparks told you. It's not safe for you to go in alone."

"You're going to protect me," I said off-handedly. After a pause, I added, "You better go on and do your thing once we're ashore. I'm headin' for the red-light district."

"What's that? There's no such thing in Eureka. I oughta know, it's practically my hometown."

"Every town this size and bigger has a red-light district, especially if it's on a seacoast."

Hatcher glanced over toward us just as I stood up and began to put my shoeshine kit away.

"You boys seem to be hittin' it off pretty good here lately," he said in a loud voice. "Have you announced the event yet?"

I looked down at Miranda, who was still sitting on his bunk. "Is this jerk supposed to be funny or what?"

Hatcher walked toward us, popping the towel at various targets along the way. "What was that, Red? Was you addressin' me?"

"Forget it, Hatcher," said Castleberry. "We've got other fish to fry tonight."

I picked up my blouse and started to put it on.

"But I can't forget it, Buster," said Hatcher, popping the towel at the foot of my bunk. "Look, this asshole's planning' on goin' ashore in dress blues."

The buzzard face of the deckhand was suddenly within a foot of mine, and as he spoke he jabbed his forefinger into my chest. I took a step backward and he noticed the double row of ribbons on my left breast.

"God damn, look at that, Castleberry!" he spat.

Hatcher was at least ten years older than me and had the scars of a dozen bar fights on his face and arms. He was tall and rangy and broad-shouldered, and freshly-showered he smelled like a mule.

I took another short step backward and said, "I don't know what your problem is, Ugly, but I'm telling you to get out of my breathing space."

"Oh, my my," said Hatcher, eyeing me, with the towel held back at ready. "Hey, Buster, Pretty Boy here is threatenin' me."

"Leave him alone, Hatcher," warned Castleberry. "You want to git restricted to the ship? We've got plans for tonight, remember?"

"Looks like your luck is holdin', Red," growled Hatcher. "But one of these days—I'll get around to you."

"Anytime you can manage it," I said.

He turned and headed for his foot locker, and I put on my new dress blouse. Miranda said, "Red, dressed that way you had better stay on Broadway and go no place but the center of town. Whatever you do don't go down on Second Street. You'd just be askin' for trouble."

"So that's where the red-light district is," I said with a chuckle.

"Forget it, kid." When I was fully dressed and had my wallet looped over the front of my trousers, I faced him and asked, "Are you really that afraid of the Portuguese?"

"Damn right I am. They'll kill you."

"Well, don't worry. All I'm going to do is drink a few beers. I would ask you the name of a good bar, but I'll bet you've never tried any of them out."

"I know one you'd better stay out of. The Triangle. That's the one place in town you don't want to go. It's a Portygee hangout."

"Then that's where I'm heading. I'll bet it's the hottest place in town." I headed for the hatch in the forward end of the quarters, and he fell in behind. Over my shoulder I said, "I'll bet it's a Coastie hangout, too."

"It's where most of the fights start. Somebody gets killed in there every once in awhile."

We went down the passageway and mounted the stairs that led topside. Chief Larkin, standing at the port lifeline, saw us come out upon deck and burst out laughing. About that time Chief Robinson showed up, wondering what was so amusing.

"If that don't beat anything I ever saw! Look, Miranda's holdin' Red's hand!"

"Somebody had better keep an eye on 'em while they're in town," said Robinson. "Them dress blues of Red's will start trouble."

"Don't it bother you that your man has taken up with that pretty little kid?"

"It don't bother me. I think Red feels sorry for him. Speakin' of which, I wish you'd let up on Miranda."

"He's a fuckin' girl, and a goodlookin' one at that."

Robinson turned to leave, "I think I'll get dressed and walk up to the Triangle. You better come with me, if you know what I mean."

"Hang on a minute," said Larkin, nodding. "I'll go with you."

Out on the dock Miranda brought out some photographs and began holding them up in front of my face, one at a time. I soon realized he had something in mind.

"Are you saying you know all these girls?" I asked, stopping to take a look at a Polaroid of a tall brunette. "This one is something else!" It was a posed, frontal view of a very young naked girl.

"That one's my girlfriend. We're going to get married when she graduates from high school."

"Why are you showing me a nude picture of your wife-to-be?" I complained, handing all of the pictures back.

He shuffled through the pack and handed me one I hadn't seen. "Take a look at this one."

I was about to shove it back at him but instead grabbed it and stared. "Your twin sister?"

He nodded. "That's Tonya." He shuffled some more and handed me another picture of her. "What do you think about her?"

"Well," I laughed, "she's the spitting image of you."

He nodded and put the pictures away. "Red, I need to tell you something."

We were on a nameless street that led toward the main part of town, and as we walked I was keeping an eye out for a street sign.

"What's bothering you?"

"That guy Hatcher. He's one mean bastard."

"I could tell that the first time I ever laid eyes on him," I said with a laugh. "I've seen his kind before."

"He fights dirty, my friend. "He an' Castleberry gang up on someone every once in awhile out on liberty, and when they do they really do a number on him. Jenkins had to go to the hospital after a run-in with them, and when he came back they made his life so miserable he finally asked for a transfer." After a pause, Miranda added sadly, "Jenkins was the only friend I had on the ship."

"Well, Tony, I suggest we put all of that and our other cares behind us for now and have a good time. By the way, do you ever have a good time?"

He laughed nervously, "I guess I don't until I'm about a mile from the cutter."

"Tell me, how'd you get those pictures of your intended?"

"I had to promise her I wouldn't show them to anybody." He glanced at me and laughed. "I wanted the pictures for you, not me."

"For me?" I burst out. "Why in the world—?"

Ahead us, coming in from the right, was Second Street. This far out it was hardly more than a wide road, but two blocks away it became a double row of flashing red and green neon signs and curb-to-curb motorized traffic. There was no longer any doubt where the red light district was.

We joined the pedestrian traffic on the left sidewalk and almost immediately I saw the Triangle. It was a hotel-and-bar strategically located at the corner of Second and Inyo Streets. Four stories high and built of a rugged-looking brown brick that gave the place an antique look. The full-length swinging doors opened out onto both thoroughfares; and while we stared into the darkened interior, one of the doors swung open, releasing a great blast of hot Portuguese music.

"Let's git out of here!" insisted Miranda. "Come on, let's go over into town and find a movie!"

"Why don't you go, Tony? I want to check out this place!"

Miranda had the look of an old mother hen as he stood there staring at me. Finally, he shrugged his thin little shoulders and said bravely, "No. If you insist on staying, I'll stay with you."

I nodded quickly, shoved the right door back, and penetrated the wall of cool, foul air and loud music. In a way I was enjoying Miranda's discomfiture. He had obviously lived a very sheltered life and needed some exposure to a man's world. In fact, he needed to rid himself of some of that fear he was carrying around with him. I led the way past the packed bar to a booth in the back, all the time analyzing the various exotic smells and insisting aloud that these were very much a part of the romance of bars.

The stench of laborers' sweat, old puke, stale farts, and rot-gut whisky, I philosophized, was just as important to the total picture as were the bartender and the waitress and the music. It had, I insisted, a positive connotation, for had any other smell met us at the door it would have seemed wrong, and the spell would have been broken. Thus, a great deal of the excitement of anticipation would have disappeared instantly.

"Well, as far as I'm concerned, it could go ahead and disappear," said my young friend. "Where did you pick up all that stuff?"

"The United States Coast Guard has landed," said a husky female voice at my shoulder.

I smiled at Miranda and without moving said, "Ah, the Voice on the Radio and the Face in the Boat! I forgot to ask your name."

"But I know yours."

That quickly brought me to a standing position. I turned and faced the next booth and its single occupant. "Would you join us?"

"That might not be a good idea, brave man." The beautiful face that I was barely able to make out through the general gloom of the place and the cloud of cigarette smoke was unsmiling, and, indeed, seemed very sad to me. "Some of my cousins might not like that."

Miranda had begun to hammer on my shoulder. "God, Red, let's get out of here!"

"Do you let your cousins decide where you will sit?" I asked.

"It is you that I am concerned about. My cousins just don't like Coasties. Why did you wear that uniform? Are you that ignorant of the local scene?"

"That's what I've been tellin' this hardhead," moaned Miranda.

"Let's have a drink," I said, "right after I find out your name."

"I am Rosa Rita," she said with a faint smile, "and you are Red. Could I talk you into leaving this place and going back to the Coast Guard ship? Anytime now the *sheet* is going to *heet* the fan, if you understand my French."

"I just left that ship," I said. "Have just one drink with us and then we'll go, okay?" When she did not reply and appeared about to fly away, I put my lips close to her left ear and said in a soft, deadly-serious voice, "We're not bothering anybody, and the day will never come when I'm afraid to sit and have a drink in an American bar in an American city. Tell your cousins that."

"You could end up in an American graveyard," she said, pulling back. Then she got out of the booth stood facing me. Her head barely reached my shoulders. "I must say, Red Head, you are bigger than you look at a distance."

I found her hands and folded them into mine. "You're trembling."

"There are some very unhappy men in this bar," she said, moving into our booth and taking me with her. She kept tugging until we were against the wall. "That uniform is telling them that you wish to make trouble."

Miranda was shaking his head sadly and staring at me.

Suddenly, Rosa Rita smiled brightly, tossed her head nonchalantly, and called above my head to a passing waiter. When he turned, she held up three fingers.

"Will you buy me a beer?" she asked, her face not six inches from mine. "And perhaps your young friend would put some nickels in the jukebox?"

"Of course," I said. To myself, I said, How do you figure the female mentality? I leaned near her and whispered, "You are so beautiful!" Her hands suddenly grasp mine and again I was surprised, this time at the strength in her long fingers.

"Slow down, sailor," she smiled, moving back an inch. "You are also beautiful, but you are also in enemy territory. I do not wish to witness a slaughter."

Still grinning stupidly and gazing into her eyes, said out of the corner of my mouth to Miranda, "Order us three beers and go play some music."

"Play some music?" cried my little friend, incredulous. "In the juke box?"

"It is a *toca-discos*," said Rosa Rita, now full of smiles and speaking in a devil-may-care tone of voice. She pointed toward a dark corner, then turned her finger toward the bar. "Tell the bartender I like Lucky Lager."

"Go on, Tony, play something lively. What do you like, Rosa?"

"I do not care what you play, *amigo*. Perhaps *Mi Poca Chiquita* you would like." Rosa, now in a ball in the back of the booth, pulled my head down until her lips touched my ear. "It is too bad, this thing between my people and the Coast Guard, Red. But I truly wish you and your friend would go to another place, perhaps to another part of town."

At the bar a number of dark, bearded faces had turned about and were staring in our direction.

"Why do your people all look so glum?" I asked. "Don't they enjoy drinking beer? They all look like they're on their way to a funeral."

"I wish you hadn't mentioned that," moaned Miranda, getting out of the booth. "Listen, if I'm not back in two minutes, come and carry the remains back to the ship."

"They are not glum," pouted Rosa Rita, "but merely tryin' to decide what to do with you." A waiter showed up with three Lucky Lagers. She snatched one and drank from even before I could pay the man. "I tell you what, brave one." She studied my face seriously, her right elbow on the table and the bottle in her hand steadied as if she were about to drink. "I think if I tell my brother what kind of fellow you are just maybe you get back to the ship in one piece tonight."

"Which one is your brother?" I asked, watching Miranda work his way slowly across the room.

"You do not see him, but he knows you are here."

"Well, I don't need any help to get back to the ship. Thanks anyway."

"Speaking for yourself, as usual," said Miranda, already back from the jukebox. He slid to the back of the booth across from the girl and me.

"You do not like what is going on with the Coast Guard, do you?" asked Rosa Rita. "I could tell that you have a dislike for this boatswain's mate, Larkin."

I nodded slowly, looking at her, "I don't know what can be done about him, but something has to happen. He can't go on doing what he's doing."

"He is lucky to still be alive."

"That's what I was going to ask you. Why haven't the fishermen waylaid him in an alley?"

"He has been badly beaten twice, but now he is cautious. He carries a gun whenever he leaves the ship, and he always keeps bodyguards with him."

"Even with Larkin gone, your people would not like the Coast Guard," said Miranda. "You people just will not abide by rules and regulations."

"Ha!" burst Rosa. "Rules and regulations!" She tossed her head angrily, then turned on Miranda. "The men who own the boats know when it is safe to go out. They do not need nursemaids to tell them everything. And that Chief, the one who always inspects the boats, he does not go by the rules."

"What I saw on that one inspection tour was enough to convince me," I said, nodding. To Tony I said, "Didn't you say he pulls that stuff every time he goes on an inspection tour?"

"Sometimes it's much worse than it was when you went out," nodded Miranda. "I think falling in the drink slowed him down a bit this last trip."

"He sometimes rapes girls that are on the boats," said Rosa Rita. "I have been told this many times, and I could tell by the look in his eye that was what he planned, just before he fell."

"It wouldn't have happened," I said.

Rosa began to push me out of the booth, to make room for her departure. "Here, Red, you keep this place warm for me." She pushed her beer toward me. "I will be gone only a second." And before I had finished telling Miranda how I felt about that last remark he had made, here she was winding her way through the crowded room.

"Red," pleaded Miranda, "I'm askin' you for the tenth time—"

"Pretty soon," I said. "Stop worrying. Let's see what she has on her mind."

Rosa Rita was leading a handsome young Portuguese man by the hand, and her face looked pale in the gloom of the bar. I stood up and waited.

"This is my brother, Ricardo Montreya. He is as hardheaded as you are, and maybe even as brave."

I put out my hand and when he refused to take it, I said, "I'm glad to meet you, Rick."

Ricardo glared at me angrily. Obviously, he was humoring his pretty sister by coming to our table; but a wrong word or gesture on my part might be all it would take to set him off.

"Shake hands, Ricardo," said Rosa, hotly. "I want the two of you to be friends. Red, do not call him *Rick*."

"This man has come lookin' for trouble," said Ricardo. "And he has come to the right place."

"Tell him you will not call him that," said Rosa, looking at me sternly. "And tell him that you did not come here to make trouble."

"Okay," I said, smiling. "Ricardo Montreya, I am not looking for trouble. If you're referring to this uniform, it happens to be my country's uniform. And if—"

"Red!"

"He is very hardheaded," said Ricardo, nodding and putting out his hand. "Jus' like me."

"Good!" exclaimed Rosa, nudging me. "Shake! Shake!"

"You hooligans cause my people much trouble," said Ricardo. "You keep the men from putting food on their families' tables. Why do you do this?"

I looked at Rosa Rita, my face suddenly very hot.

"I tried to tell him you just got here, that you don't approve of what is going on. But he has admitted that he is hardheaded, too."

"We do not like the regulations," Ricardo went on, "but we could live with them—if we was given a chance. As it is, whether our boats are seaworthy or not makes little difference. It is all up to that Chief asshole that drinks too much and uses threats to get into the bed with our women—right in front of their fathers and husbands. If we give him enough wine an' crawl on our bellies—"

I nodded, looking at Miranda. "Is that true, Tony?"

"Yes, it is."

"Are all of the inspections done by Chief Larkin?" I asked, still looking at Miranda.

"Sure. Who else?"

"Have you actually been on one of the tours when Larkin has—taken advantage of a woman?"

Miranda sighed and looked down. "I'm afraid I have. More'n once the coxswain and me and old Robinson have had to wait in the small-boat while the Chief banged some chick."

"Why haven't you put him on report?"

"Who, me? You've got to be kiddin'! It'd be my word against his and Houston's—and later on he'd just plain kill me!"

"I tell you what is goin' to happen," hissed Ricardo.

"You listen to Red!" snapped Rosa. "He is good man, an' you do what he says!"

"There is goin' to be—one dead Chief Asshole!" said Ricardo. "First time he leave the ship alone."

"Listen, Ricardo," I said, "give me a little time. I just shipped aboard the cutter, and it's going to take me awhile to learn the ropes. Maybe I can put a bug in the Skipper's ear. Maybe if Miranda and Houston went to the him and told him what's going on."

Ricardo's big shaggy head nodded slowly, but there was no relaxation of the muscles in his face. "I buy you a drink, okay?"

"No, please!" whined Miranda. "He promised me, no more beer!"

"We'll have one on you," I said, grinning at Ricardo. "Maybe if these peckerwoods in here see you treating me they'll put their daggers back."

"I think this American sailor is not so dumb as he looks," laughed Rosa Rita, giving her brother a playful kick. "The two of you should drink a Lucky to friendship."

　　　　　*　　　　　　　　*　　　　　　　　*

During the week that followed, I spent a great deal of time keeping an eye on the Chief Boatswain's Mate and gathering what information I could about him from the crew. No one, with the possible exception of Chief Robinson, liked him, not even members of his own deck gang; and the general impression I got was that Larkin had his bluff in on everyone. The officers did not question his tactics, evidently, relying upon him for a great number of things; and the department heads among the noncommissioned officers simply steered clear of him. Two inspection parties went out that week, both led by him; but Chief Robinson was asked to handle the radio end of things both times.

On Friday afternoon the inspection team returned at least two hours earlier than usual, and it was obvious from the look on Robinson's face that something untoward had happened. I was on hand to see him climb out of the boat and head off toward the radio shack without a word to anyone. Ordinarily, he would have been cutting up and making jokes about *them wild Portygees.*

A few minutes later, I stuck my head inside the shack and asked him if he cared for some coffee.

"Yeah, come on in and set the coffee down. I've got something I want to tell you."

"What's up?"

"Well, for one thing, I'm sure as hell glad I'm gettin' off this barge! I can't take much more shit like I saw today."

I delivered a mug of steaming coffee to the Chief and settled in the second chair with mine. He picked up the coffee and sipped cautiously.

"I be damned if I know how Boats gets away with the stunts he pulls on these inspection trips! For what he did today he oughta get ten years!"

I swiveled around and stared at Robinson.

"First, he got so drunk he couldn't see to nail up quarantine notices and, second, he—"

Robinson, too overcome with emotion to finish what he was saying, sat there shaking his head in disbelief. He would not look at me.

"I swear I can't believe what he did. You ready for this? He fucked a young Portygee kid while her boyfriend and her mother and father and all the rest of us looked on! I just about puked!"

"He had never done this before when you were with the team?"

"Hell, no!" shouted Robinson, glaring up at me. "Well, he may have down below deck, but not right in front of us. He always wrestled with whatever woman or girl was aboard, but generally he was so drunk he couldn't git it up. As far as I know he never actually went through with it when I was present! But today, while me and Miranda went through our routine, he and this fisherman disappeared into the quarters below. First thing we knew this wild-eyed kid—she couldn't've been more'n thirteen or fourteen—busted out of that compartment screaming like a mad hyena! And she didn't have a stitch of clothes on her! Ran out of the pilothouse and down the deck and just as she was about to jump over the side Larkin caught her!"

Something in the pit of my stomach turned to jelly at the thought of that enormous man raping a little girl, and for a time I just sat there and stared at Robinson.

"That's when the rest of us got into the smallboat and the coxswain started up the motor. Finally, we got to hell outta there!"

"It probably wouldn't be a good night to go on liberty." After a time I said, "Can you blame the Portuguese for beating the hell out of every Coastie they catch away from the cutter?"

"Listen," said Robinson, red-faced and shaking with anger, "I would-n't put it past them to try something stupid, like—!"

"Like boarding us?" I said quietly.

"You're damned right! If something aint done real soon, there's goin' to be a full scale war in these parts!"

I shoved my coffee back and stood up. "You're going to the Old Man, right?"

"It'd be my word against his," sighed Robinson. "Houston will back him up, and Miranda won't back me up."

"Let me talk to Miranda. He'll back you up."

"No he won't!" snapped Robinson. "That little fucker's so scared he wouldn't say a word if you put a pistol to his head."

"Let me work on him, just the same," I said and beelined it out of the shack.

Hatcher

◆

Miranda was right where I knew he would be, on the bow of the cutter. He was gazing forlornly out across the bay, his young girl's face troubled.

"How's it going?" I asked placing my hand on his shoulder.

"You know what we were talkin' about in the Triangle Bar, with Rosa Rita and her brother? Well, man, it's too late for anybody to do anything now."

"What do you mean?"

"The Chief climbed on a little broad today right up on deck, where the whole fishing fleet could see!"

"That's what I wanted to talk to you about."

"This time he went too far! He raped that little girl, while the father and everybody, even the girl's boyfriend, looked on! Everybody pleaded with him, but of course it did no good. And when she got away from him she jumped over the side!"

"What're you saying? She tried to drown herself?"

"They hadn't found her when we finally got Larkin in the boat and returned to the cutter."

"Oh, my God!"

"Boats spent ten minutes tryin' to nail up a quarantine notice, even though there wasn't anything wrong with that boat! And all that time they were diving and searching for the girl."

I took my little friend by the shoulders and whirled him around so quickly he almost lost his footing. "Listen, I want you to come with me and Chief Robinson to see the Old Man. Will you do it?"

He did not hesitate. "No way, Red! The Boats would kill me. You and Robinson might get away with it, but he would crucify me!"

"So you're just going to let this shit go on and on."

"There's no way I can stop it! Nobody can stop it."

"You're disgusting," I said, removing my hands from his shoulders. "I've wasted my time on you!"

"Come on, Red!"

"'Come on', hell! You're a miserable coward!"

"Would you—?"

"Nobody's going to hurt your precious hide. You and I and Robinson can hang this bastard from the yardarm. He'll be drummed out of the service for sure."

I continued to glare into Miranda's big, tear-filled eyes. Then I became aware that a few feet away, leaning against a lifeline, Hatcher and two other members of the bridge gang were watching us with wide grins.

"Now, that is quite a romantic little scene!" called out the big-mouthed deckhand. "Hey, Red, you two makin' out these days?"

I felt my body stiffened. I looked at Hatcher. "Not now, Buzzard Beak."

"Oh, ho," he said. "If not now, then when?"

"Just mind your own business."

"And pay no attention while you and Miranda carry on right out here in public?" laughed Hatcher. "At least you could go rent a room someplace."

I turned around and faced Hatcher. He was asking for it and sooner or later I was going to have to invite him out on the dock. But this was not the time. Taking down Chief Larkin was more important than this pile of deck crap. Summoning all of my willpower, I headed toward the stern. Hatcher and the deckhands fell in behind me, shouting and clapping their hands. As we neared 'midships on the port side, Chief Larkin popped from the hatchway and headed for the gangplank. He was decked out in dress blues.

Hatcher and his cronies suddenly disappeared into the passageway leading to the messdeck, and Miranda came up and stood looking at me. He was tearing badly and when he spoke he had to choke it out.

"Okay, I'll do it."

"You'll tell the Skipper what you saw?"

The big boatswain's mate lumbered across the gangplank. He was so heavy the two-by-twelves swayed and groaned beneath his enormous feet.

"He's going ashore alone!" burst out Miranda. "Maybe—"

"I think this is the first time in my life I've actually wanted to see a man walk the plank," I said. "Come on." On the way to the radio shack, I said, "He's as drunk as a hoot owl from all that wine he drank today. The thing I don't want to see happen, though, is some Portuguese getting blamed for his murder. It's bound to happen, sure as hell, and it just might be Ricardo."

"More than likely it'll be the first fisherman he runs into. They'll all be waiting for him."

"Well, there's nothing we can do about that. The bastard deserves to die and just maybe nobody'll be blamed." At the door of the radio shack, I added, "But it just doesn't work that way, my friend. Somebody will have to pay, and the feud will go on. Whoever takes Larkin's place will be out to get the Portuguese."

Miranda stared at me, open-mouthed. "I hope you're not stupid enough—"

"Catch you later!" I took off at a gallop for the crewsquarters, with Miranda right behind me, yelling all the way. There would be no time to shower and shave, or even to go by the office and get a liberty chit. And this time I would not be bothered with my little friend.

When I emerged on deck five minutes later, there was no one in sight. Larkin, of course, had disappeared up Broadway; but I knew only too well what his shore routine was. He would undoubtedly check in at the

Triangle, where his habit was to linger just long enough to make the bartender nervous and to antagonize whoever happened to be in the place. Then he would move two blocks over to the redneck Irish bar, *Hooter's,* where he would spend most of the evening. He had a reputation for being a ruthless, dangerous man, one who carried a pistol in his coat pocket and, drunk or sober, could hit what he aimed at.

While I was still half a block from the *Triangle,* I began to hear the sounds of a brawl! A chair came hurtling through a window onto Second Street, bringing with it a lot of glass and the Lucky Lager neon sign! This was quite naturally followed by a great increase in noise, part of which was a high-pitched female voice cursing in Portuguese! I made out the word *hooligan.*

One cautious glance between the swinging doors that faced the intersection of Second and Inyo confirmed my suspicions. A gang of Portuguese fishermen had waylaid Larkin and were doing their best to beat him to death!

Throwing caution to the wind, I stepped inside the bar quickly and ducked to one side, just in time to avoid a hurtling Portuguese! At least six more of them were in a huddle in the middle of the barroom, and from inside that crowd came the outraged voice of Chief Larkin. And when his head suddenly shot up above them, I saw that his face and neck were bloody and his dress blues were in tatters.

"Here goes nothing," I said, quickly removing my neckerchief. The noise was deafening, and nobody was paying me any attention. I climbed upon a table near the front doors and began shouting.

I repeated "Wait a minute!" several times, while I was busy fashioning my neckerchief into a blackjack. "Just a minute! Stop the fighting!"

A bottle came end-over-end above the heads of the brawlers, narrowly missing me. Then, as a great deal of the attention was shifting from Larkin, it became deathly clear to me that instead of stopping this mob I was merely offering myself as the sacrificial lamb!

Too much had gone under the bridge for any of them to listen.

From my vantage point on that table, I saw Rosa Rita and her brother standing with a small crowd off to one side. They were not taking part in the massacre, but then it was obvious they were not needed. Rosa Rita spotted me and began shouting something that I couldn't make out. At that moment I felt hands clamp onto my legs!

I raised the neckerchief and whirled it once, like a lariat; and when the roll of dimes in it hit the first fisherman, I heard Rosa Rita scream. Another fisherman had begun clutching at my right leg, and his angry face came up just in time to glimpse my little surprise. For a very brief moment I saw the startled look on his face, just before his eyeballs rolled upward, and this time it was he who screamed. Still another fisherman, this one fully aware that I was using a very long blackjack, lunged in, caught the dimes just above the right eye, and went backward.

I had not stopped shouting and, of course, I was doing a great deal of wild dancing on that table. Now, with each swing of my neckerchief, I began to call out, "Back off!"—and whatever seemed appropriate at the time. Each time a head would come into reach, I would make the necessary adjustment to my swing, and at the precise instant the forty-seven dimes made contact, I would shout, "Back off, *amico!*"

The men standing over Larkin suddenly straightened up and headed in my direction, tripping and falling every which way over unconscious bodies. The noise was such that I could just barely make out the *whapping sound* a half-pound of silver makes when it bounces off a very thick skull.

"Now, listen to me a minute!" I yelled, narrowly missing a head that came in close. "You kill this man and you'll be charged with murder! Let me take him back to the ship!"

Something zipped past my left ear, landed on the floor near the door. I saw what it was and felt sick at my stomach. Turning about quickly, I was in time to see the man who had tried to kill me. There was shock on his face, no doubt from having missed me.

"Didn't you hear a word I said?" I bawled out, bringing my dimes around in a wide, sweeping arc. The moment I realized I couldn't reach him, it occurred to me with a shock that my mission as a peacemaker was now secondary to my need to lay that knife-thrower out.

This swarthy gentleman, anxious to correct his mistake, brought out another knife and began moving in my direction, probably to make certain he did not miss a second time. I danced to the edge of the table and swung the dimes as far out as I could. The sound that followed was clearly audible throughout the room.

Because, suddenly, the racket had ceased!

The *whapping sound* and the feeling that was transmitted up the neckerchief to my right hand and arm brought a warmth and a satisfaction to the pit of my stomach that is difficult to explain. It was very similar to the feeling that a mediocre baseball player receives when his bat encounters a ball at just the right moment and the sound rings out across the ball park to the hushed stands. Like the homerun hitter, I did not even have to look to make sure of the result.

Ricardo, with Rosa Rita at his side, had moved into the center of the room, with his arms raised high for attention. He began to shout in Portuguese, ending with, *"Sabe?"*

The Chief, lying in a pool of his own blood, was still rolling about and trying to get up; and the fishermen who had gotten too close to my makeshift blackjack, were also beginning to move. A man in a black raincoat and spoke to Ricardo, who nodded and turned to me:

"Do you need help with this pile of shit?"

At this point, Chief Robinson and Miranda appeared at the open double doors, waving at me. I said to Ricardo, "Thanks, but we can get him back to the cutter."

Ricardo put out his hand and I shifted the neckerchief to my left and took it.

"That is a lethal weapon you wear around your neck, Red."

"It's my little equalizer," I said, taking Rosa Rita's outstretched hand. The look on her face sent a warm feeling through my body, and for a moment we stared at each other. Then I leaned down and barked, "Get up, Chief. We're going to the cutter!"

"I don't know if I can," he said, surprising me. He sounded very sober and, after a mighty effort, he managed to get to his knees.

I grabbed one of his hands and Chief Robinson took the other, and after another struggle the big man rose to his feet and put an arm over my shoulder. I looked at Richardo and nodded and we moved toward the door.

*   *   *

The moment Larkin staggered across the gangplank of the Cutter *Alert*, the Old Man popped out of his stateroom and started bellowing. Much of what he said was incoherent to us on deck, but it was clear at once that Larkin's days aboard the ship were numbered. The Skipper had been appalled at Chief Robinson's account of the inspection tour, and he had insisted on hearing everything Miranda and Houston had to say. And when the coxswain, Houston, had denied being a witness to any of the Chief's misdeeds, the Old Man had threatened him with death and dismemberment, finally getting from him additional damaging information.

So it happened that, one week later, two chief petty officers aboard the *Alert* received their transfer papers on the same day. Old Sparks, heading for the Ozarks of Arkansas, was all smiles and handshakes; but the once mighty chief boatswain's mate neither looked at nor said a word to any of the crew or officers as he crossed the gangplank. He was on his way to the brig at the Alameda Naval Air Station, where he would await a General Court Martial in San Francisco. The chief witnesses against him would travel down aboard the *Alert*, which just happened to be scheduled for an annual drydocking at Pier 5 on the Embarkadaro a week before the big trial.

Indeed, it was a joyous occasion for the crew of the cutter. Even the Old Man was in a holiday mood, and as the taxicab pulled away from the dock, on its way to the bus station, he went up to the bridge, flipped on the PA system, something no one had ever seen him do before, and made a speech in which he outlined plans for getting underway for San Francisco Bay. About a week from then, he finally admitted.

Afterward, I went to the messdeck, filled a mug with coffee, and headed for the radio shack. Chief Robinson's departure had left me in charge, and it dawned on me that I was not only in charge of the radio shack but the inspection tours as well. I knew I would genuinely miss the old reprobate, whose tattered Sears and Roebuck catalog still sprawled open on the typewriter at the operating position. Of course, as far as the work and the responsibility of the shack were concerned, I did not think I would miss him at all. During the time I had been aboard he had done almost nothing except plan for his chicken farm down in the boon docks.

Larkin, on the other hand, had been a blight on the morale of the ship, and his absence was like a breath of sweet, fresh air.

Hatcher, made even bolder and more obnoxious by Larkin's absence, remained a burr in my side, never letting up from morning chow until lights out whenever we happened to meet on deck or in the quarters. He would begin each day with some crack about Miranda and me, how our night had gone; and from that point on he would needle me for a show-down. I had adopted a *turn the other cheek* attitude, having decided that I had too much to lose now that I was radioman-in-charge. I simply could not afford to jeopardize the best assignment the Coasties had to offer a swab like me.

My part in the rescue of Larkin from the Portuguese fishermen had remained a secret, as far as the crew and officers of the *Alert* were concerned; and although Miranda had been there for the finish, no one was about to believe anything he might have to say about me.

One day Tully overheard a discussion in the messdeck that sent him looking for me. "What the hell gives?" he burst out the moment he saw me. "You afraid of that vulture Hatcher?"

"No, I just don't like Captain's Masts."

"Hell, take him out on the dock! That's the Coast Guard way. And one thing for damn sure, Hatcher's not goin' to leave you alone until you two tangle."

"Thanks, Tully, but I would like to avoid having to fight him."

To Miranda one day I said, "It sounds to me like the Neanderthal has made a career of picking fights with people. That's probably why he's still a deckhand."

Miranda looked pained, and it was obvious that he had something to say that was distasteful to him. "Red, you're going to find out anyway but I hate to be the one to tell you."

"What?"

"Everybody aboard thinks you're yellow. Hatcher's known up and down the coast as a good fighter. He's proud of the fact that he's never lost a fight. And he's made it very clear that you're afraid to fight him."

"I know all that," I snapped. "But I don't want to mess up my record, Tony. This guy just isn't worth it."

"But going out on the dock wouldn't *mess up* your record."

"The hell it wouldn't."

Miranda frowned. "I keep forgettin' how ignorant you are of the Coast Guard. You think it's just like the Navy, but it's not. There's a lot of stuff you don't understand." He was getting wound up. "For example, if you told old Hatcher to go on out the deck with you, the officers wouldn't do a thing about it. Of course, if you got banged up and had to go to the hospital, you wouldn't make any points with the Old Man. But about the worst thing you can do in this outfit is refuse to meet someone on the dock."

I shook my head, "You can't beat a man into the dock—and not have it effect your record. Why don't *you* go out on the dock with him?"

"But, Red, the dock's off-limits to any kind of interference from the officers! The Old Man won't lift a finger one way or the other. That's just the way it is in the Coast Guard." After a pause, he added, "He wouldn't lower himself to ask me out on the dock."

I straightened up and stared at him. "How about we met on liberty and ended up in a civilian jail? Wouldn't the brass frown upon that?"

"This aint the deep sea Navy, Red. Somebody on the ship would bail you out, more'n likely. What happens on liberty is not held against you, unless it effects your performance on the cutter. If the police or Navy SP's picked you up and threw you into the brig, the Skipper or whoever happened to be the O. O. D. would see to it you got transportation back to the cutter."

"But wouldn't I be on report?"

"Not unless you embarrassed the ship, did something illegal, like stealing or raping a young girl. But, Red, this is not the friggin' big ship Navy."

"Yeah, I know. It's the friggin' hooligan navy. Come on."

In the messdeck we found Tully leaning across the counter painting a glowing picture of the change that had come over the town of Eureka since Larkin's departure. He had hit three bars the evening before, including the *Triangle*, and— (At this point he spotted me) —it was his opinion that if somebody he could spit on would go just a little bit easy on the poor fishermen with his inspection tours, things would finally settle back to normal.

"They'll get a fair shake," I said, defensively, "But I can't turn my head entirely."

"Maybe you could take into consideration the fact that them Portuguese fishermen are among the world's best sailors," snapped Tully. "Hell, they aint a bunch of civilians goin' out in flat-bottomed john boats. We come in an' lay a lot of shit on 'em they think they don't need."

"You seen Hatcher lately?" I broke in.

At that point Hatcher, Castleberry, and Benton crowded through the forward hatch and bellied up to the coffee urn, making so much noise Tully turned back into his galley in disgust.

"Well, look what we've got here, boys! Hey, Sparks, I been intendin' to ask you something. What's Carmen here like in the sack?"

"Hatcher, what say you and I visit the dock?" I asked, casually.

Hatcher's mouth dropped open. Castleberry lost control of his big crock mug and it fell with a crash to the deck.

Benton yelled, "Sooeee! Did you hear that?"

"Did I hear you right, asshole?" demanded Hatcher, his eyes still round with surprise.

"You heard me. Let's go."

The big mangy deckhand slammed his mug down on the counter and walked stiff-legged around his cronies toward me. Over his shoulder he crowed, "Watch this, boys." He poked his forefinger toward my chest and laughed. "There's no goddamned place in the Coasties for queers like Red here and Carmen Miranda!" To me, he hissed, "I say you stop seein' each other in public, or find a way to get out of the Service."

When his long, crooked forefinger neared my chest, I grabbed it and jerked, snapping it out of place with a popping sound. With an agonized scream, he wrenched back; but before he could get out of reach I poked him in the throat with two fingers bent at the second joints. This caused him to leap back with both hands in the air.

"Hey, ever'body saw what he done!" screamed Hatcher, working with his two fingers to get them back in place. "For that I'm goin' to fix that pretty kisser of yours!"

I moved toward him, putting my face within two inches of his. "Listen, you ignorant moron, I said get your ass out on the dock! We'll see whose got a yellow streak!"

"Come on, Hatch," said Castleberry. "He's really askin' for it!"

Tully appeared at the end of the counter, beaming. "All right, clear the messdeck, everybody! Hatcher, you know the rules!"

"I know the rules all right!" cried Hatcher. "I think he jerked my finger out of place!" He started toward the forward end of the compartment. "I'll be waitin'!" With that he turned and disappeared through the forward hatchway, followed by Castleberry and Benton.

Tully, his big round face suddenly a picture of doom and gloom, shook his head sadly, all the time looking at me. "Listen, Red, I don't know what you've heard about Hatcher, but he's one dirty sonofabitch on the dock. He'll bite your ears off, gouge your eyes out—do anything that comes handy. And, boy, if you're not careful he'll maim you for life." Turning to Miranda, he said, "Better pass the word. This could go down as a goodun."

"I've fought his kind," I said, feeling a rush of adrenaline. "I grew up with pug uglies just like him."

Tully shook his head, obviously not convinced. "It was bound to happen. I knew it the first time I saw him watchin' you and the kid. I say kill the sonofabitch if you can."

"Tony's scared to death of him."

"Well, until you came along Larkin and Hatcher both was after him all the time." Tully put his hand on my shoulder. "Listen, I want you to expect dirty fightin', gougin' and kickin'. He'll do anything it takes—"

I nodded. "I'll try to keep out of his way."

"Hatcher fights barroom style, goddamnit! Which means *no holds barred*, as they say. God, what a sorry bastard he is." He looked me, his face tight with worry. "All I've got to say is you'd better take that neckerchief of yours along with you for this one."

I did a double-take. "Where did you hear about that?"

"Hell, don't you think I know the folks down at the *Triangle?*"

Miranda jumped in with, "Red grew up with a lot of big brothers, and he held his own with them."

"Yeah, well, the people he grew up with wasn't tryin' to kill him."

"That's what you think," I joked. "When we fought, it was for keeps."

Of course, he was right and we all knew it.

*   *   *

Some ten minutes after my challenge to Hatcher the two of us, stripped to the waist and without shoes or socks on, stood facing each other on the dock. The crew had formed a circle around us; and on the bridge three of the four officers milled about, pretending not to be at all interested in what was about to happen down on the dock.

Word of the fight had somehow leaked to the dock workers, and little knots of them had begun to assemble. On the ugly old buoy tender tied in front of the *Alert* a number of its crew had gathered on the stern to watch.

Tully, a good six inches shorter than Hatcher and me, stood between us with arms outstretched and short, pudgy fingers resting on our chests.

"Okay!" he shouted. "Listen up! Red here is new to the Coasties and so might not know what to expect!"

"I can tell him what to expect!" shouted Castleberry. "He's about to git the holy shit beat out of him!"

"Shut up!" bawled Tully, waving his hands. "Red, when I step back, the fight begins. There are no rules except that either one of you can end the whole thing by raising your hands."

"I'll tell him another way he can end it!" laughed Benton. "He can lay down pretend he's out cold!"

Tully, looking at Hatcher sternly and said, "When one of you goes down an' stops movin', the other one leaves him alone!"

"Why, sure, Mommy!" chuckled Hatcher, falling into a crouch.

"Okay, go at it."

The instant Tully stopped talking Hatcher moved quickly, lashing out with his right. It whizzed past my face, as I lowered my head and began to weave back and forth, pivoting at the waist. He was fast and confident and liked to do a jig, throwing lefts each time his feet touched the dock. I easily dodged his wild, longer punches and brushed aside most of the jabbing. Grunting his disgust at being unable to connect, he lunged at me just like the brawler I knew he was, and for his trouble caught a solid right that sent him to the dock.

We had been at it about thirty seconds.

He leaped up, embarrassed, and began yelling, "Take your medicine, Navy! Stand up and fight!"

I paid no attention to him, of course, and continued to weave and duck.

Some of the deckhands of the *Alert*, taking their cue from what he had said, began to shout, "Navy!" Somebody called out, "Lay down and play dead, Red!"

Of course, I had not expected anyone, with the exception of Miranda and Tully, to take my side. To the crew of the *Alert* I was not only a new man but ex-Navy, and it was only natural that they would be rooting for Hatcher. To them this was a grudge fight between the Coasties and the Navy.

"You goddamned idiots!" shouted Tully, looking about him at the jeering crew. "You ought to be hopin' this asshole gets what's comin' to him!"

Hatcher, for a time, did his best to reach my face with his left, undoubtedly wanting to bloody me up, leave some scars; but finding that my arms were a bit too long for him to do that with impunity, he soon began to change his tactics. It soon became clear to me that he just wanted to put an end to the fight quickly, with one mighty haymaker. Again and again he walsed in for the knockout punch; but each time he did so I feinted to one side, coming back with quick short jabs to the neck and face. And just as I had expected, Hatcher's temper began to rise toward the boiling point.

"You bastard, stand up and fight!" he shouted, hoarsely, aiming a mighty right cross at my head. He had not led with his left and, so, was slightly off-balance when the blow missed its target. For a brief moment the entire left side of his face was exposed. It was the break I had not expected from this seasoned barroom brawler.

Up to this point I had thrown only one right punch, and this had been enough to convince several of the spectators that I was no slugger and therefore did not have what it would take to put Hatcher away.

Then old Hatcher's guard went down and I threw a right at his chin.

Every slugger, whether fist-fighter or professional boxer, lives for that split second window of opportunity. And I knew when I felt my fist connect with his jaw it was a humdinger. It was not the best right cross I had ever delivered, but it was solid and backed by most of my weight.

And it was enough to break old Hatcher's jaw and, as it turned out, end his promising career as a Coast Guard boxer.

It would be discussed and debated in the messdecks and crews' quarters of the U. S. Coast Guard for years to come, finally making it to the East Coast and even to a loran station in Newfoundland. And as it passed from eyewitness accounts to hearsay and gossip, that punch was to become the big brother of all knockout punches, a lucky *golden* punch, thrown at just the right instant that caught Hatcher off guard and laid him out cold.

The solid cracking sound of bone against bone echoed up and down the dock, reaching the crew of the buoy tender (as I was to learn later). All eyes were glued on Hatcher as his feet left the dock and he plummeted into the circle of onlookers. He was straightened up for a brief moment, but it was obvious at once that he was out on his feet. Those who had seen him fight before could not believe it.

Then a mighty shout went up, as Hatcher was revived and taken back across the gangplank to a table in the messdeck. The O. O. D., Lt. Bertinelli, called the Eureka City Hospital for an ambulance, since the ship had no means of transportation of its own. Later, he nodded to me with a glitter in his eyes.

It was a curious thing that although *two of my knuckles had been knocked down*, as they say in fist-fight circles, I was feeling no pain. That would come later and I would once again swear that my fist-fighting days were over. I would argue, as I had many times in the past, that you cannot teach a man a lesson by hitting him with your fists. You can only make an enemy of him for life; and the joy that you get from that one lucky punch, if it happens, is not worth it.

Hello, Frisco, Hello!

———————— ◆ ————————

The Old Man of the Coast Guard Cutter *Alert,* Lt. Comdr. Mike Miklokowski, leaned across his desk and snatched the brass voicetube from the bulkhead. "God damn it!" he bellowed into the flared end, viciously lashing out with his foot at his wastebasket, which was just out of range. "Bertinelli!" Hearing nothing at all coming from the tube, he remembered that the other end was plugged. He put his mouth inside the flared end and blew savagely.

Shortly from the tube came a hesitant reply.

"Speak up, God damn it! Who is this?"

"Lieutenant Mosely, Sir!"

"Git Bertinelli here on the double!"

"Yes, Sir!"

During the two minutes that it took his Communications Officer to get dressed and make it to his cabin, the Old Man glared angrily at the sheet of paper lying on the center of his otherwise barren desk. And when Lt. Bertinelli, still hatless and tieless, knocked and was ordered inside, he shouted, "What the hell is this, Mister?"

The lieutenant inched forward, craning his neck.

"Hall's request for transfer, Sir."

"I know that, god damn it! What's it doin' here?"

"Uh, begging your pardon, Sir, but he—"

Miklokowski's fist came down hard on the request. "What I want to know is why in hell did you sign such a thing? Aint you aware that—I mean—the circumstances?"

The Old Man's mouth clamped shut at this point, and when he opened it again an entirely different voice came out.

"Lieutenant, we've got a goddamned good crew on this ship right now. Things are goin' along rather smoothly for a change. We've completed a difficult year, and I for one was lookin' forward to a little R and R in Frisco prior to starting all over ag'in. Now, from what I've heard our present radio operator played a vital part in straightenin' out the problem—with the fishermen."

"Begging your pardon, Sir—"

"You disputin' that?"

"No, Sir! I was just going to say that's why I thought we ought to approve Hall's request. That and the fact that he has performed his radio duties admirably."

"Hell, Bertinelli, don't you know you have to hang onto the good ones and git rid of the worthless ones? This is right where Hall needs to be. And if he had any sense he'd know that."

Lt. Bertinelli had straightened up and was standing uncomfortably at attention in the center of the room.

"Relax, god damn it. You make me nervous."

"What do you want me to do, Sir? I doubt that I can explain to him that his transfer has been denied. And even if I could I've already signed it and he's already—"

"Git him in your quarters an' butter him up. Tell him he's vital to the operation of this ship. Tell him you're recommendin' him for a rate change. Talk him into tearin' up that paper."

"But, Sir—"

"We're headin' down to Frisco in a couple of days, an' I want this matter settled by the time we git there."

The lieutenant later found his friend Lt. (jg) Harold 'Dusty' Rhodes in the wardroom ordering coffee and pie. He settled in next to Rhodes at the long dining table; and when the steward looked his way with raised eyebrows, he nodded.

"The Old Man ought to be in the Maritime Service," he said, matter-of-factly.

"That's where he came from, you know."

Bertinelli laughed incredulously. "Well, then, how did he ever become a lieutenant commander in the Coast Guard?"

"The war, my boy, the war. Lots of strange things happened back then. I imagine, if the truth was known, old Miklokowski's pretty nervous these days about being retired from the Service."

"That would explain why he's so hell bent on hanging onto this radioman. You wouldn't believe what I just received in the way of an order."

"Nothing would surprise me, where the Old Man's concerned. He's one ornery sonofabitch."

"He told me to offer this kid a rate change to RM1 if he'll remain aboard."

Rhodes became momentarily unable to talk because of an obstruction in his throat. Finally, he said, "But you can't do that! I mean you can offer it to him, but you can't make good on it. He's got to be at least four years away from that."

"I think Hall's smart enough to know that such a promise would be a lie. He would never go for it."

"What're you going to do?"

"I don't know. I thought maybe you might have a suggestion."

At about the time this conversation was taking place, I was seated in my swivel chair reading for the tenth time a radiogram from District Headquarters. Miranda drifted in and I handed it to him with the remark that I was taking them up on their offer.

Miranda read the radiogram, which was a request for volunteers to go to the Coast Guard aviation radio school in San Diego. I watched his face go through a metamorphosis. Reading Tony's mind was a very simple matter of paying attention to his face changes. What passed in his heart came out loud and clear on it. Now, it went from relaxed and happy through suspicion and doubt to alarm. And when he raised his eyes from the paper he looked like someone who had been terribly wronged.

"But why, for Christ's sake? I thought things were going just great!"

"Why, you ask? Why not, I say! Don't you realize that's the opportunity of a lifetime! It's tailormade for me. I have always wanted to gad about the country in a helicopter, and I'll bet that's what I'd get if I went through that school."

"You want to leave the *Alert?*" he cried, incredulous. "This is the best duty in the Coast Guard right here!"

"Sure, it's good duty, maybe the best, but think about it, being a radio operator on some helicopter or PBY! I've had quite a bit of training in aviation, you know. And I'm really looking forward to that sixteen weeks of aeronautical radio school before I'm assigned to something."

But Miranda was not interested in such talk. All he could think about was the imminent departure of his best friend and protector.

"Maybe the Old Man won't approve it," he said, brightening up. "And you might not even qualify. Ever thought of that? It says here you've got to take a series of tests and score high on them."

"Well, that's true," I admitted, sorry that he had to bring that up. "I'll have to pass some tests. But the Old Man's got to approve my request for transfer. This is a priority message from the Big Brass at DHQ. And if you'll look at it again, you'll notice that it says that Second Class Radiomen will receive first consideration. If I get it, I'll be at the Alameda Naval Air Base at least a month, right there in the Bay area."

"The Old Man doesn't have to do anything. Nobody can make him transfer you."

"Whose side you on, anyway?"

"Look, we've got a good thing here, you and me, goin' on liberties together an' bein' buddies and such. Don't you enjoy the bull sessions up on the bow at night? And you know the pictures I showed you? You can have any those in that bunch."

"Thanks, Tony, but I've got plenty of pictures of pretty girls."

"Yeah, but how many pretty girls do you have, right here close, in the flesh?"

"Tony, you can't *give* me one of those girls! And even if you could, I prefer to pick and choose my own girl friends."

"I guarantee any girl in that stack of pictures, and you won't find prettier or sexier ones in Frisco."

"What if I chose your twin?" I asked, maliciously.

Miranda's face broke into a smile. "Want to hear something weird? Promise you won't tell anybody?"

"What?" I demanded, suspicious.

"Promise me that this will go no farther than you."

"Okay."

"First, Tonya got her hair cut just like mine. She wanted to find out what you're like, I've told her so much about you, so she talked me into letting her take my place here on the ship a couple of times, just for the day. And one day the ship went out and she had to spend the night in the quarters."

My mouth had dropped open now it began to go up and down.

"Remember the first trip you took up to Sand Point? That's when it was."

I sat there remembering that night, remembering and becoming more and more upset. Finally, I burst out, "Tony, I know you're lying. You and I sat right here in the shack for an hour and shot the bull."

"You and Tonya sat here. She told me all about it. And up on the bow that night and down in the quarters later on."

All I could do was stare at him and protest, "Are you serious?"

"Yes. She told me she thought you would really be great in bed. Listen, if you'll promise to stay aboard, I'll get her to switch places with me tonight and you can find out what she's like."

"You would go ashore and exchange clothes with Tonya?" I said just above a whisper. My adrenaline was going lickety-split.

"After lights out she would climb into the sack with you."

At this point, Houston, the coxswain, stuck his head inside the shack and said that Mr. Bertinelli wanted me to report to the wardroom.

I got up to leave. Miranda was obviously enjoying my embarrassment. I could feel the heat in my face, a sure sign that I was blushing. Making certain that Houston was not standing outside the door, I said just above a whisper, "Don't get me wrong, Tony, I think your sister looks great and I'm sure she would be fine in the sack, but you're built much better."

As I went through the hatch, I glanced back and laughed. Tony's face was a bright red.

When I made it to the wardroom maybe two minutes later, Lt. Bertinelli waved and smiled at me, like we were old buddies. Then he rose from the table and excused himself to the two officers at the table.

"Follow me, Hall," he said, brushing past me in the doorway. "This will take just a minute.

When we were inside the lieutenant's stateroom and the door was closed, I said, "Sir, is it about the request for transfer?"

Bertinelli nodded, trying to look excited. "I talked to the Old Man, and he's convinced the ship can't make it without you. No kidding, he wants me to talk you out of this crazy scheme of yours."

"Pardon me, Sir," I said quickly, "but my mind's made up."

"I'm sorry to hear you say that. The truth of the matter is that my recommendation doesn't mean a thing unless the Old Man agrees with it. You stay aboard and I'll promise you as soon as the time requirement is met you'll become First Class."

"Sir, if I make it through this aviation radio school, I'll automatically be advanced to First Class. If I stay aboard this cutter, it'll be another couple of years, at least."

"Will you give this some more thought? Say until we get to Frisco?"

"According to the radiogram, I've got to put in for this school right away or it'll be too late. Is there anything else, Sir?"

Bertinelli, looking pained, shook his head. "No. No, I guess not. That'll be all."

*   *   *

The CGC *Yacona,* freshly painted and flying holiday pennants, showed up late on the afternoon of March 2. Its crew, most of whom had never been in Eureka, seemed overly anxious to go ashore and check out the town. Over dinner aboard the *Alert* that evening Lt. Comdr. Miklokowski briefed the skipper and executive officer of the *Yacona* on the local situation, strongly advising them not to start something with the Portuguese fishermen.

"Things are goin' along all right for the time being," he said. "Stir it up and there'll be hell to pay."

The Skipper of the *Yacona* winked at his Exec, then said to Miklokowski, "Aw, Mike, we'll keep it just as it is until you get back. Don't worry about a thing."

The next morning we lost no time getting underway for the big annual pilgrimage to Frisco. Everybody was in a holiday mood, and even before we cleared Humboldt Bay, we knew it was going to be one of those rare days along the northern California coast, for that time of year. It was cloudless and fogless and therefore brilliant, and the crew of the *Alert* crowded along the starboard lifeline in their shirtsleeves to talk about liberty in the Bay Area and watch the Humboldt Bay Lifeboat Station disappear. That finally accomplished, all but a few of the more excited and anxious ones headed for the messdeck for breakfast.

On Cloud Nine because of a piece of paper in my left shirt pocket, I stuck it out in the radio shack and maintained radio contact with the *Yacona* until static bursts finally forced me to sign off. At that point, I tuned in the calling frequency of NMC, District Headquarters, and asked for a signal report and permission to send one priority message.

Miranda drifted in from his lookout watch on the bow and wanted to know why I was grinning stupidly.

"I just received word from Mr. Bertinelli that I'm leaving the ship as soon as it docks at Pier 5. Tomorrow morning I'll be at Alameda taking a physical."

"Can't I go with you on liberty tomorrow night?"

"As a matter of fact, Tony, I'm going to a wedding tomorrow night. And I was given permission to invite you. But, before the wedding, I've got an errand to run—by myself."

"Why by yourself?"

"Heck, I'm not required to give out that kind of information. But if you have to know, I've got two hometown buddies in the Bay Area; and tomorrow I plan to round them up and party heavy, before the wedding." I poked my sad young friend in the ribs. "You don't ever party heavy, remember? You would be bored to death."

"Okay," he said, turning sullenly toward the door. "If that's the way you want it."

Feeling in a devilish mood, I said, "Now, if you just happened to be Tonya—!" While he glared at me, I added, "Come to think of it, I'll bet you are Tonya!" I eyed him up and down.

"How do you know I'm not, Smart Aleck?"

"Well, you look like her and you sound like her—but she has a special smell about her." I began to sniff in his direction.

"Go to hell, Red."

Watching Miranda slump out, I noticed for the first time that he was *built* very much like his sister, especially in the breast and bottom areas. For a moment I considered the possibility that just maybe I was watching Tonya slump out." That sobered me a bit.

In one corner of the radio shack sat that enormous old transmitter, with two kilowatts of RF output. The thought suddenly occurred to me that it just might be possible to raise a ham operator in the Bay Area on that thing. If I could do that, was it not highly likely that the ham would be gracious enough to deliver a couple of landline messages for me?

I was well aware that it was risky business to fire up a Coast Guard transmitter on amateur radio frequencies; but, then, wasn't life a risky business at best? Lt. Bertinelli could not read the International Morse Code when it was being sent beyond five words a minute, even if he should happen to drop in. And what were the chances anybody aboard the *Yacona* would tune across the particular ham frequency I would be using? I would have to make my transmission time short, use a phony call sign, and know exactly what I wanted to say before I began.

It took the TDE five minutes to warm up to operational, and by that time I had settled into the twenty-meter ham band on the Hallicrafters receiver and found a vacant space. A number of QSO's were in progress on that very popular band, but there was no telling how long I would have to eavesdrop before I would be lucky enough to identify a ham from the Bay Area. My best bet was to address the entire band.

With a tightening of the muscles in my lower intestines, I zero-beat a vacant spot on the band and began to tap out "QRZ FRISCO DE W6RED K" with the brass key, taking it slow and easy to attract all types. Even without glancing at my RF output I knew the signal I was sending into the ionosphere must be dimming lights in the Bay and playing holy havoc with a wide swath of the twenty-meter band.

Almost at once my efforts were rewarded. Ted, W6LVF, whose QTH was Richmond, broke in with "QSA 5" and wanted to know what the scoop was. He had not heard a signal that strong in all his born days, he confided. And no such noise, he joked, had been heard in that part of the country since the spark-gap transmitter. I told him it was home-made and experimental and would he relay two messages for me, one to Government Island, Alameda, and the other to the Coast Guard Tug at Fisherman's Wharf.

"No problem, old buddy. Fire away."

*   *   *

The Big Sur was shrouded in heavy fog, calling to mind Thornton Wilder and the romance of small boats, heavy fog, and bell buoys. We drifted past, feeling our way, looking for San Francisco. We found it by following the buoys and beelined it for the center of the Golden Gate Bridge. On such a morning, without the magic of a brilliant rising sun, it looked exactly like what it was, an ugly rusting old red bridge. We passed close to Alcatraz; but the Coast Guard Tug and Fisherman's Wharf, only a short distance away on our starboard, were hiding behind a dense fog bank. Not long after that we cut in close to the Embarcadero and found Pier 5. Visibility was about ten feet.

In dress blues and shiny black regulation shoes, I left the ship as soon as the gangplank was out, heading down the Embarkadaro toward the Bay Bridge. In my left breast pocket was a roll of twenties, what was left of two complete paychecks; and at the top of my spine, sewn cunningly into my neckerchief, was a slender pocket containing some thirty-seven dimes.

I walked down the center of the dock, my hands in my peacoat pockets, alert to the slightest sounds from all sides. I could see the planks beneath my feet but that was about all. It was quiet for the most part, the only sounds being those from some distance away, the muffled groans of fog horns and the occasional high-pitched squeal of a tug in the harbor.

On my right were the piers, at which ships from around the world were moored, bearing names that I could only occasionally make out, names like *Slovidna* and *Rastag Daz* and *Cai Li Ya*. It was, I found, quite difficult to keep my eyes away from them.

From behind me, almost from the moment I stepped off the gangplank, I was hearing or perhaps imagining the sound of soft, hesitant footsteps keeping pace with my own. Of course, the moment I paused to listen they ceased.

Hardly had I walked a block before I began moving into areas of fog so dense I could not even see my feet. It had not occurred to me that the soup would be so thick; and realizing that if I wandered too far to the right I would fall into the Bay. To the left, I knew, were the endless warehouses, and soon I was bouncing off these and making my way by guessing and feeling.

I became convinced that someone was behind me! I was certain of it and, after a time, I decided that it was not another sailor going ashore on liberty. It was a stalker, someone that was aware of me and meant me bodily harm.

"Who's there?" I called out, stopping suddenly and turning around. "I know you're there, mate!"

But to my ears came no human sound at all. It was like being suspended inside a pitch black, sound proof chamber of some kind.

I quickly removed my neckerchief and, holding the two ends in my right hand, took a step backward. At that moment something touched my right shoulder! *Something solid!*

"Hey, buddy, could you—?"

My heart had stopped altogether, but out of pure instinct I brought the chunk of dimes around in the direction of the voice! It encountered only thin air.

"Get away from me, whoever you are!" I shouted, swinging my long blackjack again. And again it found nothing but dense fog.

Then, from a short distance behind me, how far I could not be certain, came a stern voice. I couldn't be sure, but it sounded like, "He's mine, goddamnit!"

Were there two wharf rats following me?

Then, no mistaking it, I heard, "Matey, for a sawbuck I'll see you make it to the Bridge." The speaker was quite close to me!

Hearing rapid footsteps approaching, I ducked against one of the buildings and waited, keeping my blackjack at ready. It was a good move, evidently, catching both of the bums off guard. Because while I stood, not breathing, with my back to a metal wall, the two collided in the fog!

There followed a brief scuffle and a great deal of cursing and threatening. One of the two began to plead for mercy in a high sing-song voice. I glided quietly along the side of the building, still gripping the two ends of my neckerchief. Within minutes I found myself beneath a floodlight, the first of many along the last quarter of a mile to Market Street. There I replaced my neckerchief, checked my roll, and waited for my heart to slow down.

Next time, I told myself, I would carry a pistol or talk someone into going ashore with me!

* * *

The last leg of my journey to Fisherman's Wharf and the rendezvous with Bill Archer and Gene Goodrich was made in a taxicab, an extravagance that I justified on the grounds that I was running late and not at all certain my two buddies would still be waiting around for me. The cabby pulled up to the front door of the Harbor View Lounge, almost tipping over a gumball machine.

I paid him and went inside. It was dark but after a short time I was able to go on a search of the place for Coastie uniforms. The place was already crowded but I did not see a single uniform of any kind. I paralleled the long bar, hoping to get the attention of one of the busy bartenders. Failing that, I found a barstool.

Almost immediately a thin, pale face appeared across the bar from me. "What'll it be, mate?"

"I'm looking for two Coasties—"

At that moment the sound of a piano caught my attention. It was coming from the back of the lounge.

The bartender nodded. "They've got quite a party going back there. The *maestro* is wearing a Coast Guard uniform, and I think there's another one back there."

I hurried down the bar and veered to the left, found Goodrich in a booth by himself. At a baby grand a crowd of six or eight well-dressed women were blocking my view of the pianist. Goodrich was ready for me with a strong case against Archer's social behavior.

"There's gonna be trouble, Red."

A waiter arrived and I ordered two drinks. Goodrich was holding an empty glass.

"Tell you what," I said, "let's have one drink, grab Archer, and head for Chinatown."

"See all of them women at the piano? Each of them is with a man. An angry man who is at this very minute trying to decide whether he will kill Arch or just beat him senseless."

Archer suddenly shifted from a rather light-hearted version of a Chopin concerto to a most provocative version, his own, of *The Okie Boogie*. Which had the instantaneous effect of bringing a number of well-dressed men to their feet, all of them were facing toward the piano and the milling, giggling women.

"Hoh, oh," I said, getting up and heading for the crowd at the piano. I sidled between two women with raised drinks, bumped into another, and finally reached Archer's shoulder. Some hateful things were said to me, but I ignored them and grabbed Archer by an arm.

"Hey, Red Dog! You made it!"

I yelled into his ear, "In case you're interested, the party is moving! We're out of here!"

It had always been my considered opinion that Archer's hearing was even worse than his eyesight. On this occasion, he looked me in the eye and continued to grin and pound on the piano. There was no sign at all that he had heard my message.

I jerked him to his feet, upsetting the bench on which he had been sitting, and headed through the crowd toward the door. The angry women came after us, pounding me on the back and shoulders with their clenched fists and trying to grab hold of Archer. Some of the slower ones began throwing cocktail glasses, as we broke into the clear.

What followed was total confusion. Goodrich took the point toward the door, and I followed as best I could, dragging Archer by one arm. He had somehow managed to get a cocktail, probably from one of the women, and was trying to drink it all the while the world was exploding around us. Then, despite the obvious advantages of having us out of that place as soon as possible, one of the bartenders threw himself in our path, insisting that Archer had to pay his tab.

Somehow, with only minor bruises and contusions, not to mention the loss of two of my twenties, we made it through the swinging doors and found ourselves surrounded by a busload of tourists from Iowa who were headed for the lookout point facing Alcatraz Island. I glanced back, caught a glimpse of the front entrance of the Harbor View. It was alive with young men in black suits.

We hurried down the street, which was only half a street, with no buildings at all on one side. This was the street of small markets and restaurants that ran from the intersection to Pier 45, with vats of live seafood at the curb.

I felt a painful need to explain to my two friends that we should be on our way to Oakland if we were going to make it in time for the wedding. Goodrich was neutral on the subject, and Archer was convinced that we should go back inside the Harbor View and party.

"Let's vote," said Archer.

I shook my head quickly. "I went to too much trouble. I know you two don't know this swab that's getting married, but will you take my word for it that this is one party we cannot miss?"

"Where we goin'?" demanded Archer. "Chinatown? I've heard a lot about a bar up in that direction called the *Paper Doll*. Got any money left, Red?"

"Come on!" I shouted. "We're going to Oakland. I'm getting a cab!"

Goodrich looked at me for a moment, grabbed one of Archer's arms, and said, "I guess he means business, Curly Bill. Let's follow him. Besides, we're broke."

At the intersection of Embarcadero and Caliente, on the corner facing the Harbor View Lounge, we caught not a taxi but a bus. Which just happened to be going directly to the Terminal Building. On the way there and across the Bay Bridge and through a sizable chunk of east Oakland, while Archer sobered up, Goodrich brought me up to date on what he and Archer had been doing. Just as started to tell about the Portuguese fishermen, the fight on the dock with Hatcher, and my eminent transfer to the Coast Guard Aeronautical Radio School in San Diego, I realized that we were about to disembark from our bus. It had stopped in front of *Ted and Roy's Hooligan Bar*, which (I was guessing) could not be far from our destination of the evening.

Peg o' My Heart

◆

By the time we reached the fifteen-hundred block of east Oakland Archer had joined the living and wanted to know where we were going. Goodrich wanted to know why I had insisted on leading him and Arch all the way across the Bay and into the ugliest part of Oakland. Who was this friend throwing the party?

"He's a quartermaster on the *Alert*," I said. "I'll introduce you to him when we get to the party."

"What I want to know," growled Goodrich, "is why are we going to this party? Is he something special?"

"Actually, no. Let me just say that this is one party we couldn't miss. It's a long story. Trust me."

I could have told them that this quartermaster was the son of a very rich Oakland businessman, that he had a reputation on the cutter for throwing very expensive parties that were attended by very pretty chicks.

By my calculations the party had been going on about three hours when I finally we saw the place, about a block ahead of us. It had a number of big neon signs out front, proclaiming the place to be the *C & E Club*, but not one of them was on. The whole block looked dead.

"Man, we're going to spend all night looking for this dude," said Archer. "You don't know where he lives, do you?"

I had not mentioned to my friends the minor detail that we were looking for a lounge, not the quartermaster's house. So at this point, having heard the definite sounds of a party behind the darkened doors of the C & E Club, I said, "Let's ask about my friend at that place."

"Are you kiddin'?"

When we reached the door, I pounded on it and stepped back.

"Nobody's going to open that door," complained Archer. "That's a private party in there."

I pounded again, harder this time.

Suddenly, a small panel in the heavy door slid to one side and a pair of eyes appeared. I moved in close and said, "Pardon me, Sir. We're looking for a party in this neck of the woods."

"Say the magic words."

"What do you mean?" I said, faking bewilderment. "A password?"

"You got it, mate. Give me the magic words."

"Well, hell," I said, looking around at my friends. "I thought this might be the place." Then, turning back to the door, I blurted, "*Semper fidelis.*"

"Wrong. Good night."

"*Semper party!*" called out Archer, grinning mischievously. "Come on, Red, let's get out of here!"

"Wrong again. You boys git lost."

"How about *Semper paratus!*" I suggested, innocently.

For a time, the eyes did not blink and no words came out of the hole in the wall. Finally, "I guess it's okay, but maybe you was just guessin'." The door swung back slowly. "Keep it down. This's a highbrow party." A man, whose neck was wider than his head, appeared in the doorway, looked us over, and backed up, taking the door with him.

"You don't say!" I joked. "I thought it was Cheesy Macklin that was throwing the party."

"It's the Macklin family that's sponsoring this party." The big man suddenly grinned, "I guess you could say Mister Macklin's the Big Cheese in this end of Oakland. Cheese is his business." Then, confidentially, with an arch in his eyebrows, he said, "You boys may be in over your heads tonight."

"Let us be the judge of that," I said. "Where do we put our hats?"

The entrance room was rather small and looked like a foyer to a modest residence, but from there on it was an entirely different story. Across a deep-carpeted floor filled with tables and chairs that disappeared finally in the hazy distance was a bar that occupied the entire right wall. This very large room, lighted only by candles, was occupied by only a half-dozen couples that were seated at tables covered with white linen. From a distance came the distinctive sounds of big band music.

"I am impressed," I said, stopping dead in my tracks. "What next?"

The band, without a pause or transition, eased into "Stardust Melodies."

"This just goes to prove you can't judge a book by its cover," I said. "I thought old Macklin got his nickname for the way he smelled, not what his father did for a living. Come on, let's join the revelers."

The instant we moved past the little group gathered at the tables in the front part of the lounge area we received another shock. Here most of the guests were young ladies in long, expensive dresses and young men in tuxedos; and they were shuffling about on a large wooden dance floor. Several Coasties in dress uniforms were sitting in a knot at small tables near the band, without female company!

"Well, would you look at that," complained Archer, nodding toward the swabs. "We ended up in the wrong place, after all."

"We're at the right place," I scolded. "Come on, let's join that bunch of hooligans over there." I spotted Tully and headed toward him. Then I saw Miranda and Houston. With them were two quartermasters and a yeoman from the *Alert*, and all were sitting straight and sober.

"Don't say a goddamned word," said Tully when I walked up. "Good liquor, good music—What the hell more can a man ask?" It was very obvious that he was re-thinking his decision to attend this party.

A waitress showed up and discretely stood to one side until we were ready to order. I glanced at her and she smiled and said,

"You've got to be Red. Mr. Macklin told me to keep an eye out for a sailor with a lot of red hair."

I nodded, wondering why Macklin was singling me out, since we weren't particularly good friends. As if she had read my thoughts, she said, "He wants to introduce you to someone. Would you follow me?"

"Could we have a drink first? We've just hitch-hiked all the way from Fisherman's Wharf." I turned to my two friends, who had found empty chairs. "Beer all right?"

"Yeah," said Archer, "Bring us out some Lone Star."

This was meant to be a joke, but the girl frowned and shook her head. "We don't serve that, I'm afraid."

"Bring us any kind of beer you've got," said Goodrich, "as long as it's lowbrow."

"We do have Lowenbrau."

"They'll never know the difference," I told her. "I'll take the same."

The girl, looking a bit flustered, left quickly.

"I don't think any of us said the right thing," commented Archer, grinning and tearing. "Nice lookin' chick, don't you think, Red?"

At that moment I spotted the host, a thin, pimply young man dressed in a tux. He was bending over one of the tables on the fringe of the civilian crowd, talking to two young women seated there. He was blocking my view of them, but when he straightened up and nodded in my direction, I felt my heart falter. Even at that distance I knew I had just caught sight of royalty.

"Look," said Archer, "Red's got that look on his face."

"Shut up, Bill," I hissed, unable to take my eyes off the young lady, whose large brown ones were now focused upon me. At a distance of at least fifty feet I could feel the electric shock of instant and total infatuation! I could see only her upper body, but what I could see was pure perfection.

Macklin, with a final nod at the two girls, turned and began to make his way toward me. In his tux he did not look at all like the scroungy Quartermster Third Class on the *Alert*.

"Red, hi. I'm very glad you could make it!"

I nodded, accepting Cheesy's clammy hand. "I'd like you to meet two hometown friends of mine. Archer, the grinning one, and Goodrich. Sorry it took us so long to get here."

"Listen, Red, I've got a favor to ask of you. When I was explaining to my family about the members of the crew that I'd invited, my cousin, over there at that table, insisted on knowing all about you. I guess it was the red hair, but it seemed like the more I talked about how you trimmed old Hatcher's sails and all that stuff at the Triangle Bar the more she wanted to meet you. I finally had to promise I'd introduce you to her if you showed up at the weddin'. Is that okay with you?"

Archer leaned over and whispered into my ear, "Don't do it, Red. If she's this guy's cousin, she's probably a sweat hog."

"Your cousin, you say?" I asked. "Sure, I don't mind."

"Ask him if she looks anything like him," whispered Archer.

"That's her over there at that table, the small brunette," said Cheesy, pointing. "She's the one looking this way."

At that moment, while my heart was doing a flip-flop and Archer was choking on the words he had just said, the band settled into *Peg O' My Heart,* causing a number of couples to rise and go to the dance floor.

"I see her, Cheesy," I said, just above a whisper. "Introduce me to her."

Macklin led the way happily. Apparently, a load had been lifted from his shoulders. When we reached the table, he put his hand on the shoulder of the larger of the two girls, who was built rather solidly in the neck and shoulders. "This is my cousin Clara, who lives in Fresno." I nodded and said something, and Cheesy moved his hand to the other girl's shoulder and said, "And this is Melissa, my cousin from Richmond. Melissa, this is my very good friend, Red."

Suddenly, she was on her feet and headed around the table toward me, smiling and extending her hand.

Stupid things were going through my mind, and birds were singing and butterflies were dancing about in my stomach. All the silly things poets had said about star-crossed lovers and love at first sight were no longer corny.

"I've heard so much about you."

Her voice was deep and rich and sexy, and I was a tongue-tied Gatsby facing his Daisy. It was the first time in my life that I was afraid I might say or do the wrong thing in front of a pretty girl.

I took her hand, feeling my insides rolling about like I was on an eighty-three footer in gale-force winds. Up close she looked even better than she had at fifty feet away. And her dancing brown eyes were like magnets drawing me to her, encouraging me to take her into my arms and kiss her. Somehow, I resisted that urge and just stood there like a stump and tried to clear my voice.

"Look, he's blushing!" she snickered, squeezing my hand.

"Would you like to dance?" I stammered, half-hoping she would refuse. What if I stepped on her foot?

She nodded quickly and glanced at her cousin at the table, whose expression had softened. Clara nodded first at Melissa and then at me, and seemed quite pleased, which instantly caused me to change my opinion of her. Everybody, it seemed, was smiling at us. I glanced across the room at my buddies and they were beaming stupidly. I did not want to think what I looked like.

"I love this song," she whispered into my ear as soon as we were on the dance platform. "It's my very own song."

"I think it's the first time I ever heard it," I said.

I could feel her body stiffen as I spoke. She was quite obviously astonished that I could not remember ever having heard *Peg O' My Heart*, which, she said, was the Number One song on all the popular charts. Her voice, which was no longer husky and sexy, turned my insides to ice. She suddenly wanted to know what kind of an isolated and ridiculous world I had come from.

"The same world your cousin comes from," I said, completely taken aback. And just a little on the defensive. "Sorry, but this just isn't the kind of music I listen to on the cutter."

"Then what kind of music do you listen to?" She seemed close to tears, and although we continued to dance she had pulled herself away from me.

"Look," I pleaded, "I like it. In fact, I love it. And I don't have the slightest idea in the world why I haven't heard it before."

"You're just saying that. Malcolm should have told me you don't like good music."

We were looking into each other's eyes, and suddenly I became aware that the music had stopped and I was still trying to drag her about the dance floor. I had never felt so miserable in my life.

"I swear I like it. What in the world's wrong with you?"

The instant these words were out of my mouth I knew I had made a major mistake.

"Never mind. Take me to my table." Her voice now was cold and hateful and her beautiful face had hardened into something I could not stand to look at.

"Who is Malcolm?" I asked, clinging to one of her hands and leading her through the crowd that was milling about on the dance platform.

She turned her tragic face upward toward me and batted her tear-filled eyes like the end was near. "Thank you for—the dance. And I'm also sorry about the song."

"My God," I sighed, to no one in particular. "What's wrong?"

Again I could have kicked myself. There was decidedly something wrong with her, but what fool male between the ages of six and sixty would say such a thing like that to such a lovely creature?

Her cousin, who did not bother to look me in the eye when we approached the table, now had a sullen look on her face; and glancing across the room toward Tully and my hometown buddies, I suddenly realized that the world could be a cold and ugly place. They were nodding and grinning in my direction, obviously trying to cheer me on. Without another word, I crossed the floor and fell into a chair between Goodrich and Archer.

"You beat all," said the former, elbowing me. "Dancing with the riff-raff that way."

"Yeah," agreed the latter, faking chagrin. "If there's an ugly woman around, Red'll find her."

"Shut up, both of you. That's the girl I'm going to marry."

"Oh?" exclaimed Goodrich. "What about that little ole tomboy down in the River Bend?"

"Yeah, Jamie Lee," agreed Archer.

Quite suddenly I felt cold all over. I had shut Jamie and Jody and Alice out, just as Melissa had shut me out. I would go through life without true love.

"With you bastards around I don't need a conscience," I said.

"Pathetic," said Goodrich, looking justified.

There was movement at Melissa's table, I noticed. A strikingly handsome man in a tux had showed up and was offering his hand to her. He had a great head of wavy black hair and a very arrogant Roman nose; and, instantly, I hated his guts.

"Oh, hoh," said Archer, staring straight at the other table. "The pretty canary is about to escape into the hands of the big ugly vulture."

"Look at that guy's shoulders," sighed Goodrich.

"They're padded," I said. "Underneath all that is skin and bones."

"Yeah, an' he's wearing stilts," said Goodrich. "But looks like she's pretty impressed."

The tall-dark-handsome Lothario led Melissa to the edge of the dance floor, taking six pairs of eyes with him. They made a striking couple, I had to admit. The most beautiful girl I had ever seen was dancing with the tallest and most handsome man in the room.

"I sure as hell hope he likes *Peg O' My Heart*," I mumbled, "for his own sake." When my buddies glanced at me, I tried to grin. What I wanted to do was go retch.

"What's goin' on?" demanded Goodrich. He leaned across me and looked at Archer. "Did I miss something? That's not what the band's playing." Then to me he said, "Did you and that girl have a spat about that sorry song?"

"All I said was that I hadn't heard it before. She made a big thing out of it, like it was some kind of test. Just because I had never even heard it before, she threw a fit. The stupidest thing I ever saw."

"But you didn't like it, did you?" insisted Archer. "No wonder you dropped her so quick."

"Are you nuts? I didn't drop her. She dropped me. She's a high-class girl, and I'm lucky to have the chance to dance with her. Country hicks like you and Goodrich wouldn't understand girls like her at all."

"But you would," said Goodrich. "Shit, man, she'd make a lunatic out of you inside of a week."

"She wouldn't need a week," I admitted, soberly.

The band began *Begin the Begeen,* and everybody at the table watched as the tall young man took the petite brunette into his arms once again and lifted her to the platform. It was the most painful scene I had ever watched.

"Look what he did," said Archer. "You gonna stand for that, Red?"

Nobody at the table was having a good time, it was obvious. They were sipping beer like it was tea, and not one of them had had the balls to go ask a girl to dance. I rose, feeling like a lighted fuse, and said to no one in particular, "Wait for me."

"Don't start trouble," warned Goodrich.

I worked my way around tables and chairs past Melissa's table. Clara saw me and, for a moment, looked startled. Then she suddenly frowned and straightened up. She had decided I was up to no good and as I began to circle the dance floor, her eyes followed me. I was uncertain what I was about to do, but I knew I could not continue to watch that Latin scarecrow continue to put his big hungry hands all over Melissa.

The thought of leaving the place never entered my mind. And, likewise, it never occurred to me that I had absolutely no rights where this girl was concerned.

At the edge of the platform I stopped, having lost sight of them. They were somewhere near the center of the dance floor, evidently, hidden by other dancers. I continued to circle impatiently, refusing to look back at the two tables of Coasties. I told myself that it did not matter at all what they were thinking. What did matter was how Melissa was going to take it when I—

Suddenly, they appeared not two feet away, and Melissa was staring in disbelief at me, her face pale and drawn! Without hesitation I stepped upon the platform and clapped my right hand over the tall kid's shoulder. I had to reach to do it; and sure enough, beneath the expensive blue serge jacket I felt nothing but padding and a thin bone.

"May I cut in?" I said, in a voice that I did not recognize.

They stared at me in amazement, while around them couples continued to dance, paying us no attention.

"This is not that kind of party," scolded Melissa, looking quite pleased all of a sudden. "Maybe you can have the next dance."

"It's all right, Peg," said the young man. "Is this Red?"

I looked from one of them to the other, startled. But before I had time to mull over just what was transpiring, Melissa pushed the tall one away and fell into my arms with a happy giggle. "Go on, Lyle. And thanks," she said, hugging me. Then, while Lyle looked on, she faced me and mouthed, "Were you jealous?"

The little vixen, I thought. She enjoyed making me miserable. No girl had ever made me feel that way before.

"I don't have the least idea what's going on," I said. "Why did he call you *Peg?* I thought your name was *Melissa.*"

At this point I was just a bit giddy, quite the happiest I had ever been in my life. There remained, however, a tiny cloud of suspicion that I might have been betrayed. I had been told that her name was *Melissa*, a very beautiful name that fitted her perfectly, when all the time her real name was *Peg* and some songwriter had written a song about her and called it *Peg 'O My Heart.* If that were true, then I had surely been tested and found sadly lacking.

Here, I thought, holding her exciting little body tighter, is a very complicated female. And it was very scary how easily she could make me miserable.

"You're not supposed to know what's going on," she laughed. "But I'll tell you just a little of it. Lyle's my brother. Isn't he a dear, sweet, wonderful guy? He just happened to drop by and ask me to dance. Know what he told me? Oh, I've been called *Peg* all my life because my middle name is *Elizabeth.*"

"That makes perfectly good sense."

"Know what he said?"

"Well, yeah, I guess. No, I don't know. What?"

"He said I had been ridiculous and cruel for making such a thing about a song and that real sailors never cared much for stupid things like that. He also said that you are the handsomest man in the room tonight."

"He did not, you little cut up."

"He got you to ask me to dance again, didn't he? I guess I forgive you."

"There was nothing at all to forgive," I pouted.

The words were out of my mouth before I could stop them, and I felt my insides turn to ice-water. I braced myself for the worst.

However, instead of her body stiffening and her face turning cold and hateful, she wrapped her arms around me, placed one of her feet on one of mine, and began to climb! Just when I was certain I had completely ruined everything between us, she was as happy as a lark! I glanced around to see if anyone was watching us.

"Oh, God!" she sighed. "Hold me, Red! Squeeze me!"

"Don't you want to dance?"

"I am so glad I found you, you handsome devil! I've looked all of my life for you, and when I least expected it here you are in the flesh!" She wrapped her free leg around me and pressed her other one into my crotch. "I am never going to let you go!"

We danced that way for a time, attracting no attention whatsoever. I was careful to maneuver us about the side of the dance floor away from the nosey Coasties. Who were undoubtedly wondering why they had come to this party. I knew I would catch it from Goodrich and Archer later.

"I know," she sighed into my ear irrelevantly, sounding as if she were responding to something I had said. "You're such a gentleman, Red! I want to know everything there is to know about you, where you came from and where you're going, all about your tastes in music and art and literature and—!"

"When will I see you again?" I agonized, crushing her to me. I had felt of a variety of female bodies before but never one so soft and at the same time firm and agile and alive. It was like clinging to a young cougar that had been declawed.

"Oh, don't worry. You won't get away from me, now that I've found you!"

*   *   *

Government Island lay exposed in the early morning sunshine, a sight no young and impressionable youth should have to witness before breakfast; but on this morning after, this D-Day-Minus-One, I saw only beauty and warmth and homely goodness. To me it looked like an old and very dear friend ready to see to my simple needs and provide me with a comfortable place to while away the twenty-four hours left before I would report to the hospital at Alameda Naval Air Station.

At the Main Gate, I spoke affably to one of the two men there about my plans to become an aviation radioman. It was the kind of thing I never did. But on this occasion I could not help myself.

The world had taken a ninety-degree turn for me, no doubt about it, and things would never be the same again. Not only was I about to embark upon a very exciting career, but I had met (and won) what had to be the most beautiful and interesting girl in the entire world.

Ask not for whom the bell tolls.

Later, at Personnel, Eugene Tuney Goodrich accepted my orders with disgust written all over his face. "Tomorrow's the big day, huh, Red?" he asked, looking into the manila envelope that contained the orders. "You will keep away from whores and prostitutes and ladies of the street prior to the physical, I presume."

"That reminds me," I said, "I'm expecting a phone call. Could you send someone to the barracks for me when it comes in?"

"No incoming calls for enlisted personnel," he said quickly, mechanically.

"You heard me, old buddy," I warned.

"We don't accept any calls for enlisted personnel, and that's the truth, Red. Want me to take a message for you? I can do that."

I turned toward the door. "If you have any notions of ever bumming liberty money off me in the future, or being invited to great parties by me ever again, you'll send someone over when the call comes in."

"Can't do it. Against the rules. By the way, that party was the worst I have ever attended in my entire life, bar none."

"I'm warning you, Butt Head."

The call came just after noon chow while I was taking a stroll down by the docks. A yeoman striker from the Personnel Office came running down the street between the barracks buildings with the news, adding that it was a girl with a very sexy voice.

Walking very quickly, about a foot off the ground, I took the lead back to Personnel. There I was told to use the phone at the end of the counter. Goodrich was nowhere in sight, but I had no doubt that it was he who had sent the yeoman-striker for me.

My heart was pounding as I moved toward the phone. I put out my hand for it, aware that an officer had just entered the room. Hesitating, I turned and faced him. He was wearing a lieutenant's bars on his collar.

"What the hell's going on?" he asked, unkindly. "Who do you think you are?"

I slowly lifted the phone, all the while looking him in the eye, and said, very softly, "Hello."

"Jorgensen, what's that sailor doing on the phone?" shouted the officer.

At this point, Goodrich came sailing into the room and lined up in front of the officer. "Mr. Soldolski, Sir, the Skipper of the CGC *Alert* called and said he wanted to talk—"

"Oh," said the lieutenant, doubtfully. He turned first in my direction and then toward Goodrich. "What did you say his skipper's name is? I never heard of anybody named *Soldolski.*"

"Lt. Commander Miklokowski, Sir," I corrected.

"Oh, right. Okay, go ahead."

I said again into the phone, "Hello." Then, adjusting the thing to my ear, I realized that she was already halfway through a sentence.

"—took you so long?"

The voice was dripping with honey goodness, but the words I soon realized were not. What she was saying translated into *adios, farewell, I'll not be seeing you*—if you don't get your act together.

"I can't believe you would be so awful, Red, to keep me waiting here like just any ole girl off the street that you might be dating. I thought we really had something going."

I looked at the lieutenant, who was eyeing me suspiciously from ten feet away. Into the phone I said, in a very respectful tone of voice, "Sorry, Sir, it's against regulations for an enlisted man to receive calls here."

"Why are you talking to me that way?" Peg cried, heartbroken. "Never in my life—!"

"I'm very sorry, Sir," I said, in my sexiest voice. "No doubt about it, Sir."

"I get it. You don't want to talk to me. You've decided that this is the way you'll get rid of me."

"Oh, no, Sir, nothing like that at all!"

"Well, then, if that's true, tell me what your personal opinion of me is. Do you like me just a little?"

"Oh, yes, Sir, I do. I think—"

The lieutenant, still looking at me, turned and said something to Goodrich.

"I think you're wonderful," I whispered, "and I'll call you tomorrow right after my physical."

"What did you say? You think I'm *what?* I couldn't hear that last at all."

"I said—"

At that point, the lieutenant lifted his right hand high and with head lowered like a fighting bull barreled it toward me, saying as he did so, "Sailor, let me talk to your Commanding Officer!"

Startled, I lowered the phone into its holder, just as the lieutenant's hand clamped onto it. Peg's voice was still ringing in my ears.

"I'm sorry, Sir, I believe he just hung up."

"But I was still hearing a voice!" snapped the lieutenant. "Who in hell was that on that phone, sailor?"

"It was the Commander, Sir," Goodrich assured him. "I'm pretty sure it was, because I took the call myself."

"Well, I'm certain what I heard was a very high-pitched, feminine voice. The Commander Miklokowski I remember—"

"Oh, he gets a little high-pitched when he's upset, Sir," I said. "And he's real upset right now."

"I always thought Miklokowski was an old walrus."

"That's just when he's in a good mood, Sir," I said. "He can get very high-pitched when he's upset."

*　　　　*　　　　*

From Personnel I beelined it to the barracks building, suddenly feeling an urgent need to investigate an itching in my crotch. There, to my amazement and disbelief, I found a small patch of redness on one side of my penis. Perhaps, I reasoned, it was some kind of rash, undoubtedly picked up on some stool. Scratching didn't seem to relieve it at all; but, returning to my bunk and stretching out, I managed, after a time, to put it out of my mind by going back over what Peg had said on the telephone.

An hour later the itch was again demanding attention. Refusing to scratch or even rub the inflamed area, I walked quickly back to the head in the rear of the barracks and dropped my dungaree trousers, now very much alarmed. What I saw was no longer a small red patch. My miserable instrument, now a beet red and swollen beyond recognition, appeared to be retreating into layers of red, puffy skin, giving the appearance of a reluctant box turtle pulling back from a naughty world.

"Oh, my God!" I burst out. "What has happened to you?"

The only reply from the mute and blatant abomination between my legs was an almost imperceptible and involuntary flinching motion that instantly brought tears to my eyes. Feeling real panic now, I carefully eased the trousers up, buttoned them, slid the belt through the brass buckle, and cinched it down. "Gangway," I whispered pathetically, and headed for the front of the barracks. I moved as quickly as I could, with only one fully operational leg. The other had become little more than a crutch that served to balance me on my way to the Sick Bay.

My only hope now was that I would not meet or be observed by anyone who knew me.

But it was not to be. My luck had run entirely out. Good luck, as they say, generally comes in threes; but bad luck, once it starts, can go on and on forever. Suddenly before me was none other than Yeoman Second Class, E. T. Goodrich, one of the two men in the Bay Area who was capable of carrying incriminating news back to the home folks and girl-friends in Oklahoma.

"Hey, Red, you saved me a trip!" he called out, while he was still some distance away. "Where you headin'?"

I said nothing, having nothing at all in the world to say to this sucker.

"Why are you hobblin' along like that?"

Ignoring him, I continued moving toward the dispensary as expeditiously as possible. But to keep certain parts from rubbing against something, I was being forced to waddle, much like an old man with hemorrhoids.

"Red, quit clownin'! Word just came in. Alameda wants you right now. A Jeep from Transportation is on its way."

I hurtled an expletive or two in his direction but continued looking straight ahead.

"Why are you clowning?"

"None of your business. Don't you have something to type?"

"Where are you going? The Jeep will be here real soon."

"Where does it look like I'm going?"

He fell in beside me and we walked on toward Sick Bay.

"I'll lay you odds it was Sunshine," he said, finally.

It was a curious thing, but I had not even thought of Sunshine. I had carefully gone over my amorous involvements with Jody and Jamie and Alice and Darleen, and the Blue Top Girl, whose name I could not remember, in great detail; but not once had I given any thought to that wild little tease from Atoka, Oklahoma. With whom I had partied seriously just before enlisting in the Coast Guard.

Indeed, I had wined and dined her night and day for about two months prior to that last date, spent more than a hundred dollars on her for beer alone, and, finally, a week or so before we left, she had spent a night with me at Alamo Courts, in Ada. Up until Goodrich had opened his big mouth, I had considered Sunshine one of my signal victories as a Ruptured Duck, not as my Waterloo.

"Sunshine, my friend, was a virgin. It wasn't her."

"I hate to tell you this, Red, but I know for a fact she was no virgin."

"You tell anybody about this and so help me I'll personally put out your lights."

"Hey, my lips are sealed."

An hour later, after fifty-nine minutes of agony in the waiting room and a ten-second glance at my penis by Dr. Lt. Comdr. Bonebrake, who was wearing the silver clusters of a full commander on his white jacket, said casually, "Where the hell you been, sailor?" His voice was not unkindly. "Vallejo?"

I said nothing, standing there like a half-wit while he busied himself with creating a specimen and staring at it under a microscope. And when he finally spoke again, his voice betrayed no hint of the tragedy he was about to lay on me

"Looks like you're about to reap a few wild oats, my boy."

"Will that knock me out of radio school, Sir?" I blurted.

The broad butt of the officer swung around facing me, and for a time I could hear nothing but snickers and giggles coming from him and the pretty little nurse he was blocking from my view.

Finally, he swung back around and, wiping a grin from his face, he said, "You must put such things out of your mind for a time. I'll see if I can get you in over at the U. S. Marine Hospital, in San Francisco." Then he turned to the grinning nurse and said something that I couldn't hear.

"Wait in the next room, sailor boy," she said.

I sighed, all of the spunk and vinegar taken out of me. I wanted to ask her if she had something that would relieve my problem short term, but instead I tucked my tail between my legs and dragged out to the waiting room.

Five minutes later I was on my way back to the barracks with a tube of salve, some pills, and a note to Personnel. Goodrich, who had left me at the door of the dispensary, was waiting on the little stoop.

"What'll I tell you know who if she calls back?"

"Tell her I was transferred to Newfoundland."

Something to Remember Me By

♦

After two days flat of my back, with no liberty and no telephone calls but with a relayed message from Cheesy Macklin that his cousin wanted nothing more to do with me, I finally received orders to check back in at Sick Bay. Following a complete physical, I went by Personnel and turned in the Sick Bay report, refusing even to look at Goodrich.

To his credit he had visited me a number of times, but I had maintained a great deal of restraint in his presence.

"Did you decide whether to kill yourself or not?" he asked before I could turn and reach the door. "Still waitin' till you get your strength back?"

Later that day in the barracks he needled me until I blasted out, "Why did it have to happen to me? Compared to you and Arch, I've practically been a celibate! I had one girl all that time at home and you two had several, even while you were shacking up with your regular girlfriends."

"The gods like you and want you to straighten up your act. They don't care about Archer an' me."

"Git out of here! Go back to your own barracks!"

"Are you tryin' to tell me you never got into the pants of any of those girls that pestered you all the time? How about Darleen? I know you slept with her. Remember, I was at that overnight party in the woods."

"Sure, I slept with her but she asked me not to do anything and I didn't. I could have but I didn't."

"Come to think of it, the gods may have given you that to teach you a lesson. I never heard anything that stupid in my life."

At evening chow I made it halfway through the line before dropping out and returning to my bunk; and the next morning I ignored chow call. Around nine o'clock Goodrich showed up at the barracks with a brown manila envelope.

"Get ready, Red. A Jeep from Transportation will be by to get you in ten minutes."

"Where am I going?" I asked. "Surely not back to the *Alert.*

"Well, since you're doomed anyway, the Coasties have decided they don't want you around anymore. They're dumping you over the Bay Bridge this morning."

"Shut up, you worthless no-good-for-nothing *yeoman.*"

"Ouch. That hurt. Just remember, it is you that's going to the hospital, not me."

                    *   *   *

The U. S. Marine Hospital, located on a lovely hillside overlooking San Francisco State Park, was full of Merchant Marine sailors and a colorful collection of derelicts from around the world. But, I was to learn, I was the only Coastie in the place. I was assigned to Ward C, on the fourth floor, with twenty-seven other VD victims; and one quick glance assured me that I had gotten myself into something of a mess. Most of the naked men in the room were full-bearded, wrinkled, and loudmouthed, especially about the fights they had won and their sexual conquests.

I wanted nothing at all do with anything sexual, and how these old dudes could brag about what they had done to this and that female was beyond me.

Curiously enough, however, even the crustiest of these old salts left me alone, as if they had been warned with a pistol to their heads that I was not to be pestered. Maybe it was because they had not seen many clean-faced, innocent boys like me; or, more likely, because I was too unbelievably vulnerable and naive.

Immediately, I was nicknamed *Kid*.

That first day and night I resisted all overtures of friendship from the motley residents and the clean white nurses alike, refused to go to the dining room for meals, the crafts room for crafts, and the reckroom for a game of dominos. On the second night, when I was in the depths of despair, I was visited by a very pretty chocolate-brown nurse, who seemed to take an instant liking for me. Her name was *Lilli*, and, I was to learn, she was the favorite of every man in that ward.

For a long time that evening she sat on the side of my bed and talked to me in her low, husky, South of the Border voice, finally convincing me that I still had something to live for, that indeed I had probably picked up my 'problem' from some stool.

Lilli, I decided, must be an angel sent from God; and when she laid her hand in mine, I knew it was so. She was without a doubt the most beautiful and charming young woman in the world, so soft and mature and loving. Her skin was dark, her smile bright and honest, and her starched and brilliantly white uniform a perfect fit for her absolutely stunning body. *But, thank God, I felt nothing at all in my genitals all the time she was with me!*

Even before I saw her up close it was clear to me that she was beautiful and desirable to every man in the ward. Even the old men who were too sick to sit up and look at her greeted her with proposals of marriage as she moved down the double row of beds. Even so, I was not prepared for her *up close!*

She entered the large room like a gust of spring air, singing out, "Coffee time!" And it wasn't until the needle hit me in the butt that I realized it was just her way of preparing us to brace ourselves. If she had not been so beautiful and soft and warm, I would have undoubtedly called her a few names for tricking me with that cruel euphemism.

Coffee time indeed!

I could not remember having seen her before that second night, perhaps because I had been very feverish and, at times, delirious. And it was certainly the first time I had heard her sweet voice call out those words. I had actually expected her to deliver a cup of coffee to my bedside, and so mellow and soothing was her voice I was planning to drink some of it, for her sake. But about the time I was thinking what a nice thing it was for this pretty young Latin-American girl to do, delivering coffee to sick sailors, firm, strong hands flopped me over on my stomach and popped a long needle into my buttock!

Following my outraged bellow and the burst of laughter in the ward, she asked me in a kindly voice, "What were you expecting, Sailor? Do you want some coffee?"

"No! Thank you."

"Oh, ho-ho-ho!" she laughed, patting me tenderly on the swollen pecker. "You are a very young and naive boy! That is just what I say when I enter, to let everyone know it is time for the shot!"

"I know that now."

"I am so very sorry."

Then she moved on to the next bed, and I could follow her progress down the ward by the groans and yelps from the fortunate men who were receiving her attention. What an absolutely delightful creature, I thought, once the pain of the needle had worn off. Indeed, that second night in the ward I decided that I would be willing to experience any amount of pain as long as she was there to hold my hand.

It was perhaps twenty minutes after she had left the ward, long enough for me to drift off, that I felt her hand on my arm and turned to see her *climbing into bed with me!* The ward was dimly lighted, but I could see her clearly—as could every swab and bum in the place!

In the next bed toward the back of the room was a hook-nosed Greek named *Georgio*, whom I knew already to be cursed by oral diarrhea and egomania. From the moment I had settled in two days before, he had rattled on about the places he had been and the women he had laid.

Now, he raised himself on one elbow and said, "Hey, Kid, you want I should come over there and hold your hand while you do your thing?"

The girl paid no attention to him at all, and soon she was settled next to me beneath the sheet.

I turned my head and hissed, "Keep it down, Homer! For once, just shut up!" Turning to the pretty face beside me, I whispered, "You're the first person, besides that nut next to me, that's even looked in my direction since I came in here. Could you tell me how long I'm going to be in this—place?"

Her warm hand had searched out mine and, as if we were already lovers, she began caressing it tenderly. "I really have no idea. Maybe two, three weeks. But this is actually not a bad place for you right now. There is a beautiful green hillsides facing the ocean, where you can walk in the evenings, and a great crafts building, where you can learn many good things to do with your hands."

I decided then and there that I had never known anyone like her. She was indescribably fascinating, so warm and sensitive and *angelic*. Her skin was so soft and cool it actually felt *slick* to the touch. What a breathtakingly beautiful girl, and yet I could not think of this without remembering and agonizing over my disability. Worst of all, she knew about it.

"And," I sighed, "there is you."

For a time she did not speak, and when she did it was with a sigh. "I won't get to see you much—but, yes, there is of course—me."

"I think I've died and you're an angel."

"No!" she laughed. "Do you really think you would go to Heaven if you died? But we agreed that you got this," she put her hand on my penis, "from a stool."

"Nothing like this has ever happened to me before. I swear."

"Yes, I know. Well, goodbye now. I will come and see you again."

"Is that all you do? Deliver coffee?"

She laughed and the sound sent thrills through my body, even, for a brief moment, unto my enormous, flawed penis. "No, in other places I take temperatures and see that the medicine is taken."

*   *   *

Before I knew it I had settled into the routine of the mighty U. S. Marine Hospital. Lights came on at five each morning for the first round of medication, and that was followed immediately by breakfast and crafts, which lasted until eleven. After a free hour for letter-writing and gazing into space, the *guests* of this Shangra La ate again and returned to crafts. At four-thirty we were given some real free time, during which we could stroll about the campus-like grounds or read or write letters home.

I spent most of my spare time wandering about the grounds, hoping to catch a glimpse of the nut brown maid in the skin-tight nurse's uniform.

Somehow, certainly without actually saying anything that could be construed as a promise or a proposition, that girl had made me feel special, that down the road there just might be a chance for me to begin afresh with her. Her appearance beside my bed shortly after nine almost every night gave me strength and resolve, and, in time, brought back my manhood.

Her full name, I learned after a week, was Delilah Morita Lolita Nuñez. She had lived in San Francisco since she was a little girl; but, like everybody else in California, she had been born someplace else. I loved to listen to her crazy brand of English, which had been picked up in the streets and back alleys of Frisco. Analyzed later, most of it didn't make much sense; but at the time she was actually talking there was no doubt about what she was saying. She was, she told me quite happily, a lot of different things, all put together with love.

"Like what?" I asked, irreverently, absolutely fascinated.

"Like does-it-matter?"

In time I was to discover that Lilli had been attracted to me momentarily by my youth, my vulnerability, my crazy way of talking (She confessed that she had not been able to make much sense out of my words when she first saw me), and because I was after all an *untouchable*. She never mentioned a boyfriend or a husband, but I came to believe that her thing was to bask in the spotlight of everybody's desires, that she had no ulterior motives where I was concerned. She was much too beautiful and exciting to be completely alone, without men.

Every day, after evening chow, I returned to Ward C with the mouthy Greek, Georgio, who bedeviled me mercilessly about my *leetle problem* (which was actually smaller by a long sight than Georgio's own). I had made the mistake of asking the Greek's opinion about my malady. I had, indeed, skinned down and presented my very swollen membrane for his buzzard-curious inspection. Since no medical person had bothered to tell me anything specific about my VD, certainly not the name of my malady, and since I had never seen or experienced anything like it before, I quite naturally turned to the very friendly fellow in the next bunk who apparently had the same problem.

Georgio had immediately announced to the entire ward, "Hey, everybody, listen up! The Keed here has a classic case of *syphilis!*"

The memory of that moment was to remain crystal clear in my mind from that time on. I had been unable to say a thing in response. After everyone in the ward had taken a look and agreed that, yes, that was indeed a classic case, I had further compounded my mistake by moaning to the Greek, "That can't be! Are you certain?"

"Oh, yes, but yes! I ought to know, I've had thees sam thing myself at least twice!"

The first thought that went through my mind was that I would go blind at an early age, and the second was that all of my off-spring would be born blind, deaf, and half-witted. Later, I got around to worrying about what the tender young things back home would think if they ever found out my secret.

"But do not worry too much, Keed! I am certain they may have caught eet in plenty of time."

"What do you mean?"

"I can tell that eet ees in eets early stage weeth you, I think, and so the medics can stop eet in eets tracks. Now, if you had held back and tried to doctor eet yourself, eet might really have geet you."

Everybody in the ward was nodding and agreeing, keeping straight faces. In time I had to admit that Georgio knew a lot about venereal diseases, especially syphilis. For a solid week he talked about nothing else. He had read and evidently studied deeply in that subject, committing to memory every conceivable kind of statistic and technical term.

He spoke always to the entire ward, was completely incapable of holding his tongue on any subject, and had no control at all of his temper. He loved nothing better than to get the entire ward gathered around him for a two-hour monologue on some unpredictable subject. Regardless of the topic that popped into his head or was raised by someone else, he always dominated the evenings in Ward C. He won all of the arguments in which he took part, sometimes by logic and statistics but more often by volume and foul language.

After my initial profound hatred for Georgio, I slowly came to admire two things about him, his very black and very thick beard and his remarkable vocabulary. This noisy descendant of Socrates had a command of foul language that surpassed that of any Navy boatswain's mate I had ever run across. Every other word he uttered was a colorful expletive that he had picked up from his innumerable mysterious travels about the world, and of course he did not restrict himself to the English language.

From the beginning I distrusted Georgio's word on almost all subjects, but it never occurred to me to question his knowledge and experience concerning my *leetle problem*. That was not something one would lie about, I had decided.

"You think I am a' ignoran' Greek, hey, Keed?" he began one evening. What seemed like a long time ago I had learned not to ignore such a remark when it came from this fellow. All such beginnings were just warming-up exercises for him. He was preparing his victim, me, for something much more important.

"No, you are definitely no ignoramus."

"I am no ignoramus, you will come to see," he said matter-of-factly, ignoring my concession. "I have read all the great books of the world, sailed all the oceans leetle and big, an' screwed every kind of woman with no exceptions. Do you know that there are only seven female body types, my fran? Only ze seven zat zay have."

Georgio's English ranged all the way from gibberish to formal English, and there was very little consistency or logic about his various accents and mispronunciations.

"But there is an infinite variety of pussy types. Each and ever' one of them is different, like the fingerprints. That is why I am always so anxious to deck a new one, to see what kind of a' interior she has. Which brings me to your problem. Do you know, for example, that syphilis first arrived in Europe from the New World aboard the *Pinta?* No, it ees true. Not the other way around. You did not know that, hey, Keed?"

"Yes, I knew that. You told me that."

"That is actually so. The pilot of the ship called the *Pinta* caught it in the New World and took it to Europe, where it has enjoyed a great career ever since.

Many of my evenings began in a similar way, with Georgio accusing me of thinking he was an ignoramus. And I was always polite to him and managed to put up with him, no matter what the topic was. Others in the ward, prior to my arrival, had shut Georgio up by crying or puking or throwing things at him.

Only once did I lose it with the Greek.

One-on-one he was sometimes not hard to tolerate; but whenever he had an audience, he could become unbearable. On that one occasion, when I could no longer take Georgio's insults and wisecracks, I rose up in bed and threatened to knock his block off. Georgio had laughed and raised such a ruckus several nurses and a doctor rushed in to see what was happening. But the Greek's audience was crowding around waiting for the fight to begin, making it difficult for the forces of reason to get through. When they finally did, I was straddling Georgio, with my right fist clinched and cocked.

"He ees gonda keel me!" he screamed at the doctor. "This keed he ees crazee! He needs to be put in a cell all by himself!"

"Calm down, Georgio. Nobody's going to kill anybody!" said the doctor. He waved at the nurses and they transferred me rapidly back to my own bed and tucked my sheets about me so tight I couldn't move. One of them patted me on the head and said, not unkindly, "Now, Kid, you stay where you belong or I'll make you wish you had."

"Make that hairy ape keep his mouth shut then!" I shouted.

Soon all was quiet, making it possible for the doctor and the nurses to leave. By this time Georgio had forgiven me completely and was launched into a relatively safe topic that would take us right up to lights out and Lilli's Coffee-Time visit.

*   *   *

Until the last minute of my stay at USMH, Georgio teased and tormented me with his lying and exaggerating and practical jokes. Even so, some kind of friendship had developed between us. In my dress blues and carrying only my small dittybag, my seabag having been taken down by an attendant, I paused at the big swinging doors leading from the main reception room to the front parking lot for one last look toward his window. And there he was, my hairy Greek nemesis, waving and grinning frantically at me from a fourth floor window.

"Hey, Keed, I think I will miss you when you are gone!"

He had maintained up until that very last moment that I would never leave the hosptial. Like him I was a permanent guest, he had told me again and again. And on that last morning he had behaved like a small, stubborn boy, refusing to accept the fact that I was cured and therefore out of there. His high-pitched Greek voice had echoed about walls of the fourth floor and penetrated all the way down to the first level reception areas.

"Yeah, well, start missing, old buddy!" I yelled back, walking out to the parking lot. "God help the sucker that gets my bed!"

Nevertheless, I knew I would miss the loudmouth.

Considerably sobered by my hospital experience, I crossed the Bay Bridge on the electric train in some kind of daze. I had no notion at all where I stood with the Coast Guard. The Cutter *Alert* would be back in Eureka by this time; but, of course, there would be no going back to that. Old Miklokowski would die and go to hell before he would take me back. His attitude toward *screwing around,* as he called it, was legend.

The future looked bleak for me, to say the least. Even the return to Government Island to await further orders was repugnant to me. There I would have to put up with Goodrich.

Mechanically, indifferently, I watched Yerba Buena Island flash by on my left at the mid-point across the Bay; and thirty minutes later I found himself standing at a bus stop, waiting for transportation to East Oakland. Finally, I alighted from a bus half a block from *Ted and Roy's,* on East Fifteenth Street; and without even so much as a glance in the direction of the little hooligan hangout, I trudged the quarter of a mile to G. I.

When I stuck my head through the door at Personnel, Goodrich, at the front desk, waved and called out, "Buck up, fuck-up! The beer's on me tonight."

"No beer for me. I want to get out of here. When do I get my orders?"

"What did they say you had?"

"Do you have my orders?"

"I asked first."

"Go play with yourself." With that, I turned and started for the door.

Goodrich called out, "You're still attached to the *Alert*, Red. Your bus ticket will be ready in the morning."

The next morning early my yeoman buddy came by the barracks and told me in no uncertain words to get out of bed and go to chow with him. I did and once he had me mellowed a bit with strong coffee, he confessed that he did not feel sorry for me at all, that what had happened could have happened to any of the three of us, and that I ought to stop thinking about the past so much and get on with it.

I told him I would handle it and he was not to lose any sleep over it.

A Jeep was parked at Personnel when we walked up from the messhall, and I knew it was for me. I followed Goodrich inside and picked up my travel orders and voucher, and when I turned to leave he stuck out his hand.

"Reckon old Soldoski, whatever his name is, will take you back?"

"Miklokowski. He will kick my butt off the *Alert* as soon as I get there. I'll be back down here tomorrow night."

That afternoon, with a tightening in the upper intestines, I alighted from a taxi half a block from the cutter and stood contemplating the pretty little 125-footer. The first person to show his head was Miranda, who shouted at me and rushed down the dock and grabbed my hand. This, however, was followed by silence and a look that I knew only too well.

"Okay, what's wrong?"

"The Old Man's hoppin' mad at you, Red! He would kill you with his bare hands if he thought he could get away with it!"

"The old fart," I said, "what does he know about anything?"

"A radiogram came about your flunkin' out of the school."

I stared at him. "I didn't *flunk out of school!* I had to go to the friggin' hospital!"

Miranda nodded quickly. "I know. He wants you to double-time it to his cabin."

"You know how I feel about that kind of thing."

"This time I think you'd better, Red."

I went below, with Miranda right behind me moaning the entire time that both of us would be in trouble if I didn't get myself up to the Captain's cabin right away. He was the Gangway Watch and he had been told to send me there first thing when I arrived. In the messdeck, with Tully looking on with a frown, I siphoned off a mug of coffee from the big urn and sat for a time sipping it absentmindedly. Several members of the crew gathered around, trying to get up enough guts to ask me some questions. But the look on my face must have shut them up. Finally, a deckhand wanted to know what it was I had picked up.

"Syphilis," I said calmly, looking at him. "And I'm still contagious."

"Holy shit!"

"Where'd you git it, Red?" asked Houston.

Everybody was fidgeting and had a pained look on their faces.

"Actually, all I had was the claps, which I caught in the head on this ship," I said. "I'm surprised all of you haven't got it by now."

I finished my coffee and went to the crew's quarters and stretched out on an empty bunk on my back. Losing out on that special radio school was a hard pill to swallow, but the black mark on my record for coming down with the clap was even worse. There was no reprieve from that. It would go with me from then on, until my discharge from the Service. And, of course, the Old Man was going to boot my ass off the *Alert*. No question about it. And that would not help things.

Miranda sat on the nearest bunk and agonized.

"You can handle it, Red. A lot of fellas git the clap. And the Cap'n can't kill you. It's against regulations."

"*Handle* what, little buddy?" I said with a laugh. "Do you really think I'm worried about that old windbag of a Merchant Marine sailor? I don't give a damn what he says to me. I'm out of here and so that's that. Sticks and stones, you know. If he tries anything more than that, he'll get a chance to find out what the U. S. Marine Hospital's like for himself."

Putting up with the Old Man's cursing and screaming was just another pill, one of several that I would have to take as a result of the little mistake I had made. But the thing had happened, and I would just have to make the best of it.

"The reason I didn't go straight to the Captain's cabin was not what you think, Tony," I said, getting up. "I thought I would time my visit to coincide with his big meal of the day. Besides, I was just a bit wound up, if you know what I mean. It wouldn't have been a good idea to go in on him half-cocked. I thought that long bus ride would do it, but it didn't. There's no telling what I might've done if I'd had to listen to all that shit right away."

Miranda smiled, looking at the deck. "I knew you weren't scared of him, Red. Heck, you took old Hatcher."

"How is old Hatcher?"

"He transferred to an Indian cutter while we was at Pier 5. The *Escanaba*, I think."

"Serves him right."

When I made it to the passageway leading to the Old Man's cabin, I saw the ship's steward delivering a steaming hot tray of food on a special-built mobile serving table. My timing could not have been better. The Old Man was just sitting down to his evening meal, and oh how he hated to be interrupted when he was eating. I stopped outside the polished and pampered door, with the brass nameplate and the elaborate brass knocker, trying to suppress a grin. He was a very big eater and had, on more than one occasion, left word with the gangway watch never to bother him during evening chow. Miranda, thinking only of his responsibility to deliver me to the Old Man, had forgotten completely about that standing order.

I waited there until the steward left and I knew the Old Man had had time to get at least one bite into his mouth; then I knocked three times hard with my knuckles, ignoring the official knocker. No sound came from inside. After a respectable wait, I knocked again, this time with my clinched fist. Suddenly, from inside came the sound of the heavy serving table being rolled about the wooden deck. That was followed at once by a loud, disgruntled blast that sounded something like *SHAT!*

"Who is it, goddamnit? I'm eatin' supper!"

"Hall, Sir!"

After a considerable pause, "Well, goddamnit, come in!"

I turned the brass knob and swung the door inward. The Old Man was standing humped over at his desk, in the act of moving the tray farther out of his way.

No effort had been spared in the fittings and arrangements of this cozy little nook. It was a sailor's dream, a sanctuary fit for Lord Horatio Hornblower, done entirely in mahogany, brass, and silver.

The tray was heaped over with smoking food. A thick steak, grilled well-done, had just received a generous application of A-1 Sauce. The sauce bottle, with the lid missing, was still on the tray. Also on the platter was an enormous baked potato sliced down the center and piled high with sour cream. To one side a stack of French garlic bread waited beside a small China saucer piled high with rapidly-melting butter.

"Goddamned fuck-up!" blasted the old sailor, dropping back into his swivel chair. His regulation U. S. Coast Guard napkin was lying open on the deck, and the wheel tracks of the mobile table were upon it. "I said somethin' like this was going to happen! Born fuck-up! An' I knew if given a little rope you'd hang yourself to the nearest yardarm!"

I had settled at parade rest in the center of the little compartment, with the serving table between us.

"A goddamned disgrace to the United States Coast Guard, goin' out and whorin' around with ever'thing you could find and bringin' back your dirty fuckin' disease to my ship!"

I was on the verge of saying that I had whored with only one very small Oklahoma girl, but thought better of it just in time.

"What! What did you say?"

"Nothing, Sir."

Red splotches had begun to pop out on the Old Man's face.

"What the goddamned hell did you say, Mister? You tryin' to be funny with me? Do you think this thing's over?"

I looked at the steak, which had stopped smoking. When I looked up, the Old Man was also looking at it.

"When I heard about your little trick, I asked myself what punishment would be appropriate for a fuckup like you. I thought about sendin' you to a lighthouse up in the North Atlantic, where there'd be no chance for you to screw around. You need to be isolated from the rest of mankind!"

"Pardon me, Sir, but have you've already signed the paperwork for my transfer?"

"You smartass bastard! You think you pulled a good one, don't you? But you're gonna git precisely what you deserve, and my conscience won't bother me at all when you're gone! I called the District and asked what was open for a someone like you, and guess what?"

I had turned back and was looking at the food on the tray. The entire meal, which had looked so appetizing only a few minutes before, so neatly and expertly spread out on the snow white linen tablecloth, was now cold and dead. Except for the butter, which had been sliced into neat little spats for the potato. It had warmed up and turned into a greasy pool and was threatening to run onto the table.

The Old Man's big red face appeared about to explode. He was glaring at me and waiting for me to ask the where and the what of his transfer. It was quite obvious to me that he wanted to dangle me over the pits of Hellfire a little longer. I had visions of Jonathan Edwards' spider suspended over such a place.

Finally, he burst out, "You're going to the *Taney* ! How does that grab ye?"

"Yes, Sir," I said, keeping my voice steady, emotionless.

"You do know about the goddamned *Taney*, don't you?"

"I understand it's one of the finest cutters in the Service, Sir."

"Yeah, well, you'll 'understand' something else once you're aboard her. They know how to take care of pretty little boys like you aboard that ship."

"Yes, Sir."

"Git to hell out of this room! I don't want to see you again, ever! Go find the yeoman and git your orders and git off my ship! And if you ever step foot back aboard, I'll personally see to it that you're thrown overboard!"

"Very good, Sir!" With that I turned and left, slamming the door.

Outside, Miranda was waiting with his mouth already flapping. "Red, I could hear the Old Man yellin'! What'd he give you?"

I shrugged. "Well, first, he said to me, *Git thee back into the tempest of the Night's Plutonian shore! Take thy beak from out of my heart, and take thy form from off my door!*, right after that he said I was going to the CGC *Taney*."

"Holy shit!"

"Well put, my boy."

The CGC Roger B. Taney

◆

The Coast Guard Cutter *Taney* looked like a glorified Navy destroyer, with one serious exception: She was as white!

I stood on the dock at Government Island and watched this paragon of ships come in from weather patrol, thinking that here must be the finest-looking thing in the United States Coast Guard. Having heard a great deal about the old *Taney* during my wait at G. I., I had expected her to look a lot leaner and meaner. Maybe even have a few barnacles on her behind. But except for her size she looked a lot like the two Indian cutters that had been moored at the dock when I showed up from Eureka.

No doubt old Comdr. Miklokowski had been right, that I would have to toe the line aboard this ship. This had decidedly not been what I had had in mind back a few months before in Oklahoma when Bill Archer, Gene Goodrich, and I had chosen the Coasties over the U. S. Navy. One important reason we had decided on the Coast Guard had been the belief, based upon rumor and hearsay, that there would be very little spit-and-polish, no Captain's Inspections, and no uniform-of-the-day.

I was about to lift my seabag and throw it over my left shoulder for the trip across the gangplank when somebody aboard the *Taney* yelled at me:

"Hey, mate, pick up that goddamn bag!"

The one who had done the yelling was standing just forward of the gangplank. He was a big pot-bellied man wearing dungarees and a Chief's hat. An ensign, quite obviously the deck officer, and the swab on gangway duty had turned and were glaring at me like I was some kind of scum.

"You too fuckin' lazy to carry that bag?"

I hoisted the bag and got it settled on my shoulder.

The Chief grimaced and turned to say something to the officer.

I adjusted my golfball cap just so over my right eye and set out for the gangplank, taking my good old easy time. The Chief turned and glared at me. At the foot of the gangplank I paused and said, "Permission to come aboard, Sir." The ensign returned my salute and I went up the plank. At the gunwale I saluted the fantail and gave him my name and rank.

I was decked out in brand-new gabardine bell-bottom trousers and a close-fitting blouse, and my cap had been sculpted by a real pro. Across my left breast were two and a half rows of ribbons, one of which represented the Bronze Star Medal. There were three tiny bronze battle stars on the Asiatic campaign ribbon.

Just as the CPO came up, red in the face, I dropped my bag over the end of the gangplank to the deck and followed it. He stood there studying me while I fished my orders out of my ditty bag and handed them to the ensign, who passed them on to the enlisted man.

The Chief focused upon my ribbons. "So you're Hall," he growled. Then he took a look at my papers to be sure. "The *Taney* gets all the fuckups," he observed to the ensign. To me he said, "The word here is you was booted off the *Alert.*"

"Chief—" began the ensign.

"When Husbands finishes signin' you in, Hall, we'll have him escort you to the quarters," said the Chief, ignoring the officer. Without another word he turned and waddled off toward the bow.

The ensign, speaking loud enough for the CPO to hear him, said, "Husbands, take this man to the crew's quarters and see that he gets settled."

Husbands, in undress blues, was wearing the shoulder patch of a Radioman Third Class. I did not like his looks. For one thing, he was overweight and soft-looking. For another, the expression his face said plain as day that he was God's gift to the universe.

Without a word to me, as soon as he had logged me in, he headed aft toward the nearest hatchway. I hoisted my seabag on my shoulder again and followed, the heat rising in my face. He disappeared down a ladder and I, have picked up the scent of fresh coffee, followed my nose straight to the messdeck.

There were a number of enlisted bunched around a table in the big, low-ceilinged room playing cards; and when I dropped the heavy seabag and the ditty bag against a bulkhead with a bang, they stopped talking and stared at me. I went to the rack of mugs beside the urn and selected one and filled it with the thick black stuff, wondering how old it was. Evidently, I had been smelling the urn next door in the Chief's Mess, or perhaps the wardroom.

When I turned and glanced at the group, nobody was paying me any attention except a kid in new dungarees.

"Welcome aboard," I said, setting my coffee on the end of a table close by and dropping to the bench beside it. He nodded, surprised. I lifted the mug and sniffed, thinking how true it was that every ship I had ever signed aboard had a personality all its own. The *Alert* was a nice, warm, friendly kind of place, with a homey atmosphere, where a stranger would have no trouble striking up a conversation with any-body aboard. A new swab crossed the gangplank and everyone that saw him just naturally gravitated in his direction, ready to lend a helping hand. The tug, at Fisherman's Wharf, was a good-time Charlie kind of place, where somebody was always trying to buy you a drink or feed you or take you to a party of some kind.

The card players were from the engineroom, no question about it. Some of them had been there recently, I could tell, judging by the grease smears on the sleeves of their dungaree shirts and the strong smell of diesel oil emanating from them. Without an introduction, I knew a number of things about them from past experience. As a group they were a combination of the Ku Klux Klan and Alabama rednecks, especially on liberty guzzling beer. I never knew one that could not hold his liquor, and to engage one of them in a conversation, drunk or sober, was like dealing with a deaf mute. Because it was a well-known fact that none of them knew shit about anything aboard ship but the engines.

The coffee was so strong and ancient it had already begun to turn to mud. Without having taken even a sip, I got up and returned it to the tray beside the urn.

"Which way's the crew's quarters?" I asked the kid, who had decided to keep away from me and was circling the room. He had heavy black eyebrows and a weak chin, and it was obvious that he was still just a striker, the lowest thing in the engineroom. He glanced at me doubtfully then pointed toward the stern of the ship. "Down that passageway. What division you in?"

That surprised me. Here, now, was the first sign of curiosity I had seen since going aboard. I showed him my shoulder patch.

"Yeah. What's your rating?"

"I'm a Chief," I said, disgusted.

Two or three of the card-players looked up and groaned. One of them said, "Shit, Stokes, don't you know what that patch on his arm says? He's a *dit-dah* boy."

*   *   *

Even though it was still short of lights-out by two hours, the enlisted men's quarters was abuzz and asnort with the sounds of sleeping men when I dragged my seabag through the hatchway. Leaving it beside the hatch, I went in search of an unoccupied bunk, suddenly very ready to call it a day. There were several empty bunks, not one of which had a mattress and pillow.

At the gangway watch station I found only an enlisted man, a kid without a rating patch.

"I need a mattress," I said, without preliminary. "There are no mattresses in the quarters."

"Better see the Chief Boats," he said.

"Where would he be?"

"Right behind you."

I glanced around and faced the big, pot-bellied boatswain's mate, who, it seemed to me, was spending a lot of time at the gangplank. To my question about a mattress and a pillow, he said, "I thought you'd come cryin' to me about that. What'd you do with the one that was issued to you?"

"No such thing was issued to me, Chief. I shipped over from the Navy, and a seabag full of clothes was all I got."

"Don't tell me that. It was issued to you along with all the other stuff."

"Well, if you say so. One thing for sure, I don't have one."

"Well, I guess you're gonna learn a little lesson, smart boy. You'll have to make-do tonight. Tomorrow notify your division chief, and maybe you'll be able to requisition one from Stores. If so it'll cost you the full price of a new mattress."

"Thanks a million, Chief."

Back in the darkened quarters, I selected an empty bunk near the forward end and distributed the contents of my seabag on the springs. Then, using my ditty bag as a pillow, I stretched out in the clothes I had worn aboard and closed my eyes.

By six o'clock the following morning, stiff and cold, I was topside, waiting for chow call. I had changed to dungarees, white golfball hat, and polished black Navy shoes. Nobody but the gangway watch was stirring, of course, and he was in no mood to talk. For a time I leaned over a lifeline and studied the dirty green water that lopped gently against the ship's hull, wondering what my chances were of ever getting a transfer from this shit barge.

I still had the better part of two years to go on my hitch, and the thought of spending it on this chickenshit scow was not a good one. According to the scuttlebutt, there were only two ways to get off the *Taney*. You either had to die or serve out your hitch and refuse to re-enlist.

From behind me came the sound of shuffling feet and, before I had time to turn around, the first friendly voice I had heard since leaving the *Alert*.

"Guess you're the new sparks."

The speaker turned out to be a solidly-built swab in faded dungarees, maybe four or five years older than me, with very black hair and sad eyes. His clothes hung loosely about him, and the cuffs of his shirt were buttoned at the wrists.

"Name's Janssen. Somebody in the messhall told me you came in last night. Welcome to the *Roger B. Taney*."

"Thanks, I'm Hall."

Janssen wanted to know where I had bunked. After I told him the where and the how, he said that some of the men were sleeping on two mattresses and that he would see to it that I had at least one before the day was out. Here, I thought, was an unhappy man. Happy sailors took pride in the way they dressed, and most of them tended to act just a bit cocky. This aging first class radioman failed on both counts.

"The Chief told me to look you up and get you settled—and keep you out of trouble till he could get around to you. After muster, we'll go up to the shack and I'll introduce you and I or somebody will show you the equipment and explain the routine."

"I guess it's pretty well known that—"

"Uh, yes, I'm afraid so. The Coast Guard's a very small outfit. Scuttlebutt gets around fast." He leaned on the lifeline and stared at the water. "We've got a couple of green-behind-the-ears pricks in the department," he said after a time. "Don't be surprised by anything they say or do. Young punks fresh out of school. Know-it-alls. You won't have to be told which ones they are. They'll give themselves away the first time they open their mouths."

Then, as the PA system cut loose with *reveille*, he added, "Let's go eat."

We made our way quickly toward an open hatchway near the center of the ship. A piercing boatswain's whistle, sounding chow call, was followed by, "Now hear this! Chow down for the Starboard Section."

"Sounds like the Navy," I said.

"This is the Navy," he growled. "Wait till you get a load of our Captain. You'll think Admiral Bull Halsey has shipped over into the Coast Guard. In fact, Gorman's nickname is also *Bull.*"

I had heard about Commander Gorman, and none of it was comforting.

"You fuck up on this scow, and he'll have you for breakfast."

"Don't worry, I'm going to keep my slate very clean," I said with a laugh. "All I want to do is serve out my time and retire."

"Me, too," said Janssen. "But you'll need more than good intentions. There are some real bastards aboard this ship."

We took our place at the tail end of the chowline, and Janssen said, "Here we go again. A man that spends twenty years in the Service uses up about nineteen of it in some kind of a line."

Later, after chow and muster, I followed Janssen to the radio shack and was introduced to the *dit-dah* gang. In addition to the salty old Chief, whom everybody quite naturally called "Sparky," and Janssen, there were four of them.

"Red," said Sparky, after the introductions, "comes to us from the United States Navy." He was keeping a straight face, but that didn't fool me for a minute. "Maybe some of you peckerwoods," he glanced around at the three youngsters in the group, "will learn something from him."

He stopped, chewing on his lower lip, waiting for some kind of response. I could tell that the men had not been impressed, much less pleased, by the comment about my Navy background. They were scattered about the shack, some sitting and some lounging against the equipment with arms folded. Sears, the first class on watch, grunted and nodded at me but said nothing. Husbands, one of the three third class operators, had already spread the word that I had slept on bare springs the night before. At this point he said:

"Big shit, huh?" He turned and grinned at the other two third class radio operators.

"Keep your fuckin' language decent," said Sparky. "Did I say anything about Red here bein' *big shit?*" He swiveled about in his chair and looked at me. "This is a weather ship. Do you know what I mean by that?"

I nodded tentatively but said nothing.

"Oh, you do, do you? You ever been on a weather station before?"

"*On* a weather station?" I asked. "No, I guess not. But I've heard quite a lot about weather ships."

"Well, listen up and I'll tell you a little about what you're in for. First, we cruise out about halfway between Frisco and Honolulu. Takes us three days. Then we kill the engines and sit dead in the water for twenty fuckin' days and twenty fuckin' nights, taking weather information. And during that time it is our duty to send all of that shit back to Frisco—in five-digit code groups. You aint never held down a radio watch until you've sat on your can for four hours with a brass key going full blast."

He was enjoying himself, and his eyes never left my face.

"Yeah," said Husbands, "it sucks."

"Shut up," said the Chief. "Nobody asked you." Turning again toward me he said, "You done much CW?"

"Not in awhile. Some during the war."

"Well, you'll stand watch with Janssen. He can show you the ropes and let you get in some practice before the shit starts. Sears here is goin' on leave; so it'll be four-on and eight-off once we leave the dock."

"Day and night?" I asked. It was out of my mouth before I could stop it.

Everybody laughed, even Sparky, who, I had decided, was mostly threat and bluster. He popped out of his chair and began to rub his hands, "Okay, then. We've all got something to do; so let's do it. The ship will be getting underway in about an hour. Red, stick to Janssen. Husbands, you and Podscoff and Ceccarelli finish up that job you started yesterday with the paint brushes."

"How about puttin' Red on that job with us, Sparky?" asked Husbands. "Don't you think he could use a little fresh air an' sunshine?" He exchanged winks with the other two third class operators. "How about it, Red?"

"Let me do the job assignments," snapped Sparky. "If I did put Red on that job, he'd be in charge, asshole; and then where would you be, after that remark? You've got the brains of a pissant."

Husbands was scowling again. "Shit, all I said was he looks kind of pale and maybe some sunshine might do him some good."

"He just finished a tour of duty in the hospital," said Sparky.

"Oh?" laughed Husbands. "Well, now, let me guess why he was in there!"

"Git your ass out of here!"

"Aye, aye, Sir!"

"Don't pay no attention to that smart ass," said Sparky. "He thinks he's still a civilian."

While Janssen was showing me the equipment and explaining this and that about the shack, I noticed that one of the speakers was apparently not attached to any of the receivers. When I laid my hand on it and looked at him, he volunteered that it was a direct pipeline from the bridge. With the flip of a switch it was possible to hear everything going on in the pilothouse. A bit later, as the ship prepared to get underway, Sparky turned the volume up on this so that he wouldn't miss anything.

Eventually, the word came: "Now, hear this! All hands, prepare to get underway! Bosuns, man the lines!"

"Come on, Red," said Janssen. "Let's get some air. All serousness pretty well stops while we make our way out of the Bay. Besides, I like to take one last look at trees and houses before all that green water takes over. Sitting in one spot in the ocean isn't quite the same as plowing along toward some destination."

"Maybe you could tell me something more about this weather station business. I think Sparky left out a few things."

"Yeah, well, where do I start? We're relieving the *Chautauqua* in three days; and twenty-three days from now the *Escanaba* will relieve us. That's the routine."

"So we spend twenty-six days out and better than a month in?"

"That's what could and should happen, and does happen to the other two. But it generally does not happen to the *Taney*."

"Why is that?"

"Because we've got a *gung-ho* skipper who likes to play at being in charge of a ship at sea. We spend considerably more time out there than in here. Take for example what happened right after our last patrol. We'd completed our twenty days and had been back in port maybe three days when the news came that one of the *dit-dah* boys on the *Escanaba* had committed suicide. Well, naturally, Comdr. Gorman volunteered to go out and relieve the ole *Esky*."

"You mean pick up the corpse."

"Heck, no. I mean *relieve*. We took the rest of the *Escanaba's* watch. The kid that had slashed his wrists was doin' fine in the Sick Bay by the time we got there."

"What's wrong with the Skipper?"

"My theory is that he craves to be the kingpin, which he is as long as we're at sea; but when the ship's in port he spends most of his time at home with a wife, who bosses him around. Can you blame the man for wantin' to be at sea?"

We made our way down the metal ladders to the main deck and lined up on the starboard bow at the lifeline, just in time to see the weather-men in their bright yellow outfits come aboard. There were three of them, and they were being followed by a ton of luggage and equipment.

"Talk about good duty," said Janssen. "These guys have it made in the shade. All they do while we're out is take some readings from their instruments and pass them on to the Communications Officer. On the way out and coming back they just stroll about like passengers. We're the workhorses."

"Yeah," I agreed, "but I wouldn't trade jobs with those deckhands down there." I pointed toward the scurrying seamen. "Theirs has got to be is a thankless and endless job, trying to please that chief boatswain's mate."

"Well, before you get too sympathetic for that bunch of good-time Charleys, wait till you've stood a couple of weather watches. That poor kid that committed suicide aboard the *Esky* was no freak. I knew him well. He was as sane and happy to be alive as any of us; and I, for one, know exactly where he was when he decided to slash his wrists and jump overboard. Sending five-digit word groups gets to you real fast, especially on lonely mid-watches. And in case you don't know it, you're being groomed to take over one of the watches."

Hearing a light rapping sound, I glanced around and saw Janssen's right hand giving it hell. He was drumming some kind of message on the lifeline with the middle finger of his right hand! I had caught myself doing that same thing once upon a time, way back during WWII.

"You sending out for help?" I kidded.

"Yeah, for sure. I do that without even thinking about it. In fact, I hear code just about all the time, while I'm in the sack, in my dreams, even when somebody's talking to me. Somebody honks a horn several times and I read whatever message there is in it. *Dahdit-didahdit-ditty-dah-dah.*"

"*N R U T?*"

"Yep. That's old *Taney's* call sign. Better get used to it."

"Listen, I know what you mean," I said with a laugh. "It'll be my luck to sign off with the *Alert's* call sign, right under Sparky's nose."

"It won't happen but once."

Over the loudspeakers came the words everyone had been waiting for: "Cast off all lines!"

As the ship made its slow and careful way out into the center of the Bay, we stood there watching but saying nothing. There was no telling what was going through Janssen's mind, but as with every ocean voyage I had ever made, there was quite suddenly a mysterious, warm feeling deep inside me. It began the instant the ship freed itself from its mooring eased away from the dock.

Going to sea, to me, was like a purging, a shucking off of undesirable habits and weaknesses. And part of it was a feeling of pity for landlubbers, especially city dwellers, who measure out their lives on concrete and asphalt.

The bleak old barracks buildings at G. I., which at first seemed to be moving away from us, began to lose some detail. It was a decided improvement as far as I was concerned. Alameda Naval Air Base, with its windsock flapping in the breeze, was on the port side; and dead ahead was Treasure Island, that man-made extension of Goat Island in the center of the Oakland-San Francisco Bay Bridge. Shortly, in the distance and off the starboard bow, I spotted Alcatraz Island, a solid chunk of ugliness shrouded by fog; and about the same distance off our port bow was Fisherman's Wharf, where Archer would more than likely be sacked out aboard the Coast Guard tug.

By this time most of the off-duty crew were lined up along the port side to catch a last view of the San Francisco skyline. There was Coit Tower, a blaze of white well up Telegraph Hill, and, equally brilliant in the morning sunshine was the big Coast Guard Twelfth District Headquarters building partway up the more gentle slope to Chinatown.

It was a picture, I told myself, that would remain indelibly etched in my memory. This alone was reason enough to forsake family and friends and ship-over into the Coast Guard.

"I've got a wife over there on that hillside," Janssen broke in, pointing toward San Francisco State Park.

"A wife? Somehow I can't imagine you married."

"See that ridge, with the row of white houses?"

I followed his finger. There were a million white buildings.

"Look to the right of that water tower."

I nodded, "Oh, yeah! That's where you live?"

"No, that's where Lindy lives. I go over to see her as often as I can, but the Skipper doesn't make it easy."

"So? What's your wife like?" I continued to search for the row of small white houses.

"She's all right. Prettier than I deserve, understanding. And since I can't get liberty too often, we worked out a signal."

"What kind?"

"Pretty soon you'll be able to make out the flagpole. She flies a Coast Guard flag—except when she's having a period or when she's not at home."

"For when you come in from weather patrol?"

He nodded. "And even when we don't leave the dock. All I have to do is get on one of the harbor frequencies and ask some sparks that's passing that way to look for the flag. If it's a red flag, I know she's having a monthly."

"Does she have them pretty often?" I could not help but ask.

"As a matter of fact, I started keepin' a record. Not too long ago I began to get the feelin' that that time of month was coming along too often." After a long pause, he added, "But when she runs up a red flag, I stay away."

Weather Station Fox

$\blacklozenge$

According to Sparky, who knew everything about everything, the *Taney* would shut down precisely at 145 degrees west longitude and 30 degrees north latitude, a distance of 1,091 land miles from San Francisco and approximately the same distance from Honolulu. That, he said, was Weather Station Fox.

Nobody was about to dispute his word.

About noon on the third day out from Frisco word was passed that a lookout had spotted the *Chautauqua*. She already had a head of steam up, so to speak, and it was obvious from the shouting and waving on deck that the *Taney* was more than welcome.

As the gap narrowed between us, a signalman on the Indian cutter blinked out the following message: "Don't worry about a thing, we'll take care of your woman while you're out here." At least that's what I think he sent. I was standing on the bow looking over my shoulder, and he was sending just a bit fast for me.

While we treaded water gunwale-to-gunwale and transferred two large bags of mail, someone on the bridge of the *Chautauqua* yelled, "How's Frisco? Did you leave any women for us?" The reply from our bridge was, "Frisco burned down the other day. You'll have to settle for Vallejo!"

"They're tellin' the truth about taking care of our women," said Janssen, looking chagrined. "Coast Guard women, as a rule, keep about three steady boyfriends."

During daylight hours all the way out from Frisco the *Taney* had been in a constant state of discombobble. Comdr. Bull Gorman, it seemed, liked drills. And even though most of the crew stood both day and night watches, only those who had been on midwatches were excused from these.

It brought back fond memories of a cruise I once had on a Navy tin-can, only the shinola we went through was for real.

Immediately following morning chow each day, our Skipper, standing tall and handsome in starched white shorts and a short-sleeve shirt on the bridge with a pair of binoculars strapped around his neck, would nod and over the PA system there would issue a loud "Clang-clang-clanging!" This would be followed by the Deck Chief's announcement (It would vary very little from day to day), "Now, hear this! All hands! Fire drill! Man your duty stations!" One day it would be the Damage-Control Drill, another day the First-Aid Drill. Two of the most unpopular drills were the Abandon-Ship Drill and the Boat Drill, because these required going over the side and burning up some calories.

Between the twice-daily drills (morning and afternoon) there were clean sweep-downs fore-and-aft, in which all enlisted personnel not on watch participated, Captain's Inspections (always when the men were least expecting them), and General Quarters. It was all very exciting and invigorating, and it did accomplish one positive result: Everyone looked forward to the four-hour watches.

Another revolting development for me, totally unexpected and surprisingly far-reaching in its effect upon my quality-of-life, was Janssen's dislike of coffee. During our first watch, which began just after we passed the Faralon Islands, I made the mistake of delivering a steaming hot mug of the stuff to him. I mean, how was I to know?

That first night out began for me on a distasteful note and went downhill from there on.

Just as a quartermaster began banging out eight bells over the PA system, signaling the change of watches, I went to check on Janssen. He was sound asleep in his bunk, and while I was trying to wake him, Husbands called out from his bunk, "Where you from, Red, Arkansas?"

About to lean over and give Janssen a shake, I glanced at the big soft-looking Saint Bernard and saw that he was reading a Harold Robbins paperback thriller with a naked woman on the cover. The book was lying open and face down on his chest, and behind him, sprawled out on their bunks, were his two mangy friends, Ceccarelli and Podscoff. Both were grinning stupidly at me.

"Oklahoma. Where you from, California?"

Caught off guard, Husbands stared at me for a time. I could almost hear the slow, rusty wheels inside his big shaggy head turning slowly.

"Yeah, as a matter of fact I am. But how'd you guess?" Taking up his book, he pretended to read.

"It was no guess. You look like a fruitcake, you talk like a fruitcake, and you behave like a fruitcake. *Ergo*, Husbands, you had to be a fruitcake." After I gave Janssen a shake, I added, "And since all fruitcakes come from California—"

Husband's face, now red as a beat, slowly rose above the book. And if looks could kill, I would have been a dead swab.

"Look, you gonna hold that remark I made against me forever?"

"Let me tell you something, Slug." I looked at Janssen and winked. "You made a mistake smarting off to me the way you did. You didn't know me from Adam, but like every asshole I've ever met from the State of California you just had to show out."

"Shit."

"Yeah, shit. Think about it. And from now on stay off my case."

Podscoff had turned on his side and eyeing me.

"You're one tough cookie, huh, Red?" he snickered, rolling over and looking at Ceccarelli. "Do you suppose this old salt layers his hamburgers with gunpowder or something, Chet?"

"Either that or maybe he layers his gunpowder with hamburger!" came the reply.

"I'll be seeing you three farts around," I said, turning toward the open hatch. "Maybe we'll have a work detail or two together."

"Oh, so, now he threatens!" cackled Podscoff, romping on his bunk. "We are to be afraid of His Eminence!"

"If you've got any sense, you will," said Janssen, sitting up in his bunk. "But then that would be asking too much."

After the dead air of the quarters, it felt really great topside; and for a brief time I stood facing the salty breeze coming down the port side from the bow. When Janssen finally popped through the hatchway, I was leaning against a lifeline thinking about the three jerks down in the quarters.

The ship was clipping along beautifully, and Comdr. Gorman, thank God for small favors, was finally settled in his quarters just below the bridge. I had spotted him entering it shirtless and hatless a moment before, doubtlessly on his way to his bunk. He might be planning something for the wee hours of the morning, but it was a safe bet he was calling it a day.

It was dark as pitch topside, with not a star showing, and the ship was rolling gently from side to side. I stared at the lively wake we were leaving, my mind wandering back to the little scene in the quarters. It was now clear to me that I was going to be forced to have it out with those three. As long as we were on the ship, however, I would not be able to lay a hand on them. Their little mind games and practical joking would no doubt continue, especially when no officer was around.

Janssen showed up, announcing himself by clearing his throat. He was eating a sandwich.

"It's about that time," I said. "You up for this?"

"No way. I could have used about eight more hours of sleep."

He took the lead, talking over his shoulder about what I could expect on the watch. We were checked out with NMC, Twelfth District Base Radio, and, more than likely we would have nothing at all to do for the entire four hours. That sounded all right to me, but he seemed to be dreading it. To myself, I said, "This is going to be a piece of cake compared to what I went through on the *Alert.*

Just outside the radio shack, after climbing all that way, he stopped and said, "Why don't you go down to the messdeck and get us some sandwiches and whatever else Cookie might've put out?"

"Excellent idea," I said, leaning against a bulkhead and faking exhaustion. Paying absolutely no mind to me, he disappeared into the shack.

What the heck? I was enjoying the fresh air, and the exercise was good for me. I tripped down to the messdeck and lined up behind a mob of swabs. Quartermasters and motormacks were joggling each other for the cold cuts, all laid out neatly on regulation Coast Guard metal trays on the serving counter. After waiting my turn, I dived in and began piling bologna, cheese, onions, pickles and ham slices on thick slices of bread, ending up with two Dagwood sandwiches. From some of the more squeamish this brought good-natured grunts and groans.

A grinning quartermaster said to me, "You takin' that up to Janssen? Be sure not to forget the coffee."

"Hey, don't you worry about that!"

I wondered at the snickering that had followed that question but dismissed it in my anticipation of a feast up in the shack.

Cookie had thoughtfully left some paper sacks on the counter, along with plastic spoons, forks, and knives. I stuffed my creations into one of the larger sacks and headed for the coffee urn. Could I handle two mugs and that heavy sack up the those ladders? I remembered that Janssen hadn't been drinking coffee with his sandwich a few minutes before; so I did not dare show up without a big mug for him.

It turned out to be something of a juggling act, but I managed two large mugs of coffee and the paper sack of sandwiches up those three flights without a mishap. And when I set all of this down beside my watch buddy, he turned and glared at me, shoving the sack back.

"No coffee, Red. I can't stand the stuff. I can't even stand to smell that crap. Smells like skunk piss."

"You're kidding, right?"

"No way. Come on, let's get into this thing."

That he also did not smoke, drink, chew, dip, or gamble meant little or nothing to me; but the news that he couldn't tolerate the presence of coffee was a blow that left me dazed and sick at my stomach. It meant not only complete abstinence for me four hours running, twice every twenty-four hours, but also no breaks for either of us during our watch! There would be no excuse at all to get out of that stuffy shack for some fresh air occasionally.

I set the two mugs outside the hatchway, wondering how he managed to survive in the messdeck. That place reeked of strong coffee twenty-four hours a day. What he needed was a private stateroom, where he could be served individually.

No, he needed a caretaker.

＊   ＊   ＊

Since the weathermen had not collected information that day, there was no real business for Janssen and me on that first watch out to Ocean Station Fox; so Janssen insisted on showing me how to tune up the big Collins transmitter, which was a brand that I had not seen before. Still shook up over his taboo on coffee, I sat sullenly by and pretended to doze off. If the stolid, slow-talking Janssen noticed my inattention, he gave no sign of it. All of the operating frequencies had been typed on a sheet of paper and placed under glass next to each of the two positions, a particularly helpful thing, I thought; and after Janssen had finally stopped talking and demonstrating, I spent an hour checking these out on the Hallicrafters receivers.

Perhaps two hours into the watch, with head phones strapped on but turned away from his ears, my watch mate settled into a magazine he had brought with him from the quarters. He had given me a split-phone watch to monitor; and, wearing my phones like a collar, I moved about the shack poking into things. The ship had stopped rolling and the long, slow hours of a night at sea were upon us.

"Are you nervous or something?" he asked. "If you think this is bad, you're really in for it."

"*Bad?*" I laughed. "If I died and went to Heaven right now, it could not be much of an improvement! This is what I consider great duty!" Then, unable to resist the opportunity, "Of course, in a radio operator's Heaven there will be coffee."

"Yeah, I know," he said, nodding and looking tragic. "It's the shits. But, do you know, I think I prefer this to a day watch. At least at eleven o'clock at night you don't have much traffic through the shack. And the Chief sure as hell aint going to come nosing around."

He had not heard a word I said.

I was about to make another stab at explaining how I felt about being at sea on a good ship, but it occurred to me that this fellow would not understand. He wouldn't even try. To him all of this was a bore, a terrible routine, something that he had done so many times he couldn't remember it ever being exciting. He was undoubtedly a nice guy, a straight-shooter, a good man to have as a friend; but he had become jaded with the Coast Guard and weather patrols.

Static crackled and spewed from three directions. To me it was like listening to an old and dear friend whispering to me, a reassurance of the continuity of things, a promise that just over the horizon great and mighty things were happening.

For a time I tried to imagine what it would be like sitting on a patch of ocean for twenty days, with absolutely no intention of going anyplace. Just sitting. No one would be looking for us and we would be looking for no one. But, what with the drills and Captain's inspections, none of us was likely to die of boredom.

During my snooping about the shack, I discovered a small panel of speaker- and mike-receptacles inside a cabinet. They bore the labels *A*, *B*, and *C*.

"What are these? Is it possible they go to speakers somewhere?" I wanted to know. "Are we hooked up to the PA system?"

"Why do you ask?"

"Just curious. Is there a way to pipe music and stuff to the crew?"

After stalling for five minutes, he pointed to a row of jacks over one of the positions. Somehow, I had overlooked these. And, curiously, they had the same labels as the speakers. "Just make damned sure you never plug something into Gorman's speaker by mistake."

"Which one is his?"

"Never mind."

"Come on, you know."

"Okay, it's *A*. But, also, stay away from the others. Unless the Chief says so, do not, I repeat, do not bother them."

"Wouldn't the crew appreciate a little Stateside news and music once we settle in at Weather Station Fox?"

"They might, but you'd get your ass in a sling if you engineered it."

"I was just curious," I said with a grin.

*   *   *

After the *Chautauqua* disappeared over the eastern horizon, I stayed topside, gazing at the vast blue void above (The overcast had finally disappeared) and the endless green water between us and the horizon. Only a small flock of gooney birds, some of which had joined us the day before, remained to keep us company. The surface of the ocean was, at midday, glassy smooth; and the sun beat down upon us without mercy, sending all that were not assigned to deck details below to the messdeck or the reckhall.

Sparky had issued a new watch schedule, which coupled Husbands and me. Because Janssen had given him a glowing report of my behavior while on watch, he had decided to put me in charge of the shack during the midwatches. I could have kissed him. Husbands had been on a previous weather patrol but had had very little actual operating experience. And, of course, since he was only a green third class radioman straight out of dit-dah school he was not expected to transmit classified weather messages in code.

I did not let on how pleased I was with the new watch schedule, but Janssen looked at me and said, "Let the good times roll." It was the closest he had ever come in my presence to a sense of humor. "Now, you can stink up the shack with that skunk piss.

The idea of having to spend four hours at a sitting with Husbands was made tolerable by the fact that I would be in charge. Besides, of the three knotheads he was the least obnoxious. Janssen would be with Podscoff, and Sparky himself would break in Ceccarelli.

Sears' absence was working a real hardship for the old Chief.

"Red, I thought it would be a good idea if you'd take the midwatch, on a regular basis," he said. "That way you'll miss most of the weather stuff at night, and Janssen or I will always be around during the noon watch to help out if we're needed."

"We've got the fuckin' midwatch from now on?" groaned Husbands.

Sparky whirled on him with, "Till I say otherwise!"

As far as I was concerned, Husbands and I had gotten the best of the three watch schedules. The twelve-to-four watches would mean very little monotonous sending of coded word groups and practically no involvement in the Skipper's drills. Coming off the midwatch, we would be allowed to sleep until lunch; then, after the midday watch we would have free time, for the most part, until our next watch.

During the awkward pause following the Chief's outburst at Husbands, I asked a question that had been bugging me ever since I had signed aboard. "Would somebody explain to me why the weather information has to be sent in digital code groups? Why can't we just send it plain language?" My reasoning was that sending it plain language was quite easy, compared to coded groups, every character of which had to be exactly right or the decoding would be screwed up. It was such an obvious question I was caught completely off-guard at the Chief's reaction:

"That's just about the stupidest dumb question I ever heard! You from the sticks or someplace?"

"It's not stupid," said Husbands. "Red's got a point. Why'n hell do we have to bother with five-number code groups, like it was something the Russians might want to get their hands on? Who in the fuck cares who gets this stuff and finds out what the weather is like out in this shithole of an ocean?"

"Husbands, go check out a scraper and a wire brush! Anybody as stupid as you are needs fresh air and exercise! I want you to get back to that job on the smokestack. And I don't want to hear anything more about this! Got it?" Then, turning to me and speaking almost civilly, he said, "All I've ever been told is that the purpose of our assignment out here is to gather weather information for the U. S. Weather Bureau and send it with a priority classification to the U. S. Coast Guard Base Radio Station in San Francisco. Why it has to be in numbers and not just plain coded letter-groups I don't have the slightest notion. But, of course, as you know, it is against regulations to send classified information in plain language, peace or war. If you don't know that, maybe we need to have a long talk. Even oral transmissions have to be in message form, fully approved by the Communications Officer."

Janssen broke in with, "I was under the impression the only Coast Guard experience Red's had was on the *Alert*. I'll lay you odds no coded messages ever went out of that rowboat. Am I right, Red?"

"Well, yeah, but the way you put it sounds almost like a criticism," I said with a laugh. "You really want to know what it's like handling the radio on the *Alert*? First off, I didn't stand a watch. From day one, even while there were two of us, I had to be in the shack all the time when the ship was at sea. When I needed coffee or food, someone from the bridge gang or the cook himself delivered it to me. On rare occasions, when we weren't expecting anything at all, I would pipe whatever frequency I was monitoring into the pilothouse and hit the sack. Then when a call came in, whoever was handy would pick up the mike. All of it was plain language, of course."

"Yeah, sure!" scoffed Sparky, scratching his head. Janssen, too, was grinning. "Plain language?"

"We knew everybody up and down the Coast; so when we'd get a call, it would generally be addressed to one of us personally. The sparks that handled harbor frequencies at NMC would begin with something like, *Hey, Red, you awake?*"

"Goddamn!" laughed Sparky. "For a breech of regulations like that on the *Taney* you'd get twenty years in the brig! Did you ever have to send any CW, Red?"

"Just once, all the time I was aboard."

This brought a laugh from everyone in the shack.

"Sounds like some hooligan outfit to me," groaned Sparky. He slapped me on the shoulder. "Go keep an eye on Husbands."

*   *   *

During the second half of the patrol almost everybody aboard ship had a countdown calendar near his bunk, religiously marking off the days. For recreation we had a choice of pool and ping-pong, if we were willing to wait in line. Swimming was never brought up in my presence, and my one visit to the ship's library was my last. The dog-eared old action-packed thrillers I had read back when they were new, and the one or two mainstream novels in the collection that I would have enjoyed reading had been cannibalized.

Finally, the twentieth day dawned. It was a Wednesday and the crew, after having shown no sign of life for at least a week, was abuzz with excitement. If our relief showed up on time, we might possibly make it into San Fran Bay by the following Saturday early enough for liberty.

And to brighten things even more, word had been passed that the Pay Officer would be waiting for us at Government Island.

Sure enough, about nine o'clock that morning the *Escanaba* was spotted on the eastern horizon, looking like an Aussie frigate heading for a celebration of some kind. Flapping happily in the slight breeze she was stirring up was a line of pennants and signal flags that stretched all the way from the point of the bow to the top of the mast amidships; and, as she drew near, the crew of the *Taney* began to pour it on heavy. Did they think they were headed for a friggin' party?

We received from them three fat canvas bags of mail, from which I hoped to get enough reading matter to keep me busy for three days.

On the way in work details were suspended and drills were a thing of the past. I fell into the habit of spending a great deal of time on the bow with Janssen and a quartermaster by the name of Harry Doscher. Except for the two Indian cutters, we hadn't seen a single ship the entire time we had been out, though it was possible some may have passed during the night. Except for gooney birds, the only life forms I had seen were the regular flights of passenger planes to and from Honolulu. And when one of the big birds would zoom low, to salute the ship, Husbands would invariably say, "Just think, Red, if we were on that thing, we'd be in Frisco tonight." Even when they were headed westward, he would say *Frisco*. And after a time, when I had learned to overlook his fogginess, I would invariably reply, "Who wants to be in Frisco?"

Early that Saturday morning, right on schedule, there appeared in the fog- and mist-shrouded distance the Faralon Islands; and these were shortly followed by the jagged outline of the northern California coast. By the time the Golden Gate was in sight, looking like a giant golden crown across the harbor entrance, the entire off-duty crew was running around topside acting like little undisciplined boys. For once, the Skipper was not present on the bridge to squelch the tomfoolery.

Perhaps he was sulking in his cabin, dreading to go home.

Husbands, bouncing with excitement, trailed along behind me to the starboard side of the ship to watch the landing at Government Island. The boatswain's mates and their deckhands scurried about, screaming at each other and doing their best to appear important, just in case someone on the beach might be watching them.

Leaning over the lifeline and gazing in the general direction of the Personnel Office, I said, "You know, Hoss, the sailor is just about the most fortunate of human beings on this earth."

"The fuck he is. Being a sailor sucks."

"Think about it," I said, dodging a monkey's fist that sailed within inches of my head. "Going to sea makes a man's appetite for just about everything on land keener and keeps him excited and alive to the creature comforts."

Husbands shook his big shaggy head. "I can't wait to git out of this fuckin' outfit. Give me Fresno and mother's food."

"The ancient philosophers were right," I continued, poking him in the short ribs. "Man suffers from moral, spiritual, and physical bankruptcy."

"Maybe," said Husbands, trying not to listen. "I wonder when liberty's gonna happen? Man, I can't wait to get some cold Lucky Lager!"

"When we get too much of a thing, we quite naturally turn away from it. Nothing, not a single thing on God's green earth, is good when it's repeated or experienced over and over again. Isn't that right? The steak-eater finally has his fill of steak, preferring chicken or some other meat eventually to a New York strip cooked medium rare. Ice-cream, consumed daily, becomes just so much mush in the mouth. And females—once you've had your fill of them—are a real pain in the butt."

"Stow it, Red!" shouted Husbands. "There's no way on God's green Earth I'll ever get my fill of women!"

"But you will, if you're unlucky enough to fraternize with them on a daily basis. The young, tender female, reputedly God's greatest blessing to Mankind, loses one by one her charms and attractiveness after you have known her for awhile and becomes, finally, just another skirt."

"Shit! I'm payin' no attention to you, Red. You dit-happy or somethin'? I'm out of here!"

"Hang on, old buddy!" I pleaded, good-naturedly, catching the big, soft arm of my shipmate. "What I'm getting at is that the sailor, by the very nature of his calling and pursuits, is blessed above all other of God's creatures. Whether instinctively or wisely (Who is to say?), he follows a calling that makes it possible for him to love women and other things perpetually and without any let-up at all. And if he doesn't know it to begin with, he learns one of the great truths of human existence, a truth that saves him from physical, spiritual, and moral bankruptcy. You see, his time at sea in the company of other men absolves him of these shortcomings, renews and even sharpens his appreciation of God's great gifts. The steak is even tastier than before, wine and beer brighten his outlook on life quicker, and even a mediocre, washed-out, stringy-haired, narrow-butted little female is, for him, a miracle of delight and beauty—at least for a few days or perhaps even a week. By then it is time for him to return to sea."

"Nobody is listenin' to you."

"Abstinence makes the heart and the palate and, god bless America, the penis grow fonder."

The Piper Pays

◆

There was one thing I liked about the *Taney* when she was in port. It was the peace and quiet that descended upon the ship very soon after docking, a result of the mass exodus of the crew for east Oakland. Even the officers, who had wives and children scattered around the Bay, couldn't wait to get off the ship and into civilian clothes.

In order to avoid the idiotic bragging and storytelling that went on in the crew's quarters as the men spruced up for a night at a nearby bar, I hung out in the radio shack until everything had left. Then, in leisurely style, I would go below and shower and shave and put on my undress blues, in anticipation of the quarter-of-a-mile hike to *Ted and Roy's* for a beer.

As it turned out, I was one of the few members of the crew that stayed aboard ship at night. This was not something that Cookie and his messcooks encouraged, especially on weekends. They refused to cook a full meal, of course; but for the men on gangway watch and the engineroom they grudgingly put out cold cuts and pickles and loaves of bread. The coffee urn went untended from Friday afternoon until Monday morning.

But I did not mind the cold food as much as I did the pointed remarks the duty cook would make about people that didn't have sense enough to go on liberty when they had the chance. Generally, I would be the only one not on some kind of a watch; so the remarks were obviously aimed at me.

One evening shortly after that first weather patrol I went across the bridge to *Ted and Roy's* with the innocent intention of having maybe two beers at most and a peaceful night's sleep back in the crews quarters. Cookie, in a foul mood because he was on duty, had fired a broadside just over my head to the effect that any man that would stick around the ship when he could be ashore enjoying the company of women had to be *a queer or something*. I had learned a long time ago that the one person aboard ship a sailor does not cross is the cook; therefore, instead of taking one of his own dishpans and beating the belligerent cook over the head with it, I got out of there fast. And ten minutes later I was still fuming when I straddled a barstool at *Ted and Roy's* and ordered a draft beer.

Ted, the rawboned half of the establishment, wiped a circle on the bar in front of me and set a big, ice-cold stein in the precise center of it.

"Hard day, Red?"

"What makes you ask?" I was surprised that he had even bothered to speak to me. I took a long drink, studying the foul-smelling beer.

"Just a wild guess. Last time I saw you you was feelin' pretty good."

I stared at the half an inch of foam still on top of the beer, trying to remember.

"You broke one of my chairs, remember?"

"What do you want, more money?" I asked, still refusing to look at him. "Have you forgot that I settled up with you for that?"

"You settled up with my partner, who evidently didn't know how much them chairs cost. But I aint saying you owe me anything."

"Yeah, well."

A big, round-shouldered, sour-faced motormack that I had seen on the *Taney* moved in on my left, on the side toward the front door. I knew by the smell he was a grease-monkey before I glanced around and spotted the shoulder patch.

First an elbow and then a knee and finally a shoulder jostled me, the last causing me to bump my beer hard. At this point I turned and examined the swab's profile. Ted hastily wiped his way to the motormack.

"What'll it be, Jackson?"

"Make it a boilermaker. And tell Red here to quit crowdin' me."

"Oh, shit," sighed Ted, glancing at me and wiping up the pool of beer in front of me. "Is it going be one of them nights?" For a moment he wiped furiously, unwilling to leave the two of us alone long enough to get the beer-and-bourbon drink for the motormack. "Now, Jackson, I'm warnin' you to behave yourself. Red is mindin' his own business."

"He bumped me twice, in case you didn't notice," said Jackson.

"You picked the wrong night, Ugly," I said quietly, rolling around on the stool. "Ordinarily, I'd avoid shit like you."

"Aw, God!" groaned the bartender.

It is a sad fact of life, but there are some people that you cannot reason with, and I suddenly decided that this motormack was one of them. So instead of trying to talk my way out of something, I brought the heavy stein around squarely into Jackson's startled face! The motormack and all of the beer mug except the handle flew across the floor, followed at once by me. And for some reason I was about as mad as I ever get.

"How much do you want?" I said, straddling him and letting him have it in the jaw. "You came in here looking for it, didn't you?" I hit him again hard, this time squarely in the nose. Blood spurted across the deck.

The little bar was crowded with Coasties, most of whom were from the *Taney*. Two big motormacks, friends of Jackson's as it turned out, leaped forward and grabbed my arms and pinned them behind my back.

"Git off me!" bellowed Jackson. He was bleeding like a stuck pig from the nose, and there was an ugly gash over his left eye that was beginning to bleed.

The two apes pulled me up and turned me to face Jackson, who got to his feet and squared off at me. He was as broad as a barn and built solid. I had no intentions of standing there and letting him beat on me.

Someone yelled, "Hey, turn old Red loose! Let him defend himself!"

Ted had circled the bar and was in the middle of things, demanding that we split up and move outside.

Jackson, who was a little taller than me and a good one hundred pounds heavier, had time to throw one punch before I finally wrenched my right arm free and fall backward. The punch glanced off my shoulder, and, righting myself, I realized I was facing the pug ugly that was still clinging to my left arm. I hit him twice in rapid succession before he went down, his face already covered with blood. Whirling, I landed one on the sucker that had been holding my right arm, knocking him across a table.

All this time Jackson was trying to get at me, around Ted.

"All right, all right!" I heard Ted yelling. He showed up in front of me, just as I prepared to meet Jackson head on. I let go anyway and he ducked and stumbled backward, into the motormack.

"By God, I'm callin' the police!"

The fifteen or twenty Coasties in the bar were by this time on their feet yelling, and I heard one of them shout, "Give it to 'em, Red!" Someone grabbed Ted, trying to keep him away from the phone.

One thing I had never been able to tolerate was somebody holding me while somebody else pounded on me; and this, coupled with Jackson's unprovoked attempt to lay me out and cookie's remark about queers had worked me up to real mad. Mama used to tell my five older brothers, "Never get Wesley real mad at you, or somebody will get hurt."

I bounced from one to the other of the motormacks, giving each a knuckle sandwich. Jackson, a bit slow on his feet, finally showed up in front of me with his bloody face, snorting and spitting first to one side and then to the other. I hit him twice in the kisser with my left, readying him for ole Johnny Come Lately. My right fist began its assent down close to the floor, and when it landed in Jackson's left ear, it sounded like Papa felling a four-hundred-pound pig with a club.

All was suddenly quiet in the little bar.

I staggered over one of the motormacks and climbed on a barstool. Everybody began to return to their seats, but no one made a move to help the three motormacks. Jackson's helpers were sitting up, wiping, but he was taking up a lot of room on the deck.

"Give me a shot of something," I said, looking at Ted. "Have you called the police?"

"Not yet." He poured me a double shot of bourbon, and I noticed that his hands were trembling. "I sholy did intend to, but I just didn't quite have time."

After a great deal of confusion caused by chairs and tables going back where they belonged and loud arguing about what had just taken place, things began to settle down considerably. Jackson was hauled off to the head by his buddies, and I waited around to see that he made it through to the street all right, once he was cleaned up. I was no longer interested in settling for two beers and bed; so I ordered a boilermaker, chatted with Ted about what a rotten day it had been, and I kept a wary eye on that door in the rear, just in case Mr. Jackson wanted to pick up where we had left off.

"God damn it, Red!" complained Ted, "Ever' time you come in here hell breaks loose. You broke two of my chairs this time!"

"You've got that a might wrong," I said, calmly. "I broke no chairs of yours tonight." I downed some beer and glanced toward the head. "How much do you reckon those two chairs would cost to replace?"

"Hell, a hundred bucks at least!"

The head door opened and the three motormacks came out, led by Jackson. He took one look at me and started to head for the street door.

"How much money you got on you, Slug?" I asked, putting out my hand. To Ted I said, "We just got paid."

"I think you broke my nose."

"Hmmm," I said, "is that all I did? How much jack you got? You owe Ted one hundred and fifty dollars." Glancing at the other two accomplices, I added, "The three of you, that is. Divvy it up, boys." None of them had a word to say, apparently, and were anxious to move on. One of the two sidekicks, I noticed, had a great bulge in his blouse pocket.

Without a word, I slid off the barstool and removed, after a brief scuffle, a roll of bills from it.

Ted's eyes, slightly bulging, were glued on the money, as I began to row up twenties on the bar. "What're you doing, Red?" he asked, incredulous. "You can't—"

"Now, Ted, you seemed anxious to collect for the damages awhile ago. These boys caused the damage. Am I right? So they are the ones who will have to pay for it." I carefully placed the seventh twenty on the bar and began to look for a ten. "You don't expect me to pay for something that I didn't cause, do you? I have no idea how this boy managed to accumulate so much money, but we'll let the other two give him their shares in this."

"Red—" began Ted and stopped.

Jackson, after an evil look in my direction, motioned to the other two and they left. All eyes in the bar followed them out the door.

Ted gathered up the money. "You're on the *Taney* now, right?"

"That's right."

"Well, all I can say is you'd better take out life insurance."

I nodded, feeling of the weight on the back of my neck. "I did that quite awhile ago."

*   *   *

Although Husbands was a Native Son and not quite as smart as an ox, I had found that I could tolerate him. Most of this third class's problem, if one could overlook his ignorance and stupidity, was his habit of trying to be funny and failing miserably. He had grown up with boys smarter than him, and in order not to be thought stupid he had worked hard at being a wisecracker and a practical joker.

Of course, once we were tied up at the dock, he received a three-day pass and headed for Fresno and his mother's cooking. And since there was no flag at all in front of Janssen's house, my only other friend on the ship had decided he should find out what was going on.

Tied up at the G. I. dock, the *Taney* turned out to be a far different ship from the *Taney* at sea. The Skipper, who slept ashore, would show up in time for morning muster, make a little pep talk about hard work and perseverance, and disappear into his cabin, leaving the Department Heads to extract as much as possible from their charges.

Sparky had one project that endeared him to his men and got him a lot of attention from the other Chiefs, the never-ending scraping and painting (but not necessarily in that order) of the exterior bulkheads of the radio shack and the smokestack. He liked to point out that his 'left-arm rates' had to work just as hard as any of the 'right-arm rates'.

And until I came along Sparky had assigned only the lowly third class operators to the really difficult work on the scaffolding. It was, to say the least, a noisy and thankless bit of drudgery. The first class radiomen, Janseen and Sears, would hang out in or near the shack, just in case the Communications Officer happened along; but the Chief himself rarely visited the place during the painting and scraping.

The first morning after Husbands returned from his week-end pass, Sparky delivered a little speech that shocked the daylights out of me and sent my watch mate through the overhead. New things had to be tried out, our salty Chief told us. Instead of sending the three third class outside with scrapers and paint brushes, why not send the new man, who was not a first class yet, and Husbands, who was not only a third class but an asshole to boot? We were, after all, a pair, was the way he put it. Janssen and Podscoff were another pair, and Sears, who would be back from leave any day, and Ceccarelli were a third pair. And since Janssen and Sears were not expected to do manual labor, it would have to be Hall and Husbands on the smokestack.

The reasoning was completely lost on me. And all Husbands could do was sputter and cough.

I could understand how painful it must have been for Husbands, seeing his buddies sitting around the radio shack drinking coffee and reading magazines while we worked out in the hot sun. One morning, unable to take it any longer, he confronted Janssen outside the shack about the unfairness of the whole thing.

"What're you bitchin' about, Husbands? You'd be out there anyway, one way or the other. As for Red, I think he's got a gripe coming. But the Chief gets these hairs once in awhile. He told me he thinks of us as teams of two and since Red's junior to me and Sears and, since Podscoff and Ceccarelli are assigned to us respectively, it had to be him and you."

Husbands was waving his hands, erasing everything Janssen was saying. "It's at least a three-man job!"

As soon as Janssen had gone on into the radio shack and closed the door (to shut out the noise of our scrapers, as well as Husband's big wolfy voice), I said, "If that's the way the Chief wants it, Hoss, don't sweat it. Actually, it's not bad out here as long as we've got some shade. And, personally, I would rather Ceccarelli and Podscoff not join us."

Hearing heavy footsteps coming up the ladder, we turned and saw Chief Boatswain's Mate Mackey huffing and puffing toward us. Seeing me, he called out, "Where you goin', Red?"

I had no idea what he was getting at, and furthermore I was startled by the almost-chipper tone with which he spoke.

"You aint runnin' from Jackson, are you? Heh, heh."

"Not likely."

"That's what I understand. Say, Red, next time we run into each other down at *Ted and Roy's*, I want to buy you a beer. That sonbitch Jackson had that comin' to him."

At that moment Ceccarelli and Podscoff, grinning broadly, came out of the radio shack, headed no doubt for coffee.

"Well, how about this?" asked Ceccarelli. "Looks like old Red's found something to do that's on his level." Then, laughing hysterically, they dived down the ladder.

Podscoff paused at the landing to say over his shoulder, "Hey, Harold, have fun!"

"What the hell goes on?" demanded Chief Mackey. "You gonna take that crap, Red?" When I said nothing, he shrugged and entered the radio shack.

Ten minutes later, Sparky came out of the shack and Mackey was right behind him.

"Uh, Hall, I want you to take charge of this project. Turn your paint brush over to Ceccarelli or Podscoff, and see that the other one has a scraper."

"Right," I said, exchanging a wink with Chief Mackey.

"Well, kiss my butt," said Husbands, shaking his head.

When Sparky and Mackey left, I said to Husbands, "You want to have some fun?" I asked. "Follow me."

We found the two third class radiomen sacked out in the crew's quarters, reading comic books. Ceccarelli was lying on his side with his butt hanging over the edge of his bunk. As we approached, he craned his neck, looking first at Husbands and then at me.

"Git up to the radio shack!" I snapped, kicking Ceccarelli's extended foot.

"Hey, that hurt!" he complained, pathetically. "I'm goin' to the Chief about that!"

"Did you hear me?"

"Leave me alone. I don't feel like gettin' up just now."

"Oh, you're gonna get up, all right! You can count on that."

"Go take a flyin' suck at the moon."

"Is that the way you want it?" I said with a laugh, clamping down on one of his bare feet with both hands and balancing myself for a mighty yank.

"All right!" the third class yelped, wallowing out of his trough and, feet first, dropping to the deck. "What do you want?"

"I'll tell—!"

In the blink of an eye and out of nowhere Ceccarelli's little birdlike fist slammed into my chin. I went down fast, with hardly any sensation of pain or even an awareness that I was falling, I suddenly found myself flat of my back on the deck—with a hole in the left side of my skull! I had ricocheted off one of the metal bunks on the way down, and now black clouds moved in rapidly, turning out the lights!

Later, after Husbands half-carried and half-dragged me to the head and ran cold water over my bleeding skull and still later after he and the other two third class radiomen lifted me like a sack of flour and carried me to the Sick Bay, where my scalp was cleaned and a spot the size of a silver dollar shaved and stitched up, I learned that I had evidently land-ed on one of the small steel chainhooks on Ceccarelli's bottom bunk, after falling almost full-length!

Cecil Ceccarelli, who hailed from a little town fifteen miles west of Fresno, had lashed out blindly, landing the luckiest punch of his life; and when I came to he was bending over me, his large, watery blue eyes slightly bulging. He never intended to do something like that. It had just happened and he hoped I wouldn't hold it against him. It was a terrible thing on his conscience, and he could not understand why my head had to land where it did.

I spent the rest of the day in or near my bunk, confined to quarters, while Ceccarelli, Podscoff, and Husbands pretended to scrape paint. Periodically, one of them would dash into the quarters to see how I was doing, to deliver cold drinks and get pills or something for me. On one occasion, I roused, looking at Ceccarelli from between half-closed eyes. "You still pretending to work up on the smokestack?"

"I am workin', Red! Just like if you was there yellin' at me! You gonna be okay?"

Either a complete *metamorphosis*had occurred or Ceccarelli was one hell of an actor. I couldn't believe what I was hearing.

"Hah. Get out."

"Yeah, but I'm real sorry! I didn't mean to do it, Red!"

While I was recuperating and Ceccarelli was running back and forth fixing me up with anything I wanted and a few things I didn't want, all the while claiming to be working like a slave topside, I became convinced that this miraculous change in the boy was not temporary. Day followed day with no let up, and, indeed, within a week I was beginning to think his attentions were getting out of hand.

"I really thought I'd killed you, Red," he moaned one day. "Man, do you realize how close I came?"

"Aw, forget it," I told him. "My head's harder than that."

It was a very odd thing. Previously, the three of them, Husbands included, had worked together to make life miserable for me. They knew better than to try something alone and in the open; but together, one of them lying and the other two swearing to it, they could get away with murder. That was evidently all in the past.

One day I learned that Ceccarelli had not only refused to side with Podscoff against me but had gone out of his way to save me from a Captain's Mast.

It was a Wednesday, three days before we were due to head out to another weather patrol, and the entire radio gang had been detailed to put an extra coat of white paint on the big forward smokestack. The four of us, Husbands, the other two third class radiomen, and I, were suspended about ten feet above the bridge deck on a two-by-twelve scaffolding, each with a paint bucket and a brush. Husbands was farthest aft, I was beside him, and the other two were on the forward end, where I could keep an eye on them. All they wanted to do was prank, splash paint and destabilize the platform.

Below us, Sears and Janssen would occasionally duck past the paint zone, fresh from the galley or on the way there. Sears would be carrying coffee on the return trips and old Janssen would be hanging onto the sandwiches; and, of course, both of them would be enjoying the sight of four unhappy dit-dah men balancing on a precarious platform. Since I was in charge of the detail, it was my responsibility to see that the three jerks under me did not kill themselves or make a mess below.

On a number of occasions one or the other of the buckets had come close to toppling off the scaffolding. On one occasion, the Chief himself had emerged from the radio shack just in time to spot one of them on the verge of tipping. He let out a high-pitched scream, and I managed to catch it in time. But that incident left me nervous and irritable, for I could see clearly where this was heading. And sure enough, a few minutes later, the platform gave a sudden jerk, Podscoff screamed, and my own bucket tumbled to the deck below!

"Look out below!" warned Ceccarelli, nonchalantly.

"Oh, shit!" screamed Husbands, grabbing hold of me with a shaking hand. Podscoff and I were in the center of the board, without support or hand-holds of any kind; and, forgetting for the moment about his bucket, Husbands had grabbed me with one hand and the after line that supported his end of the board with the other. The end result was that his bucket tipped over!

Immediately below us was the wardroom, where several officers were having a coffee break. I balanced precariously on the two-by-twelve, like a cripple trying to water ski, contemplating the mess below on the deck. From Ceccarelli's bucket had burst a mighty river of white oil-based paint, and this had begun to fan out across the deck, breaking into a dozen or so creeks and rivulets. All of which had to be cleaned immediately, if not sooner. But as fickle fate would have it, Mr. Randle, the new Communications Officer, chose that particular moment to arrive below the project. I glanced down just in time to see my bucket do a neat flip-flop and land squarely on the officer's head!

Mr. Randle, unluckily in this case, was a very agile young man, well-known in the commissioned ranks as a sprinter. Realizing that he was in a danger zone, he leaped the precise distance necessary to catch a second bucket, this time on his right shoulder and back!

All of this occurred in the blink of an eye. Then for perhaps a full minute silence fell upon the scene, broken only by the *splat-splat* of thick One-Coat Enamel landing on the deck below. Miraculously, both

Ceccarelli and I had remained on our scaffolding. I looked down into the terrified face of Mr. Randle, who had begun to whimper softly. He was frozen to the spot where that third bucket had caught him, still not fully aware of what had happened. He brushed tentatively at himself, looking wild-eyed.

Sparky, followed by Sears and Janssen, arrived on the scene, yelling and pointing upward toward us. I understood nothing they were saying. Several deckhands rushed up and gave aid to Mr. Randle, who finally calmed down enough to make an impassioned speech, directed at the four of us on the two-by-twelves. He promised that the one or ones responsible for the two buckets that landed on him would face nothing less than a Deck Court Martial!

Scraping and painting the CGC Taney's stack! (August, 1947)

Miraculously, two buckets still remained on the platform. The onlookers below, after moving out of harm's way, began demanding to know just whose bucket tipped first? From a crouching position, I turned and glared at Podscoff, who was pointing anxiously toward Ceccarelli.

"It wasn't my bucket!" screamed Podscoff. "This one's mine right here!" He pointed toward the one nearest him on the scaffolding.

"Shut up," said the Chief. "Whose bucket fell on Mr. Randle, Red?"

"Well, it sure as hell wasn't mine!" yelled Podscoff, so relieved to be in the clear on this charge he was leaning nonchalantly against the line at his and Ceccarelli's end, causing the board to sway back and forth.

"Red?" screamed the Chief. "You got a mouth?"

"It wasn't his fault, Chief," said Ceccarelli. "I saw it all."

"Who belonged to that first bucket?" demanded the Chief, glaring at Husbands.

"Well, that one was Red's, Chief, but Podscoff pushed us away from the stack and caused that bucket to tip!" explained Husbands, looking at Ceccarelli for support.

"What caused yours to tip?" pursued the Sparky. His long-nurtured hatred of Husbands was close to the surface.

"That same push, Chief!"

"Go to your quarters and stay there, all of you!" shouted Sparky. "You'll be called to give your side one at a time." He turned to leave and then stopped and glared back up at us. "Before you go anyplace, git this goddamned paint cleaned up! You miss one fuckin' flyspeck of a drop and I'll see that all four of you are restricted to the ship for a month and put on a ration of bread and water!"

As I climbed down to the passageway, I said with a laugh, "That might not be so bad, you know."

"*Not so bad?*" complained Husbands. "What're you talkin' about?"

"Well, think about it," I said, looking up at him. "If we get restricted to the ship for a month, that means *restricted to quarters*, right? How long is a weather patrol?"

"Twenty days."

"How long does it take us to go out and back?"

"Oh!" exclaimed Husbands. "You mean that we could spend the entire weather patrol—off duty. No watches?"

"But," I added sadly, "what if we're not restricted at all but put on bread-and-water—"

"Aw, shut up!"

        *   *   *

The Deck Court Martial that everybody expected me to get did not take place, simply because Mr. Randle could not convince the Exec that it was justified. It was, finally, Ceccarelli's detailed account of how Podscoff had caused the whole thing that reduced my case to a Captain's Mast. Husbands was also put on report *for carelessness and insubordination.* The Captain's Masts were set to follow muster two mornings after the incident.

Husbands was devastated. The very thought of having a Captain's Mast on his unblemished record scared him out of his wits. He kept looking at me and shaking his head pathetically.

"Red, have you ever had a Captain's Mast?"

"Yeah, sure."

"What's it like?"

"Nothing to it. You just stand in front of the Skipper and he pulls out his pistol, takes aim, and shoots you."

"Oh, shit, be serious."

"That's what I've heard about the Captain's Masts on the *Taney.*"

We the condemned went to breakfast that fateful morning, the center of attention on the messdeck. Husbands' stock on the open market had risen considerably, a thing that both shocked and pleased him; and shipmates who had never spoken to me before wanted to shake hands and slap me on the back. We had done a courageous thing, everybody said, dropping all that paint on an officer's head. The consensus was that we should be given medals.

Podscoff, of course, could not understand how Husbands and I could be heroes, while he was suddenly an outcast. He kept repeating to anyone who would listen that all he had done was tell the truth. Maybe he should have lied about it and taken the blame!

But that just wasn't his way.

When the three of us lined up to dispose of our trays, I noticed that Husbands hadn't touched his food. His face was whiter than the undress whites he was wearing for the upcoming occasion, and his hands were trembling. We filed out, going to the section of the quarterdeck where the Communications Division would be mustered at eight o'clock.

Sparky, looking genuinely chagrined, positioned himself in front of Husbands and me. I couldn't tell whether he was going to blast us or shake our hands.

"I hate to tell you this but Gorman will probably throw the book at you two."

"Thanks, Chief, we appreciate your heart-warming words," I said with a grin. I was beginning to feel butterfies in my stomach.

"What the hell you lookin' so happy about, Red? Don't you know this'll go down on your record and follow you wherever you go in the service?"

"What's one more blemish, more or less? Besides, we are innocent."

"Hell, you're gettin' exactly what you deserve," he said, poking me in the ribs. "Good luck, both of you."

After the piping from the bridge and the hasty straightening up of all lines and the Department Heads going through their "All present or accounted for, Sir!"—and, finally, our summons over the PA system— Husbands fell in behind me and we went immediately to the door of the Captain's. I noticed that Husbands was standing at attention. Neither of us spoke to the guard, nor did he bat an eye in our direction; but after a time he glanced at his watch, turned, and rapped on the door. Without waiting for permission to enter, he opened it and stood back for us to enter. We lined up facing Comdr. Gorman, who sat at a large desk, on which were two manila folders. A thick one and a thin one.

Fifteen minutes later we were back in the messdeck drinking coffee, surrounded by a dozen shipmates. It had been an amazing experience for both of us, and Husbands was ecstatic about the outcome. He let everybody know that he was proud of himself now that he had faced a court martial and lived to tell about it. At one point he turned to me and boasted, "Hell, Red here, with his reputation, could've gotten Alcatraz!"

"What, exactly, did you git?" demanded Cookie, looking at me.

Husbands glanced at me and burst out, "Well, Red was docked a month's pay and restricted to the ship for a month!" Then he dropped his head and admitted that all he had got was a reprimand and the advice that he should avoid the company of sailors like me.

Restricted

◆

My second trip out to Weather Station Fox aboard The *Roger B. Taney* began on a Saturday night, close to midnight. Janssen and Podscoff, with less than an hour to go, had the first watch. At eleven-thirty, about fifteen minutes after we cleared the harbor, the senior member of that team said to the junior member, "Better go wake Red and Husbands."

"Do I have to?" moaned Podscoff. "I'd almost rather stand their watch than git close to Red when he's sleepin'."

"Wake Husbands and ask him to wake Red."

"Okay, but if I do neither one of them will make it up here in time to relieve us."

Podscoff slumped out and, taking his time about it, dragged down to the crew's quarters. He went first to Husbands and poked him hard, "Hey, Tub! Time to relieve the watch!" And although there were sleeping swabs on all sides, he was not keeping his voice down. The fist that he had been expecting and was prepared for turned into a foot that came out of nowhere. He stumbled backward, received another kick from unknown quarters.

I was fully awake by this time, of course, as was just about everyone in the quarters. He moved in my direction and from a distance of five or six feet he whispered loudly, "You awake, Red? It's time for you and Tub to go on watch."

"Yeah," I said.

"Will you make sure old Tub's awake?"

I didn't answer. My mind was already on the ship's departure from San Fran Bay and what Husbands and I had to look forward to during our watch. The ship was rolling gently from side to side, and there was a slight vibration coming from the engines. I swung out of my bunk and felt the cold clamminess of the steel deck against my bare feet.

I went over to Husbands, who was sound asleep, and shook him violently.

"Get up, Hoss. It's reality time."

"What is it?" he asked , sounding shocked. "I don't want any breakfast, but thanks anyway." He turned over and faced the bulkhead.

I sat down on the Native Son's bunk, giving him a poke in the backside. "I don't care whether you want any breakfast or not, but I cannot leave you down here sleeping. Come on, let's drop by the messdeck for some coffee. You can sleep on watch. as usual." I got up and waited, hands on hips. "Don't you want to go up and relieve your old buddy, Podscoff."

"Hell, no!"

By the time we reached the messdeck, Husbands had decided he was starving to death, and it became necessary for me to drag him away from the piles of cold cuts and potato chips. On the way up to the shack I reminded him that when you relieved Janssen you did not enter the shack with coffee. "After we settle in, you can drop back down and get us some coffee and sandwiches."

The radio shack was full of people when we walked in. The Chief, presiding over a hastily-called meeting, sat in one of the swiveled and anchored chairs at the long desk that occupied the forward end of the room. Janssen, still on watch, sat at the other position with earphones strapped around his neck; and Sears and Lt. Randle were leaning against the starboard bulkhead listening to the Chief. Podscoff was lurking just outside the hatch, waiting for Husbands to relieve him.

The Communications Officer turned to me and said, "I guess you think your restriction turned out to be a joke, Hall. It occurred to me you might be planning to sleep that time off in your bunk."

"Sir, am I restricted to my quarters, or just the ship?"

"Your restriction has been lifted. But, of course, the Captain's Mast will remain on your records."

Sparky nodded, trying to look distressed.

"Well, I just wanted to drop by and wish everybody a good patrol."

"Thank you, Sir!" said Sparky. "Everything's shipshape here. All watches will be covered." The second the hatch closed behind the lieutenant, he turned to me and said, "You ought to try to put on just a little with the officers, Red. Especially the Com Officer. God damn it, don't you know anything about diplomacy?"

"Don't you mean *brown-nosing*, Sparky?" I asked. "I have a little problem with that kind of shinola. Besides, in no time at all I'll be a civilian."

"Ha!" he scoffed. "You're a twenty-year man if I ever saw one."

"Well, I guess we're out of here," said Janssen. Turning to me, he said with the semblance of a grin, "Thanks for holding off on the skunk piss. What does Husbands think of that stuff?"

"I don't have the slightest notion, but he drinks Dr. Pepper morning, noon, and night."

Two minutes later Husbands and I slid into our radio positions. I strapped a pair of earphones around my neck and, glancing at him, motioned toward the hatch. He groaned at the sudden realization that he had to climb all those ladders, but eventually he got up and shuffled out. I could still hear him groaning halfway down the passageway.

Thirty minutes later he was back with two half-mugs of coffee and three thick sandwiches. He had eaten two, he said, on the way up, so I could have two and he would have only the one. I looked at the coffee and frowned. He then explained that it was next to impossible to carry two heavy mugs in one hand up all those steps without spilling a little.

"Did your parents encourage you to join the Coast Guard, Hoss?" I asked, taking a sip of coffee.

"Yeah, you bet they did. Dad thought it was a great thing, because he was in the Coasties during the war. And Mom couldn't brag enough about me to the relatives." He took a long drink from his bottle of Dr. Pepper, his great, flabby brow a network of furrows as he tried to remember such a distant past. "Boy, do I ever miss Mom's cookin'!"

"No doubt about it," I nodded, reaching over and tapping his gut. "But I'd say you're saving you folks a lot of money by being here. In fact, I don't see how any family of modest means, as you say yours are, could afford to feed you for very long."

"That's funny," cackled Husbands, banging his bottle on the glass desktop. "Dad said just about the same thing a couple dozen times."

The ship gave a great shudder, like a wet dog, and there followed a slight rolling sensation to the starboard.

"We're no longer landlocked," I observed. "Think you can keep an eye out for Sparky and other authority figures?"

He looked startled: "Now, Red, you're not plannin' to do something illegal."

"You know," I said. "We talked about piping some music to the mess-deck and reckhall. It's midnight and every officer except one is sound asleep in his nice wide berth."

I took my phones off and laid them face up on the desk; then I opened a cabinet door beneath the typewriter and flipped a speaker switch. Husbands sighed noisily and turned the volume up on his head-phones, removed them from his neck, and hung them over his chair back. Then he got slowly to his feet and headed for the hatch.

"I wish we had a listening device of some kind out there in the pas-sageway," he said. "Then maybe I could enjoy the music, too."

"You'll enjoy it just as well out there as you would in here," I assured him, concentrating on the tuning dial of a Hallicrafters receiver. "What kind of music are we in the mood for this fine morning?"

"I'm tellin' you, Red, you're takin' a helluva chance. What if Mr. Randle just happened to be wherever you're pipin'? He won't even bother to add two and two. He'll beeline it in here."

"Well, in the first place, he never leaves Officers' Country after dark, and in the second place, if he did and heard our music, I would claim that it was all your idea."

"Hah, nobody would take your word for that."

"Are you saying our superiors would take the word of a lowly, insignificant, irresponsible third class radio operator over the word of the radioman-in-charge of the watch?"

"Who just happens to be a lowly second class radio operator with a marred and scarred service record."

"Nevertheless."

*   *   *

About a week into the patrol, when every enlisted man aboard the ship knew about my illegal poaching on the radio broadcast band, I encountered Jackson and some of his friends on deck, taking in the sunshine. It was a rare sight and for a moment I gawked. Motormacks, I knew, did not like sunlight and fresh air. But there they were, sprawled around the forward gun emplacement, each with a cigarette in his mouth; and when one of them punched Jackson and pointed toward me, the big cheese of the engineroom called out, "Hey, Red, got a minute?"

"Wait till I git my knucks," I kidded. "How's your jaw?"

"Pills says I'll never be able to pronounce the F-words again." He rubbed his chin. "You tuning' in music down to the messdeck durin' the midwatches?"

"Hell no! That's illegal."

"I know that," sighed Jackson, looking pained. "But scuttlebutt has it you're doin' it anyway."

"Husbands talks too much."

"Scuttlebutt also has it you and Husbands always stand the mid-watches, like we do." He glanced about at his friends. "We was thinkin' that if somebody with some balls was runnin' the radio shack, he could pipe a little of that music to us."

"You really would like to see me busted back to Apprentice Seaman, wouldn't you?"

"Hell, no. I don't hold no grudges about that little two-second fight you and me had. Can you do it?"

"Pipe us in something lively," said Varner, one of the two that had held my arms at *Ted and Roy's*.

"You're hooked up to the PA system, right?" demanded Jackson. "Ever' place on the ship has a speaker attached to that thing. All you'd have to do—"

Husbands came dragging up.

"Why don't you ask my assistant to do this naughty little favor?" I asked. "He's already in trouble with the brass."

The motormacks laughed and Jackson stood up and put his arm around the massive shoulders of the Native Son. "How would you like to be a real hero on this ole bucket, my good man?"

"He's already that," said one of the motormacks. "I about shit my pants when I heard he deliberately dropped a bucket of paint on the Communications Officer's head!"

Husbands lifted Jackson's arm up and away from his shoulder, wrinkling his nose and stepping back.

"All you've got to do to be a greater hero is hook the engineroom up to that music you're piping during the midwatch."

"I don't anything to do with that," said Husbands. He turned and faced me. "Red, I would not trust these dudes, if I was you."

★ ★ ★

Two nights after the music came on in the engineroom Husbands suddenly leaped from his lookout post near the radio shack door and yelped, "Shut it down, Red!"

"Who is it?"

"I don't know, but just do it!"

About two seconds after I had flipped the switches, in walked Winton, a quartermaster, carrying a papersack. I motioned him to the empty chair at the long desk, and he took it without a word. Husbands followed him and stood looking hungrily at the sack.

"How's things going, Red? All quiet on the western front?"

"Couldn't be quieter. What's cookin'?"

"You hungry?"

"I am," said Husbands, reaching for the sack.

The quartermaster handed it to me. To Husbands he said, "I've just got two pieces, and they're both for Red here."

I opened the sack and sniffed.

"Man, is it ever dull up on the bridge tonight. Somebody said you—"

"I don't know," I said, frowning suspiciously. "Whose on watch with you?"

"Just Wilkins. You know ole Wilkins. Nice fellow."

"Radarman, right? Who's the O. O. D.?"

"Mr. Langston! He's the one that sent me down here."

"You're full of crap!" said Husbands. "Red, don't believe that! No officer is—!"

"I shit you not, Red! He brought the pie up from the wardroom and told me he wanted me to deliver it. Right after we found out about the music bein' piped to the engineroom, Mr. Langston said he wouldn't mind having music during the watch."

"How'd you and Wilkins find out—about the engineroom? Huh, huh, huh?" demanded Husbands. "That was supposed to be on the Q. T., right, Red?"

"Anyway," said Winton, "Mr. Langston said for me to come down and see if you wouldn't mind piping us some music. I thought of the apple pie myself last night and suggested it to him."

I raised my hand, signaling *enough*. "Okay, but just till about three-thirty. I don't want my relief to find out about this." I wheeled around in my chair, searched for and found a phone jack labeled *Bridge*, plugged it into the control panel, and flipped a switch. "You're in business. Hoss, go get us some fresh coffee to go with this pie."

"I can't. I gotta watch out for the Chief."

"Forget about the Chief," I scolded. "How many times in his twenty-four years in the Coast Guard do you reckon he's arisen during the mid-watch and checked out the radio shack?"

Husbands left, complaining, and within two minutes he was back, breathless, "Sorry, Red, but you was wrong!"

The Chief barreled into the shack in this undershirt, sputtering. I was sprawled out with my feet across the other swivel chair reading a *QST* magazine, and Bing Crosby was reaching way down into his breadbasket for *Far Away Places*.

"God damn it, Red!"

I lowered my magazine and reached over and turned the music down, trying to appear unperturbed.

"What's up, Sparky?"

"You sonofabitch! You've done it this time!"

"How so?"

"What in blue blazes do you think you're doin' in my radio shack?"

I raised my eyebrows, faking innocence. "Standing a watch?"

"For this little stunt you'll git it right up the old bohunkus!" With that he wheeled and dashed out.

There were consequences, of course, but perhaps not the kind the Chief intended. Within about ten minutes I went on report and was relieved of my duties in the shack. This time I was *confined* to the crews quarters. Husbands was sent to get Sears, who had to take the rest of the watch. This, of course, saddened me. I had assumed that Sparky himself would take over the watch.

Then, as the days went by, while I lay in my bunk (reading *QST* and *The Amateur Radio Handbook*), the two first class radiomen, Sears and Janssen, had to stand four-on and four-off watches, since the Chief had decided not to participate. It was his way of punishing me.

A good week later, when the Chief finally realized that putting me on report would one day translate into another Captain's Mast for me, which, in turn, would translate into a great deal more four-on and four-off duty for his first class radiomen, he sent a request through channels that the charges be dropped. This was approved, at which point he returned me to the regular watch schedule—with a new partner. (Husbands had voluntarily confessed that he was in on the music scandal, in order to be confined to his sack. Instead, he was paired with Janssen and told that his Captain's Mast would be delayed until we arrived back at G. I.)

The chief, once a prissy little man with a satisfied and benevolent expression on his face, now prowled about the ship all hours of the day and night, looking uneasy and depressed. His visits to the radio shack were frequent and unpredictable, especially during my watch. According to scuttlebutt coming out of the wardroom, the Old Man had dressed him down over the music incident, even hinting that he just might be incapable of controlling the men beneath him.

At one and two in the morning he was apt to drop into the shack, swear a bit and disappear, his face the picture of disaster.

Podscoff, my new watch buddy, in some ways even more mule-headed than Husbands, decided he would take no orders from me. After all, he pointed out, I was in Dutch with everybody, especially the Chief, and therefore deserved no respect from him. And since the Chief did not dare put anybody else on report, he (Podscoff) would do just as he pleased on my watch. In his opinion, he should have seniority over me, since he had been aboard the ship longer and had an unblemished record.

Instead of forcing the issue, I decided to teach Podscoff a lesson. I knew this kid was incompetent in all phases of the operation of a radio shack; and quite by accident I learned on our very first watch together that he was mortally scared of speaking into a mike to the headquarters station, NMC, in San Francisco. Straight off, the first time the Base called, I contrived to be on another frequency, thus forcing Podscoff to respond. And hardly had he recuperated from this when a messenger straight from the weather center dropped in with six pages of columned, five-digit code groups, which had to be sent to NMC using International Morse. It was a Priority One message, of course, and no errors and no repeats could be tolerated by the decoders in Frisco.

I ignored the third class completely, pretending to have my hands full on another frequency. He stared at me, rattled the mike, hissed, and finally began to whimper. I watched him out of the corner of my eye, saw him fondle the brass key, tentatively tap out *N M C*. Suddenly, he flung the earphones at me and sprang up.

"Red, goshdangit! I can't do this! NMC's callin' us! And I can't send that long message in code—without a mistake!"

"But you said you ought to be in charge of this watch," I said, casually. "Okay, take charge. Tell NMC you've got a Priority message for them. Just remember, if you fuck this up they'll send you to the deck gang."

The Radioroom of the CGC Roger B. Taney (ca. 1947)

The O. O. D. Jeep

◆

There was an indefinable something in the air, something electric yet disturbingly pleasant and exciting. All sounds of activity on the dock had ceased long ago, but the messcooks on the *Taney* had unceremoniously dumped six cans of first class Coast Guard garbage over the stern. And this, of course, had brought in at least three score and ten white-and-steelgray seagulls, swooping and screaming their heads off.

They were, of course, totally unaware that it was Saturday afternoon and time for another three-day liberty in old Frisco town.

Especially below decks, where Cheesy Macklin, the latest man to ship aboard (from the CGC *Alert*), and I were slumped on our bunks engrossed in a penny-ante poker game, there was electricity in the stale, heavy air. Both duty sections had been granted liberty, leaving only those on restriction and those unlucky enough to draw the gangway watches.

It was something like the aftermath of a great battle.

"What time you got?" I asked, studying my cards.

"What difference does it make what time it is? We're stuck here."

"I think I should have been on that liberty list," I said casually.

"What about me?" After a minute or so, Cheesy looked up quickly and said, "You tryin' to be funny? You don't deserve bread and water."

Cheesy's thin, pinched of face turned accusingly on me. Sitting there in his starch-splotched and tattered dungarees and old dirty white T-shirt, he was the picture of hard luck and self-pity. "You *did* fuck up, you know. And all I did was git caught in your presence at the wrong time, for Pete's sake!" He slammed a card down. "Man, I gotta stop foolin' around with the likes of you!"

"Go ahead," I said calmly and raised two fingers. "Hit me."

"I mean you're bad luck, Red. I get classified with you and I'll never get ashore ag'in."

"Like I told you, Cheesy. You go your way and I'll go mine."

"I'd appreciate it if you'd stop callin' me that."

"Then stop calling me *Red*. What time you got?"

From the forward end of the quarters Ensign Hargschriemer called out, "Either one of you on the gangway?"

"No, Sir!" called out Cheesy, without looking up.

The shavetail ensign was suddenly standing over us. "How about you, Red?"

"You heard the man," I said casually.

When I glanced up, Mr. Hargscriemer, a brand-new graduate of the Academy, was glaring at me.

"What's that, sailor?" he snapped, his face beginning to turn red. "What did you say to me? I didn't catch that."

"Don't you have a copy of the duty roster, Sir?" I asked, innocently. My hands were poised above the pot for Cheesy to show his cards.

But Cheesy's mouth had dropped open, and he was staring at me in disbelief.

"There you go ag'in, Red!" he whispered, hiding his mouth behind his cards. "Why can't you just once—!" Noticing that Ensign Hargscriemer had turned and was staring at him, he jumped off the bunk and stood at attention, facing the officer. "Uh, I don't know, Sir, who's on the gangway, Sir. Mebbe Delancy—"

"Stow it, Macklin!" snapped Hargschriemer. "I wasn't addressin' you!" Just as Cheesy slumped back to the bunk, he yelled, "Stand at attention, sailor!"

I took my time about laying the cards down and getting up; but Cheesy once again leaped off the bunk and stood rigid before the officer, his thin, excited chest puffed outward. His eyes, however, were glued on me.

"Not you, Macklin! Hall, you're on report!"

"Yes, Sir," I agreed, still speaking in a casual voice. "I shore am."

"You're on report for insubordination."

"I do believe that is one of the complaints pending 'gainst me, Sir."

"You some kind of glutton for punishment, sailor?" Hargschriemer demanded. "You *want* another Captain's Mast?" His face was now brick red, and he had begun tossing his hands in exasperation.

I motioned to Cheesy to return to his seat and resume playing. Then, as if I were speaking to a good friend, I said to the second most recent arrival on the ship, "Well, not exactly, Suh." I swung my legs off the bunk and stood up, facing the pasty-faced ensign. "But I am rather anxious to hear just what you're goin' to say at this Captain's Mast. Are you goin' to tell the Skipper you came into the enlisted quarters and asked that stupid question? Cheesy here heard it, too, you know. Are you going to admit that your were out of uniform and unaware of who was assigned to the gangway watch?"

Hargschriemer was perhaps a year or two older than me, but I knew for a fact that he was an ensign straight out of New London, Connecticut, with no sea duty on his record at all. During the war he had worked in the packaging and mailing division of his father's shoe business.

And he was, at his tender age, an alcoholic.

"That," said Hargschriemer, "will be about enough out of you. Get up on that gangway watch!"

"What time you got, Cheesy?" I asked, turning to the terrified ex-quartermaster and ignoring the officer altogether.

The ensign wheeled and barreled off, his back stiff with resolve. Cheesy, letting out a chest of air, fell back on his bunk. "Man, if you don't beat anythin' I ever seen in my whole life! Don't you know that officer'll be on *my* tail from here on out? I wish I had never laid eyes on you!"

"Tell you what," I said, looking him in the eye. "How about you and I mosey over to San Pablo after awhile and find out what's goin' on at that big Saturday night hillbilly dance there? Wouldn't you like to mix with civilians tonight?"

Cheesy began to choke and shake his head vigorously.

"You do have the wherewithal for a liberty, don't you?"

"You talkin' 'bout tonight, Looney Toons?"

"I shorely am. Where's my hat? You in—or out?"

Again Cheesy let out a chest full of air. "What are you talkin' 'bout? You got some idee about gettin' off this scow and goin' on liberty? You're on the gangway watch, you're restricted to the ship, you don't have a liberty chit or gate pass, and now you're on report!"

"Nah, I'm not on report. Yet. We're going to San Pablo," I said, looking beneath my pillow. "I'm pretty sure I can get off this island. Where's my cap?"

"Man, that fuckin' officer's probably up there right now puttin' you on report—and you talkin' about liberty!"

"You in or out, ole buddy?"

"It don't make no never mind, anymore," said Cheesy, his voice beginning to break. "I'm a cooked goose anyway. You got a plan?"

"Yeah, well, this is still a free world you know. We're not prisoners of war."

"Hah! That won't even git us off the ship."

I crossed the quarters to the forward hatch, without looking back. Cheesy, grumbling, followed at a safe distance.

"Feel that magic in the air?" I said over my shoulder.

"What magic? All I feel is butterflies down around my navel."

"Hear that hillbilly music? Smell that poontang?"

Cheesy waited until we were topside at the gangway before saying, "I feel nothin' and I shore as hell don't smell no poontang! What I do smell is impendin' doom—for you, you Southern fried looney."

The afternoon sun had lost its hold upon the peaceful docks and the row upon row of olive drab quonset huts on Government Island. Chow call was being piped over he PA system at the base, but there was not a sign of life anywhere. The crews the CGC *Taney* and the CGC *Escanaba*, which was tied up astern of us, had already crossed the narrow bridge from Government Island into East Oakland, most of the partiers on their way to *Ted and Roy's.*

When we reached the quarterdeck, I went to the narrow, recessed shelf where the ship's log was lying open and lifted the tethered duty pencil from its slot. "Let me map out the evenin' for you, Cheesy, old boy," I said, brandishing the pencil as though I planned to sketch out my scheme in the official logbook. For a moment Cheesy poised over that sacred text in an attitude both curious and animated. He was certain I was about to commit some foul misdeed.

"You better not write *my name* in that book!"

"When Hargschriemer passes out—" I began, looking up.

"You're nuts!" howled Cheesy. "What makes you think he's goin' to pass out?"

"As I was saying, when our esteemed leader passes out, we'll go down and put on our undress whites." I looked disapprovingly at Cheesy. "Before that, even as we speak, you'd better jump into the shower, get at least one layer of whatever that is off you. Then we'll secure the help of a friend of mine, borrow some transportation, and depart this island paradise."

"Oh, no, we aint! Not me! No, no! Not on your life! Not in a million years! Man, you gotta be crazy!" He kept looking about as if he expected trouble already, even before we had made a move.

"What part of the plan do you object to? Is it the shower that's botherin' you?"

"Hell, no!" he snorted. "It's the whole thing! You ready to spend the next ten years on Mare Island that's botherin' me!"

"At the very worst," I cajoled, "you'd lose a stripe. What's your rating right now, Cheesy?"

"Apprentice seaman. I used to be a Quartermaster Third Class, before I met you!"

"Well, there you are. You're now as low as anybody can get. If they busted you any farther, you'd be a civilian."

Cheesy glared about suspiciously, bending his nose and snerfing at what he considered a most cruel and unjust world. "On the CGC *Alert*," he whined pathetically, "I was a member of the bridge gang but now, after one liberty with you, I'm in the deck gang of the worst ship in the entire Coast Guard. Oh, how I hate this hooligan outfit!" After a pause, he added, "But, Red, I signed up for a four-year hitch. They'd never let me out!"

"You've got three years to go. I know, you told me." I turned from the log and started to put my arm around his shoulder, but thought better of it. "Would you like to go back to your old job with your papa's cheese factory?"

With flared nostrils and head wagging energetically, Cheesy burst out, "Durn right I would! I didn't know when I had it real good!"

"One more little court martial would send you straight home. You might get there in time to win back that wife that left you."

"It'd be my luck to git sent back to boot camp."

I turned to the log book and began writing. Cheesy leaned in close to see what I was doing. Suddenly, he burst out, "What's that you're writin' in the Book?" His voice was painful to my ears. "Don't you put *my* name in that thing!"

Ignoring him, I said, "But, as I see it, we've still got one little problem."

"I don't want to hear what it is—because I aint gonna have anythin' to do with your scheme."

"What we need is some kind of pass to get us through that gate. One of us has got to make a trip to Personnel, right over there." I pointed toward the nearest quonset building on the island.

"Huh! Don't look at me! I'm restricted to the ship."

"But just about now the ensign is going to turn on his music."

"What does that have to do with anything?"

"That is his way of blocking out the world. His door will be bolted and he will be there until he comes out of it in the morning. Keep an ear tuned in his direction."

Suddenly, from Officer's Country came the banging of drums and loud drinking music. I grasped Cheesy by a bony shoulder and turned him toward the gangplank. "Go over to Personnel and see if Goodrich is still in the office. Remember Gooch? Think Humphrey Bogart in undress whites. Tell him you and I need something to get us through that gate. A letter maybe, on *Taney* stationery, if possible. Tell him I said we'll leave it up to him to figure something out. He owes me one. Tell him that. Remind him that I could ruin him back home if he lets me down. When he gets mad, tell him I was just kiddin'."

Cheesy was shaking his head all through this, and when the crossed the gangway he was still shaking his head. His last intelligible words were, "But when I do this I'm hittin' the sack!"

I stood for a time facing across the gangplank. A white Jeep was parked to the left of it. I had never seen anyone drive that vehicle, except the enlisted man who delivered it from Transportation each time the *Taney* tied up at G. I. That it was gassed up and in tiptop condition I had no doubt, and what a shame it was that nobody ever took it out for a spin.

It had a fresh coat of glossy white enamel, and on the strip of metal below the windshield were the letters *O O D*, in brilliant red.

"Hmmm," I said, stepping upon the gangplank. "I wonder—"

As if drawn by a magnet, I crossed the gangplank and circled it, seeing (actually looking at) it up close for the first time. I noticed that the key was missing from the ignition switch and that little puddles of water remained in the floorboard from a recent wash. The deck gang, I knew, kept the thing very clean against the possibility that the O. O. D. might wish to drive over to the Personnel Office, a distance of less than half a city block.

While I was still examining that white beauty, Cheesy came rushing across from Personnel to inform me that Goodrich had flatly refused to write anything, and so (Cheesy was wearing a tentative grin) my little scheme was kerflut.

I took him by the shoulders and faced him back toward Personnel. "Now, don't you take him seriously. We're hometown buddies and he's not about to refuse me anything. That was just his way of saying, Okay, give me ten minutes. I want you to go back over there and wait around until he hands you the pass."

"Red, he's not going to do it."

"Sure he is. Tell him we're headed for the Okie dance in San Pablo, and he's invited."

On his way, Cheesy screamed over his shoulder, "What's wrong with you? You know it's against regulations for the gangway watch to be on the dock! Or anywhere else but on the ship."

Without raising my voice, I said, "Now, don't you worry about that. Let me see if I have the key to this fine automobile. I started around the ring (that went with the job of gangway watch) and found it at once.

I hardly had time to reach my post back aboard the *Taney* when here came Cheesy, followed at a respectable distance by Goodrich. Neither of them asked permission to come aboard or saluted the Union Jack. Gooch's first words were:

"There's no way I will aid and abet criminals one day before the Sabbath."

"Then you're on report," I said. "For failing to ask permission to come aboard and, most seriously, for refusing to salute our Jack."

None of this, of course, had any effect on my old hometown buddy.

"You would never get away with it, and then I'd be brought in on it."

"That's where you're wrong. Listen, besides the liberty chits we'll need something to get us through that gate—with that Jeep." I nodded across the gangplank.

Goodrich and Cheesy turned and stared at the Duty Jeep as if it had just materialized out of thin air.

"You try something like that and you will surely be sent home in disgrace," said Goodrich. His tragic, droopy eyes suddenly popped open: "So that's it. You want a court martial, not a piddling little old Captain's Mast. You want to go back to Garner's Pool Hall and pick up right where you left off. Why don't you get Archer to go along with you?"

"Listen, you will not be implicated in this. You owe me, you know."

"I don't owe you that much."

He was weakening, no doubt about it.

"Listen, be sure to write something believable on *Taney* stationery that'll get us through the main gate. And don't forget to sign Gorman's name to it. Will you do it, old buddy?" When he said nothing but just stared at me, I yelped, "Okay! I won't forget it! And while you're doing that, I'll check on old Hargey." I turned to leave, then added, "Maybe you could say something about taking the Jeep out for repairs. You'll think of something."

Cheesy followed after me, complaining that I had completely lost my marbles and that he was not going to have anything else to do with me.

"You're already in this thing, mate," I assured him. "Now, keep it down. That ensign might still be conscious." We entered the port hatch into Officer Country and stood for a time listening. From behind Hargschriemer's door came the soft strains of a very old and sad song.

"What're we listenin' for?" asked Cheesy.

"The music to stop," I hissed. "He plays LP records. When the music stops and doesn't start up again, we'll know he's out cold."

"We could be here all night."

But within minutes the music stopped and did not start up again (We gave it a couple of minutes to be sure), we left quietly the same way we had got there. Goodrich was nowhere to be seen; so I knew he was over at Personnel getting us fixed up. I had had no real doubts about that boy.

"For this event," I said to Cheesy, "we'd better wear our dress blues."

"I can't. Mine still has the petty officer patch on the shoulder."

"You'll be forgiven."

When Goodrich showed up, carrying a long white envelope, I said, "The plan is to put on our dress blues, drive the Jeep to the gate, show the watch our papers, and head on down to *Ted and Roy's*. You'll follow as soon as you can, afoot since you don't want to be associated with us."

"I'm also not any part of this forged document."

"If you're not at the rendezvous point by nine o'clock, my passenger and I will proceed without you. Is that understood?"

"Listen, Red, I'd like to go to San Pablo and take in that hootin' an' hollerin' at Maple Hall with you, but I met a real nice girl here awhile back an' I'm spendin' all my shore time with her. She's a nurse in Oakland. Pretty soon I'll come up for promotion, and—"

"Nine o'clock, old buddy."

With the letter were two liberty chits. I placed these in one of my peacoat pockets, dropped the ring of keys on the watch desk, and tripped across the gangplank. Goodrich was right behind me.

"You really think you'll get past the Main Gate? More than likely they'll arrest you. But if by some miracle you make it off G. I., do you actually believe you can traipse all over the Bay Area and make it back here before the O. O. D. of this ship wakes up?"

"You know what they say. *Que sera sera.*"

When I did not try to argue with him, he added, "And when you get caught, I'm going to categorically deny any knowledge or involvement in this thing. Besides, who would believe you if you claimed that a respectable yeoman from the Base stole *Taney* stationery, wrote that lie, and signed Commander Gorman's signature to it? Cheesy, evidently, aint going with you. Smart boy."

"Yes, he is. He just needs a little more urging. Besides, this paper specifically includes him and will get us both through. By the way, Archer will give me hell when I show up without you."

Goodrich laughed, "You never miss a bet! You would lie to my face to get me to go along! You have no idea what he's doin' tonight."

"He's meeting us at *Ted and Roy's* on or before nine. Do you think I would stick around that dump just for you?"

As soon as Goodrich left, headed for the sack, I got into the Jeep. After a time, here came Cheesy.

"Okay, I'll go with you. What've I got to lose? But I know we'll never git across that bridge. They'll probably take us straight to the nearest brig." He got in beside me, peering around the steering wheel. "The key's missin', right? So I guess that'll put an end to your little scheme."

I stuck the key beneath his nose. "I am the official *Taney* gangway watch, you know. And as such I have access to all the ship's keys when the O. O. D. is incapacitated."

I inserted the key and turned it. The engine came alive with a roar.

"San Pablo, here we come!"

I straightened myself in the driver's seat and took the steering wheel in both hands, like an amateur. "How do you put this thing in reverse?" I ground some gears, found first, and the Jeep began to climb the piling that separated us from the strip of water between the dock and the *Taney*.

"Owwwww!" screamed Cheesy, bracing himself. "Don't you know how to drive this thing?"

"Well, I know it has forward gears and reverse gears. At least that's what somebody told me."

Cheesy stood up, holding onto the windshield and peering over the dockside at the strip of water just a few feet away. I eased the Jeep into reverse and backed us far out away from the cutter. Goodrich had stopped and was enjoying my silliness; but poor old Cheesy, as soon as he realized he had been taken, put his mouth to my right ear and yelled, "You know, it's a curious thing to me why a guy like you ever needs to go to a bar to git drunk. You haven't had a drink in at least a week but you're actin' like you're dog drunk!"

"And you're way too serious, my friend. Lighten up."

The Jeep zipped across the asphalt in the direction of the Main Gate, with Cheesy hanging onto his hat.

"This is never going to work!" he wailed, as we slowed for the gateway watch. "Why did I let myself get mixed up in this thing? They'll take one look at that piece of paper and we'll be in the brig!"

The gate watch, in dungarees and a dyed golfball cap and carrying a clipboard and a pencil on a string, emerged from the small building at the main gate. From inside the sounds of a baseball game issued.

"Who's playin'?" I asked, faking profound interest.

"Let me see your authorization, mate," snapped the watch, obviously anxious to get back to his game.

I took my time with the folded page of paper, taking it from the envelope with careful deliberateness and handing it over almost reluctantly. Then, just as the swab's hand was about to clamp onto it, I pulled it back to see if it was right side up.

"Give it to me!" he snapped. "No need of takin' all night!"

"Sorry to take you away from your game."

"Never mind about that. This says you are taking a prisoner to Mare Island. This him?" The watch turned and looked suspiciously at Cheesy.

"Geez!" burst Cheesy, squirming uncomfortably. "Red—!"

That information had also given me a start. It had not occurred to me to peruse what Goodrich had concocted to get us past the Gate! What else could be in that letter? I felt like leaping out of the Jeep and chasing him down. No doubt he was out there in the darkness watching!

However, without batting an eye, I grinned stupidly and nodded. I could just see my former buddy back there laughing his ass off. "Yeah, this is him. Mean sonofabitch, actually. Struck an officer."

"No shit?" The gate watch was visibly impressed. "He don't look very mean."

Cheesy, red-faced, began to climb out of the Jeep, the words he was screeching coming so fast it was impossible to make much out of them. I reached up and clamped onto his baggy pants and pulled him back to his seat, calling out to the watchman as I do so:

"Hey, buddy, could you give me a little help here? You got any cuffs?"

"I've got some nylon rope inside the shack," he said, slamming Cheesy brutally back into his seat. "Here, hold him down till it git it."

"All right all right all right!" Cheesy began to scream, thrashing. "I knew I should've never mixed myself up in this business with you!"

When the gate watch came back with the cord, I said, "Better tie him good. He's one devious sonofagun."

"He sure don't look it," repeated the watch, shaking his head. "But you just can't go by looks anymore."

Cheesy was saying over and over, "No! No! No! No!"

When we had the prisoner securely bound and anchored to the Jeep, the watch, having forgotten his ball game, said in a neighborly tone, "When do you expect to make it back, mate?"

"Oh, I really can't say, to be frank with you. It could take till two or three in the mornin'. Mare Island's a long way from here, you know. And then there's the redtape."

The watch nodded, sympathetically. "Well, good luck."

Cheesy, quiet at last, glared around at the scenery. He was frothing a bit at the corners of his mouth.

"If you make it back before say eleven, bring me a slug of something," said the watch. "I've been on this island for a week without a thing."

"You got it. Catch you later, buddy."

I eased the Jeep into gear and we went on across the bridge. I could feel the eyes of the watchman following us. Cheesy was sitting straight and uncomfortable and looking dead ahead through glazed eyes. When we finally cleared the bridge and made the left turn at the intersection, he screamed, "Red!"

"Hey, man, that was the only way I could get us out of there!" I complained, faking shock at his attitude. "Goodrich threw a curve with that statement about taking a prisoner out. I swear to God I didn't know anything about that."

"Well, pull over and take this crap offen me."

"Let us wait just a bit. With you loose we might look suspicious in an O. O. D. Jeep. *Ted and Roy's* is right around the corner down there."

"Dad blame it!" shouted Cheesy. "I mean now! I don't want to be seen thisaway!"

"Now don't get your bowels in an uproar! It's right down there!" I brought the Jeep in to the curb in front of an ancient sign that proclaimed, *Ted and Roy's*.

"Come on, Red! Move us away from here before somebody comes along! I don't want to be seen tied up like this!"

I removed the key from the ignition, hopped out onto the sidewalk, and headed for the door of the pub, leaving him with mouth ajar. Once inside, I stopped and peeped back around the door to see what my prisoner was doing. Cheesy had evidently scrunched down on the floorboard of the Jeep, but after a time I saw the top of his white golfball cap rising slowly above the door.

Ted and Roy's and the C & E Club, East Oakland, CA (July 4, 1948)

The Chase

◆

Just as I was turning away from the door, assured that Cheesy would be all right in the Jeep, two swabs from the *Taney's* bridge gang entered *Ted and Roy's*. They walked past me to the bar without a word and I followed, trying to be inconspicuous. I glanced at the clock behind Ted's head. Plenty of time for a draft or two before giving up on Archer. And Goodrich, too, for that matter. He would never be able to go to sleep knowing the two of us had gone to an Okie dance.

One of the two who had just entered was Whitey Blanton, a radarman that liked to gossip; and the other was a pale, thin kid named Carlin or something like that, also a member of the bridge gang of the *Taney*.

Blanton glanced at me and said, straight faced, "You know anything about the *Taney* Jeep outside?"

"Sure!" I said with a smile. That's my transportation tonight."

"Yeah, yeah! Wouldn't you like!" scoffed Carlin.

Blanton eyed me doubtfully but didn't say anything.

"I'm taking a prisoner to an Okie dance over in San Pablo."

"Shit, mate, you're not doin' anything of the kind," sneered Blanton, looking around for a table. "Come on, Carl, it's gettin' deep here."

"For one thing," said Carlin, looking disgusted, "there was no prisoner in that Jeep. And for another they would never turn it over to you for a second." He looked at Blanton for support.

"I thought you was smarter'n that, Carl," growled Blanton. "He's tryin' to make a joke."

"Oh, but there was a prisoner in that Jeep," I assured them. "Go take a closer look."

While Blanton scowled, Carlin scooted for the door.

"You're Hall," said the radarman. "Aint you restricted to the ship right now?"

"Now would I be in here sipping beer if I was?"

Carlin came rushing back. "He's right, Brian! There's a dad blamed prisoner in that Jeep."

"You boys in the mood for San Pablo tonight?" I asked. "I've got room for two passengers."

Blanton went to the door and peered out. When he came back, he said, "Come on, Harold, let's move over in that corner there out of harm's way. In about a minute this place is gonna be swarmin' with SP's."

"All right, you're not invited then," I said with a laugh.

Suddenly, Curly Bill Archer was standing beside me, grinning and nodding. "What's that Jeep doin' outside?" he asked, settling on the stool Blanton had vacated. "You wouldn't have anything to do with it, would you?"

I caught Ted's eye and nodded, pointing at my beer and lifting two fingers.

"I have proper authorization for that vehicle!" I said, lifting my glass. "Here's to life, liberty, and the pursuit."

Goodrich, shaved and slicked down, showed up at Archer's elbow, looking a bit spooked. He had evidently overheard my remark about the Jeep. "And I was the one that gave it to him!"

The other owner of the place, Roy, was standing in front of us eyeing me suspiciously. "People are tellin' me you swiped that pretty little white Jeep out front. That true? If so, I reckon we won't be seein' much of you around here for awhile."

I pretended to be taken aback at his words. "I didn't steal that Jeep! Ask these fellows. Stealing is wrong."

"Well, I just don't want no ruckus in here tonight. When they come for you, leave peacefully."

I set my stein down and started for the door, saying over my shoulder, "Since Roy doesn't want us in here, fellows, let's hit the road." I went out, did a double-take and whirled, pushing Archer back into the room. Goodrich collided with him.

"Back me up!" I said. "Whatever I say, nod and agree. Got that?" I turned back toward the door and we filed outside.

Standing on the sidewalk peering down into the front seat of the Jeep were two white-helmeted Navy Shore Patrol. Cheesy, his face a pale green in the light that glared down from the *Ted and Roy's* sign, was looking back at them from the floorboard of the Jeep.

When I walked up, one of the SP's asked, "What is this man doing, tied up here in front of this—bar?"

"He's my prisoner," I admitted, removing the wrinkled and soiled envelope from beneath my blouse. It had slid out upon the bar a few minutes before into some beer suds and was a bit damp. "This is where I apprehended him, after he leaped from the vehicle. I never frequent such places, myself. But as I turned the corner down there, the prisoner, after giving his word to me that he would behave himself, jumped out and ran down the street to this miserable den of iniquity."

He took the sheet of paper, frowning, and handed it to the other SP, who produced a flashlight and held the paper up for closer scrutiny. "I suggest you get on your way," he said, not unkindly. "Do you need some assistance?"

"As a matter of fact," I said, I could use some handcuffs." When the one with the flashlight shook his head and lowered his eyebrows, I hastily added, "Perhaps I could talk these two fellows here into assisting me. They're off my ship."

"Good. Well, better be on your way."

"Maybe you've got an extra armband," suggested Archer.

I vigorously erased that and hustled my two friends into the backseat of the Jeep. "We surely will be on our way. And thanks a lot, fellas."

All the time I was getting the prisoner to calm down and the Jeep started, those two fine-looking Shore Patrol watched critically. Archer, who never knew when to keep his mouth shut, called out, "I don't reckon he'll get away from the three of us, mates!"

I eased the Jeep out into traffic, saying under my breath, "Keep it down!" Once we were out of sight of *Ted and Roy's* and the SP's, I floorboarded the Jeep and headed east on East Fifteenth Street, hoping I would find the highway to Richmond and San Pablo, eventually.

Long before this was to happen, however, I became acutely aware that our vehicle needed some serious attention. I pulled in at a Shell service station.

"What's up?" asked Gooch. "Is this a liquor joint?"

I began to remove the nylon cord from Cheesy, who had begun to blubber pathetically. An attendant angled over toward us from the two-car garage attached to the station and asked if he could help us with something.

"I want out," said Cheesy.

To the attendant, I said, "Two things. My tail lights seem to have a short in them, and could you tell me how to get to the highway to Richmond?"

"If you think I'm gonna go with you, Red, you've got another thought comin'."

"Two blocks the way you're heading and make a right. As for the lights, why don't you pull over to that empty slot at the garage?"

Cheesy had climbed out of the Jeep but as I eased toward the garage he kept up, assuring me that he was finished with me forever.

Before we left, with Cheesy back beside me in the front seat, the attendant, a quiet young man covered with grease, not only repaired the tail lights but filled the almost-empty gas tank and replaced a windshield wiper that was in threads.

"What do we owe you?"

"Just the gas is all I'll charge you for," he said apologetically. "That'll be three dollars even."

I stuffed a twenty into his outstretched hand and said, "Keep the change. Do you suppose you could forget that we paid you a visit this evening? In case somebody came along and asked."

"I will swear that I never saw a single white Jeep this whole night."

"If I live to be a hundred," said Goodrich, proudly, "I'll never figure out where ole Red gets all his money! I swear, we make as much as he does but he's the one that's always flush."

"Speaking of which," I said, maneuvering out upon the wide empty street, "we had better look for a package store or this party's on the rocks. I am not about to drink that stuff Archer's carrying around."

Two blocks down the street I spotted the Highway 80 sign and Goodrich spotted a package liquor store. Of course, the latter was located across the eight busy lanes of the former. Traffic had picked up considerably, but I managed to whip out upon the highway and do a wobbly-S maneuver across to a brightly-lighted one-gallus liquor store. "One of you stay with the prisoner," I said, leaping out.

"Hey!" yelled Cheesy. "I'm no prisoner anymore!"

"The hell you say," I barked over my shoulder. "We're deliverin' you to San Pablo. Dead or alive. Makes no never mind to me which."

"Aw, come on, Red!" he whined. "Cut it out!"

"I'll stay with him," said Goodrich, "if you'll git me a Red Dot."

Curly Bill, tearing happily, was right behind me. We entered the makeshift shack and found ourselves facing a large grinning woman.

"What'll it be, Mateys?"

The woman had a face rolling around on layers of fat; and once she had gotten our attention she retired and watched us from one corner of the room, her little Poland China eyes shining with the knowledge that part of the big roll in my blouse pocket was about to be hers.

"Just point me to-*wards* the bourbon likker," sang out Archer.

"Let's see," I said, "we'll need four pints of Four Roses."

"Well, all right!" laughed the lady. "You boys out on the prowl tonight?"

"I reckon," I nodded, grinning and looking her over as if I were really interested. "We're Coast Guard Seals. Been at the North Pole. Just got in."

"Oh, my!" she squealed, straightening up. "The North Pole?"

"You're the first woman we've seen in over a year," Archer confided.

"I do declare!" She got to her feet, sucked in her belly, and ceremoniously put a hand to her breast.

"Maybe you'd like to come along," I suggested, winking at Archer.

"Gawd I wish I could!" she screamed excitedly, plopping a bottle of brown liquor on the end of the counter for us to consider. "But I got an invalid husband at home and I caint leave him very long at a time."

"Aw, we wouldn't keep you away that long," pleaded Archer, pretending to be hanging upon her every word. He punched me in the ribs, "Better not keep this goin' much longer. She's beginnin' to weaken." He said this just above a whisper, turning his head so that the big lady couldn't see him. Then he turned and said to her, "I've slept with nothin' but walruses for a good year!"

"Listen, Honey!" she blasted, beginning to turn red. "I've got—"

"I didn't say you was a walrus!" Archer laughed, sidling toward the door. "Come on, Red Dog, I think she's lookin' for something to hurl." He opened the door, ready to dive for the street. "Ma'am, I saw a whale once that was sexier lookin' than you!"

Like two powerful black beacons the woman's little round eyes followed Curly Bill toward the door, and at the last second she raised her right hand high and flung something. It missed its mark but took out a shelf of knick-knacks not more than six inches from his head. On my way out I grabbed a handful of cigars and two pints of black-label bourbon that were on the counter. Bent double and moving quickly through the maze of narrow aisles, I stuffed these into my peacoat pockets.

"Keep the change, Ma'am," I sang out, tossing a ten-dollar bill in the air above my head. "You have a nice evenin', you hear?" At the open doorway, but still not entirely out of harm's way, I yelled back, "I personally think you're better looking than a walrus!"

The woman was scanning the shelves for something cheap she could throw as I slammed the door to behind me.

At the Jeep I handed the cigars and bourbon to Goodrich. "When will I ever learn to leave that kinky-haired nut back there at home?" I started up the Jeep, accepted back one of the bottles, which he had opened and was shoving at me, and backed us out of the parking space. "I swear, he does not know how to behave around ladies."

Archer leaned from the back seat and said, "You know what they say about that." He was grinning like a possum eating peach seeds. "That was no *lady.*"

I drove with my foot on the floor all the way to Richmond. Cheesy had finally taken a sip from one of the bottles but had refused another until somebody let him pay his fair share. Archer responded not at all to this line of reasoning, and Goodrich refused to accept money for the booze on the grounds that it did not belong to him.

*   *   *

The parking lot at the Maple Hall Emporium was full, and for a good mile in every direction cars and half-ton trucks lined the streets and avenues. I drove up and down every lane, but all slots were filled and nobody was leaving.

"Park this thing!" complained Curly. "The night is gettin' away from us! Man, there are loose women in there just waitin'!"

"Yeah," agreed Gooch. "But not for the likes of you."

"All right," I said, "you want to park that bad?" I stopped the Jeep at the front end of a row of vehicles. "Get out and move one of those pickups out of my way." While my three passengers thought this over, I added, "And make sure said pickup is far enough away so the driver won't know for sure who got his place."

After a bit of mumbling and grumbling, the three of them got out and eased a big Chevy four-by-four out of its space and down the aisle of vehicles about two hundred feet. People were coming and going, and there were little knots of men sharing bottles at the tailgates of several pickups, but nobody paid any attention to them. I whipped the Jeep into the slot, ceremoniously took the key from the ignition, and climbed out. Goodrich was standing in the center of the aisle waiting for me.

"You just can't do anything legal, can you?" he said.

"Weren't you one of the ones that wanted to park right now?"

Cheesy came up carrying a paper sack.

"What's that?" I asked, suspiciously.

"A bottle," he said. "It was right there in the seat of that Chevy, behind the steering wheel."

"Take it back, stupid. Now, that would make somebody mad."

"What kind is it?" asked Curly, coming up.

"It doesn't matter what kind it is!" I snapped. "Take it back. We can afford to buy our own likker." While the matter was being studied, I added, "I just don't want to make somebody mad at us."

"Since when did you become sensitive about somebody getting mad at us?" asked Curly, innocently. "Hey, Cheesy, give me a slug of that before you put it back."

At that point I glanced at Cheesy. He was standing with his shoulders raised up around his ears, shivering.

"Where's your coat?"

Cheesy moaned pitifully, "I think it blew out of the Jeep. You drove awful fast, Red."

"Give me that bottle, Half-wit. Since you don't have a coat to put it in, I'll have to hang onto it for you."

It was nearing midnight, which meant that most of the urban cowgirls would already be inside, looking for men. From the blast of noise that issued from the PA system and the big double front doors, the entire countryside was suddenly made aware of the fact that Bob Wells and His Texas Playboys were about to commence *The Rose of San Antone.*

"Come on!" I said, "I want to hear that up close."

At the ticket window Cheesy reluctantly shelled out twenty dollars for the cover charge. Then the four of us filed through the big double doors to the checkout counter. Taking my peacoat off, I caught the eye of a slender blonde, and offered it to her. When she reached for it, I said, "Would you handle this gingerly? Hold it right side up. There's—"

"Yes, I know. I'll take care of it for you, Sailor." She grabbed it from me and, when it sagged to the counter, she began laughing. To the other girl working there she said, "Would you believe this? There's got to be at least a gallon in this one!"

"Yeah, well," I said, nodding, "just you remember that. And don't let any of it get away."

It was shoulder-to-shoulder inside, and the noise was deafening. I led the way down the left side of the dance floor toward the bandstand. Tommy Duncan was crooning and Bob Wells, grinning broadly, his huge white Stetson pushed back on his head, was putting in an occasional high-pitched "Ah, *ha!*" at the right places.

When the music stopped, I said to Goodrich, "Why do we go to so much effort to put ourselves through this? Neither of us likes to dance, and you know as well as I do Curly is the only one that's going to find a woman."

"Look," he said sadly, pointing, "he's already found one."

So the three of us sat there watching Archer move about the floor, dancing with one girl after another. On two occasions we worked our way back past the coat room, picked up the peacoats and booze, and went out to the parking lot. We were sitting in the Jeep passing the bottle when Archer finally staggered out and began to look for us. We watched with interest while he went up and down between the rows of vehicles, looking neither to the right or the left. I commented on his inability to see more than three feet in front of him, and Goodrich mentioned the miracle that had got him past the eye test back in Oklahoma City.

When we finally could not sit there and watch any longer, I eased the Jeep out of its slot and we began to follow him. When he suddenly whirled and almost ran into us, I leaned out and asked if he wanted a ride or did he prefer to hitch-hike back to the tug.

Somewhere between San Pablo and Richmond the tail lights on the Jeep began to flicker again. Without consulting the others, I decided to beeline it back to G. I. It was getting quite late, and some of my go-to-hell attitude had disappeared. And, although I knew it was a remote possibility, I began to think I just might be able to return the Jeep to its parking space beside the *Taney* before the O. O. D. came out of his stupor.

We were almost to the outskirts of Oakland when Archer tapped me on the shoulder and calmly asked, "What's that astern of us?"

I peered into the rearview mirror.

Goodrich, who had taken Cheesy's place in the front with me, turned and peered between Curly Bill and Cheesy. "Looks like the Law to me. I believe it's the Oakland Police."

Archer did not even bother to look. He said, casually, "I wonder what's on his mind? We're not speeding or anything, are we?"

I had the Jeep floorboarded, which on a level stretch of highway translated into about sixty miles an hour. Thinking, logically, that the police might not be interested in us (After all, we were not civilians), I began to change lanes, putting as many vehicles between us as possible.

Even at one o'clock in the morning the traffic was heavy.

Goodrich then contributed, "I'd swear a California State Highway Patrol has nudged in right behind that Oakland City Police."

"They're not after us," I said. "Neither one of them has turned on a red light."

"Let me out of the vehicle," said Cheesy, who had evidently done some serious sobering up in the past couple of minutes. "I'm no part of this illegal operation."

"My guess is they're just cruisin'," I said. "They may suspect something but they don't know a thing."

"They know we're speedin'," said Goodrich. "Of course, we're not going any faster than anybody else on this road."

I had decided that I would do a left at the next intersection, to test the waters. If they continued on, we were in the clear and could back track and go on to *Ted and Roy's*, where I planned to dump my passengers.

"Hold onto your hats!" I called out. We were coming up fast on an intersection, and we had the green left-turn signal. "In about ten seconds we'll know whether"!"

We were not in the left-turn lane, but at the last possible moment I whipped the Jeep to the left and we went careening around onto Lexington Avenue. Nobody was behind us! I opened my mouth to shout, "Hallelujah!"

"Hoh, oh! Hold it!" moaned Goodrich. "If I'm not badly mistaken, there's a Navy Shore Patrol behind us now!"

Almost before he got that out of his mouth, Cheesy added, "Yeah, and that Holstein has fallen in behind him, *with his red light on!*

"You know what this means, don't you, Red?" cried Curly.

"Yeah," I said, dryly. "It means I've got to drop you three someplace real fast."

"Hah!" yelled Goodrich. "Like where? With two carloads of constabulary behind us?"

"Three," corrected Cheesy. "The Oakland Police is back on our trail! Slow down and I'll jump!"

I had a vague idea where we were, but I knew for sure that we were a long way from East Fifteenth Street. "Hang on!" I yelled, taking a right on two wheels into a residential neighborhood. At an intersection I saw a street sign. We were on Purvis Boulevard, which, I knew, ran through a black section of the city.

"There's only one member of the constabulary behind us now!" shouted Goodrich.

My last maneuver had caught the Oakland Police and the Highway Patrol by surprise, causing them to shoot on past the turn; but the Shore Patrol vehicle, also a white Jeep, roared around the corner and came barreling after us. I knew that Purvis eventually cut down past Government Island, and I also knew that I would have to do some wild maneuvering into back alleys and down one-way streets if I hoped to let my Coastie buddies off in the clear.

"How could he be gainin' on us?" complained Archer. "He's in a Jeep and we're in a Jeep!"

"He's in a better Jeep," observed Goodrich. "It's probably souped up. This thing is ready for the boneyard."

It was true that on every straight away the SP Jeep was narrowing the distance that separated us.

From Purvis we cut down a narrow side street that, I thought, would take us near *Ted and Roy's*; and for a moment it appeared that we had gained some valuable distance on the Shore Patrol.

"Hey, Red, did you see that sign back there?" asked Goodrich.

"What sign?" I yelled. The street was deserted for four blocks ahead of us, and as of that second there was no one behind us.

"That *One Way* sign."

"Hey!" I laughed, riding high on a burst of adrenaline, "that explains why the *gendarmes* are no longer behind us!" The truth was until that moment I had no idea we had taken the wrong direction on a one-way street.

"Yeah, well, Hot Shot, you'd better look ag'in!"

Seeing traffic approaching ahead, I whipped to the left down an alley and took a right on another one-way street, this time straight for *Ted and Roy's*. A block away from that oasis I swerved the Jeep in close to the curb and stopped, in front of an abandoned building. "All right, mates, this is where you get off! *Ted and Roy's* is right down that street!"

Goodrich went first. I slapped his outstretched hand. "I'll catch you later!" Archer was airborne when our hands met, and Cheesy went over the back, waving and yelling:

"I'll visit you once a month!"

My plan was to do some maneuvering through back streets, coming out near the bridge. My adrenaline was zinging along a mile a minute. The truth was I had never felt better in my life!

The Jeep and I roared down one street and up another and, and only occasionally did I catch sight of a white Jeep behind me, sometimes headed in the opposite direction. And, believe it or not, we (the Jeep and I) actually made it to the G. I. bridge without a tail, and I thought what a hoot it would be if I could get across and return it before all that stuff caught up with me.

But it was not meant to be. Before I was halfway across I saw in my rearview mirror a most saddening spectacle, the other white Jeep whipping around a corner on two wheels and straightening out behind me, in full pursuit!

Then, ahead of me at the Main Gate of Government Island, I saw another heart-stopper. Four swabs in undress blues wearing SP armbands had fanned out across the road and were crouching on one knee! And each of them had what appeared to be a short-barreled shotgun aimed in my direction!

I slowed the Jeep to a snail's pace, which seemed the appropriate thing to do under the circumstances. Huge spotlights and floodlights had been rigged especially for this occasion, evidently, because I could not remember ever having seen the place so bright, even in the daytime. Some distance from the shotguns I stopped the Jeep and waited.

"Git out of the vehicle!" came a shout from the line of crouching swabs. "With your hands up!"

Then an enlisted man in dungarees and wearing an SP arm band and carrying a Navy Colt .45 in his right hand, rushed up to me and shouted, "Turn it off and git away from the vehicle!"

"Listen," I protested, "I'm *returning* this Jeep, okay? It's in considerably better shape than when I borrowed it."

But no one wanted to discuss the issue. Immediately, everybody swooped in upon me. High brass in full dress uniforms, who had been waiting back in the shadows, and SP's in tailormade dress blues were soon joined by the Oakland Police and the California Highway Patrol. And in no time at all there was standing room only on the G. I. end of the bridge.

I was hauled roughly out of the Jeep and escorted to the gangplank of the· *Taney*, where Lt. Comdr. M. P. Hazelton, the ship's Executive Officer, was waiting to read me my rights. There, in the presence of two dozen swabs and officers, he said in a trembling voice:

"Hall, as of this moment you're restricted to the ship!" He was trembling with rage and seemed to be waiting for me to say something. "Who in hell do you think you are, steeling the *Taney's* Jeep?"

Ensign Hargschriemer, looking pale and drawn, was standing beside him. He leaned in and said quietly, "He was already restricted to the ship, Sir!"

The XO whirled and glared at the ensign. "You keep out of it! If you had been on the goddamned ball, he would never have gotten off with that Jeep in the first place!"

*   *   *

Two days later (It was a fine Tuesday morning) I was standing at one of the port'les in the ship's laundry watching Alcatraz Island go by when Cheesy showed up with a cardboard box. He had combed his hair and put on a clean tie-dyed T-shirt, but about him there was still a dead-horse odor.

"Thanks, buddy," I said, taking the box. "Did you manage to pick up everything I had on the list?"

"No problem. It's all there, including the Russian novels."

I nodded, backing away instinctively. "Now, I'm ready for twenty-six days of peace and quiet. No midwatches and no shit details."

Husbands appeared in the open hatchway, already talking before I was aware of him. "Well, you finally managed it, didn't you? You made them so mad they restricted you even while we're at sea. They're goin' to punish you by forcin' you to spend the entire weather watch in this terrible place, with only a stereo phonograph and a steady stream of friends to keep you company. You don't get to scrape and red-lead the stack with me, you don't get to send all those weather messages back to Frisco, and, sorrow of sorrows, you'll miss out on Sparky's hour-long pep talks on the joys of serving under him."

"Yeah, aint it the shits?" I said with a grin.

"And another thing. You've got Limburger here to run errands for you, deliver food to you three or four times a day and keep you supplied with coffee."

"Actually, I don't think this is such a *terrible* place," argued Cheesy. "It's nice and warm in here, and it smells good."

"Speaking of which," I jumped in, taking another step backwards, "how about you scoot out of here? Check back in an hour, okay?"

After Cheesy left, Husbands pulled up a chair to my hastily-rigged desk and reached for a do-nut.

"Why is he at your beck-and-call all of a sudden?"

"I did him a favor the other night."

"You mean you saved him from a court martial by running off and leavin' him outside the gate without a pass?"

"Well, it seemed like the thing to do at the time."

"I understand Ensign Hargschriemer's bein' transferred because of that trip you took. The Exec told Sparky he went a bit lenient on you, gave you a Deck Court instead of a Summary Court, because you had brought to light what the ensign was doing while on O. O. D. watch."

I poured coffee into two big Navy mugs and handed one of them to Husbands.

"And, too, I practically overhauled that Jeep, put in a new tail light, had the headlights adjusted, got it lubricated, and brought it back in with a full tank of Ethel."

"You ought to be decorated."

The Norwegian Freighter

—————————— ◆ ——————————

In some ways my restriction to the laundry was the best thirty days of my Coast Guard career. It was, for the most part, quiet and private, which are two luxuries enlisted men in all branches of the Armed Services do not often enjoy. It is true that I had frequent visitors during the day, especially when nothing was going on topside, like drills; but there was plenty of time between these for me to read and write letters and nap. Cheesy never let me want for anything, and Husbands saw to it that my little valet didn't wear out his welcome.

Anyway, the twenty days went quickly and the first thing I knew we were on our way back to Frisco. When were only an hour or so from the Golden Gate, Cheesy showed up to tell me that I was free to leave the laundry and return to my quarters. With his help I immediately gathered up the sizable collection of things (books, magazines, two radios, a deck of cards and a chess set, a coffee pot, six mugs, bedding, clothing, and so on) which had accumulated during that month at sea and taken them to the crew's quarters.

Then Cheesy, Husbands, Ceccarelli, and I positioned ourselves along the port lifeline to watch Government Island take shape. Also tied up at the long dock were the Indian Cutter CGC *Chautauqua* and the much smaller air-sea rescue cutter the *CGC Yacona*.

On the bow of the former several enlisted men had assembled and were waving their hands, apparently at us.

"Something's going on," I said. "Nobody ever paid any attention to our arrival before."

"I'll bet they're waving at you, Red!" screeched Cheesy.

"Why, because I got thrown in the can for a month?"

"Because you defied the brass," said Husbands.

From the forward hatch behind us Janssen called out, "Guess what, Red!" I turned, startled at the tone of his voice. "Have you seen the liberty roster?"

"Hah," I said. "Why should I look at that?"

"Because you're on it." He put his arm over my shoulder. "Correct me if I'm wrong, but aren't you up for a Summary Court Martial?"

"Deck," I said. "Are you sure my name's on that thing?"

"No doubt about it. And Sparky told me to tell you you'd better get your ass off the ship in a hurry—before they discover their mistake!"

"You're sure now? No kiddin'?"

"I wouldn't kid about a thing like that. If you don't believe me, look at this!" He removed a folded sheet of paper from his shirt pocket.

It was a copy of the Duty-and-Liberty Roster. Below the official letterhead of the cutter were two columns of names, one labeled *The Duty Section* and the other *The Liberty Section*. And, sure enough, about a third of the way down on the latter, where it was not supposed to be, was my name!

"How could this be?" I marveled, handing the roster on to Husbands.

"Well," he laughed, "it's just a guess but I think Sears had something to do with it. He's good friends with the yeoman that types these up, and I happened to hear him saying something about you at the time that list was being typed up. Something about *balls*."

"Liberty Call will be sounded about fifteen minutes after we dock," said Janssen. "Better get a move on. The bridge gang's already laughing their asses off about this *snafu*, so the word will get around fast."

I dashed for the open hatchway, my mind whirling with *if's* and *maybe's*. If the O. O. D. or some other officer didn't take a close look at that roster. If no enlisted man inadvertently or otherwise gave me away. If I could just get across that gangplank and through the Main Gate! Just maybe I could turn this *snafu* into one hell of a final liberty. Before the long arm of the law got its clutches on me!

Perhaps it was, as Janssen thought, the work of Sears. But there was also the distinct possibility that the O. O. D., who just happened to be Ensign Hargscriemer's replacement, had failed to put me on report, since I had just spent thirty days of restriction in the laundry.

One thing for sure, somebody would be walking the plank for this.

I went below to the crew's quarters and laid out my undress blue uniform and a change of skivvies. The thought had occurred to me that I would have to work this thing just right—or that slip on the roster would not mean a thing. First, I would have to attend morning muster, which would occur shortly after the docking. Nobody would be allowed to leave the ship until that little ritual had been completed. If I put on my undress blues, the *liberty* uniform of the day at G. I., that might attract the attention of some officer who knew me personally. But then again it might merely suggest to those interested in my case that I was on my way to see the Captain. To be sure, somebody would be dispatched to get me very soon after muster—and I could not afford to be aboard ship when that happened.

I ran into the head and examined my face. My barely visible red stubble could wait until I was ashore, I decided; but I felt like garbage and needed a shower badly. It would have to be the fastest on record.

The radio gang was already lined up when I emerged onto the quarterdeck. I took my place between Husbands and Sears and kept my eyes straight ahead. The plan was to duck out of there as soon as the whistle piped the end of muster.

Husbands kept muttering something to me out of the corner of his mouth, but I paid him no attention. Just as I was about to bolt, Sears nudged me and said just loud enough for me to hear, "I say give 'em hell, Red. What do you have to lose? They won't bust you but one rank, and they're gonna do that anyway."

At that point, the boatswain's mate on duty blew his whistle and I headed for the gangplank, expecting my name to be announced over the PA system at any second. I paused for the gangway watch to check my name off the roster, and with a snappy salute to the O. O. D., I hopped onto the gangplank and saluted the fantail.

The short hair on the back of my neck was standing at attention as I scooted past the O. O. D. Jeep and other parked vehicles. But so far so good. I walked smartly but without any visible sign of hurry cross the grinder (a seemingly long stretch of no man's land on this occasion) to the row of barracks buildings. Then, turning a corner, I headed directly for the Main Gate.

I was wondering if the landline had been hooked up between the *Taney* and the Gate. With my heart in my throat, I lined up behind a Chief Boatswain's Mate with three rows of ribbons on his left breast. He was giving the gate watch a hard time. The kid, dressed in brand-new dungarees and more than likely straight from boot camp, had failed to salute some officer who had just driven through. Also, he had been too lax about checking out liberty chits, and he had a *smart-ass* look on his face that needed to be wiped off.

I waited, feeling my lower belly muscles tightening into knots.

"Listen, Chief—" I said, apologetically.

"Just a goddamned minute!" the Chief bellowed, whirling and giving me an icy scrutiny. "You assholes on the *Taney* think you ought to get special treatment here at G. I. Why is that?"

"Hey," I said with a shrug, tossing my hands in the air, "I'm from the *Chautauqua*."

"You tryin' to be funny, Mate?" he said, his voice a deadly purr suddenly. "Didn't you just come off the *Taney*?"

"Nope. Look, all I'm tryin' to do is get through this gate so I can go visit my sick old mother in East Oakland."

"Well, hell, why didn't you say so?" he said, hotly. And turning to the kid, he bellowed, "See if you can check this one out right!"

The bridge from G. I. was incredibly long on this occasion. I wanted to run but once I was through the gate I forced myself to walk normally. The thought occurred to me, as I reached the high point on the bridge, that I was making too much of this thing, that nobody of consequence on the *Taney* would care one way or the other whether I went on liberty or not.

Once I was out of sight of the Main Gate and only the masts of the *Taney* and the *Chautauqua* were still remained visible, I began to worry that the O. O. D. would dispatch someone in the Duty Jeep to pick me up. I would not be completely in the clear until I was our of east Oakland.

Across the street from *Ted and Roy's*, I caught a bus to the electric train stop near the Oakland-San Francisco Bay Bridge, feeling like an escapee from a maximum security prison. The adrenaline was working overtime, and the world was my oyster.

I had all day to reach Fisherman's Wharf, since Archer would be on duty until sixteen-hundred hours. On the electric, zipping across the Bay at fifty miles an hour, I worked our my itinerary: I would breakfast on Market, take a trolley car out to San Francisco State Park and spend some time on the beach, and, after lunching at one of the mobile fast-food huts, stroll over to the U. S. Marine Hospital and pay a visit to Georgio. Who knows, maybe I would run into Lilli.

＊　　　　　　＊　　　　　　＊

Archer, in dirty dungarees and wear an ancient golfball cap on the back of his head, was working over a huge pile of heavy lines, trying to remove the knots. He was apparently the only member of the tugboat crew on the pier; but tourists were all around him, either plugging quarters into the telescopes aimed at Alcatraz Island or standing over him watching what he was doing.

For a time I joined the tourists and listened to their corny questions and his whimsical answers. He did not look up, even when one of the tourists was right in his face. The fact was old Curly Bill's mind was someplace else, perhaps on the big night ahead. That is, providing Goodrich had heard about my escape from the Roger B. and relayed it to him.

Eventually, I said something and he looked up, startled.

"Well, hell, how long you been standin' there?" He stood up, tossing the line to the dock. "Come on, it's quitin' time." He stuck out his grimy hand and I refused it. The tourists backed away, smiling. They had just seen something but they weren't sure what.

"Goodrich said you would end up here. Did you actually jump ship?" He pushed me toward the gangplank of the tug. "Listen, tonight's on me and him, okay?"

Faking a heart attack, I said, "Either I heard wrong or the end of the world is at hand!"

"No shit." He was tearing badly and grinning like a drunk, but I knew he hadn't had a drink. "I got paid today. Give me a couple of minutes to get cleaned up." On the gangplank, he said, "I've got a bottle under my bunk. While I'm showerin', pour us a couple of slugs. I've already got the entire evening worked out."

"Does it include breaking the law in any way?"

The joke here, of course, was that Curly Bill was incapable of planning anything out, much less one of our evenings.

We went through the galley, where the cook was busy at a big coffee urn. He looked around briefly at Curly, then turned on me.

"Well, hell. How's the world been treatin' you, Red?"

"Never better. How's it going with you?"

"Not bad. How about some mud?"

"Don't let any of that stuff pass your lips, Red," advised Curly. "It'll corrode the lining of your stomach—"

"Just for that you'll get no breakfast in the mornin'," growled the cook. "O worthless one."

Ignoring him, Curly said to me, "Get two glasses and follow me."

The cook nudged me with his fat belly, "My favorite drink is Irish coffee, about half-and-half.

What's he got to offer?"

"I have no idea, but he's treating tonight and I dare not slight him."

I caught up with Archer, who handed me a pint bottle with a green label on it. I took one swallow of the foul stuff and handed it back, tearing. The evening was launched, and the fact that I was facing a court martial but somehow legally but very temporarily ashore on liberty made the possibilities seem enormous. While he showered and put on a uniform, I relaxed on a bunk and listened to him tell about the fifteen-day leave he had taken while I was in the laundry of the *Taney*.

"What was home like?" I asked when he was standing before me dressed and ready to go. "Did you see anyone I knew?"

For a long moment he looked at me, grinning and tearing.

"Red, you need to go home. I swear everywhere I went somebody was mad at you. Everybody just about except Darleen."

"What vicious lies did you spread?" I went into a fighting crouch. "What did you tell my folks?"

"Exactly what they wanted to hear, that you're getting out of the Coast Guard and going back to college." He turned and ducked through the open hatchway. "Come on, we're supposed to meet Goodrich at the Harbor View."

On our way through the galley, I poured the rest of Archer's bottle into the cook's big coffee mug. He lifted it in salute, his face deadpan. I caught up with Curly, who was outlining his plan for the evening. After a screwdriver or two at the Harbor View Lounge, we would make a stop in Chinatown at, as he put it, a Siamese cat house. I shot that down by mentioning the expense it would involve and the fact that he would be picking up the tab.

By midnight, and still no Goodrich, we had forgotten all about leaving the Harbor View *for greener pastures,* a phrase Curly liked to use. We had, during the course of the evening, fraternized with a number of women, who seemed to be showing up in relays just for the purpose of finding someone to buy them drinks. There were Marge and Suzie, a brunette and a redhead, who claimed they worked at the Coast Guard Building, up near Knob Hill; Jan and Allie, two blondes, who claimed to be airline stewardesses; and, lastly, a redheaded taxi driver, who offered to take us free of charge to San Pablo.

Suddenly, I became aware of a distant whistling, like that of a boat in a heavy fog bank. One long blast that seemed to last forever. Archer was nose-to-nose with the redhead and apparently had heard nothing.

I got up and went to the swinging front doors. It was quite loud, I realized, and it was coming from the tug!

"Arch!" I yelled, holding one of the doors back. The whistling had stopped and then it started again. I dashed back to the booth, grabbed my friend by the neck and shouted, "That's your boat!" He just stared at me, grinning like a half-wit. "The signal!" I yelled, shaking him.

"How many whistles?"

"That's the third one!"

Archer's mouth dropped open. "Did you say *three?*" Without waiting for a reply, he scrambled out of the booth and dived toward the door. The redhead tried to block my exit but I shoved her aside and followed.

When we reached the tug, the CPO skipper was not aboard. Most of the crew was, however, and frantically preparing to get underway. Archer, now quite sober, fell in with the deck crew, leaving me to get along on my own. In the galley I found the old cook, who insisted that I sit at the table and have a cup of coffee.

"What's the emergency?" I asked.

"Some freighter needs help." He poured coffee into a mug. "We do this kind of thing all the time."

Having forgotten completely about morning muster on the CGC *Taney* and that I was going to be in big trouble when I returned, I soon excused myself and headed for the crew's quarters, almost out on my feet. Archer, I knew, was in worse shape than I was.

Around two o'clock, about an hour after I hit the sack, I awoke in mid-air, just before I landed on my hands and knees on the hardwood deck! The tug was rolling badly, and I could tell by the noise and vibration in the bulkheads that we were moving fast! I climbed to my feet, hanging onto a stanchion, and felt around in the darkness for Archer's bunk. He was not there. After a hasty check I discovered that the compartment was completely vacant. What in blazes was going on?

Stiff and sore from the fall, I sat down and began to feel around for my shoes and socks, the only items of clothing I had removed. The shoes had slid beneath a bunk on the port side, but I was unable to find the socks.

Quite obviously some kind of emergency had developed, I decided, making my way to the hatch. There was better visibility in the narrow passageway; and hanging onto a railing, I made it to the galley, where I found the cook sitting in the same spot I had left him.

"I've got to admit you're one sound sleeper," he said, pointing a finger toward the coffee urn.

I groaned, covering my eyes with the palms of my hands. "Ahhh! Why do you need all this light?"

"Get some of that java. That'll turn the lights down some."

"What's happening?" I moved hand-over-hand along another railing to the urn, worked a mug out of a close-fitting rack, and siphoned off some coffee. "Why are we underway?"

"Something about a Norwegian freighter. The Skipper left word for you to report to the bridge when you came alive."

"Why, for Pete's sake?"

"We're evidently shorthanded."

I shook my head doubtfully, taking a mouthful of the thick, black coffee. "If he's short-handed, why don't you pitch in?"

"Because I'm the cook, matey."

"And you don't volunteer in such emergencies?"

He stared at me for a moment, his face deadpan. "Let me see if I can make you understand, farm boy. I'm the goddamned cook aboard this vessel! And I am very much on duty at this very moment! Just as the Skipper don't fuck around with my pots and pans, I don't fuck around on the bridge!"

"Right. I get your drift."

"This is where I belong, not on that slippery-assed deck!"

I took the mug to the sink and got out of there as quickly as I could.

The instant I reached the bridge, the Chief Boatswain's Mate, Donnelly, at the helm, yelled, "That my volunteer? Glad you're aboard! We could really use you here on steering!" The noise from the engine-room and the waves hitting the bow with great whams made it very difficult for me to hear what he was saying. "Archer tells me you've done some time on a small Navy boat!"

I slipped and slid across to the wheel. "It was a subchaser, Chief!"

"Yeah! Are you up to this?"

I nodded, thinking, *God help us!*

"Then take over here! Stay on this heading!"

The pilothouse on the tug was about the size of one of the *Taney's* linen closets. Perched high in the center of the tug, it looked like a watchtower sticking up above the main deck, with its row of heavy port'les that stretched from the port side to the starboard.

I caught a glimpse of three of the deck gang, dressed in yellow rain-coats and matching rain caps, down on deck doing something with lines and fenders; and the sound of their voices, fragments of give-and-take, occasionally reached the pilothouse when the lashing from the waves let up for a moment. The tug was traveling at flank speed down the San Francisco Bay, toward the Bay Bridge, but I had no idea what our destination was.

On our starboard were the endless banks of lights that had to be San Francisco, rising into the sky, because dead ahead was the string of pearls I knew to be the Bay Bridge.

The Skipper, a salty CPO (He was about thirty), had moved to the engine controls and was speaking into a mike, at first in a language I guessed was modern Danish. Then in rapid fire English he spoke to the San Francisco Fire Department! During a pause, he said to me, "Come right about ten degrees, and be ready to change to another heading real quick."

"Right ten degrees."

The tug was as clumsy as a bucket half full of water, and I had no confidence in my ability to turn the thing in a hurry. Of course, if I should run the tug into something, there was at least a ton of fenders on the point of the bow to soften the blow!

Within minutes on the new heading I began to recognize the outlines of many ships tied up side-by-side along the mist-shrouded Embarcadero. Ships of every size and description, from all parts of the world.

"I'm sorry you got caught on this tug—on this particular occasion!" yelled the Chief. "You do know what you're up against, don't you, Red?"

I shook my head, feeling a chill settle in my guts.

"You might as well know. A Norwegian freighter, loaded with animal fodder of one kind and another has caught on fire at Pier 955. She's in danger of going sky high at any minute."

I turned and stared at him.

"Yeah, for sure. And if she goes, she'll take out a sizable chunk of San Francisco." After a time he added, "Our job is to get her out of that crowded dock before she goes."

I waited for him to add, "If she goes."

He had moved up beside me and was apparently squinting at something. His head was lowered and he was actually leaning on a panel of the windshield.

"How do I resign from this outfit?" I asked.

He laughed nervously. "There's every possibility you'll miss your morning muster aboard the CGC *Taney*."

"I don't think I'll worry about that right now."

"Keep a sharp eye now. We're gettin' close."

"What am I looking for?"

Instead of answering my question, he yelled, "Right full rudder! Come around till I say otherwise!"

"Right full rudder!" I called out.

"Okay, straighten her up. We're there! I'll handle the engine controls! You keep your wits about you, now! We're goin' in fast, and I want you to maneuver us in perfectly parallel to that ship on the starboard side! And make it damned close!"

How close is *damned close*, I wondered.

It was a profound mystery to me how the Skipper had known the precise place to pull in. The fantails of the ships we were passing all looked alike to me.

"Okay, can you make out anything on the stern of that one dead ahead?"

What was I supposed to be looking for? A name? Somebody? What, for Christ's sake?

"Nothing but two small orange lights!"

"That's it! Take it easy now!"

At that point I began to make out some kind of lettering on the stern of the ship on the right of the two lights. It looked like *Dansigger* or *Dansinger*.

"That one! That's it, by Golly! Whip 'er in quick, stay on the port side of it! Not so dad-blamed close!" The Chief was working the engine controls, and I could hear bells going crazy below. The big sea-going tug was powering down fast, being outrun by its own wake!

For a heartbreaking moment I was convinced I had steered in too close and was going to ram the freighter; but the Skipper was manipulating the engines, reversing the port and goosing the starboard ahead, which was definitely helping. At any rate, quite suddenly the tug nudged the freighter and came to a stop.

"By Whilliker, Red, I want to talk to you about that landing some day!" the Skipper yelled, sounding almost hysterical.

Below, on the main deck, Archer and two other Coasties were lashing the tug to the freighter; and on the deck of the freighter half a dozen men in rain gear shouted and pointed excitedly. The Skipper, after a startled look around at me, had plunged out of the pilothouse and joined the crew below. Not knowing what else to do, I remained at the helm, convinced that I had come close to destroying the tug and was therefore on the Skipper's shit list.

In two minutes he was back. "Okay, steady as she goes. We're easing this bucket out of here!" He leaped to the engine controls. "I hope those Norwegians got rid of all their lines to he dock!" He leaned and slapped me on the back. "Here we go!" He began to ring bells in the engineroom again, and I suddenly realized he was smiling at me. "Hey, Red, we did it! I do believe!"

I could not muster up a great deal of enthusiasm at this point, despite his optimism. We were, after all, dragging that time bomb out into the Bay with us.

We began to move slowly away from the Embarcadero, heading at an angle toward the center of the Bay and the open sea. And while he joked and carried on about what we were tugging on and what a crazy night this had been, I phrased and rephrased the question: When do we cut loose from this abomination and head for safer waters?

Archer and the deck crew had disappeared inside the tug; and after we had maneuvered the freighter half a mile or so out into the Bay, Chief

Donnelly took the wheel, with the remark, "Go below and send someone up to take your place. We'll be releasing the freighter real soon."

I opened the hatch on the port side and began to work my way down to the main deck, realizing as I did so that the eastern sky was beginning to turn pale. Then, with my hand on the handle of the hatch to the galley, I saw half a dozen small ships and boats headed in our direction from the Embarcadero. That, I guessed, would be the San Francisco Fire Department on its way to the rescue!

Cookie, carrying a platter of fried eggs, grinned at me as I entered. "Here's the guy that came damned near plastering us all over the side of that Danish slop bucket!"

"Norwegian," corrected Archer, lifting his coffee in a toast to me.

"Whatever. What's important—"

"What's important is that you deliver them eggs," growled a gangly deckhand.

"I'll let you have these eggs over the head, Pissant!" laughed the cook. "If you fool with me."

"Aint he ferocious?" asked the kid, looking at me.

"Listen," I said with a shrug, "I'm staying out of it."

Later, after the eggs and the bacon and the biscuits and many cups of coffee, followed by a complete going over of the entire night, word was passed down from the pilothouse that we were out of danger. The freighter had been thoroughly soaked with seawater, and the fireboats had returned to San Francisco.

By this time it was broad daylight, and all of us were dead on our feet. I had, of course, given some thought to the trouble I was in and the choices open to me. And since these seemed to have been reduced to a rock and a hard place, I decided an hour in the sack would not make things much worse.

At the hatch that opened into the crews quarters, I suddenly found himself grasping for support, as the tug rolled violently to the starboard. Instinctively, I tried to withdraw my hand, although it meant losing my balance.

Archer flipped on an overhead light in the center of the small quarters. "You can have your pick, Red. Any bunk but this one." With that he collapsed. "Git the light."

I had not made a sound, but through the fingers of my left hand blood was streaming. He glanced up and saw the blood.

"What th' hell!" he burst out. "What'd you do?"

I was staring at my flattened, bleeding fingers and shaking my head. "The pain is just now beginning," I said. "Find me something to catch this!" The pain was still hardly more than a dull throb, but I braced myself for that moment when the numbness would begin to depart.

Archer had leaped up and started yelling: "Cookie, get something to swab up this blood!"

Cookie appeared with towels. "What blood, you idiot! Come on, Red, take that into the head. I'll find some painkiller." He wrapped a towel around my hand and led me down the passageway to a tiny head. "Well, it looks like you've got a pretty good excuse for being AOL, now."

"Quite a price to pay," I said.

The Skipper crowded into the head, wanting to know the extent of the damages. While he and Cookie examined my fingers, I asked:

"When do you think can I get—transportation back to my ship?"

"Look, you're in no danger of dying," teased the Skipper. "Just try to relax. What's your hurry to get back to that dad-blamed *Taney* anywho?"

"Yeah," agreed Archer, who had also wedged himself into the head, "I think you ought to spend a few days on the tug."

The Skipper, without a word to anyone, left and, ten minutes later, just as I stretched out on a bunk, sent word that he wanted me to report to the pilothouse. He was speaking into a mike when Archer and I lined up beside him.

"Red," he said, cupping the mike, "I've got the *Taney* on the radio, and I thought you'd better hear what I'm goin' to tell 'em."

"Thanks," I said, tightlipped, trying to ignore the pain.

"I've already told them you're here with us." He lifted the mike, "Eagle, this is Rover, come in."

Husbands' voice suddenly filled the pilothouse, "Rover, the Exec is standing by here and wants an account of Hall's most recent travels. Leave out none of the gory details."

"Wilco," said the Chief, "hold onto your hat. We had a major problem here last night. Potentially, it could have been disastrous for a good section of San Francisco. A freighter, loaded with feed and fertilizer, caught on fire and was close to exploding. We were shorthanded, so I asked Hall if he would help out, and even though he knew he was risking his life, in the best tradition of the United States Coast Guard he volunteered to go out in the Bay and fight that fire. Which, as it turned out, lasted just about all night long." The Chief looked around at Archer and me, grinning stupidly. "And, by the way, he was pretty seriously wounded in the line of duty."

For a time the only sound coming from the speaker was a mild hum; then Husbands came back with, "Very well. Thank you, Chief. The ship's on its way out of the harbor, but we'll launch the Captain's Gig for Hall. Is that a roger?"

"Hot damn!" said the Chief, covering the mike with his hand. Then to Husbands he said, "Hall's wound will be taken care of, and he will be ready when the boat gets here. We're clear."

He returned the mike to its hook. "Now, Red, that has got to be a believe-it-or-not in the annals of the U. S. Coast Guard! The *Taney's* launching a Captain's Gig for a common, ordinary, ship-jumpin' swab!"

"Skipper," said Archer, "they must really want old Red back. Mebbe they're gonna shoot him."

"Ohhh!" I moaned, unable to laugh, holding my wounded hand and blowing on it.

"I mean, think of it!" the Chief howled, slamming his hand against the helm. "You go AOL right after being busted for stealin' an officer's Jeep and end up a gold-plated hero!"

"Cut out the hero stuff, Cap'n, please," I said, grinning and shaking my head. "You went way overboard about what I did last night. That was just pure malarky."

"Hell, no, I didn't say a word that wasn't true. Not at all. The only thing I said that might be construed as a lie was your volunteering. And I'm pretty sure you would have done that if you'd had any choice." Then, with a playful punch at my midriff, he added, "Of course, I guess you could've jumped over the side."

"Hah."

*　　　　　　*　　　　　　*

So I went back aboard the CGC *Roger B. Taney* in style. The Exec and the Communications Officer were among the delegation at the starboard side of the ship when the gig was hoisted aboard with me in it. They had come out to greet and shake my hand; and before an assembled crew on the stern the Exec read a long letter full of high-sounding rhetoric, which had reportedly been written by Commander Gorman himself. Some of the words used by the tugboat skipper were repeated, but the writer of the speech had added a number of his own about my sterling qualities, concluding with the remark that here was a man who had demonstrated the true spirit of the United States Coast Guard with disregard for personal safety.

Semper paratus.

The CGC Chautauqua

◆

The *Chat,* looking brilliant in the morning sunshine, eased in astern of the *Roger B. Taney* at the G. I. dock. She had, just that morning, received a final coat of glossy white enamel at Pier 5 in San Francisco and was now ready for another turn at Weather Station Fox.

At the gangplank of the *Taney* all of the radiomen except Podscoff were present to see me off. Husbands, looking glum, stood by himself on the other side of the gangway watch, while Sparky and Janssen and Sears took turns giving their opinion of the *Chautauqua.*

"Now, that is one sorry boat," said Janssen. "Smelly as hell and loaded with cockroaches."

"And there're nothin' but chickenshits in the radio shack," said Sparky. "You'll be absolutely miserable, Red."

"I've heard the cook can't cook," added Sears with a grin.

Of course, I was taking all of this in good-humoredly, because it was a known fact that the Indian cutters were far better duty than the *Roger B.,* and that the *Chautauqua* had the best skipper on the West Coast. I was still numb over the news, delivered to me at the eight o'clock muster that morning, that I was being transferred. It was another known fact that up until now no one had ever been transferred from the *Taney.* It just didn't happen, short of death or retirement.

"Listen, I'll be seeing you fellows," I said, preparing to lift my seabag. "We'll run into each other on liberty. At *Ted and Roy's,* for sure."

"Yeah," said Sparky, "and right here on the old *Taney*. I want you to drop in on us from time to time and let us know how you're doin'."

"Sure thing."

I shook hands with him first and then Janssen. Sears stuck out his hand first and I said, "I heard you're leaving the Service."

"You heard right. I've got about another month, then I'm calling it quits. You take care, now, and maybe we can get together and tie one on sometime."

Sears, whom I had come to like a great deal, walked with me over to Husbands, who was pretending I was thin air. I put my hand on his shoulder and said, "I want you to keep Podscoff and Ceccarelli under control, Hoss."

"It's gonna be dull around here."

"Not on the *Taney*, man! Tell you what, when our ships are in at the same time, we'll go on one heck of a liberty together, okay?"

I hoisted the seabag and mounted the gangplank, did my thing, and headed for the *Chautauqua*. Goodrich, who had been standing on the dock waiting, fell in with me. His face was deadpan, of course, but I could tell that he was happy about something.

"What's so funny?" I asked, as soon as we got aboard the Indian cutter.

"Who said anything was funny?"

"Did you have anything to do with my transfer to this bucket?"

He grunted, taking my transfer papers and looking at them.

"Don't lie to me, I know you did. I don't know how you did it, but you somehow finagled this."

"How come you're not surprised I'm on the *Chautauqua*?" he countered, sounding disappointed. "I thought you'd drop dead at the sight of me on this boat."

"Heck, I knew you were being transferred before you did. News gets around fast in the Coasties, especially when you're a radioman."

"I think it's funny we both ended up on the *Chautauqua*."

"Hey, don't say *ended up* to me," I laughed. "Listen, I've got to get settled. How about checking me in?"

A few minutes later he led me down to the crew's quarters and showed me a bunk, which just happened to be the one above his. A kid in dungaree cut-offs and a white T-shirt was lying on his back in it reading a comic book.

"Kansas, how about movin' it?" he said, not unkindly.

"Forget it. I got here first."

"Go back to your own filthy mess," said Goodrich, taking the comic book. "And in about one minute you'll be bleedin' in it."

"Hey!" screamed the kid, "Who do you think you are? There's half a dozen empty bunks in here.

I'm goin' to Mackey!"

"Do it. I dare you."

"I was gettin' ready to move to this bunk!"

While this was going on, I dug into my seabag and came out with a sheet and a pillowcase.

The kid slowly climbed down, still complaining.

The bunk was close to the port bulkhead, and some previous occupant had installed a makeshift bulletin board for pin-ups a foot from the head. I took from my ditty bag a picture of a very brown young lady in nothing but overalls and, using two thumbtacks already on the board, pinned it up.

"Jamie Lee, right? What is she, half Cherokee?"

I nodded, inspecting the picture. "I took that down at Little Sandy, our favorite place to rendezvous." I reached into the ditty bag and took out another, this one of a very white girl with a bright smile and a great deal of wavy blonde hair.

"Alice Chastain."

I nodded again. "You went to school with her, right?"

"Not very long. She transferred to a private school in town. You know, she had the whitest skin of anybody I ever saw. And, as far as I know, there wasn't a blemish on it."

"I assure you there was no blemish." I brought out another picture and tacked it up.

Goodrich laughed, "Another blonde. The Ada girl."

"A real innocent," I said, nodding. "The one that spent two nights with me in a blizzard, in my brother's cabin. You remember, Darleen."

"I know, the one you took to the Saturday night previews at the McSwain. What's she drinkin'?"

"Coca Cola. That's all she ever drinks."

"I'll believe that. Where's Jody? You've got three girlfriends and all of them are blue-eyed blondes. That brown kid is Jessica's friend."

"You think you've got all the answers. It so happens she's *numero uno.*"

"I'll bet you all four of them has found a boyfriend since you saw them last. Do you ever write to any of them?"

"Virgins all," I said, ignoring his last remark. I backed away from the bunk and studied the bulletin board.

"Yeah, sure. And how do you know that?"

"That's what they told me, and you know what they say. A nice girl will not lie about her virginity."

"That's what you said about Sunshine, the little flirt that was sleepin' with ever'one in Ada. The one that—"

"Did she ever sleep with you?"

"Well, no," he said quickly and left.

I stretched out on my bunk and turned my head toward the four pictures.

∗   ∗   ∗

Sometime before I shipped aboard the *Chautauqua,* I had become aware of three old battered wooden subchasers that were moored just below the bridge that separated G. I. from East Oakland. There they sat, rotting away, a mute reminder to all who might glance their way that time is a terrible enemy of wooden ships. To me they were a reminder of the South Pacific and World War Two and island invasions and *kamikazes* and long, monotonous convoys (from Apathy to Tedium and back again).

For two grueling years, perhaps the most important two years of my life, I had lived aboard one of those narrow and dangerous little ships; and still, with my eyes closed, I could describe in detail every inch of them, from the radar dome above the yardarm to the sonar head beneath the keel.

Taking a stroll down to the mooring to see the little ships became a favorite late-afternoon pastime of mine, and on one or two occasions I was able to talk Goodrich into accompanying me. But he saw nothing romantic or exotic about the sad relics of the past. While I looked at them and reminisced, he tossed rocks at the them, grunting his disapproval each time he scored.

Then one day the scuttlebutt began to circulate that the CGC *Chautauqua* had been assigned the job of towing the three derelicts to Seattle! What's more, volunteers were being sought to baby-sit them! Two men would be assigned to each subchaser!

I couldn't wait to break the news to Goodrich. Not the news of the trip, of course, since he would have heard that already in the Ship's Office, but the news that I was going to volunteer at once and I wanted him to be the second man aboard the one I would ride. It was a wonderful opportunity to spend three glorious days riding a wooden subchaser up the western seaboard of the United States! It would be an experience neither of us would ever forget! For me, of course, it would be *déja vu* all the way!

I had my speech all worked out for Gooch and had no doubt that he would be more than willing to go along with me. After all, we were hometown buddies. I would point out that it would be wild and wonderful to have the entire run of the little ship, batching on cold rations, sleeping in the empty crew's quarters, acting out the parts of skipper, cook, signalman, and deckhand!

But the minute I mentioned taking a ride on one of those little maverick ships bareback to Seattle Goodrich exploded, "Are you absolutely crazy? That would be pure hell for three days and three nights! I want no part of it! Three days and nights without electricity or running water or heat—!"

"What do you want heat for in August, old buddy?"

"Don't try that *old buddy* stuff on me this time. You know, Red, you're as crazy as a bed bug. Have you thought this out? Have you forgotten that *volunteering* is for idiots and half-wits? I am not about to be dragged into this little nostalgia trip of yours."

"Okay, but it would have been something to tell your grandkids."

He glared at me, shaking his head. "Are you sure you want to put your name on that list? You'll be the first one, you know. And probably the only one."

"Yep. I'm going right now and turning in my name."

As it turned out, he was right, for a change. I was wrong. Nobody stepped forward, except me. Therefore, four deckhands and a motormack striker were pressed into service for the adventure, with the promise that if they behaved themselves smartly their restrictions to the ship would be dropped once we arrived in Seattle.

My partner for the journey was a string bean motormack striker by the name of Marvin Sayles, who had been volunteered by his department head. He saw no romance or beauty in the subchaser at all and, when I told him why I was so interested, he remarked that he wished the Japs had sunk all of them in the Pacific. For a moment I seriously considered sending him to the Sick Bay, but I let it pass because just in time it occurred to me that such behavior might get me scrubbed from the mission.

"Do you realize we'll be without power of any kind?" moaned Sayles, his long, gaunt face working tragically. "We'll have to eat cold cuts."

"I like cold cuts," I said. "Heck, that's what we ate most of that last year of World War Two. Let's make sure we have plenty liverwurst and onions."

"Oh, God!" Sayles cried unhappily.

"Can you send and receive semaphore?"

"What'n hell's that?"

"Signaling with flags. Do you know the Morse Code?"

We were leaning against the insubstantial starboard lifeline on the bow of one of the derelicts, the one that had been assigned to us.

"We'll have to maintain communications with the mother ship by semaphore during the daytime and blinker light at night."

"Would a blinker light require electricity?"

"I'm taking a big flashlight."

"No shit. And you think somebody on the *Chautauqua* will see you blinking it?" After a pregnant moment of silence during which we glared at each other, he said, "You're not buckin' for a Section Eight, are you?"

The E. T. D. had been set for zero-eight-hundred hours on the fifteenth day of September, three days before my twenty-second birthday. I was up bright and early that morning, pacing the main deck of the Indian cutter. For the trip I had put together a survival kit that included, besides a flashlight and extra batteries, a mess kit, a first aid kit, enough skivvies for three days, a change of dungarees, a poncho, writing materials (with which to record the memorable moments), three rolls of toilet paper, six long candles, two semaphore flags, three towels, a pocketknife, and a flare gun.

No one had said a thing about what the *Chautauqua* would furnish, but I was certain we would have everything we needed. Marvin, of course, would be expected to pack his own food and other provisions.

The entire population of Government Island and the crew and officers of the *Roger B. Taney* had turned out to watch our historic departure. The three small wooden ships had been linked together by one-hundred-foot towlines, and the lead 'chaser was secured to the fantail of the *Chautauqua*. To my delight, Marvin and I would be bringing up the rear (I had specifically requested that position), which meant that we would be some six hundred and thirty feet astern of the ship! It also meant that we would more than likely have difficulty attracting somebody's attention on the ship in case we wanted or needed something! Of course, the idea was for us to *rough it*. The mother ship would not be likely to stop for any reason, short of the death of one of us adventurers.

As the *Chautauqua* prepared to move away from the dock, Marvin observed sadly, "Hell, Red, they don't intend to communicate with us. We're on our own. As far as they're concerned nothing can go wrong. We've been drilled on safety precautions, given strict orders not to build any fires, told never to remove our lifejackets even when we're in the sack, and not to take any chances whatsoever. Our task aboard this hunk of junk is to keep an eye on the towline. If that breaks, they'll come back and get us."

"Why are you saying all this to me, Marvin?"

"I just got the idee you was upset over bein' way back here at the end. You was worryin' about signaling them."

"Are you kidding? This is exactly where I wanted to be. And I'm not worried about anything."

"It wouldn't do us any good to signal the ship, even if we could think of something to signal," he went on. "They're not going to stop the ship and come back even if something happens to one of us."

"Okay, okay! That's your opinion. I happen to differ."

When the PA system on the *Chautauqua* announced, "Cast off all lines," a rousing cheer and a few boos went up from the swabs and brass on the *Taney* and the dock.

"They're eatin' their hearts out," I said. "Everyone of them would like to be in our shoes."

"The hell you say," said Marvin. "I shore don't like being in my shoes. They're feelin' sorry for us for havin' to tow three small ships all the way up the California, Oregon, and Washington coasts. That's rough riding, mate, and when we git to Seattle, where'll we be?"

"In one of the best liberty ports in the world."

"Wrong ag'in, my friend. We're leavin' that right now."

"Man, you are negative! All we've got to do is lounge around on this little ship and appreciate the scenic wonders of the West Coast for three short days! There'll be no watches, no painting or scraping, and not one single drill of any kind. Then we'll be in a city I've heard about all my life."

Marvin stretched out on the wooden deck, placing his hands beneath his head. "One thing I'll give you, Red. You're optimistic."

"Don't try to butter me up."

Before we were out of San Francisco Bay the going began to get a little rough, especially for Marvin and me on the last subchaser. He was hanging on for dear life, which seemed to me at the time just a bit over doing it, something to impress me. But when he began to feed the fish, I stopped thinking that and felt sorry for him. He whined and took on, remarking that it seemed as if the ocean couldn't wait to get at us.

When we passed beneath the Golden Gate Bridge, I tried to focus on the vehicular traffic that was passing over us. But by this time the entire topside deck of the subchaser was very slippery, and I had to hold onto the lifeline with both hands. The little ship was rolling and bucking like a Texas maverick on the end of a long tether; and when we left the Bay and began to angle around northward, moving out a distance from the rugged coastline, the Pacific began to get rough in earnest.

Marvin, I discovered, had retired to the after crew's quarters. This despite my warning that if he knew what was good for him he would stay up on deck where he could get some fresh air. Of course, I was thinking more about what he would do to the deck down there than any discomfort he might experience by squirreling away. I had remained on the pitching and diving bow, with an arm hooked around one of the lifeline posts. And even though I was soaked to the skin and chilled to the bone, I had never been happier in my life. The view of the northern California coastline was spectacular, with one surprise after another. I had seen it aboard the CGC *Alert,* in calmer weather; but seeing it from the bucking bow of the subchaser was a whole different thing.

As I made my way aft, looking for Marvin and not finding him, I began to have a nagging fear that this kid might not be able to make it all the way to Seattle. After all, he was very seasick and he was not used to such an unsteady deck. At 'midships, I managed to time it and dive from the port lifeline into the pilothouse, certain that that was where I would find him; and when all I found was a great deal of undigested food on the deck, that's when the thought occurred to me that I might be alone on the ship.

Again timing it, waiting for a starboard roll this time, I dived from the hatchway of the pilothouse back to the port lifeline. Actually, I slid the last half of the way across the slippery latticed deck, latched onto the line with one hand, and came very close to going into the sea. My entire body and the full length of my arms went over the port side, and for a moment I was certain I would not be able to hold on and pull myself back aboard! But when the ship rolled to port the second time, I was able to grab the line with my other hand.

I refused to think about how close that call was. Instead, I concentrated on muscling my butt back over the toe rail onto solid deck. Once there I sat for a time, my legs still dangling over the side, feeling the warmth of the seawater each time we did a port roll.

In time the thought of Marvin messing up the after crews quarters, the only place on the ship where we would be able to catch some shuteye, drove me to my feet and sent me on my perilous journey.

The instant I began to descend into the darkness of the hatchway that led to the galley and the after quarters, my nose picked up Marvin's smell. Evidently, the grease monkey had begun to puke while still on the ladder, because I found the footing rather precarious. And so it was no surprise when I felt, rather than saw, Marvin lying in a pool of his own making, apparently dead. He was between the messtable and the port footlockers that supported the first and second bottom bunks on the port side.

"Hey, old buddy!" I managed, feeling a strong urge to feed some fish myself. "Get up topside! You've got to get some fresh air!"

Marvin slowly raised his head, lifting my hand with it, and began to sputter. I helped him to a sitting position and moved back for him to retch some more. Then quite clearly, he said, "I hope you have a good trip. Now, leave me be."

"Come on, let's go, man! This is the worst possible place to be in this rough weather."

"You go."

Somehow, I wrestled and coaxed him up the ladder to the fantail, where I secured him to what had once been a K-gun rack. Then I went to the bridge hand over hand along the port lifeline and fell into the Captain's chair. There, I figured, I would be above the salt spray coming over the bow and, at the same time, be able to keep an eye on the towline. Marvin, now that he was lashed down on the fantail, was no longer a concern to me.

I buckled myself in the chair and settled into a deep reverie of the old days, when flying fish and gooney birds used to land our deck. I felt sorry for the big, awkward and helpless albatrosses flopping around, their boneless legs incapable of holding them up. Suddenly, I heard a thin, agonized scream, which I knew had to be Marvin in trouble. I scrambled across the bridge, down the metal ladder, and, once again, dived for the lifeline. This time I went down the starboard side of the ship. Marvin, his skin white as a sheet, was whispering something. I bent close, straining to hear his words.

"Could you get me a sandwich?"

I straightened up, convinced that my ears were playing tricks on me. He could not possibly be hungry! I bent down again and listened, and this time there was no doubt. He had indeed requested a sandwich.

"You'll just feed it to the fish," I said. "Why don't we wait for awhile, till we begin to get our sea legs?"

"I'm starvin' to death!" he whined, already looking like death itself. "I'll stay down, right here. I can't feed the fish if I can't get up."

"That was just a figure of speech, Marvin," I said. "It's not that simple. Tell you what, as soon as we pass through this rough stretch of water I'll fix you a big liverwurst and onion sandwich. How does that sound?"

"Aaawk!"

After he stopped retching, he said, "No onions and no liverwurst!"

*   *   *

Marvin's condition remained about the same during the entire three days and nights. His early greenish pallor took on shades of yellow near the end, but I had my doubts about that being a sign of improvement. His only words after that first request for a sandwich sounded something like variations of, "Uuughck."

Being on the tail end of the expedition, I decided just off Bodega Bay, had its drawbacks. The other subchasers didn't seem to be bouncing and bucking quite as much as we were. No matter how calm the water seemed to be, we continued to do all the things a cork is capable of doing in a highly-agitated body of water.

An early hope, dashed almost immediately, was that once we were out of the San Francisco Bay entrance the going would become easier for us. The opposite happened. The minute we began to work our way northward, hugging the coast, we encountered very rough seas. Rougher than anything I had experienced in the south and western regions of the Pacific Ocean.

And I had not anticipated the indescribable *loneliness* of the trip. Marvin, of course, was no company at all. He was, in fact, about as much company as a corpse would have been. The two swabs on the subchaser immediately ahead of us never waved or paid any attention to my attempts to signal them. No doubt, they were having a life-and-death experience themselves. And only once was I able to attract the attention of a signalman aboard the *Chautauqua*. It was around dusk of the second day, and I could see the happy port'les on the big ship lighting up (Ah, civilization!). Occasionally, when the wind was just right, I was able to catch a momentary high-pitched sound from the evening's movie.

The alert signalman must have seen my pinpoint of light with glasses and realized I was trying to get his attention. He sent greetings and best wishes and wanted to know why I was signaling. Was there an emergency. I told him to tell a certain yeoman in the Ship's Office I hoped he was enjoying the trip and that I would survive this thing and personally clean his plow once we reached Seattle.

"You intend to clean *what*?" he signaled.

"Never mind," I returned. "What's the movie tonight?"

I really did not care very much what the ship's movie was going to be, but suddenly the thought of how comfortable life was just a short distance away, especially how cushy old Gooch had it, made me ask.

Ahead of me was a very dark and friendless night.

I had been right about one thing. There were no shit details to be carried out on the mission, no painting or scraping or standing some kind of watch or being subjected to drills. But aboard the subchaser there were far worse things. The headache back on the fantail, Marvin, for example. He was far worse than any radio watch. Doing without a cup of hot coffee in the morning was infinitely worse than going through a drill. Having no place to relieve oneself (except over the raring and fonching fantail), having to eat always from a can and always the same thing (The cold cuts of spam and the liverwurst and the onions were gone after the first day).

Not only did Marvin stink up everything (He ate almost nothing the entire three days yet somehow continued to vomit), he wallowed on his backside and groaned and begged for things that I could not deliver! It was impossible to clean up after him, since there was no fresh water and no soap of any kind—and not even a bucket with which to dip water from the sea!

The weather remained ugly the entire trip. It was a combination of fog, mist, rain, and cold, biting wind—without let-up. And since the little wooden ship was bobbing about like an inflated life raft going down the white waters of the Rogue River, having absolutely no ballast, there was a constant salt spray coming over the bow, covering me from head to foot every time I moved off the bridge. Once my only change of dungarees became soaked, I remained wet all the way to Seattle.

What little sleep I got during that entire seventy-two hours occurred the third night when I lashed himself to the Captain's Chair on the bridge. And I was not so much asleep as unconscious.

The picture of the two little ships bobbing about ahead of us and the big, ugly rear end of the *Chautauqua* rolling ever so gently from side to side became indelibly etched on my brain; and never afterward was I able to dissociate pain and loneliness and ugliness from that rear view of the Indian cutter.

On the third and last day, my old buddy, Eugene Tuney Goodrich, made a rare appearance on the stern of the cutter and began waving energetically in my general direction. One of the men on *Subchaser Number Two* began to jump up and down and wave stupidly, convinced that Gooch was trying to get his attention. This did not improve my disposition a great deal; and when it became apparent that my friend had not enlisted the services of a signalman, I turned my back on the cutter and said a few things toward Marvin on the fantail.

Since Goodrich did not know the ABC's of semaphore or the Morse Code, much less how to send and receive them, one wave of the hand was as good as a thousand. It simply said to me that he had given no thought to my situation at all. He had not enlisted the aid of a signal-man because he had nothing to say to me. He was comfortable in his dry clothes, had just chowed down on excellent food, and was on his way to the movie. All he wanted to do was wave and jump up and down like the lunatic on the second subchaser!

When I glanced around a few minutes later, he had disappeared into the bowels of the ship.

Just before we reached Puget Sound, my buddy finally went to a sig-nalman up on the bridge and talked him into relaying a message to me. The fog that seldom leaves that area of the West Coast was so thick I had great difficulty reading the flapping arms on the bridge of the cutter; but, piecing together the best I could, the following is what my once best friend had to say to me: "We had steak smothered in onions for chow today. Would you care for some? How about some hot coffee to go with it? Well, I must go or I'll miss the big movie that's being shown on the messdeck. Enjoy. You're doing an invaluable service for your country."

"And you're going to rue this day, ole buddy," I said.

*   *   *

To a casual tourist that rain-soaked morning, the approach to the U. S. Coast Guard Base, that endless clutter of boats and ships and old rot-ting warehouses and piles of junk that went on for miles on both sides of Puget Sound, would undoubtedly have looked uninviting and dreary. But to me and Marvin, who was now free and able to roam the deck of the subchaser, it was breathtakingly beautiful! It was symbolic of an infi-nitely better way of life, of warmth and dry clothes and freshly-cooked food and cold beer and—*sacred Mary!*—a place to lay our weary heads!

It was indeed the end of the worst nightmare of our lives.

The CGC Chautauqua

The Airline Stewardess

———————————◆———————————

After an uneventful journey south from Seattle to San Francisco Bay, the *Chautauqua* settled in at its mooring at Government Island. It was around two on a foggy morning late in September, 1948, and the crew was tired and anxious to get some much-needed rest.

But it was not to be.

Shortly after four *reveille* was piped from the bridge, followed by the announcement over the PA system that the ship would be getting underway immediately for Weather Station Fox.

When Goodrich dragged into the messdeck, a good fifteen minutes after the visit by the Boatswain's Mate to the crew's quarters, I was sitting at a table by myself drinking coffee and eating a second donut. He slumped across the table, apparently too weak to make it to the coffee urn.

"We're always lookin' for greener pastures, no matter what we've got," he said, dropping his chin into his cupped hands.

We had begun speaking to each other, albeit rather formally, back around Sand Point, on the California-Oregon border; but each of us had avoided mentioning the trip to Seattle or the reason for our strained relationship.

"Be specific," I said with a scowl.

"I'm talkin' about me leavin' the Base, where I was situated very nicely just a short time ago, until I let you talk me into requestin' a transfer. I could still be there, with short hours, and all of them behind a desk that didn't have to be bolted to the deck, with weekends off, and every night, too, if I wanted it. But no, I had to listen to you!"

"Yeah," I said, maliciously, "but just think of the fun and excitement you've had since you got out of that hole, ole buddy." After a pause, I added, "Why do people like you enlist in a sea-going outfit?"

"I had no idea this outfit was *sea-going* when I signed up."

Once he was fully awake and bitching normally, I suggested that we take a gander at what was going on topside. Neither of us had been assigned any duties prior to departure; so we were free to stroll about the decks and watch the hurry and scurry of the deck gang as they prepared the ship for sea.

"It doesn't make any sense," he said. "We could have slept on through all this. They didn't need us at all."

"Come on, the morning air will do you good."

At that moment the sound of the high-pitched Chief Boatswain's whistle penetrated the messdeck. It was full daylight by this time and, as I stood up, from the PA system came, "Shorten all lines!"

"Doesn't that do something to the ole adrenaline flow?" I asked.

"It makes my butt pucker."

"Come on, I want to watch this place disappear."

Gooch finally stood up and began to tuck his shirt inside his trousers. "Come to think of it, it was your fault I joined this outfit. Archer and I were perfectly happy till you came along. With our fifty-two twenty money and—"

"You're much better off in the Coast Guard," I said.

We left the messdeck through the forward hatch, which was on the port side, with me leading and Gooch trailing along behind complaining. We headed for the point of the bow, whence we would be able to view both sides of the Bay.

"What's to see?" he complained. "We've seen this same view two dozen times."

"I have but you haven't," I said. "Anyway, it's always different."

"Somebody's yellin' at you on the bridge."

"Hall, report to the radio shack on the double!" The man who was shouting needed no megaphone.

"It's about time somebody discovered I was unemployed," I told Gooch, heading for 'midships. I had to duck past seamen and gun mounts on the gently rolling deck.

At the door of the radio shack I was confronted by Chief Garnes, an old salt wearing a black-billed CPO cap with a brass anchor the color of seaweed. His background was U. S. Navy submarines.

"Sorry to have to do this, Red, but we've got two men here with no real experience at handling shipboard traffic. You stood watches on the *Taney*, right? Well, this is a helluva situation I've got to admit. You're third class and these two landlubbers here are second classes."

"So who's in charge of the watch?"

"Well, that's what I meant about bein' sorry. Meek will technically be in charge, but you'll have to handle the serious stuff. Think you can do that?"

"No problem. But what if we disagree about something?"

"Well, before it comes to blows, send for me."

Meek, a thin, pale kid with bulging eyes that never seemed to blink, was sitting at the port operating position staring angrily at me. Sanderson, the other Second Class Radioman, was sitting at the other position.

"If I'm in charge, Chief, he'll do as I say," said Meek.

Sanderson nodded, "According to regulations."

"Fuck regulations," said Garnes. "You two boys have to git your feet wet before you can tell somebody like Red here what to do. My God, he spent three years in the Pacific at this business, while you two played with your diapers." He beckoned for Sanderson to follow him, and the two of them departed, closing the hatch behind them. I slid into the seat Sanderson had vacated.

"Don't touch the equipment unless I tell you to," said Meek.

Without a word I stood up and facing the pasty-faced kid. His eyes seemed ready to pop out of his head. "I think we'd better get something straight right now!"

"I'm in charge of this radio shack!" he blurted. "And don't you forget it, hear?"

I took a short, quick step forward and slapped him hard across the face with my open right hand. Startled, he fell backward across his typewriter, whining that I would be sorry for doing that. I took another step and slapped him again, this time with my left. "Just give me an excuse to knock the holy hell out of you!" I warned, dragging him by the belt out into the center of the shack. "Anything at all from you and I'll remove a few teeth!"

He cried out, "I'm putting you on report!"

"Who cares?" I asked. "I've been on report before."

He suddenly began to flail away at my head with his open hands, like a girl, at the same time crying pathetically, "You're goin' on report for this, you just see!"

Holding him away from me, I said, "Better sit down at your position! If you don't I'm going to teach you a lesson you won't soon forget."

When he paid me no attention, I moved toward him, my fists doubled. He was bawling and swearing that he was going to tell the Chief. Suddenly, I stopped and let my hand fall to my sides, as if I had decided to give up. He moved in close, slapping at my face, his entire midriff exposed.

"Don't fall into the equipment!" I snapped.

Then I hit him hard just above the belly button.

With a pitiful little puking sound, he doubled, his butt going backward and his head falling into my open hands.

"*North Star*, this is Eagle One. Over."

I whirled, dropping the kid to the deck.

"Behave yourself or you'll wish to hell you had," I warned, picking up the mike at his position. "This is *North Star*. Go ahead."

"Stand by for a priority message."

"Roger, standing by."

"Message Number Two, today's date, action addressee *North Star*. Information addressee *Morning Star*. Proceed at once to relieve *Morning Star*. Break and end of message. Do you roger? Over."

"Roger your Number Two. *North Star* out."

Meek was sitting up, holding his stomach and sobbing like a girl with a broken heart.

"Get up there at the other position," I said, "and work up this message from NMC."

"Ohhhh! I'm goin' to the Communications Officer."

I whirled and glared at him, "You do and I'll beat the living daylights out of you. Listen to me, Meek, you breathe a word of this to anybody and I'll make you wish you never laid eyes on me. I mean it. Now, do as I said."

Meek took out his handkerchief and blew his nose. "You'll never get away with this. The Chief will find out what's happened."

"What will he find out? That I slapped you around a bit and you bawled like a blithering idiot? I'll give you just about two seconds to reach that other position."

"All right, god damn it. But you'd better leave me alone."

"Let me see the message after you type it up."

A few minutes later when he returned from delivering the message to the Communications Officer, his mood seemed to have changed a bit. He slumped into the starboard position, and when he thought I wasn't busy he said, "You used to be a Second Class?"

"That I did, bucking for First."

"Listen—"

I swiveled around, "No, you listen, I'm sorry I had to hit you. This is going to be a long three weeks no matter what we do; but if we're constantly at each other's throats, it's going to be a lot worse for both of us. I'm for calling a truce."

Meek nodded thoughtfully and a moment later said, "You know, it pisses me off the way we're always in the dark about things."

"Like what?"

"This extra patrol, for example. We're not supposed to be going out. What'n heck's going on?"

"What difference does it make? We have orders to head out, and when the Base wants us to know the why of it we'll be told. The *Escanaba* evidently developed a problem, something pretty serious I guess, to cause them to abort."

"Well, why didn't Base give us the reason in that message? What's the big secret?"

"Hey, that's the way the brass do business."

*   *   *

Three days later, as we neared Weather Station Fox, Chief Garnes took a position beside me at the lifeline on the starboard side of the ship.

"Listen, Red, I wanted to ask you about you and Meek. How're things goin'?"

"Couldn't be better, Chief."

"Well, that's the very conclusion I had reached. But I guess what I want to know is what'n hell happened during that first watch? I thought you two would go at each other's throats."

"We just had a long talk and agreed that it would be smoother sailing if we get along."

"Yeah, well, I'm glad to hear that. And, Red, whatever you said to Meek, it must've took. He's changed a hundred percent in the past three days. Hell, he's friendlier and more respectful toward ever'body."

I straightened up and pointed toward the western horizon, "That's got to be the old *Escanaba*."

The Chief nodded. "I wonder why the lookout hasn't spotted it. Probably asleep up there."

"We're at least three hours ahead of our E. T. A. What do you think has happened, that the Esky needed a relief?"

"Who knows? Maybe the skipper got homesick. Can you make out the blinker light?"

"Hang on." I began to call out letters, TKS FOR RELIEVING US EARLY XRAY OUR CASUALTY STILL IN BAD WAY XRAY WE OWE YOU ONE XRAY OVER.

"Somebody probably went loony toons," said the Chief, tossing his spent cigarette butt over the side. "Five'll git you ten it was a sparky."

We could hear the blinker light banging away on the bridge.

"I'll bet I know what our signalman is sending back," said the Chief. "He's askin' what'n hell's wrong with the casualty. Right?"

"Okay, here comes the reply to our question: AN ENLISTED MAN IN THE ENGINEROOM HAS ACUTE APPENDICITIS. OVER."

*   *   *

Sunny days followed, during which I whiled away a lot of time reading Balzac and Stendhal, hardback editions that I had picked up in a Seattle bookstore-coffeehouse. And although I managed to write my kid sister a short letter, I never quite got around to Jody, Darleen, and Alice.

Each day was an exact replica of the one before; but, I noticed, every one of them marked a noticeable decline in the morale of the crew.

While most of the swabs fussed and fretted in the crew's quarters, some of them arguing over decks of cards and some of them just arguing, I spent a lot of time topside with a book, gazing off at the horizon. The ship's library was a single bookshelf of tattered hardbacks by writers like Jack London, Herman Melville, and James Michener. I had read them all. After sundown Goodrich and I would drift up to the bow of the ship and talk about the ones that got away. In time Meek started showing up with a friend from the Ship's Office, named Fromer.

At the beginning of the second week, something happened that solved the boredom-and-apathy problem and came close to changing the direction of my life for good. I was working busily on the ship's newsletter at one of the two typewriters, at the same time keeping one ear on the NMC frequency and the other on a commercial radio station. Meek was asleep in the starboard position and beginning to snore. Quite unexpectedly there came from one of the wall speakers a voice that brought me to attention. At first I was certain only that it was a man's a voice, somewhat garbled. At the beginning of the watch, as usual, I had tuned one of the receivers to the local commercial aircraft frequency, which until then had netted nothing. It was the speaker connected to this receiver that was emitting the voice.

I hastily adjusted the tuning knob of the receiver.

"Hello! Coast Guard cutter! I know you're down there because I can see you!"

I was having difficulty believing my ears. I glanced at Meek, who was blinking and yawning, and staring at the speaker.

"Did you hear that?" I asked.

"Is it somebody in trouble?"

"Coast Guard, this is United Air Lines Flight Niner-Two-Zero, San Francisco to Honolulu! Come in!"

"If I was you, I wouldn't touch that with a ten-foot pole!" warned Meek, sitting up straight. "It doesn't sound like an emergency. Garnes would skin you alive if you let yourself get into a plain language communications with an aircraft."

"But it might be an emergency," I said, already tuning and zero-beating a transmitter to the frequency. "Then I'd be court martialed for refusing to answer."

"You'll sure as heck be court martialed if you get on the air with plain language and there's no emergency."

I did not believe that for a second.

"This is the Coast Guard cutter. How can I be of help?"

"Well, howdy, down there! Thanks for returning my call. This is the skipper of ole Nine-twenty, ridin' side-saddle right now and gettin' ready to turn in. Just thought I'd see if you guys was on the ball down there!"

"You are in trouble," said Meek, getting up and beginning to pace the deck. His eyes never left my face.

Placing a hand over the mike, I said, "You keep it quiet and there will be no trouble."

"Hey, don't worry about me. It won't be me that'll tell on you!"

"Into the mike I said, "It gets a bit lonesome down here on these mid-watches, Skipper. You wouldn't have a pretty hostesses standing by, would you?"

"Why, I just might have!" came the reply. "Stand by one."

"How many times you been busted, Red?" asked Meek, shaking his head sadly.

"More times than Carter has little liver pills." I laughed and added, "Stop worrying, Meek. This is not a court martial offense."

"Hey, Coast Guard, you ready to talk to somebody real pretty?"

"I am ready," I said. "Put her on."

For a moment there was only a mild hissing sound on the aircraft frequency; then a soft, husky voice said, "Hi, Coast Guard, what are you doin' down there?"

"Getting ready to go to Mare Island," sang out Meek.

"Just sitting here talking to you," I said with a laugh. "Thinking about beautiful women and Stateside duty."

"That and nothing else? Well, my name's Denise. What's yours?"

"My friends call me—"

I put my hand over the mike and called out to Meek, "What's your first name?"

He had gone out into the passageway, and my question must have caught him by surprise because right after he said, "Charles," he demanded to know why I was asking.

"My friends call me Charles, Denise," I whispered into the mike.

"Well, Charley, did you know it's a beautiful moonlit night? I bet you haven't even looked out."

"As a matter of fact!" I laughed.

"Listen, I've got to go, Charley."

"What's your hurry?" I protested. "Listen—"

The skipper was talking again, "Yeah, Coast Guard, Denise says bye. We'll be back this way day after tomorrow." The frequency went dead.

"I wonder what time day after tomorrow," I mused.

Meek was staring at me wide-eyed. "Why did you want to know my name?" he demanded. "It sounded like that girl was callin' you *Charley*."

"You didn't think I was going to give her my name, did you?" I said. "Now, if you go blab this to anyone and it'll be you that will have to explain, not me."

"I told you I wouldn't be the one to blab," he whined. "But you had no right to give my name."

"From now on you're the lookout. Nobody sneaks up on us when we're monitoring that aircraft frequency."

"I can't guarantee that. Someone might tiptoe up the passageway."

"Then you'd better put your chair outside in the passageway."

It suddenly occurred to me that somewhere in the radio shack there should be an up-to-date listing of the airlines' regular flight schedules and operating frequencies. I glanced up at the shelf where the transmitter manuals were kept. Meek knew exactly what I was thinking.

"Over there," he said with a grimace.

After some digging, I discovered that United Air Lines Flight 920 made regular flights each Monday and Friday to and from San Francisco and Honolulu at about the same time; and, after a bit of head-scratching, I settled upon zero-two-forty-five, as the time they would be overhead. Almost exactly in the middle of our mid-watch.

Two midwatches later I had just glanced at the clock when the airliner skipper, whose name turned out to be Mike, checked in.

"Halooo, down there, Coast Guard cutter! You got your ears on?"

"Sure have," I said. "Charley speaking."

"Well, Charley, my adventuresome lad, are you ready to speak to the prettiest girl in the sky?" Mike was obviously amused by the diversion this ocean-to-sky blind dating was creating, and his match-making role in it.

"Hi, Charley," came Denise's soft voice. "Are you going to spend the rest of your life on that same spot in this great big ocean?"

"Hi, Denise. Someday I'll be back in Frisco. Where do you live when you're on land?"

"Why, Frisco, honey. Would you come and see me sometime?"

"Sure will! Just say the word."

"Sorry to cut this so short, Charley, but I've got to run."

Meek was at the open hatchway, sighing unhappily. I signed off and muted the speaker.

"You know that nobody ever calls me Charley. That is not my name and if the Chief ever finds out what's going on, he will know who's behind it."

"Just maybe," I said, tapping nervously on the desktop. "That girl has the sexiest voice I ever heard. Meek, old top, can you judge the looks of a girl by her voice?"

"I'll bet she fat and ugly."

"I don't think so. She's working for a major airlines. They wouldn't hire somebody like that. I think she's as pretty and sexy as her voice."

At the outset of the third exchange, Mike suggested that I pay the stewardess a visit in Frisco. She could talk about nothing else, he said. Denise, when she came on, began to open up about herself. She was, she said, between boyfriends, had an apartment near Golden Gate Park, and loved to go dancing and sailing. Each item of information she gave about herself had to be followed by something about me. I told her I was also between girlfriends and that I liked to dance and sail.

"Would you go dancing and sailing with me?" I asked.

"Yes," she laughed nervously, "that might be fun." But she did not commit herself to a date. And when I asked for her address, the skipper broke in and said that something had come up and he had to terminate the connection.

As our time at Weather Station Fox drew to an end, I began to worry that I would never hear from my mysterious sweetheart again. All I knew about her was her first name and that she had an apartment in San Francisco, near the Park. And that she had the sweetest voice west of the Pecos.

Word had circulated about the ship, at least among the enlisted, that I had been holding a regular schedule with an airliner, that I was, indeed, *courting* one of the hostesses. The Chief cornered me one day and began joking about what happened to radiomen who *moonlighted* over the airways. Before I could say anything, the Communications Officer, Lt. Flores, walked up and demanded to know if the scuttlebutt was accurate about a member of the radio gang and the airline stewardess. The Chief guffawed at such an idea, assuring the officer that no such thing would ever happen in *his* radio shack. The lieutenant laughed and said that as long as it occurred on the midwatch he saw nothing wrong with it. The Chief pursed his lips and nodded, but said nothing.

"But I advise you to tell your men to restrict their amorous activities to that particular watch," the lieutenant added, glancing at me.

On the evening before we were to steam for San Francisco, I could hardly wait for the midwatch to begin. It would be the last possible chance I would get to speak to Denise for a very long time, and everything depended upon whether I could get her full name and address. I had decided that I would boldly ask her for a date, and then I would insist upon a time and a place to rendezvous.

A gnawing question had to be faced. Was she playing some kind of game with me? Her goal in life, she had told me, was to become a movie actress. Was she practicing on me? Her voice had been so very sincere, and I was certain that she was not faking when she told me that she couldn't wait to talk to me each time the plane flew out from San Francisco. On the return flights, which arrived over Weather Station Fox around noon, we could not even say hello to each other.

Fifteen minutes before the plane was due to fly over us, I barked at the disgruntled Meek to take up his position outside the hatch. Since he was obviously responsible for the scuttlebutt that had been going around about me and Denise, I had not bothered to tell him what the Com Officer had said. What he did not know would not hurt him. "Keep especially alert this time," I warned, "because I think the CPO just might have something up his sleeve."

There hadn't been a crackle out of the speaker for two hours; but at exactly two-forty-five I pressed the mike button and called the air liner. Nothing. On pins and needles, I waited five minutes and called again. Nothing but static. In a panic, I put the mike down, certain that it was all over. For whatever reason, Denise had decided to end the relationship. Something had happened. Maybe there had been a change in flight scheduling.

"Hey, Coast Guard, you down there?"

More joyous words I had never heard!

"Sure am, Skipper. What's up?"

"Well, some bad news, I'm afraid. Sorry to tell you this!" His voice suddenly stopped, as if he had muffled the microphone.

A great weight had settled in the pit of my stomach. Now the truth, I thought. The game's over. Denise was just having a bit of fun to while away those midnight hours. And practice her acting skills.

"Hey, Charley, you there?" sang out Mike. "Your sweetie didn't make this trip." A long pause and then, "She told me to give you a message. You ready?"

I was so goofed up I couldn't say a word.

"She wants you to look her up in Frisco. Got a pencil handy? Here's the poop."

At that precise moment, as I readied myself for the all-important address, my anxious fingers poised above the typewriter keys, Meek began to scream from his lookout post near the hatch.

Ignoring him, I finally managed, "Go ahead, Skipper! Give it to me fast!"

The airline pilot, sensing that something was wrong, spoke rapidly, "Her name's Elizabeth Denise Mahoney! That's enough for you to find her, Charley! She's in the phone book!" The speaker went dead.

I swiveled around. Meek, with his eyes fairly popping, was standing in the hatchway, looking like death itself. And behind him, looking very amused, was Lt. Flores.

"Did you get it?"

"Yes, Sir!"

"I had every confidence you would."

Charley Meek, I noticed, was fairly gawking at me.

The CGC Bramble

◆

It was a cold, damp, ominous morning, typical for San Francisco in the fall of the year. The *Chautauqua*, finally at rest at its mooring at Government Island, looked like a ghost ship in the heavy fog that gave a gray cast to everything and muffled the sounds of San Francisco Bay. Dressed for the occasion in a peacoat, with the collar turned up, I made my way down the port side lifeline with a mug of steaming coffee in my gloved right hand. I had once again anticipated reveille by an hour and was on my way to my favorite spot on the bow.

"Wait up, Red!"

G. T. Goodrich, with only his eyes showing above the collar of his peacoat, was emerging from the hatch behind me.

"This has got to be a first," I said. "I can't remember you ever rising this early without strong provocation."

"I wanted to catch you before—uh—"

"Why are you stuttering?"

"I found out last night from Snider you're bein' transferred."

I lowered my mug and turned to stare out across the Bay. He lined up beside me and for a time neither of us said anything.

Finally, I cleared my throat and said, "Well dog my cats. Was it Mister Garnes?"

Goodrich nodded, his hangdog face looking tragic.

"Fiddle, I don't care." I sipped my coffee and after another long pause, I said, "What part did Lt. Flores play in it?"

"Well, you realize a CPO has more clout in the Coasties than a junior officer does, anything up through a full lieutenant, that is. Mr. Flores tried to go to bat for you and may have got his own ass in a sling. He finally had to admit you violated regulations by carrying on with that airline stewardess. Garnes pointed out that you were a maverick and this was just one thing you had been up to."

"Well, heck. If you'll pardon my French. What a lot of nonsense. I can't wait to get out of this hooligan outfit. Every time I turn around I get the book thrown at me."

"Well, you have to admit you was breakin' a rule, Red."

"A rule like that doesn't make sense." I took another sip of my coffee and studied the water below. "So, when is the Captain's Mast scheduled?"

"Lt. Flores saved you from that. It's just a straight transfer."

"Where to this time, Goat Island?"

Goodrich was visibly surprised. "You already knew, you joker."

It was my turn to be surprised. I quickly put out my hand for support. "Heck no I didn't know! What're you talking about? *Goat Island?* I didn't even know such a place existed!"

"Well, that's the nickname for Yerba Buena Island. You've heard of that, haven't you?" When I shook my head, he added, "That's where your ship ties up. Your new place of residence is going to be the CGC *Bramble*, which ties up there."

"Isn't that a buoy tender? An old rusty, stinking buoy tender?"

"I don't know about the rusty, but the Bramble is a buoy tender, and she does it all the way from here to the Oregon state line."

"My God, whose idea was this?"

"Red, everything that happens doesn't have to be a deliberate hit at you. The *Bramble* needed a radioman in the worst way, and you were suddenly available. I did pick up the scuttlebutt that Garnes knows an ex-chief quartermaster on the *Bramble*."

"Yeah. You know, old buddy, you're always Johnny-on-the-spot with good news."

"Don't lay the blame on me, Red Dog. Right now you'd better high-tail it to Mr. Flores' office. I was delegated to tell you that."

"Well, why didn't you say so an hour ago?"

He raised a middle finger and turned back toward the hatch. I followed as far as the messdeck, where we got rid of our coffee mugs. Then I took my time climbing the ladder to Officers' Country.

Lt. Flores opened his stateroom door to me, nodded toward a waiting chair. I settled in it and waited for him to open the conversation.

He sat on the corner of his desk eyeing me. "Goodrich gave you the word, about the transfer?"

"Yes, Sir."

"I'm sorry it didn't work out for you on the *Chautauqua*, Hall. You're being transferred to the CGC *Bramble*, which is a buoy tender stationed at the Coast Guard Supply Base at Yerba Buena Island, midway point of the Oakland-San Francisco Bay Bridge. You will be the only radioman aboard. How do you feel about that?"

"I think I would like that, Sir."

"I thought you would, and I hope you make this change—feeling that it is actually a step up for you."

For a moment I took stock of my situation. I was being transferred to a miserable buoy tender. I had not requested the transfer. No reason was being given for my dismissal from the *Chautauqua*.

Lt. Flores leaned back in his chair, smiling. "Indeed, I think this is the kind of—assignment that will just suit you. And the *Bramble* is a fine ship, with a fine record of service. And she really needs a radioman with experience and imagination. But one word of caution before you shove off."

"Yessir?"

"You'll go aboard with at least one strike against you. Make up your mind to behave yourself."

"Yes, Sir."

"I know she looks a bit scroungy, but you'll have it pretty much your own way in the radio shack. And let's face it," he laughed, "you don't do too well under the watchful eye of a CPO. You need the *Bramble*—and, evidently, she needs you. Of course, life aboard one of those things is pretty rough. I know because I've been there." For a moment he gazed thoughtfully through the porthole at his right elbow. "And something else. There's an officer on that ship by the name of Lt. Mason, who came up through the ranks, like me. He will probably give you a hard time, until he gets to know you."

"Thanks for telling me, Sir. Because—of my record?"

The lieutenant nodded quickly. "But if you watch yourself and play it straight with him, you'll be all right. I was once an enlisted man, Red. And I know only too well how one thing leads to another in this outfit. So make me proud of you. Good luck."

*   *   *

The following day an old battered Jeep showed up at the gangplank of the *Chautauqua*. It was driven by a kid whose appearance soon attracted spectators on the quarterdeck of the immaculate cutter. From his battered old golfball cap to his waist he was covered with grease smears and dirt. He parked beside the gangplank and lighted up a cigarette, staring back at the swabs on the cutter. Then, having lost interest in the grinning faces above him, he sat studying the neat and trim ship and taking in the comings and goings of the clean and tidy crew. Finally, he called out to the gangway watch:

"Hey, mate! You there, Pretty Boy!"

The man on duty at the gangplank happened to be a coxswain in freshly laundered whites, a third generation career boatswain's mate who prided himself on his appearance. When he realized that the unclean thing in the old Jeep was addressing him, he hastily glanced around to see if anybody had heard the insult. To his mortification, at least eight of his shipmates were gleefully observing the little scene from the lifeline.

"Move away from the gangplank!" he shouted, his voice failing on the last word. "Git!" he screeched.

The driver laughed nastily, "Listen, Pretty Boy, go git the transfer I'm supposed to pick up, a guy named Hill or Hull or somethin'! On the double now!"

"Hey, down there in the Jeep!" one of the spectators called out. "Better not let the Boats catch you with a lighted cigarette!"

At that moment I arrived on the scene with my gear, just in time to hear the second blast from the coxswain. After listening to it for awhile, instead of trying to explain that this was my transportation, I dropped my seabag at the gangplank, took out my orders, and logged myself off the ship. The gangway watch turned and stared at me. I shouldered the seabag, hopped upon the gangplank, and did a salty double salute, one to the coxswain and the other to the fantail of the cutter.

"Wait a minute!" shouted the watch. His face was scarlet and he was breathing hard from his recent exertion. I pointed toward the logbook and, after a brief glance, he turned back and waved. "Okay!"

The driver of the Jeep was smoking a fresh cigarette, apparently enjoying the spectacle at the gangplank. His left foot was now resting on the rearview mirror, and he had slouched into as comfortable a position as it is possible to assume in the front seat of a Jeep.

"What's cookin'?" he asked, as I raised my seabag to toss it into the back. Bending his upper body slightly, he glanced at the back seat. "Just drop it anywhere. Don't mind the mess."

Having no choice in the matter, I lowered my seabag across the seat and set my ditty bag beside it.

"Too bad about them whites, Red. But on the tender you won't have much use for them anyway."

"How about liberty?"

"Dungarees."

"I take it there is no dress code on the tender."

"What's that?" he laughed. "Oh, you mean what I'm wearin' now? Sure, dungarees. I'm not on liberty, you know." He started up the Jeep and backed away from the piling. "I volunteered to come over here and git you. Come right out of the engineroom."

I sat very straight, acutely aware that I had already picked up a bad smear on my right sleeve. The clutter and griminess of it all was unbelievable but my only protest was a very meek, "Holy cow."

"My sentiments exactly. You settled in okay?"

I wanted to ask if he intended to launch the thing into space, but I merely nodded and he gunned the Jeep in low gear all the way to the Main Gate. The high-pitched protest of the engine and the cloud of smoke we left behind somehow seemed a fitting gesture of farewell to the sane world of G. I.

At the Gate, while the Jeep smoked up the area, the driver ignored the gate watch while observing to me casually, "Man, the Coasties is takin' some mighty sad stuff these days." And although he was probably referring to the coxswain and the spectators who had assembled at the gangplank of the cutter, it was quite possible he was including me, as well. Over the roar of the motor, his voice sounded like the cackle of a rooster. "Forget about that bunch of fairies, Red! I'm takin' you to a very different kind of Coast Guard!"

I had gone into a trance and was staring straight ahead. After a time I was able to shake that mood and say to him, "Sorry about the wisecrackers back there."

"Hey, no sweat! You know what you're gettin' yourself into?" When I didn't say anything, he continued, "Actually, it's not bad. The ship, I mean. We service buoys of one kind and another, an' the deck gang catches most of the shit. Glad I'm not one of that bunch of apes."

"You're in the engineroom."

"Right on." He seemed cheered by the thought and added, "And you're the new sparks. We aint had one of them for about a month, an' he wasn't worth shit. I guess it don't make no never mind anyway, since nobody ever wants to git in touch with us by radio. 'Cept Headquarters, and the only thing we ever get from them is the same shit messages. We do the same work over an' over, so we don't need much of anything from Headquarters."

"What's Yerba Buena like?"

"Man, there aint no such place! Nobody ever calls it that. Goat Island is what we call it, and that's what it is. But it's a real island, not a man-made pile of shit like T. I. and that garbage heap G. I. I guess it's the only Coast Guard supply base this side of Seattle."

After that exchange he went into a trance of his own and had nothing to say until we were on the Bay Bridge, bearing down on the midway point.

"Hold onto your hat!" he yelled and whipped the Jeep to the right and came to a sudden stop. "I guess you know T. I.'s right down there," he said, nodding his head to the left. "Well, we're over here, on this side," he waved vaguely to our right and pointed downward. "Anybody can go to Treasure Island, but only the elite git to go to Goat Island," he joked, shifting to first gear and easing the Jeep through a gate. Then he shifted to second and left it there all the way down a steep and winding one-lane road. About halfway down the spiral, I decided that it was going to go on forever. We went through another gate and suddenly were traveling between great mounds of rusting metal and what I assumed was garbage and discarded machinery.

"What is all this stuff?" I asked.

"Garbage, mostly. Some of it's stuff we use to repair the buoys and keep them in position."

Through the dense fog and mist I saw something that caused me to suck in my breath. It would turn out to be the *Bramble*.

"Holy cow," I sighed.

"My sentiments exactly. Aint she a beauty? She don't look no better up close."

Suddenly, out of the soup, came a high metal gate with a wooden sign running across the top. It said, "U. S. Coast Guard Depot, Unauthorized Personnel Keep Out."

On either side of the road now were endless rolls of cables and buoys and unnamable junk, evidently dumped there against the time the *Bramble* or some other buoy tender would come along and have a need for it. The strip of a road we were on skirted the north side of the island, winding through the maze of clutter, most of which was painted a brilliant orange.

An enlisted man in dirty undress blues and a sad-looking old Navy peacoat came out of nowhere at the driver's honk and unlocked the gate.

"Bascum," said the driver, nodding toward the gatekeeper, "a lousy deck ape. The only man on the ship that wears blues."

I was staring past the deckhand and the rubble at the buoy tender. There it was, sitting high in the water, wide and squat and covered with rust, an unpainted glob of rusting metal, unlike any Coast Guard cutter I had ever seen. Then I realized with a shock that I had not only seen this thing before I had actually been rather close to it back in February, when I was aboard the CGC *Alert*. But on that occasion I had paid very little attention to it, my only memory being that it was a complete contrast to the clean, white air-sea rescue cutter moored behind it.

There was no movement on the deck, no gangway watch, and nobody in the pilothouse. The driver, without a word, stopped the Jeep at the gangplank, went across to the metal deck without so much as a glance in the direction of the Union Jack, and disappeared into the ship.

Then I noticed that there was no flag on either the stern or the mast! Startled, I gathered up my gear and stumbled across the gangplank, saluting the fantail and mumbling the ritualistic, "Permission to come aboard, Sir." Of course, there was no Sir around either; so I dropped my bags on the dirty deck and followed them, hopping down the two feet or so. By instinct, for no smell from below could compete with the deck stench, I soon found the galley and the messdeck. They were one and the same.

A bearded man wearing a black turtleneck sweater and dirty white tennis shoes arose from a small group huddled at one end of a table. "You the new sparks?"

I nodded, wondering if the driver had bothered to tell anyone of my arrival.

"Mr. Mason wants to see you as soon as you get settled."

"Is he the Com Officer?"

From the group at the table came an ugly chuckle. The man in the turtleneck sweater said, "We've got three officers aboard this tender, the Skipper, the Exec, and Mr. Mason. I guess you'd better report to Mason."

Another swab spoke up, "Toss your gear against the bulkhead over there. The lieutenant don't like to be kept waitin'."

The appearance of the driver of the Jeep had prepared me to some extent for the crew of the *Bramble*. One look at the little group at the table convinced me beyond a shadow of down that cleanliness was not one of the virtues of this ship. They smelled like creosote and diesel and were dressed in soiled and ragged clothing, most of which had not come from any Coast Guard Ship's Stores.

"Follow me," said the one in the turtleneck, moving toward a hatchway. "Better watch yourself. You might git somethin' on them pretty duds you're wearin'."

"Why's everybody so friendly?" I called out. "Is it my clothes?" With the exception of the Jeep driver, who had not bothered to introduce himself, I had not seen one friendly face. "Maybe if I would go find some crud and smear it all over me I could become one of you fellows."

The big swab said nothing as he mounted a metal stairway toward the bridge.

"My name's—"

"I know who you are," he growled. "Could I give you some advice, Red?"

"I'd appreciate anything you've got to say, Tiny."

"Just keep your trap shut until you have something to say."

"Hey, you got it."

We made a right and went up another steel ladder to a steel deck, took a left out onto a short latticed steel runway, and entered what could not possibly be the radio shack. Tiny assured me it was, but never in all my life had I seen a room so cluttered with junk. At some distant point in the past someone had evidently set out to paint the confusion of coaxes and pipes and stanchions in the overhead and on the bulkheads; but the job had been aborted, and over the years the white paint had turned yellow and green and black. And over this and everything else had accumulated a thick layer of dirt and grime, smeared here and there by sweating hands!

"Mr. Mason," said the guide, "here's the new sparks."

Sitting at the only operating position in the shack was a man in wrinkled khaki, with his shirt unbuttoned at the throat. Lying across the typewriter in front of him was an operating manual of some kind. There were no bars on the collar of his shirt.

"Yeah. Show him in, Simmons."

"Thanks, Simmons," I said, standing back so that the big swab could leave. Ignoring me, he lumbered off.

For a long moment the officer and I stared at each other. He picked up the aging operating manual and tossed it to the desk. Glanced back at me.

"Whatever it takes, we've got to get this pile of junk working. We've got to be able to contact the base by radio, instead of going to a pay telephone." He paused, waiting for me to say something, his face deadpan. "Do you speak English?"

I wanted to laugh at that remark, but instead I cleared my voice and said, "Sir, pardon me, but I have no idea what you expect me to say."

"Well, I guess I expect you to lighten up, mostly. Say what you think. I'm not going to bite your head off."

"Sir, I will need some time to—"

Suddenly, he was on his feet and heading for the open hatchway. "The problem is we need voice communications with NMC right away. I just wanted to let you know that the need is urgent, this crap won't work, and I'm ready to get whatever spare parts you need." He stopped and looked back at me with a grin, "The bee's on my butt as well as yours to get this stuff percolating, so why don't you check things out, make a list, and give me a shout?"

I had never heard an officer speak in the vernacular of a common seaman, especially to an enlisted man. It was a bit scary to be addressed thusly, and I resolved on the spot never to let my guard down in the presence of Lt. Mason.

*   *   *

The radio room was ten square feet of junk radio equipment. On the forward bulkhead was a built-in desk so cluttered with receivers, books, typewriter, manuals, test equipment, and one brass key that I could find no place to set a coffee mug.

On the port bulkhead, rising out of the clutter, was an enormous transmitter. It was five feet tall and bolted to the deck with L-braces, and immediately I knew I had found an old and respected friend. It was a TDE, the twin brother of the one I had wrestled with during the war.

"Why didn't your former radioman fire up this lovely lady?" I had asked Mr. Mason. It was a two KW transmitter, capable of making the monkeys in South Africa sit up and take notice!

"He didn't *fire it up*, as you put it, because it won't fire up. He spent the better part of a year trying to get it going."

"So all you had was harbor stuff, line-of-sight?"

"Precisely. Which was enough to get us permission from district headquarters to depart. But the Old Man wants like hell to be able to get out to somebody when we're underway. When we head north, we're on our own until we can find a landline."

After the lieutenant left, I replaced him in the only chair, which was also bolted to the deck, and took up the manual he had tossed on the desk. It occurred to me at that point that the *Bramble*, built like a claw-foot bathtub, must hit some pretty rough waters along the northern California coast.

Suddenly, I became aware that somebody was standing in the open hatchway behind me. I swiveled around as far as the chair would go in the crowded compartment and found myself facing a tall, sour-faced swab in his late twenties. He had the black, cavernous eyes and heavy black eyebrows of my father; and what I read in his face put a chill in my heart.

"The name's *Perrin.* I'm in charge of the bridge, and in case you're not already aware of it, that includes the radio shack."

Without hesitating, I blurted, "I think you better check that out with Mr. Mason. I've just been told I'm in charge of the radio shack."

"You're not *in charge* of anything, mate. Your job is to man the radios."

Before I could respond to that he turned and left.

For a full minute I stared at the operating manual spread across the typewriter, trying to figure out what had just transpired. I had signed aboard the *Bramble* expecting trouble from a line officer, who had turned out quite friendly. Now, from a completely unexpected source had come a different kind of trouble, from a vengeful, jealous-minded quartermaster. But why would this tall drink-of-water want to be in charge of the radio shack? I tried to imagine myself being in charge of the bridge. It made no sense at all.

I got up and took a turn around the big transmitter. The back panels lifted off easily, revealing twenty-six vacuum tubes varying in size from a thimble to a fruit jar. The power source had long ago been disconnected, of course. I began tracing power cables and coaxes. Nothing seemed to be missing there. Systematically, I hand-tested all the tubes, seating the loose ones as tightly as possible. Some of them were smoked, and one rattled when I gave it a shake. A tube tester, also of ancient vintage, told me that five of the tubes were either borderline or dead; and in a large drawer filled with radio parts, I found duplicates of all but one of these and replaced them. Then, in a tube manual, holding my breath, I scanned the pages, found what I was looking for, and wrote down the recommended substitutes for the ones I couldn't find.

"Here goes nothing." Diving once again into the huge drawer of tubes, this time looking for substitutes, I started by studying the bases, number of prongs, size and shape of the glass envelopes.

There were no exact substitutes, but I did find two that I thought just might work, according to the specifications in the manual. Then it occurred to me to glance at the schematic diagrams in the manual and check what was supposed to be against what was actually plugged in.

Just maybe, I thought.

"Well, what do you know!" I yelped. He—whoever he was—my predecessor—had overlooked an important detail! "I can't believe it!"

That former sparks, perhaps my immediate predecessor but perhaps not, had plugged in a wrong tube, no doubt thinking that it was close enough in the specs to replace the bad one; and when it had blown, he had not gone back to the transmitting parts list and ordered a proper replacement. I carefully wrote down the number of the correct tube and, once again, went to the tube manual and looked for a suitable replacement. After frustrating for thirty minutes, only to learn that none of the substitutes was available to me (a thing I should have anticipated), I suddenly realized that since it was a power tube and the initial surge of DC power was quite great, a similar power tube with more liberal requirements would likely serve the purpose as well or even better. Keeping a list of the required tubes at hand, I went back to the drawer.

And at once I found a substitute.

With a dummy antenna connected to the antenna output and fingers crossed, I plugged in the main power source and flipped the master switch.

Nothing happened, not even the *frapping* sound of a tube going to Davy Jones' locker.

It occurred to me that the other power tube, which had checked very strong on the checker, just might be a phony. Quickly, I replaced it with an identical twin of the replacement tube. If (*I grinned stupidly at the thought*) these two monsters should fire up, they would do grand things with the final emission, the RF energy that would go pinging off toward the ionosphere! Instead of two kilowatts of power, I would more than likely have *ten!*

If they didn't fire up, of course, I would be forced to send out for replacements.

In no hurry this time, I replaced the back panel and the two additional service panels I had removed, and, walking around to the front, flipped the power source.

From deep inside that big warehouse of bolts and nuts and resistors and capacitors and tubes came a pitiful little high-pitched squeal of surprise! Then, one by one, the tubes began to light up! *The monster was alive!* I squinted through the vent slits! A loud single *pop* sent me backward; but, instantly, a very healthy hum, which I recognized as the song of the final tubes, sent my adrenaline into overdrive! Tubes were glowing brightly, and the old TDE was beginning to sound well and happy!

At this point, I fell into the swivel chair and tried to calm down a bit, while the TDE slowly came to its full potential. It would need a good five minutes for this girding up of the loins, especially after so long a rest; but what a wallop it would have once it was fully alive and tuned to a Coast Guard frequency!

I was like a kid with a precious toy that no other kid on the block had, or was likely to have.

Sipping my cold coffee, my mind racing a mile a minute, I began to worry about the antenna. All the power in the world would not go anyplace without a good antenna. *What would the SWR be? If I could get the standing wave ratio down close to one-to-one—!*

Five minutes passed, according to the brass chronometer on the forward bulkhead; and, with my hand poised above the transmitting key, I decided to do a test with the dummy antenna. That at least was not likely to blow the whole thing up when I zero-beat the final tubes.

The only receiver in the shack that had any life in it was a Hallicrafters SX-25. It was tuned it to a Coast Guard harbor frequency.

I quickly searched out and found the antenna connection on the back of the TDE and tied in the dummy, feeling like a coward. Once again, with my hand suspended above the key, I said out loud to myself, "You will never know if you don't bite the bullet."

I began with the plate and carrier currents, both of which dipped nicely. "*No problemo,*" I said, fainthearted. So far so good. The monster was behaving exactly as it should. Then, holding my breath, I dipped the final RF output.

"Oh, my God!" I cried.

I stared, first at one meter and then at another, very much aware that I did not deserve the miracle I was seeing!

With heart pounding, I removed the dummy antenna and connected the coax lead-in to what had to be the main antenna. Once again through the tuning stages I went, experiencing some slight problem at times with one stage or the other; but at last I dipped the final, while holding down the mike button and staring at the output power meter.

"Hello, test," I said softly into the mike. I cleared my voice and said firmly, "Testing! Q R Zed the band. Does anybody copy? Over."

The instant I let up on the mike button, a voice burst from the speaker, which was directly above the radio position, "This frequency is restricted to official Coast Guard communications."

I could not resist laughing into my mike, having recognized the voice.

"Say something else, Collins, while I adjust my receiver! My, my, what a beautifully-modulated voice you have today!"

For a moment there was only the crackle of radio frequency energy on the frequency, what radio operators call *Q R Nancy*. Then, "Who is the unidentified operator on this restricted frequency? If I didn't know better, I'd swear it's a redheaded SNAFU on the CGC *Chautauqua.*"

"You didn't use adjectives like that the time you needed twenty bucks, old buddy!"

"Honest to God, Red, it is *you!*" After some hysterical laughter and a whapping sound that had to be his mike taking a beating, Collins' voice again filled the shack, "This time, mate, you've gone too far. When the brass finds out you're blatantly transmitting plain language on official Coast Guard frequencies—"

"How are they going to find out, Collins? Are you going to tell them? Is anyone in the Twelfth District likely to do it except somebody at NMC manning this particular frequency?"

Collins came right back with, "Here at Base, Red, we can do anything we feel like doin'. You dudes on the weather ships are the ones that have to watch their *P's* and *Q's.*"

"Which reminds me. Could you give me the radio call of the CGC *Bramble?*"

"Well, sure, but why would you want to call that tub? Surely, the *Chautauqua* couldn't have business with a buoy tender"

"Could you just give it to me?"

"Wait one." In less than a minute, he was back. "Okay, Red, here it is. I don't know why it wasn't on my list here at the operating position, but somebody evidently scratched it off—It hasn't gone down, has it?"

"The call, Collins! What is the call?"

"Yeah. It's *NRUB*. Nancy Roger Uncle Baker."

"Okay, fine, thanks. By the way, how about the phonetic call?"

After a pause, he said, "I don't think it has one. Just use *N R U B*. Oh, here it is. *Workhorse.*"

"That figures. Okay, would you give me a signal report?"

"My God, what do you need a signal report for? You're pinning my needle! The commercial broadcasting station down the street doesn't do that!"

The Fistfight

◆

The crew's quarters aboard the *Bramble* was a black hole that smelled like a Mississippi outhouse. It remained blacked out during the daytime, ostensibly for the benefit of those who stayed out all night on liberty and needed the sleep. But I was convinced it was mainly because of the filth that was lying about everywhere.

By feeling my way from bunk to bunk I was able to find my own, which always felt damp and smelled of mildew and vomit, even after I had put a freshly-laundered sheet and pillowcase on it.

Shortly after talking to Collins, formerly of the *Chautauqua* but at this time with the Twelfth District base radio station, I stretched out on my bunk to gloat over my recent triumph with the TDE transmitter. Maybe five minutes later, even before I had finished cataloging the smells and noises in that hole, there came a loud, demanding whisper from the open hatchway, "Hall, front and center!"

It was Perrin and he was waiting in the dim light of the passageway when I came through the hatch.

"The Old Man wants to straighten you out on a thing or two. It's likely he's been looking at your records."

"What is your problem, mate?"

Instead of answering my question, the quartermaster, looking as out of place on the *Bramble* as I did, turned and headed for the bridge. At the end of the passageway he stopped and glanced back. "In his cabin. Think you can you find it alone?"

"How many cabins are located right next to the pilothouse?"

"I hope he chews the shit out of you."

"Why would you want him to do a thing like that?"

The hatch that opened into the Captain's cabin, like everything else on the *Bramble*, was made of heavy, rusting metal; and once I was inside I noticed that it was outfitted with long-handled latches, for battening down.

"Hall, I want to make a couple of things very clear to you," he began without an introduction. "If you fuck up just once, I'll personally put you on bread and water and throw away the key. No monkey business on this ship."

Before me, sitting in a big swivel chair before a metal desk, both of which were was bolted to the metal deck, was a giant walrus with a handlebar mustache! He had turned and was facing across the room at me, dressed only in khaki trousers.

"Yes, Sir," I said, not entirely sure the Old Man wasn't trying to run a bluff on me.

"We don't have a laundry on this tender, but we've got a tack locker that'll serve the purpose! I damned if I'm goin' to put up with any of your tricks! Ever' ship you've been on you've fucked up. And if I didn't need a goddamned radio operator so bad, I'd never've allowed you to come across that gangplank."

"Yes, Sir."

"Now, you git your ass back there in the radio shack an' do what you have to do so we can git out of this fuckin' harbor."

"The radio equipment is working fine, Sir."

The Old Man's big Wallace Beery mouth dropped open and his little narrow-set eyes lined up on mine. Apparently, he needed some time to work out what I had just said; but after having accomplished this, he straightened up quickly, causing the chair to let out a loud squeak.

"What'n blazes did you say?"

"We're ready to go, Sir. The radio's working all right."

"Well, how'n hell did that happen? Lt. Moser just told me it would take a month to git that shit goin', providin' we could requisition a base repairman to do it!"

"It didn't need much fixing, Sir. Just a matter of replacing some bad tubes."

"Well, shit, why didn't you say so right off? Go git Castleberry!"

*   *   *

Lt. Mason, this time in dungarees, was suddenly standing in the center of the radio shack with a clipboard. "The Old Man gave me hell just now, but I'm still not certain what it was all about. You fixed the radio? Already?"

"All I did was check some tubes and do some guessing, Sir."

"Well, here's a message for Base. If you can manage it, you'll be on the Old Man's Christmas list. He started raving about the radio being fixed and nobody knowin' about it. Hell, you just came on the ship a couple of hours ago!" After pausing, he added, "Have you run into Perrin yet?"

"Yes, Sir, I have. He said he was in charge of the radio shack and everything else on the bridge. Is that accurate, Sir?"

"Could I give you a bit of advice, Red? Perrin is the light heavyweight champ of the Twelfth Coast Guard District, and it's altogether likely he could take out any of the other fighters, regardless of weight class. He is as quick and fights like it's the last one. I advise you to play it cool with him. He doesn't know a thing about radios; so why don't you just play along with him?"

"Is he in charge of the radio shack, Sir?"

"He's in charge of the bridge, and he has a right-arm rate."

"But I would like to know who's in charge of the radio shack, Sir."

"As far as I'm concerned, you are. What difference does it make?"

The lieutenant hadn't been gone two minutes when a beanpole of a swab in dirty khakis popped into the shack. He spoke with a Southern hill country accent and had a slight squint in his left eye, giving the impression that he was about to wink.

"The new sparks, right?"

I nodded, swiveling about to face him. He frowned good-naturedly and announced that he was the ranking boatswain's mate on the *Bramble* and that he had *heerd* I was quite a whiz with the *raddeo*.

"Yew need eny hep?"

"Sure," I said, enthusiastically. "I can always use some of that."

"I use'ta work on them thangs."

"Hey."

"Tried to hep t'other sparks, but he was too durned ignorant to take eny of my advice."

"'Too dumb and ignorant," I agreed, nodding again.

"Yep. Too ignorant to know when a bidey had some savvy and could be of hep to him."

"You wouldn't be Chief Castleberry, would you?"

"Shore am." The boatswain's mate began to look around for a place to sit. "Whut's thet?" He dragged an open five-gallon paint can across the room and eased his bony bottom into it. "If'n you want people to visit yew, yew'd better pick up some furniture."

I nodded, grinning, and reached quickly for my clipboard, as if I intended to make out a list. "Hold on a minute. I've got to get this to NMC."

"Durn, I thought you was gettin' serious 'bout the furniture." He adjusted himself on the can. "Yeah, I'd shore like to see yew send a message from this here layout. Don't reckon I ever seen one go out from here. What're you goner use to git it acrost the pond, flags or smoke?"

I lifted the microphone that was lying on the operating position and flipped the transmit switch. "Charlie One, this is Workhorse, over."

"Go ahead, Workhorse."

"Well, would you look at thet!" cried Castleberry. "That's the durnedest thang I ever saw!"

"Message follows. To the Commanding Officer, Twelfth Coast Guard District, from Nancy Roger Uncle Baker. Request permission to get underway zero-six-zero-zero tomorrow's date for routine servicing patrol. End of message. Over."

"Red, is that you?"

"Uh, roger, Collins. Don't you ever get a break?"

"Listen, buddy, I want to know what you're doin' on that buoy tender? None of the sparks I've talked to have a clue."

"Listen, I'm trying to get a message through to Base."

"Have you forgot how to handle traffic on a C. G. frequency?"

"Hey, I thought that was pretty formal. At any rate it's exactly what the Skipper of this buoy tender wanted sent. Do I hear a roger?"

"Well, from now on you'd better use proper procedure. You clear?"

"Not without a roger."

"Shall we classify it?"

"Operational priority."

"I never heard of that classification. Sounds like World War Two. I'll roger your priority message Number One this day's date."

"Workhorse out."

Castleberry was smiling proudly when I turned around.

"That just about brings tears to my poor ole eyes," he said. "To think, all that junk there works."

"By the way, Boats, tell me something about the Old Man. What's he like?"

The boatswain's mate studied the deck between his feet for a moment, then said, "Wal, I don't reckon he's a bad sort. Likes to spend a lot of time at sea. Hates stayin' in port."

"Then why have you been in port so long?"

"Base called the Old Man on the landline and told him his requests had to be delivered by radio, said they wouldn't accept any more requests for departure by landline. Said he had better get and keep a sparks."

"You mean—"

"He's sent two or three back. But I thank he's gonna like you, Red."

"What's Lt. Mason like?"

"Don't tangle with that'n. Sober he's not a bad sort but drunk he's a sonofagun, if you'll pardon my French."

"How about Perrin?"

"A sidewinder. Meaner'n a rabied skunk. Golden Gloves champ, sem-eye-pro for a number of years, light heavyweight champ of this district for the past five or six years. I'd rather tangle with a female Tasmanian Devil."

"That bad, huh? How about liberty aboard this scow?"

"Lots of real short ones. The problem is the Old Man likes to think we'll be goin' out at anytime. So he wants ever'body back aboard ship by midnight."

"But how about when he's not even aboard? Does he stay aboard at night?" The expression on the Chief's face had suddenly changed to grim. "Why doesn't everybody take off as soon as he leaves the ship?"

"'Cause I won't let 'em. I have to answer to the Old Man myself."

"Well, how about tonight? I wanted to go ashore and have a couple of beers."

"That might kin be arranged—right after he calls."

"'After he calls'? You mean he calls you?"

"About nine o'clock. Ever' night we're in port, right on the dot pretty near. If'n you want to buy me a couple of beers, just nod yore head."

I nodded quickly, grinning

An hour later Coast Guard Base called with a priority message for us. I took it longhand and later typed it out on an official message form. When I delivered it on a clipboard to Lt. Mason, he said, "Good work," and read and sign a copy to pass on to the Skipper.

I was still in the shack a little after nine that night when Castleberry stuck his long, skewed neck through the hatch and let out what he later confided was his 'rebel liberty' yelp. He had not shaved, changed his clothes, or even combed his mop of thick black hair; but he had found a World War Two tie-dyed sailor's cap, something that had undergone a dunking in a very questionable liquid of some kind, perhaps diesel oil.

"Yall ready?"

I was still in my undress blues, and it seemed to me that one of us ought to change into something else. But without a word I fell in behind him and we went down to the main deck.

"I wisht you didn't look so danged spruced up," he said, pausing at the gangplank. "You may be a source of embarrassment tonight."

Ignoring him, I asked, "Won't the rest of the crew be pissed off at you for not sticking around?"

"What fer? They'll be right behind us, more'n likely."

We had to foot it all the way up the steep hill to the train stop, which had to be at least a quarter of a mile from the ship; but for a change it wasn't raining. All we had to do was avoid the deep water puddles that seemed to have been deliberately spaced about twenty feet apart all the way up the hill.

"Which'll it be?" he asked as we approached the second gate. "East or west? Heaven or Hell?"

"Could you be more specific?"

"Oakland or Frisco?"

"Oh. How about East Oakland? Do you know a place called *Ted and Roy's*?"

"Never heard of the place."

The entire way, which involved switching from the train to an electric bus, Castleberry talked, oblivious to everything around him, especially to the civilians who were constantly getting in his way as they boarded and disembarked from the bus. Most of it concerned his early years back in southwest Missouri as an apprentice to a radio repairman, where he had learned all there was to know about *radideeos*.

But one of his stories was about a Coastie, a Swede Chief Boatswain's Mate whom he had run into back during the Pacific war; and this one aroused my curiosity.

"Never will forget that feller. Oley Olson was his name. Ever hear of him? Well, in some ways you remind me of him a little. Carried himself like a prizefighter, kind of swivelin' on his hips when he walked, big-shouldered, soft-spoken, always grinnin'. Best man with his fists I ever saw. One night in Honolulu he got into it with some loudmouths over a gal. I was settin' at the bar talkin' to somebody, maybe a barkeep, and the first thing I knew there was the sound of an axe slammin' into a tree trunk an' here come this ugly Machinist's Mate First Class slidin' up ag'inst the bar on his back, out cold. Well, that got my interest so I turned and watched this feller clean the plows of four or five more of them motormacks! Durnedest thing I ever seen."

The bus stopped across the street from *Ted and Roy's*. We got off and stood for a moment contemplating the new Pabst Blue Ribbon sign in the one tiny window. It and the other neon sign, which said, "Ted and Roy's Hooligan Pub," were not turned on and the place looked closed.

We stood there for a time just looking at the place, while Castleberry told how this Olson earned the Congressional Medal of Honor.

"Chief, I think this place is closed."

"Thet's the way it always looks."

"I thought you never heard of *Ted and Roy's*."

"Shit, ever' Coastie worth shootin' knows about *Ted and Roy's*. It's been here ever since before the war. Started when Ted and Roy retired from the Service about 'Thirty-seven."

The door had once contained four small panes of glass, but these had been replaced by wooden panels and left unpainted, to weather and age their way to the same dull shade of gray as the old battered door.

"Sure is quiet in there," I said, to reinforce my argument that the place was closed. I tried the knob.

It almost fell into my hand, having been wrenched about every which way until it was hardly more than an appendage.

Ted himself was waiting the bar and seemed to recognize me at once. It had been awhile since I had visited this place, but Ted smiled at me and said as if no time had passed at all:

"Hey, Red, business sure fell off bad after you stopped comin' by and breakin' up my furniture. What're you on now?"

This brought a laugh from Castleberry, who had been hiding behind me. The instant Ted spotted him, he said for all to hear, "Don't tell me you're on that sorry *Bramble!* Somebody must really have it in for you, Red!"

"Maybe I misread you ag'in," said the Chief, looking around at me at Ted. "You know this feller?"

Ted moved over and began to wipe in front of us, eyeing Castleberry suspiciously, like he might be somebody dangerous. Suddenly, he dropped the rag and stuck out his hand, "Well, hell, if it aint Hoot Castleberry. I thought there for a minute Red had picked up something off Second Street."

"Be'n awhile, huh?" laughed the old Chief, shaking hands. "This young feller here came aboard the ship today claimin' to be our new sparks, says his name's Red. You know him?"

"Hoot, where'n hell have you been? This kid took Hatcher with bare knuckles, made the *Taney* safe for tourists, stole a Jeep from an officer of the goddamn *Taney's* deck, and saved the lower half of San Francisco from goin' up in smoke!"

I caught the last of this on my way to the head. When I returned, Castleberry squinted at me profoundly and said to Ted for my benefit, "Now that you mention it, I do recall hearin' somethin' about a' ex-Navy roughneck swab that sent Hatcher to the hospital with one punch. We

happened to be in Eureka at the time an' some of the crew actually saw
that little fracas."

"Don't he remind you a little of that Swede, what's his name?"
asked Ted.

Slim's bony elbow hit me in the ribs. "Now that you mention it."

*   *   *

The day came, and not long after my first liberty with Hoot, when
the old *Bramble* eased away from the dock at Goat Island and headed
up the northern California coast. Outside the little coves and inlets it
was like riding in a big ugly barrel, and there was no honor or pride
about it.

Our reason for being, of course, was to clean up and service buoys, a
backbreaking job for the deckhands and a very noisy, ugly one for
everybody aboard ship. The days were very long and the nights were
very short, and after two weeks of nonstop hoisting and chipping and
scraping and red-leading and, finally, painting every size and style of
buoy the crew was overripe for a liberty.

Until I signed aboard the old *Bramble* the sound of an innocent bell
buoy donging away in a fog-shrouded cove was soul-inspiring, reminis-
cent of the poetry of Thornton Wilder; but in no time it came to sym-
bolize long hours of noise, fret, and bother. And, it occurred to me, if it
was enough to ruin my day, what did it do for the deckhands who had
to do the scraping and painting? Never again would I be able to see the
poetry and romance, not to mention the mystery and excitement, of
places like the Big Sur and the coves above San Francisco.

A month went by, filled with one- and two- and three-day stopovers
in a dozen coves and inlets along the northern California coast, including Humboldt Bay and Sand Point, near the Oregon state line.

For at least a week the deck gang worked the buoys at the mouth of
Humboldt Bay, and each afternoon the *Bramble* tied up next to the

CGC *Yacona* , which had replaced the *Alert* as the air-sea rescue cutter of the region. I quickly developed the habit of putting on civvies, as anything but regulation Coastie clothing was called, and going into Eureka for a few beers at the *Triangle Bar and Hotel*. On more than one of these evenings I ended up at the home of Tony and Tonya.

Eventually, the *Bramble* wallowed back into San Francisco Bay and tied up at Goat Island, the worse for wear. The scuttlebutt was that we would not make another trip until spring. That made sense because on the way up and back, we had picked up two dozen buoys, large and small, which had to be thoroughly scraped, red-leaded, and painted. Free to come and go as I pleased, I spent a solid week painting the radio shack overhead, which was a jumble of pipes and cables. Then I began the long, slow task of requisitioning supplies and equipment.

The Skipper and the Executive Officer, each of whom had a wife and a home on the beach, checked in briefly each day but never stayed aboard at night, relying upon Lt. Mason and Chief Castleberry to control the men and keep the ship safe from pirates and marauders.

For the first week or so in port I saw nothing at all of Kyle Perrin, who was rumored to be on leave. Unlike the rest of the crew, he went ashore in undress blues; and since the first day back no one had seen him. Another rumor was that he was getting married, but since he had no friends aboard and therefore confided in no one, it was anybody's guess what he was doing.

Sometime during the second week he suddenly appeared on the bridge, dressed in starched and pressed dungarees so faded they were almost white. I had just returned from the messdeck with a mug of coffee when he popped through the door of the radio shack.

"Go down and tell Castleberry you want a paint brush and some white paint. You're going to paint the pilothouse. Be quick about it."

"I finished my painting," I said, "while you gallivanted around. If you want something painted, do it yourself."

"God damn it, git off your ass and do as I say!"

I faced him, as ready as I would ever be for the little showdown that I had known all along was coming. "You get your ass out of my radio shack."

To my surprise he did not put up his dukes. Instead, he blurted, "We'll just see about this!" And with that he wheeled and left.

I put my coffee down and followed him to the bridge. When I caught up, he was speeling off to the Executive Officer, Lt. Leonard.

"Why don't you want to do some painting on the bridge, Hall?" asked the Exec, looking disappointed.

"I've got lots of work to do in the radio shack, Sir."

The Exec turned to Perrin, "He does have a mess in there. Do you think you could manage the painting up here in the pilothouse?"

"Beggin' your pardon, Sir, I don't. I've got my other two men at work in the chartroom. This man is in my department, and I want him to paint the pilothouse. Sir."

"Well, I guess you are senior up here." Turning back to me, he said, " How do you feel about spending the mornings up here and the after-noons in the radio room?"

"If you say so, Sir."

The officer nodded, smiling, then turned and went toward his state-room, which was astern of the Captain's.

"Well, does that satisfy you, big shot?" asked Perrin.

"I'll get some paint and work up here, but, I'm warning you to stay away from me. You're not my boss."

I turned and left, heading not toward Castleberry's hideout in the Chiefs' quarters but back to the radio shack. And no sooner had I stepped through the open hatchway into my own territory than Perrin was right behind me.

"I said git your ass down there and get a bucket of paint and a brush!"

I had expected as much from this sour-faced quartermaster and turned quickly, with doubled fists. "Not just yet, tightbutt. Git out of here!"

Perrin glared at me from beneath his heavy black eyebrows, looking remarkably like my old man.

But instead of taking a swing at me, he began to edge toward the hatch. I brushed past him and slammed the heavy door and bolted it.

"Now, Big Shot, make me," I said, above a whisper. "Do your damnedest."

Perrin's mouth had dropped open. Then he said, choosing his words carefully, "Evidently, no one has said anything to you about me. If you don't git your ass down to the paint locker in about one second, I'm goin' to remake your face."

"Begin anytime you feel lucky."

"Listen, I do not like to brawl, especially aboard the tender. I'm no barroom fist-fighter. I'll meet you on the dock in five minutes."

"Let's keep it private, you slimy, stuck-up bastard. Do your thing right here." My right fist shot out toward his face, falling short.

The quartermaster ducked easily to one side, felt behind him for the door latch.

"We can't fight aboard the cutter, and you know it."

"I can fight anyplace I feel like it!" I said, lunging and grabbing his wiry arms and pinning him against a metal storage cabinet. "You need to learn never to step foot inside my radio shack again! You don't belong in here, you understand?" My right knee came up into his crotch, lifting him a foot off the deck. He gasped and tried to double over, but my right fist caught him just below the left ear, sending him flat on his face to the deck.

"Out—on the dock!" he choked, turning over on his back. "We'll both git a deck court for this—!"

Then we both heard the unmistakable sound of someone working at the handles on the hatch. I straightened up just as Hoot Castleberry's long face shot into the room.

"Why the—?" he began. Then his eyes became round with surprise when he saw Perrin stretched out on the deck. "You didn't kill him, did you, Red?" Satisfied I hadn't, he grunted, shaking his head. "What'd he do, say *Boo* to you?"

"He tried to make me paint the pilothouse."

"Well, hell, that was reason enough to put out his lights. Come on, help me get him down to the messdeck. How bad you hurt, Perrin?"

"Not half bad enough," I said.

Perrin sat up, looking at Castleberry. "I want to put this man on report!" he choked out.

"You do that," I said, "and it'll be the last time you'll ever put anybody on report."

"Why don't you boys settle this off the ship?" asked Castleberry. He turned to me, "How about the dock?"

"Nothing doing," I said. "I've already got a reputation for brawling on docks. In here, with the door closed, only we will know what went on."

"Wal, Red, I'll tell you, aboard this scow I'm responsible for the likes of yew. How about someplace away from the ship?"

I nodded quickly, "I would agree to meet him on the beach."

"You've got it," said Perrin, his eyeballs bulging from the blow in the neck.

"Okay, I've got a' idee. What if I can arrange something with Ted? I'll bet we could figure out something private for you boys. How about we aim for a Friday night about nine? As soon as we can get organized?"

I nodded and we waited for Perrin to say or do something.

"Okay, make it ten," said Castleberry. "That'll give us plenty of time to get there after the Skipper calls. You boys mind if I do a little advertisin'? I reckon there are them that would lay a bet on the outcome of this thing." Then he quickly added, "It'll be strictly for people we know, Coastie enlisted, no officers. Strictly on the QT."

The CGC Escanaba

◆

By Wednesday of the week following Hoot Castleberry's proposal, Coast Guardsmen on the West Coast from San Francisco to Sand Point on the north and San Diego on the south had heard about the whole thing. Everybody below the rank of ensign, as it turned out, knew about the grudge fight that was scheduled for that Friday night at *Ted and Roy's Hooligan Pub.*

Chief Hoot Castleberry was handling both the publicity and the call-in bets from the entire area; and Ted, co-owner of the pub where it would take place, had agreed to close the establishment to the public on that occasion, for a part of the action. The two of them were selling standing-room-only tickets for twenty-five bucks each to friends and friends of friends, and they had a word-of-mouth agreement that the latter and his partner would be fully compensated for any damage that might be done to the place. As a sweetener (and a clincher), Castleberry had pressed a fifty dollar bill into Roy's hand on Tuesday afternoon.

It was, Hoot discovered long before fight time, a veritable gold mine that he had happened upon. For, as it turned out, about half of the Coasties in California had heard of the invincible Kyle Perrin in the boxing ring and a surprising number had heard exaggerated accounts of my fistfight with Hatcher, who was a well-known barroom brawler on the West Coast.

To the former, those who followed professional and semi-profession-al boxing, it seemed a sucker bet because Perrin was, after all, the champ of the Twelfth District. Who had ever heard of this redheaded kid from Oklahoma? To the latter, most of whom had either served aboard a cutter with me or had seen me in a brawl, it was bound to be a good fight to watch, certainly worth twenty-five dollars.

*   *   *

When Hoot and I showed up at *Ted and Roy's* a little before ten that Friday night, Perrin and half a dozen well-dressed people I had never seen before were there seated at the only table in the place. They were huddled over it talking and sippng cocktails. Standing at the bar with Ted were my friends Goodrich, Archer, Sears, Husbands, Cheesy, Tully, and Miranda. The latter two, I was to learn, had managed to get three-day emergency passes, under the pretext of visiting a dying friend at the U. S. Marine Hospital.

At nine forty-five Ted and Roy, backed up by hand-picked Coastie bodyguards, positioned themselves outside the front door and began gathering the tickets Ted and Hoot had been selling all week. When Ted gave the nod, the door was closed, leaving about fifty unhappy Coasties and a few curious civilians milling around outside, blocking traffic.

"All right, men, listen up!" shouted Ted, as soon as he had the door bolted. "I'm the referee of this fight. Let's all shut up now. Git back against the walls and stay there! If I see anybody make voluntary contact with either one of these boys, I'll personally boot your ass out into the street! Is that understood? This is not a boxing match, of course, and so there will be no rounds. When I give the word, the fight will begin and it'll con-tinue until one of the two is either out cold or ready to concede to the other. Okay," (He nodded to me and then turned and looked at Perrin) "git out here! Front and center! Both of you, strip down to the waist!"

"What's the purse, Ted?" someone in the audience shouted.

"This is a grudge fight. There is no purse. Side-betting, of course, is allowed. But I reckon that has pretty well been worked out."

Perrin raised his hand for attention, and on his face was a look of self-assurance and pride. I realized he was actually smiling! "The purse is the bridge of the *Bramble*. If I win, which I will, this shitface will work for me. If he wins, which he surely will not, he takes charge of the bridge gang."

Perrin's little group of friends applauded.

I raised my hand. "If I lose, which I won't, I'll fight this peckerwood everyday from now on. And no matter what the outcome is I'll never give him an inch of the radio shack." Then I quickly added, "And I have no interest in the bridge gang."

"All right, go at it!" called out Ted, positioning himself between us in the center of the floor.

*   *   *

It was immediately clear that Perrin and I were opposites, in the way we fought. He danced around on the balls of his feet as though he were tip-toeing, dancing to the right and to the left, weaving and diving. Indeed, he made an extremely difficult target to hit. Being heavier and broader, I did not shuffle about much but I did keep on the move, always toward my opponent. I fought with my fists extended in front of my face, revolving like pistons, with my body bent at the middle. And in a very short time Perrin was to learn that reaching any part of my middle was quite difficult and hazardous.

Another difference between us was that Perrin liked to psyche-out his opponent. His mouth was going from the moment we lifted our fists and squared off. A lot of it was name-calling and bad-mouthing, but it had absolutely no effect on my style of fighting. My brother Bartley had tried that on me, to no avail.

As we began to test each other, I was reminded of another older brother of mine named Zackary, skinny kid that danced around a lot and was hard to hit. Not only were the two of them built alike but they had similar moves. As one punch after another whizzed past my head, I said a silent prayer that this ugly quartermaster would not turn out to be as difficult to knock down and keep down as ole Zack had been. The only time I had ever been able to put him down for any length of time was once with a singletree from our farm wagon, which just happened to be handy at a moment when I needed it desperately.

Perrin was leading with his left, striking twice rapid-fire, then diving in with his right. Of course, about the time I had adjusted to this little technique, he changed directions to throw me off and swung with his left. He was very fast and, for his size and weight, quite powerful.

"I'm going to make sausage of that face of yours, Hall!" he told me. "You've never really been cut up before, have you? First, I'll start with your nose!" His left lashed out twice, grazing my nose both times. Then, as he pivoted and dived, my left collided with his slightly-flared Roman nose, taking him down fast.

"Is that what you had in mind?" I asked, waiting for him to get up.

The crowd had fallen silent. As Perrin started to get to his feet, Goodrich said quietly, "If that had been one of his brothers, Red wouldn't've waited for him to get up."

Someone said, "Perrin's nose is bleeding."

Perrin suddenly leaped to his feet, slinging his head like an enraged bull and lunging at me. Blood was pouring from both nostrils.

"Lucky damned punch!" he screamed at me, refusing the towel Ted was waving at him. "That's the last time you'll do that!"

I tried to keep him at arm's length for a time, giving him a chance to work off some steam. But now he was much more cautious, and wary, especially of my left. After an initial flurry, I felt blood dripping from my right eyebrow and was surprised. My adrenaline was flowing so excitedly I had not felt a thing. I touched the corner of my eye and saw blood on my hand. A lot of it. I held up a hand and Ted tossed me the towel.

It was the first time in a long time anyone had made contact with my face. My brother Bart had bloodied my nose once. Luke had laid my eyebrow open with just such a left punch back when I was in high school.

I could only guess what was going on in Perrin's head, but I was certain he was not used to being knocked flat of his back. Now, as he circled, his black eyes never leaving my face, one thing became very clear: He was angry enough to kill me if he should get the upper hand. His pride had been hurt bad, and he was anxious to prove to his friends and fans he was still the champion.

"You made a big mistake, mate!" he taunted. "You thought since I fight with gloves I can't fistfight. Well, you're going to find out in about a minute the same rules govern both!"

"Thus far all you've done is talk!" I said, returning the towel to Ted.

He bore in, striking my raised fists like a punching bag, the strategy apparently being to wear me down, force me to drop my guard. His nose was still bleeding down both sides of his chin, giving him the look of a pasty-faced clown with a red mustache.

He went back to his two-one strategy, and each time I found a little piece of his face. In his attempt to stop my forward movement with another flurry of lefts and rights, I managed to land a glancing blow on his left ear, bringing blood.

The crowd, which had been rather quiet, began to take sides noisily. From Perrin's friends came complaints that I was not fighting fair, that I was hitting below the belt. Which was ridiculous because I had not scored a single time below my opponent's chin. From my friends, especially Goodrich and Archer, came advice to get serious, stop toying with Perrin.

The noisy crowd did not effect me at all, but apparently it caused Perrin to become a bit reckless. He began diving in at me, like an amateur, his left raised high and his right cocked. I waited patiently for him to throw that right, and finally he did.

For one split second after it zinged past me, his big red nose was exposed.

There are no words quite adequate to describe the incredibly delicious feeling one gets when he delivers that perfect punch to an opponent's nose. The *feeling,* which begins at the fist at the moment of contact, is an adrenaline flow out of control that travels to the base of the spinal cord; and the *sound,* which might be described by bystnders as a *whapping,* is like a crescendo from Beethoven. It was something like hitting a home run in the ninth with all bases loaded, or dropping the winning two-pointer through the basket in the last second of a championship game.

Perrin's head hit the floor before his butt did, his face and chest covered with blood. I stood above him for a moment, saw the flattened nose and bleeding right eyebrow, which had been laid open to the bone. And, surprisingly, I felt sorry for him.

Goodrich and Archer pulled me to one side, both talking at the same time. The former wanted to know why I was looking so unhappy and the latter was saying over and over, "You took him, Red!"

"You broke his nose!" exclaimed Goodrich. "Wasn't that what you wanted to do?"

"If he's got a broken nose, he'll have to go to the hospital," I moaned. "And if he goes to the hospital, my goose is cooked on the buoy tender."

*   *   *

On November 20 of that year (1948), after two weeks at the Goat Island dock doing nothing at all, the CGC *Bramble* shook itself like a wet, shaggy dog and got ready for shoving off. The crew, having emptied their pockets and worn out their welcome all over east Oakland, seemed more than ready to breathe the fresh air of the northern California coast.

It all began for me about daylight when one of the grease monkeys came into the quarters to wake up the other grease monkeys. I was lying on my bunk, with the back of my head cupped in my hands when I heard him. He was being careful not to disturb anyone else; so I guess it must have been the strong smell of spent diesel oil he was carrying around with him.

Then someone from the bridge gang came in and began to stumble around, tripping over piles of dirty laundry and shoes, aiming for my bunk. When he came close enough, I grabbed him by the leg. It was Carnes, a quartermaster-striker.

"Red, the bridge wants you to get on the radio."

"Hey," I said, swinging my feet to the deck. That was the best news I had heard in a month of Sundays. "We're going out."

"Yeah, I guess."

I dressed in the dark, working out of my seabag. Then I went to the galley and siphoned off a mug coffee, feeling good that the ship was finally getting underway. The radio equipment was in excellent condition, and I had my routine worked out to perfection. And, needless to say, the absence of Perrin, who had not returned from the hospital, did not sully the moment.

The messdeck was swarming with smelly deckhands and grease monkeys, who differed from each other only in the quality of the smells they were gave off. They did not like each other very much, snarling and snipping whenever any part of their bodies came into mutual contact. Watching them hump around with their mugs of coffee, their faces varying from sullen to deadpan, reminded me of Edwin Markham's primitive man with the hoe.

I took my coffee and drifted about topside for awhile, eventually climbing the ladder to the radio shack. I was hardly seated when the same kid who had delivered the message from the bridge stuck his head through the door and shouted:

"Guess what? We're headin' for drydock!" And with that the head withdrew, leaving me in a state of shock.

The head came back: "Pier something or other, sixty I think, down by Mission Rock. We go there about every six months or so and get the barnacles scraped off."

Lt. Mason's was the next head to pop into the shack. "Heads up!" He tossed me a clipboard. "That goes right away, okay?"

The only thing under the clip was a brief message to NMC, Base Radio, which I dispatched in two minutes. "Nancy-Mike-Charlie, this is *Workhorse*. Priority traffic. Over."

"Go ahead, Workhorse."

"E T A Pier Sixty-three ∅9∅∅ this date." The TDE was humming contentedly, no doubt rattling the ashtrays at NMC.

"Roger your Number One, *Workhorse*. Out."

Shortly thereafter the old workhorse of the Twelfth Coast Guard District, round-bellied, rusting, bleeding at all extremities, and foul-smelling, plodded away from Goat Island and took up a heading of due south, toward Mission Rock and Central Basin.

I returned the clipboard to the bridge and went to the starboard side to get a good look at some very familiar landmarks. The deck crew below me was scurrying about trying to do the bidding of the deck CPO, one Hoot Castelberry. I thought what a break it was for them that we were going into dry dock, because with the ship jacked up out of the water they wouldn't have anything to do, and the Old Man's excuse for short liberties would be removed.

"Now, hear this!"

"Here it comes," said Bristow, Quartermaster Second Class, now in charge of the bridge, who was standing at my elbow, "the Old Man's Order of the Day, the *drydock routine.*"

"Well, it's got to be a simple one," I said.

There would be absolutely nothing for the crew to do while the ship was in, not even a gangway watch to stand. The cook and his helpers would doubtlessly close up shop during all the scraping and banging the civilian workforce would make. More than likely the Old Man would tell the crew to take a five- or ten-day leave, to get us off the ship so we wouldn't be under foot.

Someone shouted for Bristow. He left the starboard wing of the bridge in a hurry and a moment later his voice echoed about the ship, "Now hear this!" But nothing followed, except muffled background noise. Something, I thought, must be wrong.

"There will be no liberty while we are in drydock, by order of the Commanding Officer!" After another awkward pause, Bristow added, "All hands will be expected to turn to on the scraping and painting of the hull! Four-on and four-off watch schedule until the job is done! The Starboard Section will muster on the quarterdeck in five minutes!"

Somewhat stunned by the quartermaster's first words, I began to laugh by the time he arrived at the *four-on and four-off* part. Now, expelling a chest of air, I called out to Lt. Mason, who was standing in the open hatchway, "That was some kind of joke, wasn't it, Sir? Who said the Old Man doesn't have a sense of humor?"

Lt. Mason laughed bitterly, "That was no joke."

The first person I encountered on the way back to the radio shack was Hoot Castleberry, who followed me inside.

"I thought reconditioning a ship was civilian work, Boats! Is the crew of a Coast Guard cutter supposed to do that kind of work!"

"I used to think that, too," said Hoot, shaking his head sadly, "but like as not somebody over at Base got the Old Man mad by tellin' him he'd have to be in drydock for a couple of weeks. He don't like to be hung up that long."

"Well, at least, petty officers will be excluded from this work! Right?"

The old chief picked up my wastebasket and emptied the contents into a cardboard box that just happened to be handy. "Hah, you don't hear too good, Sparks!" He turned the wastebasket upside down and sat on it. "Didn't you hear that quartermaster? *All hands* means ever'body but the brass. It even includes the likes of me an' yew."

"Well, I've got a lot of things to do right here," I said with a grin. "While the crew is working on the hull, I'll be in here working on this junk."

"In a pig's eye you will."

Bristow came in and headed straight for me, ignoring the Chief. "Did you put in for a transfer, Red?"

"No, but that's not a bad idea!" I said with a laugh.

"Well, whether you did or didn't, it's here. You're supposed to report to Mr. Mason right away."

Hoot was shaking his head. "The Old Man must've found out about that little affair at *Ted and Roy's.* You can't do a goddamned thing in this outfit without every Tom, Dick, and Harry finding out about it."

When I found Lt. Mason, he was in his cabin changing into dungarees.

"Listen, Hall, I'm sorry as hell about this. You've done a damned good job in the radio shack, and I for one hate to see you go. But that's not the whole of it."

"What?"

"Well, let me see if I can explain something to you. You know the Old Man's an odd duck, right? He's scared shitless somebody beneath him will do something to put a smear on his record, something that might get in the way of his someday becoming a full commander. When Perrin had to go to the hospital with that broken jaw, he called every member of the bridge gang in and grilled them till somebody broke. And when he found out what actually went on, he called me in and told me to think up a good reason to transfer you off the ship. He knew that Base would insist on a pretty good reason for transferring you, and he sure as hell couldn't tell them it was because he had heard you were in a fight. I told him I thought you had outdone yourself in the radioroom and that in my opinion we should not get rid of you. He just about threw me out of his quarters."

"So what did he come up with?" I asked.

"First, let me make something very clear to you. The Skipper of this ship has a lot of power and influence—believe it or not."

"Yes, Sir, I believe it."

"He's capable of making a hell of a lot of trouble for any one of us, and I mean officers as well as men."

"Yes, Sir."

"Well, you've got a real black mark on your record now."

"The *Taney's* Jeep, right?" I said with a nod. "But I haven't done a thing wrong on this ship! Except that ruckus with Perrin." My head had begun to spin.

"You threatened a commissioned officer with physical violence."

"No way, Sir! I never did!"

"That's what's now on your permanent record."

"What officer did I threaten, Sir?"

"Me."

*   *   *

As all seasoned sailors know, every ship has a distinct personality; and while the CGC *Escanaba* was of the same class as the CGC *Chautauqua*, looked exactly like her from a distance, I was to learn that she differed from that other Indian cutter almost as much as the *Bramble* did. I *felt* the difference the instant I walked up the gangplank at Government Island, but at the same time I was experiencing *dèja vu* so strongly it was pushed aside.

As soon as I was signed aboard, the O. O. D. told me to report to the Communications Officer right away.

The *Esky*, although not as dirty and certainly not as rusty as the *Bramble*, looked *soiled* to me and had an odor about it that I did not like. I became aware that I was being careful not to let my seabag touch the deck, and I kept it away from the bulkheads as much as possible on the way to Officers' Country.

Lt. Mickelhaus, the Communications Officer, was not in his stateroom, I learned; so I went to the Wardroom, where I found several officers drinking coffee at the long green-covered messtable. They looked around as I entered. One of them, with the silver bars of a full lieutenant on his collar, nodded to me.

"Is Mr. Mickelhouse here?" I asked, wondering when I had seen a more unfriendly-looking group of officers.

"Hey, Mickle*house*, front and center!" called a big horse-faced junior grade lieutenant with a two-day stubble. At the opposite end of the table was an officer with no bars on his collars looked up, frowning.

He was apparently writing a letter.

"Is this the man you were expectin', Mr. Mickle*house?*" asked the lieutenant with a chuckle.

The officer nodded and motioned for me to approach. "You must be the radioman from the *Bramble*."

I admitted that I was.

"He's the one I was telling you about," said one of the officers behind me.

"The name's *Mickelhaus*, Hall. Git it straight."

Someone at the table laughed. "Is it true that you stole the *Roger B. Taney's* Jeep, sailor?"

"And why are you not still on Mare Island?" asked another officer.

"Stow your gear in the crew's quarters and report to my stateroom," said Mickelhaus. "We've got a few things to get straight."

The big horse-faced officer caught me at the door. "Before you go, I would like for you to tell us about the officer you threatened to strike on the *Bramble*." As he spoke the officers around the table became silent, waiting for my answer.

I had come to attention and was holding my cap in one hand and balancing my seabag on the deck with the other. After an embarrassingly long time, during which there was no other sound in the wardroom but that of a ticking chronometer, Mickelhaus snapped, "Go on, Hall, git out of here!"

Later, in the crew's quarters, I faired little better than I had in the wardroom. While I was adjusting my clean mattress cover over the filthy pad that had come with the bunk, one of the men in the quarters wanted to know if I happened to be the big shot that thought he could whip everybody in the Coast Guard. And before I had time to respond to that, from a corner of the compartment where a small group of swabs were playing cards, someone called out, "Maybe he thinks since he's served on the *Taney* he can push everybody on this ship around."

I wasn't about to say anything to this mob. It was better to suffer their insults and insinuations than to become embroiled in a fight so soon after shipping aboard. It wasn't until sometime later that I fully understood the resentment in the crews quarters that day. One of the deck gang, it turned out, had recently shipped aboard from the *Taney* with a bagful of stories about my comings and goings. He had carried on so much everybody had become more than a little tired of hearing any reference to me. The end result was that for weeks I received this kind of treatment.

It was not easy for me to walk away from a direct threat or a personal insult, but on this occasion I managed it. And on two other occasions within a week toughs aboard the ship sought me out with the news that they would be waiting for me ashore.

Before I was settled into the crews quarters, word was passed that the ship would be shoving off immediately, to relieve the *Chautauqua* on Weather Station Fox. Immediately following that I was paged over the PA station to report on the double to the radio shack.

The thing that sticks in my memory about that first radio watch on the *Escanaba* is how embarrassingly difficult it was to remember the call sign! I had no difficulty remembering the calls of the *Alert* and even the *Bramble*, but for some unexplainable reason, whenever I caught myself unconsciously drumming out Morse Code someplace, it was almost always the *Taney's* call sign, *NRUT*. Some calls have a rhythm to them, like the Taney's, *dahdit didahdit dididah dit*, but the Esky's *NRUE* had no music or poetry and for that reason it did not stick in my mind.

Not since *NXZ*, the base radio station at Admiral Halsey's COM-SOPAC during World War Two, had I been so taken with a call. Like that one, the *Taney's* had become a part of my thinking and basic instincts.

I hummed it, whistled it, and tapped it out on tables and the arms of chairs wherever I went (awake and asleep)!

With me on that first watch on the *Esky* was a bored and testy First Class Radioman by the name of Smellers, a man who, I was to learn, had never been anyplace, seen anything, read anything, or done anything. And, to cap it off, he buttoned his long sleeve dungaree shirt at the collar and the wrists, despite the heat in the radio shack. In a four-hour period the two of us probably did not exchange a dozen words; but since he outranked me, I kept quiet, paid attention to what he was doing and followed his lead.

Smellers, I realized immediately, was not much of a radio operator once we were away from the dock. He could handle voice communications competently, if mechanically and dully; but his CW *fist* was sloppy and unsure, not to mention slow. Furthermore, once we were on station and sending weather information back to Frisco, I discovered that he was even more inept at receiving CW messages, especially when they had a little QR-Mary mixed in with them.

Embarrassed for the First Class, I watched helplessly as he fumbled through the most routine radio traffic. He could not remember the calls of some of the message originators and had to look them up, and he was constantly asking for repeats on the messages themselves. The priority weather messages to *NMC* he sent slowly and clumsily. It was so painful for me I would leave the shack and stand at the lifeline on the starboard side of the ship during the time he was sending. He was Meeks ten years down the road.

The second night out, after a solid two hours of silence in the shack, I asked Smellers if I could tune in a little Stateside music. For a moment the First Class stared at me through watery, colorless eyes. Then, without so much as a shake of his head, he turned back to the magazine he was reading.

When we finally sighted the *Chautauqua* on the morning of the third day, to me it was like seeing an old and very dear friend. It occurred at the end of my watch and my partner was tired and sleepy, but nothing could have kept me from that starboard lifeline outside the radio shack, where I knew the sparkies aboard the *Chautauqua* would have their eyes glued. Hungrily, I searched the cutter's main deck and bridge for a long, drink of water from my hometown. The ships were going to pass each other with a considerable amount of water and a low-lying fog between them and I had no field glasses. But once, for an instant, I was quite certain I caught a glimpse of Gooch striding up a ladder toward a group of sailors on the bridge. He was paying no attention to us.

Since he was a yeoman, I told myself, and knew everybody at Government Island, he undoubtedly knew I was aboard the *Esky*. But, of course, he could not possibly have know how lonely for a friendly face I was on that miserable, tight-butted *Escanaba!*

The CGC Escanaba

The Swimming Party

———————◆———————

At best, with good friends and drinking buddies in the crew, Weather Station Fox was an endurance test. That patch of water was too far from land for seagulls and not far enough out to be popular with gooney birds. And while it was supposed to be on the direct sea and air lanes between Hawaii and San Francisco, it was a rare thing indeed to see a ship on the horizon and almost as rare to hear the drone of a commercial aircraft high overhead.

Smellers, I had decided, was worse than a knot on a log. His presence in the shack was like a boil that hadn't come to a head, a wart that while it showed no outward signs of being alive just might be cancerous. Now as bored and apathetic as Smellers had seemed at first, I was spending my four-hour radio watches staring at the First Class's stiff, uncompromising back and trying to decide what to do about him. If the ship hadn't been sitting still, *maintaining station*, one solution might have been to push him over the side some dark night. That was something to keep in mind for the return trip to Frisco.

In the meantime, the hours dragged by slowly.

On the third night, about halfway through the watch, Smellers removed his earphones and placed them beside his typewriter and stood up, refusing as always to look in my direction.

"Take over. I'm going down for coffee."

I watched him leave, thinking, *Yeah, you sorry cockroach, bring me back a mug of the black stuff and maybe a liverwurst sandwich on rye. On second thought, why don't you just stay down there and drown yourself in that black stuff?*

Smellers' coffee breaks never lasted less than thirty minutes. I watched until he disappeared into the dark moon shadow of the main deck. Then, feeling the early signs of a good adrenaline flow, I turned and went to the old Hallicrafters receiver in front of my operating position. It had not been turned on since my arrival on the ship, but I knew it was capable of picking up short wave broadcasts.

It took awhile for it to warm up, but finally I was picking up stations. I found one that flooded the shack with soft classical music, a most welcome change from the static that Smellers evidently liked so much. While the rich, heavy thumping of Beethoven's Fifth played havoc with the ten-inch communications speaker, I became interested in the antenna hook-up on the back of the receiver and discovered that it was also attached to the PA system of the ship!

Hmmm, I mused, remembering the good old days on the *Taney*. Did I dare try that little trick again?

The world was suddenly not such a boring place. I was deliberately thumbing my nose not only at Smellers, who was in charge of the watch, but Billings, the Chief Radioman and Mickelhaus, the Communications Officer. Perhaps (I grinned nastily at the thought), because of my reputation, this might be a little something the Exec and even the Skipper himself might take umbrage to.

After a few minutes of the most exciting classical music I had ever heard (because it was illegal), I plugged in a pair of earphones (thus muting the speaker) and strapped them over my head.

All right, it wasn't much. But it was something, a beginning.

When Smellers came in a good thirty minutes later, he sniffed in my direction a time or two, suspecting (I suspect) that I was listening to an unauthorized frequency. But after a brief, watery stare in my direction, which was a first, he slumped in front of his typewriter and typed something in his log. It was, of course NO SIGS, which was the only thing he could type, under the circumstances.

I was sorely disappointed that he had said nothing about the earphones. They remained strapped over my head, and I am sure he must have caught a note or two of those *civilian unregulation illegal* sounds I was enjoying so much. But there he sat, like a knot on a log, apparently not even curious enough to ask me what I was doing. Maybe he was too proud or arrogant or bored to bother. After all, it would have forced him to open his mouth and talk to me.

This, I finally decided, was intolerable. Feeling a bit of devilment rising down in my testicles, I began rolling the big dial on the Halliscratchers, looking for the commercial airlines frequencies. I expected old Smellers to lose it any minute, of course, but I did not give a tinker's damn. For a time all I picked up was a lot of QR-Nancy and some very disappointing QR-Mary. In the shelf above my head was an up-to-date listing of frequencies used by the various airlines. (I had spotted these right away the first watch I had stood.) I got it down, looked up United Airlines, and zeroed in on the Frisco-to-Honolulu flights.

The adrenaline was zinging along lippety-skit again.

I tuned the receiver to one of the calling frequencies of United and, leaving the receiver volume turned a bit high, removed my earphones and laid them face up on the desktop in front of me. That ought to get a rise out of old Smellers.

To my amazement, his only reaction was a slight twisting of the nose and an almost inaudible smerfing noise.

Squeaks and bassy noises began coming from the earphones. I glanced at Tightbutt and strapped them over my ears and adjusted the tuning dial. A rich, fully modulated male voice, sounding as if it might be coming from the cables and wiring in the overhead, said, "Hickam, this is Allied Flight Four Niner Seven. How're the skies over Diamond Head this morning?"

I was so excited I almost lost it! There was life out there, after all! Something besides a dead Coast Guard cutter was on or very near that godforsaken Weather Station Fox! We were not alone!

"Four Niner Seven, we're experiencin' no pain here. Looks like another fine day in these parts."

"Uh Roger, Hickam. Thanks."

"What's your location?"

"We're approaching the halfway mark, and below us is a little white boat, dead in the water."

"That'd be the Coast Guard cutter. I'd hate to be the poor devils that have to sit out there for a month at a time."

"It'd drive me batty."

When the carrier went off and the static and the other noise returned, I glanced at Smellers. It was obvious he had not been paying any attention to me.

"All right if I get a signal report?"

"From who?"

"Anybody that might be within hearing distance of us."

"You can't reach anybody this far out by voice, but who the hell cares? Go ahead."

I nodded, wheeling dials, zero-beating, and dipping the final tube of our TCS transceiver.

"Hey, Big Bird in the Friendly Skies of United, got your ears on?"

"That don't sound much like askin' for a signal report," said Smellers.

I glanced at him. He had turned in his swivel chair and was actually *grinning at me!* I quickly unplugged my earphones, releasing the speaker just in time. There issued forth a small metallic *plinking* noise and then the rich baritone voice of the pilot: "I've got my ears on. Come back."

"This is the little white boat below you, a segment of the Hooligan Navy, water-logged and lonely for some civilian chatter."

A peel of laughter greeted this. "I hear you, little white boat! This could not be, by weird chance, the legendary Coastie that has been known to tease United's stewardesses on this run?"

"Negativo. I have never *teased* any stewardess, United or otherwise." I glanced at Smellers.

"Well, excuse me! For a goodly time I've been listening to stories about this mellow-voiced Romeo on Weather Station Fox that defies both Coast Guard law and the laws of common decency by teasing hell out of unsuspecting hostesses that fly over him. Come back!"

Smellers was now sitting stiff-backed in his chair, all ears, and his amused watery, colorless eyes were squarely on me.

"This is all news to me, United. But speaking of hostesses, do you by any chance know a San Francisco gal that makes her living reading the headlines to lonely hooligans?"

After prolonged laughter, the pilot said, "Flushed you out, didn't I? Do I know such a gal? I listened to her carry on about you for some two or three hours one night, said you had promised to look her up in Frisco but hadn't. I think somewhere after about an hour of that I began to think she was a little wacky over you."

"She's not aboard your flight?"

"Nupe. But I expect I'll see her today. Would you like for me to pass on a word or two?"

"Just tell her I'll be out here on station for two more weeks, and I'd like to hear her voice again before I die of boredom."

"Will do, Hooligan. Say, for the benefit of my lonely passengers, would you say a few words about the wonderful experience you're having aboard that pretty little white boat?"

Smellers actually laughed at that. "Go ahead, Red. Give 'em an ear full."

"Thank you, suh, but what I have to say about this pretty little white boat and the experiences aboard same would not be fit for a civilian audience."

*   *   *

Smellers had *metamorphosed* into a halfway decent cellmate. He was from that night on easy to talk to and not at all as boring as I had surmised, disproving two theories of mine: That he had a severe speech defect and that you can tell what a book is about by its cover. Right away he wanted to know about those prior violations of the airways, specifically about the San Francisco girl.

"I'm afraid to find out what she looks like," I said (another unproved theory of mine being that you definitely cannot judge the looks of a gal by the tone of her voice). "To listen to her wonderfully soft and sexy voice you would think she's incredibly beautiful, but you know how misleading the voice can be. I've been intending to look her up for six months, but every time I get the opportunity I chicken out."

"Yeah, you're right about that. To listen to you carry on, one would think you're a nice, respectable, law abiding citizen."

"There's nothing misleading about my voice," I hastened. "For those that have good hearing."

"You want to know something? I'd heard so much shit about you before you came aboard I never wanted to lay eyes on you. Do you know how popular you're *not* on this ship?"

"What kind of shit did you hear?"

"You beat hell out of everybody that looks cross-eyed at you, even officers, you jump ship every time you're restricted, you steel O. O. D. Jeeps and go to country-and-western dances in them. Is any of that true?" He tossed his hands in the air, like he already knew the answer to that question.

"I've had a fight or two, borrowed one Jeep."

"I'm afraid you've got two strikes against you on this ship, with both the brass and the crew."

"I've had two strikes against me for quite awhile."

A good week after the chat with the United pilot, at about the time I had given up ever making another contact with that honey-voiced stewardess,

I hit the jackpot one dark and rainy midwatch. My earphones, lying face-up on the operating position spewing static, suddenly came alive.

"Hal-loo down there! Calling Charley, the Coast Guardsman! Are you down there, Charley?"

My transmitter was already on the frequency and just aching to go; so I grabbed the mike and shouted, "Is that you, Sharon Elizabeth Mahoney?"

Immediately, in a slightly different voice, the girl came back with, "Why didn't you come to see me?"

Having learned that women, especially the pretty ones, do not care for excuses and will not tolerate lies, I frankly admitted that I was afraid she would be disappointed in me, that being good radio friends was far better than not being friends at all.

"I will not be disappointed in you, silly! Don't you know that? Now, I insist on a specific time and place for us to meet. How about my house next time you're in? Please write down my telephone number and street address." She gave it without hesitation, her voice firm and insistent. "When will you be in port?"

"To be on the safe side, let's say three weeks from now."

"All right. Saturday evening, seven o'clock, exactly three weeks from now. Write it down and don't you dare fail to show up."

The signal had begun to spit and sputter, a sure sign that our UHF connection was about to play out. I hastily said my goodbyes to her and, when she passed the mike to the pilot, my thanks to him.

Smellers was looking at me and shaking his head. "Nobody in his right mind will believe any of this when I start spreading it around that you made a date with a sexy broad you've never seen on an illegal radio hookup. I heard it but I don't believe it."

"You're not going to spread anything, Willy. Hear me?"

"Fix me up and I'll keep my mouth shut."

"Fix yourself up? I don't know anybody to fix you up with."

"Yeah, maybe, but that gal you were talking to does. You want complete silence from me? Then do it." After a pause, he blurted, "Who the heck is Charley?"

Despite the change that had come over Smellers, I continued to have reservations about the *Escanaba* and its crew. It seemed that every unhappy sailor on the West Coast had ended up on this cutter. If the *Taney* had been aloof and cold, this ship was downright belligerent and antisocial. Perhaps they thought they had a special reason for disliking me, but I was convinced that it went far beyond that. To me they seemed unambitious and apathetic to a man. Well, maybe with the exception of Smellers.

There are two kinds of people in this world, those with a spark of life in them and a sense of humor and those that are dead on their feet, just waiting to be put away for keeps. For a long time I had thought you could tell them apart by just looking at them. But Smellers had proved me wrong on that.

*　　　　　*　　　　　*

On the *Chautauqua* it was a regular thing to go swimming every afternoon. You got used to hearing the PA system blast, "Swimming party stand by on the starboard side!" On the *Esky* not a word was said about a swimming party, and when I brought it up our second day on Weather Station Fox, Smellers had this to say:

"You're not aboard the *Chautauqua*, now. Forget about going swimming. I guarantee you you're wastin' your time."

"There's never a Swimming Party on this ship?" I glared at him, aghast. "Why not, for Pete's sake? Why doesn't the crew rise up and take over the ship?"

"You might as well forget it. The Skipper thinks it's too risky."

Our watch ended at four A. M. and ordinarily I did not bother with breakfast; but on that particular morning I could not sleep; so I got up, ate some scrambled eggs and bacon, and headed for the CPO quarters, aiming to do the thing right and start with the Chief Radioman.

It just wasn't done, Chief Billings told me. Forget about it. The Old Man did not like to swim, and what he didn't like you might as well forget about.

"Too risky. Somebody might drown," he said. "End of discussion."

"Why is it risky, Chief? It's no riskier than going swimming in a pool back home. Actually, it's not as risky because you just about can't drown in salt water."

"The hell you say. Don't you realize it's a thousand feet deep right here where we're settin'? Besides, I'm not the one to say whether we have a Swimming Party or not. Go to the Brass."

"Thanks, Chief. I was hoping you would say that."

When I was finally granted an audience with Mr. Mickelhaus, his response was, "Why do you want to stir something like this up? Can't you just leave well enough alone?"

"I just think the morale of the crew—"

"Then go talk to the Morale Officer. Only he would never go along with it. I know him well."

"Could I talk to him about it, Sir?"

"If you want to waste your time, it makes no difference to me. But don't tell him I'm for it." When I didn't budge an inch, he added, "That would be Lieutenant Henders."

Two days later I found Mr. Henders, a junior grade lieutenant, in the wardroom.

"I don't think the men would be interested, Hall. Can't you find anything else to keep you busy, without dredging up something like this? I don't think something like this would ever work out here in the middle of the ocean. The Captain would not approve it, anyway."

"The other two weather ships hold a swimming party every afternoon, Sir. It is really good for morale."

"And, of course, you would know about that, having served on both of them."

"Yes, Sir, I did. Could I possibly ask the Captain if it would be all right?"

The lieutenant shook his head, began to pace (We were in his two-by-four stateroom) and fret. Finally, he said, "I'll tell you what. If you can get the Exec to okay this, I'll agree to the idea. But do not—I repeat—do not say to anybody that this was my idea. I have not given my approval."

"But if you won't approve it, Sir, the Exec won't either."

"Well, there you are."

I dragged myself out onto the lush green carpeted hallway, convinced that there would never be a Swimming Party on the CGC *Escanaba*. Nevertheless, having nothing better to do, I went to the Ship's Office and asked if I could see the Exec. While I was talking to the yeoman at the front desk, the Exec himself showed up, spoke to me, and in two shakes of a dead skunk's tale I was in his office arguing my case.

"Why, that sounds like a good idea. Sure. Find Lt. Henders and ask him to drop by and see me."

The swimming party, as it turned out, attracted a lot of attention, to the absolute amazement of lieutenants Mickelhaus and Henders. Even some of the officers participated, sticking together in a little knot some distance from the fantail, on the leeward side of the enlisted men.

Sharply at thirteen hundred hours the day following my talk with Lt. Comdr. Haselton, the XO, Lt. (jg) Henders ordered a lifeboat lowered into the water, posted a man on the bridge with a carbine, and had a boatswain's mate pipe the news. One requirement was that everyone had to wear a lifejacket.

"I cannot believe," I said, shaking my head in disgust. "I for one will not go swimming in a life jacket."

"Too bad we've got the watch," grinned Smellers. "You won't get a chance to break everybody's heart by refusing to go in."

The ocean was glassy smooth, with just a hint of a swell; and, far up on the passageway that ran past the radio shack, Smellers and I watched as the screaming little boys (who had been sad old men a few minutes before) tumbled down the Jacob's Ladder into the water.

The following day, having worked out a solution to the lifejacket problem, I talked Smellers into going in with me.

"Follow me, Smerf!" I called out.

"Mind tellin' me what you've got in mind?" he shouted, strapping on his Mae West. "I'd like to be prepared for whatever."

Ignoring him, I swam to the boat, which was still in close to the ship, unstrapping my lifejacket as I went. Smellers dog-paddled up beside me and grabbed a piece of the boat.

"Who's the coxswain?" I asked.

"Search me. I've seen him run up and down the deck a lot, but—"

"Hey, mate!" I yelled, waving at the swab in the boat. "You mind if we leave these with you?" I lifted my life jacket just enough for the kid to see it.

For a minute the startled coxswain just stared; then he shook his head vigorously, "Hell, yes, I mind! You heard the word. I'd git my ass in a sling if I let you put that thing in here."

"No you won't. Nobody is paying the least bit of attention to you or what's in the boat. Let us stash these and Smellers here will get you a date when we reach Frisco. Right, Smellers?"

"A date? With a girl?"

"Heck, yes. He knows lots of very pretty young things over where he lives, close to Knob Hill."

"You swear?" He looked at Smellers for confirmation.

"He can sure do it," I said quickly.

We eased the ugly old things over the side into the boat and took off. Smellers had admitted with no attempt at humility to being a great swimmer, had indeed spent most of a midwatch building that image of himself for me. He stopped just short of saying that he was Olympics material. According to him, he had qualified First Class in boot camp; and it was nothing at all for him to swim across rivers and lakes back home. In salt water he could swim forever.

"You know about salt water, don't you?" he asked, mysteriously.

"It's heavier than fresh water, huh?" I replied, wondering where this bullshit was going.

"Well, it takes no effort at all to swim in it. Tell you what, let's you and me back off about half a mile and see which one can reach the ship first?"

"*Half a mile?* We'd never get away with it." I could not believe my ears, Smellers making a suggestion like that.

"Sure we would. It's a cinch. The man on the bridge won't be watching the men. His job is to watch out for sharks. I'll bet you twenty bucks I can beat you."

"I don't think I can swim half a mile," I said, "in any kind of water. How about one of us got a Charlie horse?"

"That's why the lifeboat's out here. You game or not?"

In no time at all, it seemed to me, we were a good half a mile out; but, I was to learn a bit later, distances out in the water are hard to judge. With no point of reference in any direction, except the ship, it seemed to me that we were floating in some limitless limbo. On all sides the watery horizon seemed to be a continuation of the sky, and in a surprisingly short time I could no longer hear the screaming and carrying-on at the Jacob's Ladder.

For the tenth time Smellers called out, "The water's really great! Aren't you glad we did this?"

"Do you get the impression we're moving farther away from the ship—even when we're not swimming?" I asked "You don't suppose there's some kind of current out this far?"

"Oh, maybe, a little. How far do you think we're out?"

"It must be close to a mile. I think we'd better head back."

"What time do you think it is? By the time we get there—"

"Just what I was thinking," I said. "You ready?"

"Remember, twenty bucks!"

We began to swim toward the ship, each of us trying to distance the other. After five minutes of furious thrashing, I could not tell that we had moved an inch! I was slightly ahead of Smellers, but it occurred to me that he had just *lost ground* and I was still where I started! And as I paused to let him catch up, I had a most disturbing bit of insight.

"Hey, I don't think we're making much headway!" I yelled, reluctant to admit what I was really thinking. Smellers, apparently disturbed because he had not drawn ahead of me, had begun to thrash the water frantically. It soon became apparent that despite his desperate efforts he wasn't closing the gap between us!

Although I could not be certain, having no reference point to judge by, I was certain we were drifting—away from the ship!

Then the shrill, but almost inaudible, piping of the boatswain's whistle reached our ears. This was followed by the voice on the PA system, *which we could not quite make out!*

I began to swim as I had never swum before; but when I finally had to rest, it was clear to me that a current, just beneath the surface, was carrying us away almost as fast as we were able to swim! Smellers was lagging considerably behind me at this point. I waved at him and he tried to shout something but began choking and spewing water!

"The boat's going in!" I gasped, but I was sure he could not hear me. "They don't know we're out here!" More scared than I had ever been in my life, I began to swim again, putting everything I had into it.

The water had become a bit choppy; and since only the upper part of our heads were visible above the surface of the water, it was extremely unlikely that anyone on the cutter would spot us without glasses. And who was going to scan that particular stretch of water with binoculars at that particular time?

I kept doggedly on, even when every muscle in my body cried out for a rest. Smellers was so far behind now I could not be sure he was still afloat. I remembered what I had bragged to the officer: "It's impossible to drown in seawater."

"Hang on, old buddy! Don't give up!" I called out, plaintively.

What seemed like an eternity, long after I had decided that the current had beat me, I became aware that I was indeed making some progress! *The ship was closer!* I could tell that the Jacob's Ladder was still unfurled down the side of the cutter. Someone was holding onto it and splashing!

For a time I had entertained the hope that Mr. Henders would check the swimming list and miss the two of us; but when the lifeboat had been secured and all the swimmers had disappeared, I knew no such thing was going to happen.

In a very short time that ladder would be withdrawn from the water, rolled up and stowed next to the toe-rail! Why, indeed, was it still in place? Whoever was thrashing about at the base of it, holding on, was undoubtedly a non-swimmer—and probably not supposed to be there. I treaded water for a moment, gathering as much strength as I could, and began to call for help. But it was no use. I was wasting my breath and what little strength I had left. Even the man at the bottom of the Jacob's Ladder had apparently not heard me.

With a final burst of strength that I did not know I still had, I inched in close to the ladder. Frantically, I reached out, only to have my hand kicked away! I tried again and the same thing happened. I tried to scream at the jerk holding onto the ladder, became convinced that he knew I was trying to reach the ladder, further that he thought this was some kind of game! He was pounding the surface of the water right in my face with his feet, and each time I put out an exhausted hand to grasp a foot he would knock it away or strike me in the face!

I caught a glimpse of his face in profile and recognized him. It was Jackson, a black messcook, a kid that liked to tease me in the chow line and then heap my tray high.

"Get away!" I choked out, weakly. "Let me—!"

Jackson suddenly recognized me; and instead of pulling back, he began deliberately pushing me away with his big feet! Great fun!

"Aw, you a good swimmah! I saw you out theah!"

"Back off, Jackson! Back off! Or so help me!"

When all of my strength was gone, at the moment when I was beginning to slip below the surface of the water for what had to be the last time, a Chief's cap appeared above us.

"What the hell's goin' on down there? Jackson, stop kickin' that man! Can't you see he's drownin'?"

It was the Deck Chief. He swung a leg over the side of the ship and skinned down, reaching out toward me. Just in time he managed to grab my right hand, the only part of me still above the surface!

The terrified Jackson began to bellow, "Chief, I swear I didn't know he was in trouble! He a good swimmah."

"It's okay, help me get him aboard."

Finally on deck, on my stomach, I coughed my guts out, all the time trying to point and explain about Smellers.

"Be quiet, Red!" scolded the Chief. "Just try to git rid of some of that saltwater."

I was finally able to raise my arm and point over the side of the ship. "Smell—!" I began choking again.

"He's tryin' to say that somethin' smells," said Jackson.

Suddenly, the Chief stood up and looked in the direction I was waving. "The hell he is!" With that he took off for the bridge, yelling over his shoulder, "Stick with him and try to get that water out of him!"

Jackson bent over me, "You gone be all right, Red. I sho' you is."

I wanted to kill him on the spot, but I decided to put that off until I had more strength.

He must have seen the look in my eyes, because he cried out, "Hey, man, I dun saved yo' mothahfuckin' life! I still savin' hit!"

Back to Paradise

◆

When our twentieth day on Weather Station Fox rolled around, right on the money there was the old *Taney*, looking like a million dollars. As dumb as it sounds, I had grown rather fond of the old bucket. I was on deck to watch her steam in, and the sight of her reminded me some of the bad times but a whole lot of the good ones. She came in close, with horns blaring and the blinker light giving it hell. I picked up some of what was being exchanged between the two bridges; but it was mostly just chit chat between the O. O. D.'s about their families; so I turned away from it and strolled up the deck, waving at a few of the *Taney* crew that looked familiar.

J. C. Lassiter, another member of the radio gang aboard the *Esky*, was in the messdeck drinking coffee when I got there. I had not exchanged a dozen words with him in the time I had been aboard. He looked up when I ducked through the hatchway and made a small effort to wave a greeting. I nodded and took my mug of coffee over to where he was sitting by himself at a mess table.

"Mister Red," he said, looking chagrined.

"Whatever," I nodded, sitting down. "I knew a fellow once named Hall," he said casually.

"Oh? I grew up on the island of New Caledonia, in the South Pacific. No kinfolk in the States."

He ignored my sarcasm. "He was from Georgia and black as the ace of spades. The first part of his name was *Wesley*. Any relation?

"Maybe. That's the first part of my name, too. Or did you already know that?"

"I hear you're on restriction. What'd you do this time?"

"I needed some time aboard ship," I said. "I requested the Captain's Mast. What's new with you?"

"You don't want to know." He studied his reflection in his coffee for a time, rubbing the small blue anchor near the top of the mug. "I opened my big mouth just like you and got ten days aboard ship."

The only thing I had heard about this guy was that he was hot-tempered and independent, a combination that the Coast Guard just could not tolerate in enlisted men.

"You disapproved of the chow," I said, trying to keep the conversation going. Although I don't know why.

"Nope."

"You disapproved of the drills."

"Nope. I happened to be doing an imitation of Mickey Mouse when he walked up behind me."

"Oh, I see. Well, you didn't have anything pressing to do on liberty, did you?"

"Listen, Red, I just got married, less than six months ago, and I can't afford to leave my wife alone for another two weeks!"

"Why not? Call her when you get in and tell her what's happened."

"Yeah, I will, but I'm not shittin' you, she's—not the kind of girl you leave alone too long." He stopped and turned a sorrowful face on me. "Can I tell you something? Have you got a minute?"

"Sure. I've got bout thirteen days."

"Okay. Well, first, I want you to understand that my wife's a knockout. Don't ask how I managed to talk her into marrying me, because I still can't believe it; but I married one beautiful and sexy girl. She's got some Spanish in her and a little Chinese, and she's built like the proverbial brick shithouse. When we got hitched, I was on a two weeks' leave from the Coasties, and we stayed naked inside a motel room the entire time, and I lost twenty-one pounds. She likes to fuck all the time. And it doesn't matter how I want it, she's willing and ready. So when I had to come back to the ship, we agreed on a couple of things. She wouldn't sleep with another man and I wouldn't sleep with another woman, that sort of thing."

"Wasn't that a one-sided deal?" I asked, forcing back a grin.

He paused, looking around like a trapped animal. "We live out on a little point of land west of Sausalito, and she can see the ships coming and going in San Fran Harbor, okay? And with field glasses I can see our house and the flagpole."

"The flag pole. My God."

"What?"

"I know somebody else with a flag pole."

"Yeah," said Lassiter, looking confused. "You do?"

"Well, I'm sure it's not the same flag pole."

After a time, Lassiter, more subdued, went on, "And when she's not having a period, she flies the United States flag."

"And when she is, she flies something red."

"No! She flies the Coastie flag."

"Okay. That sounds logical. So when she's flying *semper paratus,* you don't go home?"

"Well, I don't rush in, expecting something. We've agreed we won't do it when she's—having her period. I give her a call and when she's ready, I go in."

"So what's the big tragedy? You're restricted for a few days. So what? She'll be waiting. If you can wait, she can wait."

"Well, the last time we were in I became suspicious that she was putting out that Coastie flag a bit too often."

"Wow."

"Yeah. You see, it was out there when we entered the harbor just about one month ago. I called and waited and we had two weeks of good sex and then she began having her period. I mean I was there when it began! Now, if she's got the Coastie flag on that flagpole when we go in, I'll know for dern sure something's going on. Have you ever heard of a woman having two in one month?"

I shook my head, looking doubtfully.

"So now I've got to sit on this stupid ship one way or the other while my beautiful and sexy wife—! She's in perpetual heat, you know, and I'm gone too much as it is. She's complained an awful lot about not getting enough from me."

"Well, I wish I could help you out."

"That goddamned flag had better not be flyin'—!"

Three mornings later I was up on the point of the bow with Smellers watching the West Coast take shape when Lassiter joined us with a pair of field glasses.

"Nice day for sailing, don't you think?" I asked, irrelevantly.

"Couldn't be nicer," he said, looking sick. To Smellers he said, "I guess you've kept your nose clean and will get liberty tonight."

"I guess so." Smellers looked at me and shrugged. "You boys live too dangerously for me."

"What do you see through those glasses?" I asked.

"I see a cute little white house with a flag pole."

"I know a motormack—" began Smellers. I began to laugh and he turned to me and demanded, "What?"

I asked Lassiter, "And is *Semper Paratus* waving bravely today?"

"I'm afraid not," he said, sounding ambivalent.

"You don't say?" said Smellers. "Let me have them glasses."

About that time a yeoman from the Ship's Office showed up, wanting to know which one of us was *Hall.*

Lassiter turned around and with a straight face said to the messenger, "I didn't have a damned thing to do with whatever it is he's in trouble for."

"Nobody's in trouble," grinned the yeoman. "Hall's being transferred—to what has to be the best duty in the entire Service."

"But I didn't request a transfer," I said, testily. "If you like it that much, go in my place."

"The Communications Officer and the Morale Officer both requested it for you."

"You've got to be kiddin'," said Lassiter, disgusted. To me he said, "You're gettin' the shaft because of that Swimming Party thing."

"Better double-time it, Red," said the yeoman.

"You *double-time* it," I snarled. "I'll get there in my own good time, if you don't mind. By the way, what do you consider the best duty in the Service?"

"Find out for yourself."

"Don't hit him, Red," said Smellers. "They might transfer you to a Navy brig, someplace like Mare Island."

"Yeah," said Lassiter, "this time I'll bet they send you to a loran station in Newfoundland."

"Do we have holdings up there?" asked Smellers.

Five minutes later I was told by an officer in the Ship's Office to go pack my seabag and report back at the office for my orders. As I turned to leave, he added, "You are one lucky swab, is all I can say. Somebody must like you."

"Could you tell me who requested the transfer, Sir?"

"The Skipper of the *Alert* requested it," said the officer, smiling. "That's got to be a first, for you."

"Comdr. Miklokowski—requested me?"

"Uh, no. I believe the skipper's name is Lt. Comdr. Mason."

Still in a daze five minutes later, I ran onto Smellers loafing in the radio shack and told him about being requested by the skipper of the CGC *Alert.*

"You beat all, Red. Your orders say *proceed immediately* and yet you owe the ship about two weeks' restriction time."

"Hey, I deserve a break once in awhile. But did you hear what I said? The Skipper of the *Alert* requested me! I used to know this Lt. Comdr. Mason."

"And yet he requested you. I get it."

An hour later, with my transfer papers in my ditty bag and feeling like a million dollars in my tailormade bell-bottomed dress blues, I tripped across the gangplank of the *Escanaba* at Government Island and headed straight for the Chat. I could not leave without letting my hometown buddy, Eugene Tuney Goodrich, know I was going back to Eureka.

At the gangplank Janssen took one look at me and gawked. "Oh, my God. Are we getting you back?" He attempted a grin, which caused the seaman beside him to wheel and stare at me.

I shook my head, easing the seabag to the gangplank. "Just wanted to pay my respects, old buddy. I'm headed for the *Alert.*"

"Well, in that case, permission granted to come aboard. Weren't you on that little boat once before?"

At this point, Goodrich materialized, with his hands in the air. "Don't tell me you're joinin' us again!"

I glanced at Janssen and laughed. "No, I'm headed back to the *Alert,* but first I've got a favor to ask. Think I can leave my gear with you this afternoon and maybe tonight?"

"What?" he burst out. "How did you manage that? Didn't you leave that cutter in handcuffs?"

"The Skipper requested me, old buddy. Has a skipper ever requested you?"

Ignoring entirely what I had just said, he began complaining about how hard it was to keep up with me. "When you got transferred to the

Taney, where all fuckups and goldbricks end up, everybody said you'd be there for the duration. But not you. You managed to go to the *Bramble,* from whence no man has ever escaped—"

"I'm in a bit of a hurry, old buddy."

"It beats all I ever heard tell of. Why do you want me to baby-sit with your gear tonight? Aint we going to rendezvous with Archer?"

"I can't, not this time. I've got a date with an airline stewardess, over in Frisco."

"How'd you have time to get acquainted with one of them, what with all the court martials and captain's masts and restrictions—?"

"Never mind. Stay out of my toothpaste."

*　　　　*　　　　*

The first San Francisco telephone book I found was the old dog-eared and beer-stained copy at *Ted and Roy's.* After a brief chat with Ted at the bar, I took a stein of draft beer with me to the pay phone at the front door and began to look down through the M's, for Mahoney. I went through MacDonald, Mackey, McGillicudey, Mahaney, and there it was, the only one in the book: Mahoney, S. E., 1657 W. Poseidon Court, Number 4.

I dialed the number and waited. After three rings, the palms of my hands began to sweat ice water. On the fourth a soft, sleepy voice said, "Yes?" Somehow, I managed to identify myself. Her voice became stronger but she was not leaping about with joy. She was all alone, she said, and wanted very much to meet me. Where was I at that moment? I could take the trolley car to Sheridan and walk two blocks down the hill to Poseidon. Her apartment was on the corner!

On the way, my head began spinning, and I wrestled with the problem of how to get past the first minute or so with this sexy-voiced mystery girl? Should I act very reserved or try to be laid back? What would she do? Perhaps I should follow her lead. At the thought that she might merely like to shake hands, I breathed a sigh of relief.

Then the thought occurred that I should take flowers and perhaps a bottle of wine. What would she think of me, showing up empty-handed? I decided that I had to find a florist on the way.

A thousand questions went through my mind. Number One, what did she look like? How tall was she? How fat? Did she actually have no boyfriends at the moment, as she had claimed? I had never seen an ugly airline stewardess, nor one that was overweight or short, and I could not believe that a pretty one would be without a steady.

Finally before her door, still without the flowers, I was a mental and physical wreck, ready to bolt the moment she showed the least sign of disapproval. And I had begun to say to myself things like, "She's not the only girl in the world. If she's good enough looking to be an airline hostess, she's probably been spoiled rotten by men and therefore would be much too expensive to take out!"

I rapped three times on the top panel of her door and stepped back. On my new gabardine uniform were three rows of campaign ribbons, and I was holding a shaped and therefore very salty white golfball cap in both hands.

Finally, the door swung back. "Hold on, now!" she screamed.

Standing before me, and two steps above me, was the most beautiful girl I had ever seen. She was wearing a slouchy house dress and floppy old houseshoes, but she would have been beautiful in anything (I told myself). Or nothing at all.

That I somehow resisted turning and scooting down those steps to blissful anonymity and safety was remarkable, for her scream sounded like a near hysterical call for help! But I stood my ground and nodded, moving not a muscle.

"But—!"

"Sharon Elizabeth?"

"Yessss! I mean, *Yes!*" she nodded. "I'm Beth!"

I had spent a great deal of time flat of my back in my bunk trying to imagine just what this girl would look like. All I had had to go on were her soft, bassy, sexy voice and a few rather ambiguous remarks made by the aircraft skipper from time to time. Now, as it struck home that my feeble imagination had not even come close, all I could do was stare.

"*Truth is beauty*," I stammered, stupidly, fumbling with my cap and trying to think of something to say, "*and beauty is truth.*"

"*And that is all you need to know, on earth and in heaven*," she laughed. "You sweet dear!"

She dragged me through her front door, seated me on a divan, and skipped across the room. "Sit still," she giggled over her shoulder at a door that opened into a hallway, "I'll be right back." And she was, wearing over the house dress a silk kimono, which she had pulled tight about her small waist. She flung herself onto the other end of the divan.

"Charley!" she burst out. "Oh, God, what a surprise!" She grabbed both of my hands. "I am so absolutely knocked out! Yes, *knocked out!* You were a bit much, you know, standing there before my door—like a Coast Guard enlistment poster!"

I couldn't take my eyes off her. Her thick, lovely hair, hanging in great natural waves about her shoulders, framed a face so sweet and innocent it made tears come to my eyes. Indeed, her eyes, large and set wide apart, were like magnets drawing my own!

"Say something to me! I loved your voice on the radio!"

"Uh, I liked yours, too!"

"What do you mean?" he protested, looking coy. She knew full well what I meant. "Do you like how I look?"

Suddenly, I began to stutter: "There are no words in my vocabulary that could possibly describe how you look to me! How is it that swabs— I mean *men*—are not trying to break down your door?"

"Oh, you dear sweet beautiful sailor boy! To say that about me!" She pulled me toward her, snuggling. "I want to explain something to you. All I talk about to my friends all the time is meeting a goodlooking redheaded sailor man! I'm not kidding you! And here you are! My God, you're just what I've been lookin' for all of my life!" She grabbed my hands again and leaned back, gazing at me. "No, you're better looking than I ever imagined you would be!"

She leaped up and stood looking down at me.

"You think I'm kidding, but I'm not! I've about driven all my poor friends away with my talk about how someday I would meet this handsome redhead! He would be tall and broad-shouldered and very good looking. What color of eyes do you have? Green! Oh, nobody will believe this, this is crazy! I can't wait to show you off! My girlfriends will flip over you—so I'd better not ever let you out of my sight when they're around!"

On and on she went about how I looked. And when I was finally permitted to say that she exceeded all of my expectations, she began on how well I spoke, the quality of my very manly voice, and so on. As she spoke, she stroked my hair, straightened individual hairs in my eyebrows, traced my lips with her fingertips.

Eventually, I caught myself squirming and trying to move back from her. But Miss Beth Mahoney, still the most beautiful female creature I had ever seen, by far, moved with me, caressing my hands and arms and legs!

Waiting for an opening, I managed to say that I could drink something, if she had anything.

"Oh, yes, my sweet! Have I been rattling on too much?"

"No, no!"

"Just a minute, dear heart! I'll be right back!"

And as Sharon Elizabeth Mahoney disappeared through a revolving door at the back of the room, I let no grass grow beneath my feet on my way through the foyer to the front door! It was midnight, I was exhausted, and between me and the trolley car stop was a very steep hill. But, God bless America, I was once again a free man!

*   *   *

The Greyhound made its slow and patient way up the winding, picturesque northern California coast toward the Big Trees Country, stopping at every store and service station between San Francisco and Eureka. The time it was taking was of no importance to me. I was returning to the best duty in the Coast Guard, and I had made a pact with myself to do it right this time. No more shenanigans. I had about a year to go on my hitch, and when that was up I would return home, finish college, become a radio engineer, marry, and settle down. Maybe not in that order, of course. One thing for sure, I had to stop chasing skirts and settle upon one girl. I was wasting too much time wining and dining little teases.

This line of thinking ended abruptly when I hit upon a solemn truth: I had not been out with a single girl (or a married one, for that matter) since enlisting in the Coast Guard. God only knew, I had wanted to. But all my friends and I did was talk about picking up girls, wining and dining them, and going to a motel.

Inside the bus depot in Eureka, after a cup of coffee, I shouldered my seabag and walked out onto the cobblestone street. It was precisely the same kind of morning that had greeted me in this same spot almost exactly one year before. Nothing had changed, seemingly, not even the air I was breathing, which was cool and damp and brought to mind dead fish. The cobblestone out in the street was wet from a recent shower, just as on that other morning.

The taxi driver, who showed no signs of recognition, looked very familiar and used the very same words I had heard in March of 1947. "Hey, Mate, you need a ride?"

The docks at Humboldt Bay looked surprisingly the worse for wear, however; and the *Alert* appeared to be about twenty feet shorter than it had been.

Tully was standing on the dock at the gangplank in a clean white apron smoking a cigarette and talking to a salty-looking a CPO; and when he saw me he let out a squawk and began to waddle down the dock in my direction.

"Now, I can believe anything!" he shouted right in my face, grabbing my seabag. "The Coast Guard's sure as heck becomin' a hooligan navy, like you always said it was!"

"I can't believe I was shanghaied back aboard this scow," I said.

"You got that one right!" laughed Tully. "The Twelfth District just decided to throw in the towel and send you back here to retire. By the way, the Old Man got booted out of the Service, and we've got a humdinger of a real sailing man now! Drinks a lot but ever'body likes him. Name's Moser."

We walked down the dock to the gangplank.

"Meet our brand new boats, Red. Says his friends call him Hawk, but I reckon he don't have no friends in these parts. Looks more like a *Baldy* to me."

I stuck out my hand and the Chief took it, frowning at Tully. "After I saved his ass at the *Triangle* the other night, you'd think he could keep a civil tongue in his head. You the new sparks?"

I nodded and turned to Tully. "What's the situation at the *Triangle* these days?"

"Aw, he was just jokin'. Ever'thing's okay hereabouts. But we've got a real loser in the radio shack. Want to hear about that? He's a sour-faced kid from the East Coast, and the Skipper took a dislike for him here awhile back and wants to git rid of him. That could develop into an interesting situation, with you in there." He whacked me on the back and said to Chief Hawk, "Listen, this red-haired galoot has seen more of the Coast Guard in one hitch than I have in twenty-two years. Been on just about everything we've got here on the West Coast."

"You restless, boy?" laughed Hawkins.

"I guess I was there for awhile, but I'm not now. This is the best there is, in my opinion."

"You've got that right," said Tully, with a pleased look on his face. "Now, let's get down in the galley and have some breakfast. In about an hour I've got to get that lazy bunch of moochers up."

A few minutes later Tully informed me that Miranda had been transferred to the East Coast. "You remember that sister of his? She can dress up to look just like him."

"I know," I said, grinning. "Does she ever drop in?"

"Yeah, about ever' week or so. Them two came close to drivin' me batty talkin' 'bout you."

I was still in the messhall when the crew came dragging in. They were in a state of half-dress and truly looked like a bunch of hooligans. As each of the old hands caught sight of me, he came over and asked the same question: "What had I been up to?" Then, one by one, they drifted over to the serving bar and helped themselves to the big platter of fried eggs, bacon, biscuits, and coffee. I had just stood up and was about to leave when a slender kid came in looking for me.

"The Skipper wants to see you in the radio shack. I'm Simpkins, the sparks."

"Good to meet you." I told him my name and that I had served aboard the *Alert* before.

"I understand you're just a Third Class. So I guess I'm still the sparks."

I nodded, smiling. "Come on, let's go see the Man."

In the days that followed, we puttered around the radio shack, did a little painting, tested all of the tubes in the TDE, and replaced the two big final tubes with more powerful ones. Something I had learned from the *Bramble*. In the evenings we fell into the habit of drifting up to the *Triangle Bar* and drinking draft beer and listening to Rosa Rita sing Portuguese songs behind the bar.

Lt. Comdr. Mason dropped into the radio shack quite often to chat with me. But he had little to say to Simpkins. Once he said to the Second Class that there were other cutters that would like to have a

fine radioman like him, and he would gladly sign a request for transfer at anytime.

Simpkins, however, was not interested. He knew a good thing when
he saw it.

One day the two of us were sitting in the messdeck with Tully drinking coffee when, to our astonishment, the Skipper shot through the forward hatch and headed for our table. In his hand was a yellow half-
sheet, a radiogram delivered by the U. S. Postal Service.

"Simpkins, how would you like to get in on something really big?"

"Like what, Skipper?" Simpkins' face had turned pale.

"Here's a request for a Second Class Radioman to go to an icebreaker.
Now, wait a minute, don't shake your head yet. This thing's going to make
the damnedest journey you ever heard of—and end up no telling where.
Think of the adventure! You'll never get an opportunity like this again."

"Where is this icebreaker, Skipper?" I asked.

"Baltimore. They want a Second Class."

"Yes, Sir."

He turned back to Simpkins. "It's headed down the East Coast to
Panama, around and up the West Coast to Juneau, Alaska I don't have the
foggiest what it's goin up there for, but, man alive, what a challenge for a
young man just starting out. Simpkins, this is exactly what you need."

"I don't know," said Simpkins. "I kinda like it here."

"Shit, this is the end of the road for you! Nothin's going to happen
here, believe me. How many times do we get out of the harbor? Not a
single time in the past two weeks."

"That's what I like about it," mumbled Simpkins, glancing at me. "I
like it peaceful this way."

Mason shoved the radiogram in front of Simpkins and turned to
leave. Over his shoulder, he said, "I want you to give some serious consideration to this. And be quick about it. It's circulating all over the
Service, and I can guarantee you a lot of sparkies will apply for it."

Back in the radio shack I examined the radiogram, while Simpkins agonized over the Skipper's obvious dislike for him.

"Maybe they'd take a Radioman Third Class, with some experience," I said, feeling the beginnings of an adrenaline flow. "That would be a real kick, taking an icebreaker all the way from the East Coast around to Alaska."

"Do you really think that's a good deal?" asked Simpkins, doubtfully. "I mean, why would anybody want to take a trip like that?"

I stared at him. He really was a *klutz*. "Do I think it's a good deal? My God, yes! It's a once-in-a-lifetime good deal! I'd give anything for a berth aboard that icebreaker!"

"Why don't you put in for it then? What do you have to lose?"

"I would if I thought Mason would approve it."

"He would approve anything you come up with," said Simpkins, incredulous. "It's like he thinks you're capable of doin' no wrong."

"You're full of baloney."

"Put in for that and you'll find out I'm right."

*   *   *

The radiogram, this one directly from NMC, Base Radio, San Francisco, arrived on August 8, 1948, confirming my transfer to the CGC *Storis*, located in the U. S. Coast Guard Yard, Curtis Bay, Maryland! I stared at the half-sheet of paper, feeling a shock wave go through my body.

I handed the radiogram to Lt. Comdr. Mason, feeling sick at my stomach. Someone had mistakenly typed *RM2* after my name. The request had been for a Second Class, of course.

"What?" the Skipper demanded.

"It says *RM2* after my name, Sir."

"I know that," said Mason, testily. "You sounded so pitiful about wanting to go on this world expedition I decided to ask for a rank change for you. They wouldn't have accepted a third class radioman, anyway. Furthermore, I took the liberty of asking for an interim leave for you. When was the last time you had a leave?"

"I haven't, Sir," I said, becoming choked up.

"Well, you've got until August 31 to report to the icebreaker. Your transportation's paid for, right through your hometown; so why don't you get your butt off this ship while you've still got some spare days? You do still have a hometown, don't you?"

"Yes, Sir, I do."

Mr. Mason stuck out his hand. "God help that icebreaker."

A Decent Girl

◆

Things could have been worse. An unexpected leave of absence, advancement in rank, a train trip across the country, four girlfriends waiting for me back home, and, to cap it off, a transfer to an icebreaker followed by a voyage to Alaska via the Panama Canal!

At the Western Union Office in Eureka I wrote out three very brief telegrams. The first was to Darleen Caulfield: "Arriving in Ada sometime on Thursday the twelfth on Trailways Bus. Reserve a room for me at the Biltmore Hotel starting on that day. Love, Red."

The clerk took the half-sheet of paper and wrote the word STOP where I had placed periods. "That'll be eighty-seven cents. Should you ask for a confirmation or a reply of some kind?"

"Nope. That'll be fine just the way it is."

While he was busy with that one, I worked out another and made a copy of it: "Coming home on leave. Will call you as soon as I reach home." One of these I addressed to Jody Summers and the other to Alice Chastain.

The clerk was staring at me, doubtfully. "All these girls will be expectin' you?"

"They're just the nucleus of the reception party," I said, handing him a five-dollar bill.

"My, aren't you the one. Several girls in every port."

On the long bus ride down to Frisco my mind returned in earnest to the land of my bringing up, an area in south central Oklahoma that included two small towns in Seminole and Pontotoc counties. For the past year and a half I had devoted very little time to this area and the subjects therein; but now that I was going back, it occurred to me that I had better work out some rather definite plans.

In addition to the three girls I had wired there was a most special young lady who could not very easily be reached by telegraph or telephone. Jamie Lee, who had grown up with my kid sister, Jessica. Of course, I could have sent a wire addressed to her on the rural route.

By the time I reached San Francisco, I had decided that since Darleen was the one I had corresponded with most (She had done most of the corresponding), I would see her first, using the Biltmore Hotel in Ada as my base.

From San Francisco I took the Southern Pacific to Oklahoma City, riding first class in a Pullman coach. It was a three-day trip, which gave me plenty of time to think; and by the time I reached Albuquerque I had made up my mind to remain single, regardless of the costs. And since three of the girls had one thing and one thing only in mind where I was concerned, marriage, I would have to be strong or I would end up with a ring on my finger.

A proposal of marriage, more binding than a Deed of Trust in the small towns of Oklahoma, had to be avoided at all costs. No proposals and no engagement rings. That is, if I ever ended to go home again.

Me, myself, and I agreed wholeheartedly that I could not be *tied down* by a girl, any girl, not at this time. That would perhaps come later. But on this interim leave I was merely stopping off in my hometown (and the surrounding environs) *en route* to an icebreaker that was headed for Alaska! From there it was no telling where I would go!

In Oklahoma City I caught a Trailways bus to Ada, comforted by the fact that no one, not even Darleen, whose hometown this was, knew when I was arriving. I had deliberately kept this information from her because it was not considered *decent* for a girl to meet a strange boy at the bus station. When the bus pulled in at the depot, I was sitting behind the driver, expecting to see no one that I knew. My plan was to go straight to the hotel, which was located one block from the bus station, and take a bath, shave, and sleep for ten hours. And since it was doubly indecent in that small town for a girl to be seen near a hotel in which her boyfriend was staying, we would have to work out something.

To my astonishment, the first person I saw at the station was pale-faced little Darleen! I could not believe my eyes. The implications of this social indiscretion caused my heart to speed up considerably. To the driver I pointed out the slender little curly-haired blonde in a pink blouse and a white cotton skirt and saddle oxfords. "That's my girlfriend."

"Isn't she just a bit young for you?"

Darleen, I could tell, was scared to death, but there was a determined look in her eyes. I leaped through the door of the bus and took her in my arms, ignoring a crowd of curious and locals. She struggled weakly at first, trying to see if any of those watching us were relatives or friends; but the moment our lips touched she responded and I kissed her long and hard. And when I had quite finished, I set her back down on her feet, gathered up my seabag and ditty bag and headed for the Biltmore.

She raced and caught up with me, out of breath. "You seem—so sure of yourself!" she cried. "I sure hope none of my friends or relatives were in that crowd back there!"

"What are the chances?" I teased. "Do your friends and relatives hang out at the bus station?"

"No," she smiled, her face still ghostly pale. "But this is such a small town everyone in that crowd probably knows somebody that knows me!" She grabbed my arm. "Oh, Wesley, I can't go into the hotel with you! What will we do?"

"Sure you can. If anybody says anything, tell them I'm your steady. You did reserve a room for me, didn't you?"

"Yes, I did!" she exclaimed. "Mother would just die if she knew I had done that. And the hotel clerk asked all kinds of embarrassing questions. And he wanted cash or he wouldn't guarantee it. So I asked Daddy for the money."

"What did he say?"

"Well," she said, turning even redder, "he couldn't understand why I would be renting a room for a man I wasn't engaged to, especially a sailor. I've got to tell you my folks have a few reservations about sailors. My cousin, Nona Mae, told me never to trust a sailor, that they're out for only one thing."

"Didn't you tell your dad who I was? I thought he liked me."

"Oh, he does. Dad's a veteran of World War One, remember? And he thought you were the first real man I'd brought to the house. Actually, you're the *first man* I ever introduced to my parents."

"Come on! You can't be serious!" I glanced down at her, realized that she had filled out beautifully in the year since I had seen her. "You're eighteen years old! Or so you told me."

I stopped and set my seabag on the sidewalk. She looked as if she might take off running, but I grabbed her and pulled her tiny middle close to me and kissed her hard on the lips. When I set her down, she was breathing hard.

"Maybe we ought to wait till we get to the room," she said, with a scared little laugh. "Oh, but I can't go to that room with you!"

"Yes, you can." I picked up my gear and did not look back the rest of the way. Every person we met stared at us; and after we had passed, they turned and stared some more. And in the lobby, a dozen pairs of eyes turned upon us!

"You know what they're thinking, don't you?" whispered Darleen, looking distraught. "They think I'm a slut for going to a hotel with a sailor. Most of them, maybe all of them, know my folks, and they're thinking that here's a sailor taking the daughter of somebody they know up to his room."

"I don't know what the female gawkers are thinking, but I know what the males are," I said with a grin. "They're jealous as hell."

"Red!" she scolded.

I went to the registration desk, with her still clinging to my arm, and asked for my key. The clerk handed it over and looked toward the elevator. There was a brief exchange of glances between him and Darleen, and she dropped her head in shame.

When the elevator door closed on us, she exclaimed, "Oh, Red, I was never so relieved to get behind closed doors in my life. I hope nobody's in the hallway upstairs."

My room was Number 312, at the opposite end of the hallway from the elevator. It seemed like a city block, because I was actually having to drag Darleen along! At the door I dropped my two bags and, fumbling a bit, inserted the key. To my surprise, *my hand was trembling*. I glanced at her to see if she had noticed. She hadn't. I scooped her into my arms and carried her inside and dropped her on the bed. Then I went back and got the bags and closed the door.

" I've got bad news for you," she said when I bent over her.

I lifted her to a sitting position and kissed her.

"I'm having—"

"Me, too!" I laughed nervously, fumbling with the top button of her blouse. It was, of course, buttoned up to the throat and the buttons were tiny.

"Stop, Red. I'm so very sorry!" Just as I was about to open the flimsy garment back, she cried, "I'm—having my period!"

I blurted, "You're—*what?*" Then I added, incredulous, "You're indisposed?"

For a long embarrassing moment we stared at each other. Then she began giggling and leaped into my arms. "I've never heard it called that!" She sat up on the bed beside me, and suddenly the pained look returned to her face. "But even if I wasn't, remember you promised—"

"I remember what you promised, too," I said.

She glanced at me nervously, "I know and I meant it, as soon as—"
All I could do was stare at her.

"Oh, Honey, you do love me, don't you? You do intend to ask me to marry you!"

*   *   *

Dinner at the Biltmore turned out to be rather formal, planned that way by Darleen to dispel or at least to diminish some of the gossip that had undoubtedly been going around since the previous day. She showed up at my door about seven in a long black dress, black high-heel shoes, earrings, and a pearl necklace. She looked ten years older than she had the day before and not half as desirable. Even so, she was a piece of fine workmanship and, I had to admit, the most innocent human being I had ever known.

"Come on," she whispered into my ear, "we can't be up here long."

"Why not?" I scoffed, scooping her up, disregarding the care she had taken to look just right.

"Let's make everybody think we're just having a date, not going to bed together."

"My aching back," I complained. "The point is, *we're not going to bed together*. What do we care what they think?"

But I acquiesced, putting her down on her feet still in one piece. My uniform, just back from the hotel's laundry service, was lying on the dresser. I quickly removed my dungarees, while she blushed and checked out the two pictures on the wall facing the bed. Once my uniform was on, she turned and watched me adjust my black neckerchief just so, with the knot squarely in the bottom of the V of my blouse.

When I began to run sock over my shiny black shoes, she said with a smile, "You are *so* particular!" In a sober voice she added, "That's one of the things I like about you."

"How's your problem going?" I asked, taking her by an arm and pulling her into the hallway. "How much longer?"

"Let's don't talk about anything like that this evening. Let's just have the best time of our lives. Oh, Red, I love you so very much!"

I had wanted to take her to the Pendegast Restaurant on Main Street; but, without explaining why, she insisted that we eat at the Biltmore. It made me no never mind, one way or the other.

"I've never eaten here, can you believe?" she exclaimed. "And I've heard it's the swankiest restaurant in town."

Swankiest in town wasn't saying much, I told myself; but I didn't press the subject. We were seated, at her request, at a large table in a corner of the dining room which was hidden from curious pedestrians' view. Because of my uniform, however, everyone who entered the dining room gawked and a few actually waved. Each time someone waved or called out to us, I said to Darleen, "Somebody you know?"

"I don't think you have any idea what you've done to me," she whispered, once we were settled. We turned and watched our waiter make his way toward us across the room. "Live will never be the same again!"

"I haven't done anything to you, *yet!*"

She snickered. "Oh, yes, you have. I'll tell you after he leaves." Then kicking me on the chin, she exclaimed, "Oh, heck, I know him!"

"Could I get you something to drink?" the young man asked from ten feet away. He was tall and angular and perhaps eighteen, and on his upper lip was a smudge of something, put there no doubt to accentuate what he considered to be a mustache. "Why, Darleen, it's you!" He suddenly relaxed into a slump of hometown friendliness.

"Hello, Clyde. Red, this is a classmate of mine at Ada High. Clyde, this is Red. He's in United States Coast Guard."

"Hey, the Coast Guard! I've heard of that!"

"Hey," I said. "Clyde, I'd like to have a beer. How about you, Darleen?"

"Oh, we don't serve beer, Sir. Coffee and soft drinks and tea."

Clyde finally left for two coffees, after making it very clear that he was interested in Darleen.

That young lady, looking more flushed than before, couldn't wait to tell me,

"You've changed my whole life, Red." She laid her hand on mine. "I can't even think of a thing any more but you. I dream about you every night, and when I see a cute boy I always compare him to you. And he always comes off terribly."

"You say that now," I smiled, but what happens when I leave town? You seemed to know Clyde quite well."

"I've known Clyde all of my life, silly. He lives about half a block from my house." She squeezed my hand reassuringly, smiling, obviously pleased that I was jealous. "Daddy wouldn't let him in our house."

"Could I ask you something, my sweet? How have you managed to make it to eighteen without getting—a boyfriend?"

I was fascinated by Darleen's face, especially when she was dealing with a serious thought. It was a very accurate barometer of what was going through her mind. When something naughty or embarrassing occurred to her, it turned a most becoming scarlet; and when she disapproved of something, it became quite tragic. At this moment, it looked like death itself.

"You promised you wouldn't talk like that this evening!"

"Okay, you're right. I'll ask you later."

Around nine o'clock, after I had eaten a medium-rare sirloin that took up most of a platter, and she had toyed with a well-done one, and after dessert and a final cup of coffee (All the other diners had left long before this), I asked, "What time in the morning?"

Without hesitation, she said, "Right after breakfast."

"Why not drop by my room and go to breakfast with me?"

"I don't think that would be a good idea. It will be best if I wait until Daddy goes to work."

"Once again, how old are you?"

"Seventeen!" she moaned tragically. "I told you that in one of my letters! I'm still in high school."

"But you're a senior, right?"

"Yes, as of two months ago. I've got one more year to go."

"Well, it seems to me that your parents are treating you like junior high! When are they going to let you grow up?"

"Let's don't quarrel, Honey. I'll come to your room about ten o'clock, okay?"

"I'm taking you home tonight," I said, with finality. "Don't you think I ought to say hello to your parents?"

"Not tonight. They'll be in bed by now. Maybe you can visit tomorrow afternoon after Daddy gets off work."

The town was getting ready to roll up the sidewalks. There were very few cars still on the streets; and only a few places, like the *Hamburger King* and the *McSwain Theater*, were still open. I put my arm around Darleen's waist as we walked past the row of parked teenagers at the theater.

"Everybody in this town will know I'm going out with a sailor, if they don't already."

"Is that good or bad?"

"It will blow their minds because I've never gone out with anyone before, especially a sailor. Nona Mae told me that sailors are far more mature than most men, when it comes to women."

It was a twenty-minute leisurely stroll from the hotel to Darleen's door. There beneath the huge sycamore tree I kissed her, wondering if eyes were watching us from inside the dark house. She did not seem to care and when she began to climb up my body, I couldn't help but wonder at the metamorphosis. To test the waters, I let my hands slide down. She continued to climb until her legs were locked around my middle.

From inside the house came a noise. A lamp went on in the livingroom.

*   *   *

The following morning I breakfasted leisurely at the Biltmore, thinking about innocent little Darleen. Despite what she had said in her letters to me, about her intention to spend the night with me, I was now convinced she was just a little tease and should be placed in the same category as Jody and Alice.

It had come down to a matter of will power.

Back in my room I showered and shaved, and went about stripped down to my skivvies. And when Darleen's light knock came at the door at precisely ten o'clock, I was wearing only my white regulation Coast Guard shorts. I opened the door and stood back for her to enter. She was dressed completely in white cotton and looked like a doll, and her face was flushed with excitement.

I grabbed her and closed the door.

"Wesley, please! Let's talk!"

When my hands slid down to her little round butt, her entire body became as stiff as a two-by-four.

"I want to talk. Mother has warned me and everybody I know has warned me—not to have sex with you! Not this soon. Not until we know each other a lot better."

I held her at arms' length, looking at her.

Batting her pretty blue eyes at me, she whined, "I know I promised to spend the night with you, but Honey I've got to think about what's right for me! I love you dearly but—!"

My mind made up, I spoke very quietly, with no anger in my voice at all: "No, you don't, Darleen. Stop saying that. You love the idea of being in love with me, but you don't even know what *love* is."

Her face had become tragic as I spoke these words, and suddenly her narrow little shoulders began to shake. I dropped my hands and stood looking at her, waiting, my shorts standing out ridiculously. I knew she was very close to caving.

"My cousin fell in love with a sailor and he got her pregnant and she never saw him again!"

"Well, I guess that proves that all sailors hit and run."

"Do you really love me?"

My reply was to take her into my arms, tenderly, pressing her firmer and firmer against me. At first her body was tense and she tried to pull back.

"Oh, Red, please!"

I lifted her off the floor and lay her on the bed, tenderly, as one lays a baby down to sleep. Then, slowly, I lowered myself, straddling her. While my lips found hers, I began unbuttoning the top of her dress. Her eyes were closed and she was beginning to sob. I told her to be quiet.

"I know we shouldn't do this!" she sobbed quietly.

Her body had become stiff again and had begun to tremble. I finished unbuttoning her blouse, but even as I did so I knew I could not go on. Beneath her slip her round, firm breasts had begun to heave up and down.

"Will you—?" she began, her large, tear-filled eyes staring at me pathetically. "Will you marry me?"

I was suspended on my hands and knees above her, unable to resist looking at her beautiful little body. Perfectly proportioned, without a blemish of any kind, as far as I could see. A porcelain doll.

"Let's wait! Until—we know each other better!" she said, rolling over onto her stomach. "We'll have our entire lives to—do this!"

"Darleen, I'm on interim leave and have to report to my ship in just a few days. We don't have time to get married, don't you understand that?" When she didn't say anything, I added, "I'm going to Alaska and I don't know when I'll be back."

As she heard these words, she began to sob again. "I knew you were just here for a short time. But all we need is three days, for the blood test."

Without another word, I got up and began to undress.

At this she burst out bawling and turned over on her stomach again. I went into the bathroom and turned on the shower, disgusted with myself and feeling sorry for her. She was doing exactly what I had known she would do, and I could not blame her. I skinned off my shorts and stepped into the cold water.

If there was one thing that I knew without a shadow of a doubt, it was that I could have this girl for as long as I wanted her, without marrying her. All I had to do was go back in there and take her. She would continue to bawl, but she would not put up any resistance; and once it was over she would go to the North Pole with me, marriage license or no marriage license.

All I had to do was forget who I was for a very brief time.

The real irony was that once we made love she would never love another man. She might marry one and submit to him on a regular basis, but she would never love him. It was one of the cardinal rules by which all decent girls lived. A God only knew how decent Darleen was.

After I showered, and with water still streaming down my body, I returned and lifted her off the bed and held her close. There was no barrier between us now, physical or otherwise. She snuggled against my shoulder and said over and over again, "I love you, I love you, I love you!"

I lowered her to the bed and began to dress. She raised her head and stared.

"Pull yourself together," I said, "I'm walking you home. Then I'm to pay a visit to my folks."

*   *   *

Mary Caulfield took one look at her daughter's face and fell into a chair with an sad little whimper. She had just finished setting the kitchen table for the evening meal. Heavy, her millwright husband of twenty years, was due in from his job at the Ada Flour Mill any minute; and now, while we looked on, she twisted her hands in her apron and hyperventilated.

"Your father and I were wrong, weren't we?" she sobbed.

"What do you mean, Mother?" demanded Darleen, dismayed, her face tragic. "This is Red!"

"Yes, I know." She looked sorrowfully at me. "Well, you did it, didn't you, sailor boy?"

"Mother, nothing happened. Red's here on a very short leave."

"Yes, I'll bet he is at that. Well, he's wasting no time, I see."

"He wanted to come by and see you and Daddy."

Mrs. Caulfield got unsteadily to her feet and went to the stove and opened the oven. It was empty. She straightened up and looked at her daughter and then at me.

"We raised Darleen in the Christian church, young man. She wasn't meant for some fly-by-night sailor that was just interested in getting into her pants. You've had your enjoyment, and now Darleen's got to wait around and find out if she's pregnant. If she is and you don't marry her, what do you suppose will happen to her and the baby? Do you have any idea what that will say to this community about her and her parents? We've got a good name around here."

"We didn't do a thing, Mrs. Caulfield," I mumbled, looking at the floor.

"How can you stand here in my kitchen and tell me that? Look at her!"

Darleen had turned and was staring at me, a face tragic again. I was quite sure I knew what she was thinking, that she had let me down for no good reason, that her parents would never believe she hadn't let them down.

Whatever she was thinking, she suddenly threw her arms around my neck and began kissing me on the lips. "Oh, Mother!" she cried. "We were going to wait until Daddy got home to tell you the wonderful news!"

Mary Caulfield had stopped in her tracks in the center of the kitchen, a pan of cornbread dough ready to go into the oven.

"We haven't set the date yet, Mother, but Wesley has asked me to marry him!" She snuggled against my shoulder, sobbing. "Oh, this is the most wonderful day of my life!"

From the open doorway to the livingroom Mr. Caulfield called out, "So, young man, you popped the question!" He entered the kitchen, carrying his metal lunch box in one hand and extending the other to me.

"Oh, Daddy, Red and I—!"

"I'm glad to hear it, Princess!"

As soon as possible after dinner, I announced that I had a lot of telephoning to do and such a short time to do it. Once again I shook hands with Heavy Caulfield and waved goodbye to a tight-lipped Mary Caulfield (who had evidently read something in my face that did not jive with Darleen's words and behavior). To Darleen, I said, "I've got to spend a few days with my family in the Bend. What will you do while I'm gone?"

"Oh, I've got lots of things to do. You go ahead and visit your folks, but don't look at any of those pretty country girls. Just remember that I'm your girl now, and nobody else had better even look at you."

Five minutes after I arrived back at my hotel room and settled on the bed with the telephone there was a light knock at the door. In my skivvies, I went to the door and opened it a crack, standing to one side.

"Sweetheart, I think we need to talk."

Darleen, in bluejeans, a yellow short-sleeve shirt, and tennis shoes, stood before me like a little trooper at attention. She was incredibly desirable at that moment.

"Darleen," I sighed, "why are you keeping up this charade? They know we've already done it!"

"Can I come in?" She came in on her own and closed the door. "In case you haven't noticed it, I can't do the right thing no matter what I do. My parents *are convinced* we've done it, and that is the end of it. But all of my life I've had it drummed into my head that I must remain a virgin until I've found the right man. Well, you're the right man for me."

"Darleen, I know what you're up to, and it's not going to work. I'm not ready to get married, not right now! I'm still in the Coast Guard, and I'm on my way to Alaska."

"I can wait. That's what I do best."

"So all I have to do is say the magic words. How do you know I would—"

She put her arms around my neck. "I know you better than you know yourself," she purred. "Just say the words and I'm yours. Besides, as far as my parents and this town are concerned, I'm already yours."

Jody

———————— ◆ ————————

Jody was not in the Ada, Oklahoma, telephone book. She had moved to this little college town only because I was a student at East Central State; so the chances were good that she back at her old job at the telephone office in Konawa. I dialed the Konawa exchange, preparing myself for a good dressing down. The switchboard was as far as I got.

"Number please."

My God, I had forgotten how sexy her voice was on the telephone. "Guess who?"

After a short pause, "Sinbad."

"When do you get off?"

"Four."

"I'll pick you up at the stairway. Don't try to skip town."

"Let's eat something at the Pigg Stand before you take me to some evil place. By then I'll be starved to death. Maybe we can drive around awhile, like old times."

"Stop planning and dominating. Let's be spontaneous."

"Right after we eat."

After I hung up the phone, I called my brother Luke's house to leave a message. Luckily, he was there.

"What can I borrow that has wheels on it?" I asked, after the preliminary brotherly joshing.

"The old red pickup, if you're slumming. I could let you have my new truck if you've got a date with Jody."

"What if it's not Jody?" I laughed. "The old red one will do fine. I'm just here for a few days. Right now I'm staying at the Biltmore, in Ada."

"Can you catch the bus to Konawa? I'll leave the truck parked in front of Garner's, if I can get Christine to take it in. You know where I keep the key." Before I could respond to this, he said, "Why are you staying in Ada?"

"It's a long story, Luke. I've got thirteen days left on my leave, and then I take off for Baltimore. I appreciate the use of the truck."

"I swear, you do beat all, Little Brother. I'll put gas in the truck and remove the beer bottles."

At two o'clock that afternoon I was propped against the bar at Garner's Pool Hall drinking a long-neck Lone Star when Luke showed up in the truck. I had been keeping an eye on the street through the half-opened door.

"Christine's in the new one," he said, grinning. To the bartender he said, "Let me try a Schlitz, Jimmy."

We shook hands and, since I was the kid brother, he hit me a time or two on the back, to let me know he was still the big brother. I had a good three inches in height on him, but I was still Little Brother.

"What about tonight?" he asked. "Got a date with Jody?"

I nodded, then said, "Not actually a date."

"That's the best-looking female I ever saw. But what I can't figure is why she would give somebody like you the time of day."

"That's what I always thought about Christine and you."

"Now, you watch it, boy. If that wife of mine ever got the idee somebody thought she was beautiful, I'd have the devil to pay."

"Tell her I'll be out for supper one of these evenings."

At four I moved the pickup down to the front of the telephone office, planning to return to Garner's for a game of pool, but while I was still standing in the open door of the pool hall Jody, in tight-fitting white jeans and a soft, pale green T-shirt, bounded down the stairway and shot across the sidewalk. She was carrying her shoes and grinning happily, and as I watched her cross the sidewalk and head for the passenger's side of the truck, I decided that she was, hands down, the most beautiful thing Konawa had ever offered to the world.

Unlike Darleen, Jody was definitely no child and certainly no Mama's girl. She was a very bright and mature young woman who said and did exactly as she pleased. If she did not go to bed with me, it would be because she didn't want to, not because of family or community tradition. Both girls were blondes and blue-eyed, but there the similarities ended.

And while I had been more than a little surprised that cute, sexy Darleen could still be a virgin at seventeen, I had no doubt at all about Jody, who was year older.

As soon as I headed up the street toward her, she yelled shamelessly, "Hey, Wes! Quit stalling and take me to the Pigg Stand."

I got into the pickup and slammed the door, managing to nudge her left leg. She flung her white tennis shoes against me hard, then picked one of them up and brought it down flat and with some force upon my crotch.

I pretended to be in great pain and said quietly in a faked high-pitched voice, "Hello, Squirt."

"That's what you tell every girl that'll listen to you."

She checked her door for stability and fell against it. Then, her quick, beautiful eyes never leaving mine, she leaped at me with an energy that drove me against my door. This time I did not have to fake it. For perhaps two seconds our lips touched lightly, sending an electric shock all the way to my toes. When I opened my eyes, she was already on her side staring straight ahead, as if nothing at all had happened.

"Take me to the Pigg Stand, Jock. I'm hungry. I've been on that switchboard all afternoon without a break."

"I've never seen a girl eat as much as you do."

As I spoke, I gave her trim, solid body the once-over. She would almost make two of Darleen, but all of it was in the right places. And, reminded of vulnerable little Darleen, I decided that no ordinary mortal man was going to overcome this girl without a club—or a marriage license!

I started the truck and headed up the street past the *Temple Pharmacy* and the *Oklahoma State Bank.* I was sitting against the door on the driver's side, with my left arm extended through the window; and she was on her side, huddled in the corner the way she had done when we were in high school and she was pretending to be such an innocent and decent girl. Decent, maybe; but innocent, never. She looked like a million dollars, bunched up there grinning naughtily at me. It was a curious thing to me how she always looked as if she had just spent two hours in a beauty shop. Had she actually just come off an eight-hour shift on the telephone switchboard?

There was a time, not so long ago, when she would not bother with either her hair or her eyes. Back when I first met her, she wore her hair in a roll, like an old woman, and, to complete the picture, horn rimmed glasses and a full-length, shapeless house dress.

A number of people waved at us as we proceeded up the street, and it occurred to me that we must look like an old married couple. Certainly, we had been seen together enough in that town to cause people to think of us that way. Our very positions in the truck, with me on one side and her on the other, facing forward, suggested that we were well past the courtship stage!

"How has it been, locally?" I asked, parking diagonally in front of the Pigg Stand.

"Locally, everything is precisely the same as it was when you left like the yellow dog you are."

"I tried to get in touch with you."

"The heck you did. Don't lie to me, Jocko."

"I mean it. You had gone to visit your sister in Okie City or some-place. I tried for a week."

"A likely story. Do you mean to tell me you didn't know you were going to join the Navy the last time we were together?"

"Coast Guard."

"What?"

"I joined the Coast Guard. And, no, I didn't know. We had talked about it for a long time, but the decision to go happened rather suddenly and we left even more suddenly."

"You and those two crazy friends of yours. Goodrich and Archer."

We got out of the truck at the same time and met on the sidewalk. I had long ago given up playing the gentleman around this girl. Jody not only wouldn't wait for me to open a door for her she would refuse to go through a door under those conditions. But just let me try to beat her inside a restaurant! The penalty for that, the one time I had tried it, was a short jab to the short ribs and a kick in the chins. Of course, once the food had been consumed, she never argued over who should pick up the tab. She would head for the door right away.

"I'm starved to death."

"You said that already. And besides you're always hungry. I don't have but fifteen hundred dollars on me, and I've got to get to Baltimore on it."

"You've already got your ticket, haven't you?"

The Pigg triplets, Ima and Eura and Bea, were lined up behind the counter in the little narrow café waiting for us, the news having reached them by the usual grapevine, a customer sitting in the window booth. Even though the place was packed and the three enormous girls undoubtedly had customers to attend to, not one of them was about to move until after the ritualistic greeting. Ima, their father's favorite and therefore the spokesman of the three, squalled out, "Red, it's about time you checked in here!"

Eura, waiting her turn, squealed, "I am so glad you two are still on speaking terms."

"That's about all we are," said Jody, flouncing toward a booth. It was still loaded with dishes and used napkins; but it was the only empty place in the Stand.

Bea (pronounced Bee-Uh), whose nickname was *Five-feet tall and five-feet wide*, cackled, "Aint she a handful, Red?"

"She's hungry," I said, pretending to be concerned. "Roll out your chuck wagon."

*   *   *

That evening I parked Luke's truck on Lover's Leap, a bluff overlooking the South Canadian River, a few miles from town. It was still early, which accounted for the numerous available parking spaces.

Jody, full of piggburgers and French fries, was already resting contentedly on my right shoulder, rattling on about the wild things that had happened at the telephone switchboard that day. She was facing away from me, making serious kissing next to impossible.

I laid my arm over her shoulder and let my hand drift slowly down to where her right breast was supposed to be, but because of the awkward position we were in I couldn't be certain I was even close. After a time, without a pause in her narration, she lifted my hand and moved it three inches to the left, which probably indicated that I had not missed by very much. I tried to bend her face around for a kiss, but the best I could do was a dry peck on her cheekbone.

She straightened up finally and turned to face me in the almost pitch darkness. "Evidently, you want to kiss me. All right, none of the Frenchy stuff and get it over with so I can get comfortable. I've got something I want to tell you."

I just sat there, thinking seriously of starting up the truck and returning to Konawa. She was so clinical about everything. *Kiss me and get it over with!* I was not, at that moment, feeling any physical attraction for her. The thought suddenly occurred to me that sitting next to her was a lot like sitting next to Jessica.

But the moment passed and I sat up and took her head in my hands and pulled her to me. Wondering what it would take to break out of the mood of the moment, I snarled, "I may kiss you into oblivion!"

Whereupon she wrestled free and grabbed my ears, "No, you won't, Red Dog. You'll kiss me tenderly and you won't linger it out till both of us are dying for air."

As we kissed, not at all tenderly but quite briefly, I realized that unlike the rest of her her lips were soft and yielding.

"I want to tell you something, Stud," she said, pushing me back.

There was still no sign of life in my genitals, and I was very close to deciding that I would go on back to Ada and sleep in my own rented bed that night. To heck with my Master Plan.

"Tell away, Squirt."

"I made a decision, where you're concerned. I guess it was right after I got that telegram."

"Good," I said, actually relieved. Here it comes, I thought. Jody is about to become history.

"You're the best I'm ever going to find in these hick parts, and maybe you're the best there is in the known world. Anyway, I've decided to give you the opportunity of a lifetime."

Her hand was exploring around between my legs. It was a big first and I was so startled all I could was wait for her next move.

"Somebody's got to take my little ole tinker toy so I reckon it might as well be you." And while I was still experiencing major shock, she unzipped my jeans and rammed her hand inside, not being at all tender and loving about it. She gathered what she found up and put a squeeze on it that brought me to attention.

What she had gathered up was my entire genital repertoire, and she was able to hold it in the palm of one hand. It was then that I knew dear, beautiful Jody was history.

"Sorry, Squirt."

I did not try to rationalize or explain to myself, much less to her. I started up the old truck. Without a word she moved to her corner and rolled up into a ball, and neither of us said a word until I leaned across and opened the door for her in front of her house.

"I read somewhere how they feed you boys saltpeter so you won't fool around in the barracks. Catch you later, Dear Heart." She got out of the truck and leaned in through the window. "If you're going to be around today, drop by this afternoon and take me shopping."

On my way to Luke's house the thought occurred to me that shopping for Jody meant driving to Ada, and Ada spelled *Darleen*. Forget that nonsense. I had no brotherly feeling for that little gal.

At noon, still agonizing over what to do about Jody, I parked in her driveway and got out slowly. Perhaps I could talk her into going shopping in Seminole, which was about twenty miles in the opposite direction to Ada. Safer still would be Oklahoma City, which was another sixty miles away.

To my relief the family automobile was not on the premises.

"Hey, Red!" she called from the front door, loud enough for the neighbors on either side to hear. "Good news!"

I tried to shush her by putting a finger to my lips, but she paid no attention to me.

"We've got the house to ourselves all day and all night!"

All I could think of was that this girl did not give up easily.

"Come in, I've got a plan."

The part of her plan that involved me was for me to move the pickup truck a half block to the high school parking lot, return down the street to the alley, and sneak into the house through the back door. The reasoning being that no one would be suspicious of an old red pickup truck parked on the schoolground.

"First off," she confided to me as soon as I returned from my clandestine activity, "the dress code is nude. Get your clothes off, but fold them all up neatly so if you have to leave by the back door in a hurry you'll be able to do it in style. There's absolutely no chance of my parents coming back before tomorrow, and there's almost no chance a neighbor or one or more of my older brothers will be dropping by."

Then, while she hustled me into the pantry, where I was supposed to fold and store my clothes, she added, "But we won't take any chances, okay?"

Feeling out-maneuvered and too dazed to think of resisting, I did as she ordered. She undressed in the middle of the kitchen floor, making absolutely no effort to fold anything or even to toss any of it into a pile. I finished first and stood there, with my clothes in my hands, taking in for the first time her nude body. She was, I thought, almost too much of a good thing.

When her panties came off, she held them up with one finger and did a little curtsey. "Well, Jocko, what do you think?"

"Jody, I—"

"You like?" she asked, flouncing her butt at me. "It's now all yours. Are you man enough to do anything with it?"

Comparing her body with that of Darleen's was like comparing a slender and beautiful little prairie filly to a Kentucky thoroughbred racing mare. Her breasts were ripe and alert, creating a cleavage that I had never suspected during all the time we had known each other. Her shoulders were strong and straight, and beneath them were a ridiculously small, flat stomach and very flared hips.

For some reason I wanted to laugh, and I know that my mouth was wide open during this display. Then I heard myself saying, "Jody, I had no idea you had—so much to offer!"

"Well, look who's talking!"

She bounded across the room and disappeared into the back of the house, presenting me with a heartbreaking view of her *derriere*. I heard her two minutes later cross the diningroom, then I caught the sound of her bare feet splatting across the polished hardwood floor of the livingroom. I headed in that direction and found her in one corner of the big room bent at the waist over a pile of LP records. Against the wall was a stereo console.

The picture she presented would haunt me for the rest of my life.

"I certainly never suspected you were slung like that, Lover," she said, without looking around. "Now, stay away from me while I find us some good music. This has got to be done absolutely right."

When, I was wondering, had she looked at me? Perhaps she was trying to build up my self-confidence.

"I'm going to cook supper for us, we're going to eat at the dining room table with linen napkins, and after that we're going to listen to classical music while you smoke a pipe." She pulled out a record and put it on the turntable. "And after that we're going to sleep in a big poster bed and make love until daylight. Like decent and law-abiding folks."

"I don't have my pipe with me."

"You'll smoke one of Dad's."

"What if I don't like his brand of tobacco?"

She stood up and faced me, grinning mischievously, her lovely, eager breasts bouncing within easy reach of my hands.

"Are you going to be difficult, Stud?"

"Jody, after all this time—?"

"And don't you forget it."

"But don't you think we ought to dress for dinner?"

"We'll be dressed for dinner. You know what a birthday suit is, don't you?"

        *   *   *

The following morning early Jody prepared the orange juice while I made the coffee. Reluctantly, she admitted that it might be better if I got away before her parents returned; but she wanted me to call on her later that day. We would then work out some plans for that night. At the breakfast table, across a stack of very brown toast, we both burst out laughing at the same instant. She slapped her hand down upon the mountain of toast, and I clamped mine on top of hers.

We were wearing nothing at all, still, and I knew that while sitting fully clothed beside this girl was like sitting with my little sister, sitting across the kitchen table from her without a stitch on was definitely not the same. There was no shame on my part or, evidently, Jody's.

"Hasn't it been great?" she asked, squeezing my hand. "You're something, boy. Women all over the world are looking for something like you."

"Listen, I've got to spend some time with my folks."

She withdrew her hand at once. "So. Just as I thought. You want to get down to that little nutbrown maid."

"You know that's not true. Come with me."

"Well, sure. You know I can't do that, during the week."

"I want to introduce you to Mom and Dad."

"I've already met them, Slug, but just for the heck of it I'll go down to see them with you."

This was said so casually it took a moment for me to realize that she had changed her mind, and when I did I burst out laughing again. "You will? Can you get away from the telephone office?" Here, I thought, was one crazy, exciting, unpredictable girl.

"For you, Trigger, I can do anything. I'll take off a couple of days, and we'll make a mini-vacation of it. I want to see that little Indian's face when you tell her we're engaged."

I stared at her in astonishment. "I can't figure you out from one moment to the next."

"I can figure you out every minute of the day." She got up and poured me a fresh cup of coffee, accepting a brief kiss on the cheek for her trouble. "If you're worried about your folks' reaction, don't be. They probably like me better than they do you. I visited them a lot more than you did this past year."

"I wonder why they never mentioned that in their letters to me?"

"Maybe because I told them not to. It wasn't any of your business. I didn't go down there to impress you."

"We won't be able to sleep together," I said, grinning weakly.

"Don't you think I know that? I'll sleep with that little sister of yours, and pump her all night long about you. When I get through, you won't have a secret left in the world."

"Let's talk about your manners," I suggested, taking a sip of coffee. "You won't be able to call me *Stud* and stuff like that. And the first time you pull something vulgar, my old man will throw you out of the house."

"What kind of vulgar stuff are you referring to?"

"Oh, unzipping and taking Trigger out just to see if he's okay."

"All right, then you won't be able to fondle my teats in front of them."

My parents, of course, were overjoyed to see us both; and Jody's presence seemed to come as no surprise to them. Mother made a fuss about how skinny I was and the haggard look of my face.

"He's been through a lot," said Jody, patting me affectionately on the arm. "You and I'll nurse him back to health, huh, Mom?"

"We certainly will!" To me she demanded, "How long do we get to keep you?"

Jody beat me to the punch, "He's leaving Wednesday morning on the bus, and I think we ought to give him a big send off."

What a fine kettle of fish, I thought. I had not meant that I would be leaving *for Baltimore* on Wednesday! How was I to know she would blab that to my parents?

"What's wrong, Son?" asked Mom. "Can't you stay longer than that? Have you seen Jessica?"

I wanted to give Jody a kick in the butt, but all I was able to do was mumble, "No, Mom, I've got to leave Wednesday in order to make it to my ship on time. Where is Jessie, by the way?"

"At the Lees' for the night."

That evening Dad, settling into his favorite spot on the north side of the fireplace, confided to me that Jody would make an ideal wife. I knew what the bases were for that remark. She was perfectly built for child-bearing and she was as healthy as a horse. Two minutes later, I caught him giving her the once over. He glanced at me and said, just above a whisper, that I could do a whole lot worse. I looked him in the eye and said:

"What you see is not necessarily what you get, Dad."

At bedtime Mom quietly led Jody to the south wing of the house, to Jessica's room. And when she came back, she said, with a twinkle in her eyes, "Your bed's ready anytime you are, son. I've kept your room just as it was when you joined the Coast Guard." When I got up to leave, she added, "Breakfast's the same time as always."

"That may be a bit early for some of us," I said with a grin.

"Well, she can sleep in if she wants to!" Mom laughed. "As soon as I get the bacon and biscuits going, you'll drag yourself out of bed!"

The next morning just after five o'clock, as my mother had predicted, I took my place at the scarred old breakfast table, which had been in the family for three generations. I ate a big breakfast and left the house before sun-up, heading east on my old quarterhorse gelding, Bud. I had in mind a good fishing hole on the South Canadian River, a large flat rock overlooking Little Sandy that Jamie and I had used since we were children as a rendezvous place.

It was great to be alone, with just the horse and Old Ring for company. Once Bud knew where we were going, I let him have his head. And when we reached the spot, I removed the saddle and bridle and set them on the smooth, clean surface of the rock. Then I went and stood on the crumbling bank of the river for a time, gazing off in the direction of Jamie's house.

There was no sign of another human being as far as the eye could see.

After a time I sat cross-legged on the rock and baited a fish hook with one of Dad's red worms. The river, a quarter of a mile wide there at Little Sandy (At another time of the year it would be a mere ten or twelve feet across) was the color of chicken blood; and I knew I would be lucky to catch anything at all.

Suddenly, although I had heard nothing and Bud had given no warning, I knew I was not alone. Old Ring was sound asleep in a deep shade behind me, and my line was flapping silently in the light breeze coming up the river. I straightened up and glanced around. Floating slowly down the river from my left was the branch of a willow tree, the leaves still green, and on the other side of the river a large bird was strutting along on the beach.

Then from some distance away came, "Hey, Lover!"

Jody was riding Jessica's little mare, Blackie, without a saddle. It was a very unlikely sight, completely unexpected.

"Where did you learn how to ride bareback?" I asked when she rode up. "And how did you find me here?"

"Never mind, Big Shot. You thought you'd get off and mope, didn't you, about last night. I missed you, back there all alone in that end of the house. I kept expecting Jessica to show up, and when she didn't I thought you might pay me a visit."

"Hah! I was in the north end and you were in the south end, and Mommy dear was in between us. If I had made a move in your direction, both of us would have been tossed out on our ears."

"Well, too bad. I started my period this morning."

"That figures."

Jamie

◆

On Wednesday morning early, Jody, accompanied by my parents, Luke and Christine, and Jessica were at the *Temple Pharmacy* to see me off to the East Coast. I had spent the night at the farm, and Dad had kept his word and given me a lift into town, in my own car, an aging Ford sedan by the name of *Kilroy*. On the way we had swung by Luke's and they had joined us in his new company pickup truck.

"Promise me you'll write," said Jody. "To your mother, I mean. I felt so sorry for her never hearing from you this past year and a half." She threw her arms around my neck, and I caught a glimpse of Mom smiling happily around at Dad. "And when you get sick and tired of the Coast Guard, you and I have some serious business to talk about."

"Yes, I agree," I said, holding her close and whispering into her ear, "You brat."

"I mean it," she said, kissing me on the cheek and then a lightning peck on the lips. She quite obviously did not care who saw us carrying on. With that she moved back away from me so that others could get at me.

Jessica pulled my head down and whispered, "You half-wit, what do you think you're doing going back without seeing Jamie Lee? Don't you realize that she knows you're home?"

I whispered back, "Can you keep a secret? I'm not really leaving just yet. But I had to do something to get some time away from—*you know who.*"

"Oh. Then you are plannin' to see Jamie?"

"I'll try, Jessie"

"I'd like to brain you," she said in her normal voice, hugging and kissing me on the cheek. "When will you be home for good?"

"Aboard!" called the driver, who was crossing the sidewalk from the *Temple Pharmacy.* "All you folks going to Seminole?"

"Who's going to Seminole?" laughed Jody. "The world traveler here is headed for Iceland."

The signal had been given. Everybody crowded in on me and patted and punched me and shook my hand.

When I finally climbed into the bus, the driver said, "If you're not going to Seminole, why does your ticket say Seminole?"

"Because that's where I'm getting off, in order to go somewhere else."

"Yeah, I understand," he frowned. "You're going there but you're not actually going there."

"Jody was just joshing about Iceland."

Thirty minutes later in a Rexall Drug Store in Seminole I dialed Luke's number and Christine picked up the phone.

"He's out in the storage building, where he keeps the gasoline," she said. "Thought you left for the East Coast."

"Long story, Chris. Could you get him before he gets away?"

"Sure, hang on."

Luke was laughing when he picked up the phone. "I knew sure as heck you wasn't gone! You didn't even have your seabag or anything with you, which made me wonder why Mama swallowed that story. You trying to get away from Jody?"

"You hit the proverbial nail right on the head."

"Where are you?"

"Across the street from the bus depot in Seminole."

"Okay. Give me half an hour or so."

*   *   *

The voice on the phone was not Alice's, but it was supposed to be, evidently. For a moment I hesitated, then said, "Is that you, Chelsea?"

"How did you know?"

"It was the way you said *Howdy*. Let me talk to your big sister."

"She's out at the barn, feedin' something."

"Go get her. Tell her Wes is on the phone."

"Wes who?"

"Chelsea!"

"Okay, okay. It'll take her a minute to explain to her boyfriend that a sailor's callin' her!"

I started to say something threatening, but suddenly a very soft and sexy voice said, "Hello, Weus! Where are you? Can you come out to the farm?" Alice had picked up a phone in one of the barns.

The sound of another line opening up at that moment sidetracked my answer; but, finally, when Chelsea was disposed of, I was able to say that I would be out to get her in a few minutes, that I was in Seminole and had wheels.

The Chastain Farm was one of Oklahoma's premier thoroughbred horse ranches. Miles of white wooden fences circled and crisscrossed the place and disappeared into the trees and reappeared across the hills; and everywhere there were tall, sleek, contented mares and fillies.

Alice, in riding breeches and perched on a spirited young mare, suddenly appeared around the corner of a barn. She began waving wildly the instant she caught sight of me. I waved back and waited for her to ride up.

"Weus!" she screamed, dropping the reins and rushing toward me. "I thought I would never see you again!"

She fell into my arms, just as Chelsea burst from the front door of the house.

"Alice, you're even more beautiful than I remembered!" I told her, lifting her easily off the ground and holding her tightly. Chelsea was already tugging at my hip pocket. "Why were you afraid you would never see me again?" I protested, putting my hand on Chelsea's head and holding her at arm's length. "Are you leaving the country?"

"I'm leaving Saturday for Boston! I've got an art scholarship at Boston U.! Isn't that exciting?"

In her tight-fitting khaki outfit, Alice looked every inch the beautiful, mature young horsewoman. She had filled out considerably since I had last seen her, and it was plain that she was no longer the little girl I had gone skinny-dipping with in Lake Washita two years before.

"Let's go to Konawa and get something cold to drink," she suggested. Not waiting for my reply, she turned and glared at Chelsea. "We're not going to get any privacy here!"

"How about Seminole?" I countered.

"I'll change and be right back," she nodded, smiling. "Take Eudora out to the barn for me, will you? And find somebody out there to take care of her."

With a final double-pat on my arm, she rushed off for the house. I watched, admiring her long, slender legs and wild blonde hair that reached almost to her waist. She skipped through the gate and down the walk to the house. Here, I told myself, was a blueblood from the ground up, but a blueblood with spirit and a sense of humor.

"She really swings it, doesn't she?" asked Chelsea. "Do you suppose she's in heat?"

"Chelsea!" I scolded.

"I hope Momma sees her doin' *that.*"

At the edge of the yard was a small red convertible with the top down. It was low-slung and looked very fast. I nodded toward it, "Yours?"

"Don't I wish! Naw, that's Alice's graduation present. Know what kind it is?"

"Some kind of Italian job. A *Fieri?*"

"Now, I'm really impressed, sailor boy!" screamed Chelsea. "Daddy said nobody in this country would know what that thing is!"

On our way down to the barns, Chelsea spilled her guts about Alice. Among other things she told me that her sister's favorite pastime was talking about me and the trip I had taken with the family two summers back.

"She always ends up bawlin', for some reason. I just can't stand to see a grown woman cry."

When Alice emerged from the house, I met her at the gate and opened the truck door for her. Unlike Jody or Darleen, she expected her man to open doors. Even in bluejeans and a man's short sleeve shirt she was a very proper young lady.

"I have missed you," she said boldly, leveling her fascinating blue eyes at me. As I wheeled the pickup about and headed up the little dirt road, she clung to my shoulder. When she spoke next, her voice sounded dreamy and yet happy at the same time. "How long do you have?"

"Until Saturday. Did you get my wire?"

"Yes, finally. It stayed on Father's desk for three or four days at least!" She sounded exasperated. "He never bothers to tell me when I've got mail, probably because he's afraid it will be from some wild boy, like you."

"I thought your dad liked me."

"Oh, he does, believe me. But he thinks I'm much too young to be looking at boys. To him I'm still a little girl." After a minute, she said, keeping her eyes on the road ahead, "If you're leaving Saturday and heading for the East Coast, maybe we could travel together."

I looked quickly at her, startled. "Would your father approve of that?"

"He wouldn't have to know!" she laughed. "I've got my own car. We would meet somewhere. Would you like to do that?"

"Wow!" I shouted. "Would I ever! It's a crazy, wonderful idea! Traveling all the way to the East Coast with you! Absolutely great!"

"Are you sure?" she asked. "I wouldn't want to force myself on you."

"The question is, are *you* sure?"

I pulled the pickup to the side of the road and killed the engine. We had just topped the first ridge, and the house and barns of the Chastain Farm were hidden from our view.

"I couldn't be more sure of anything in this world!" she purred, cupping her hands around my neck and kissing me hungrily.

"Alice, you've changed so much, in such a short time!"

After awhile, she pulled back and said, "I almost lost you and no matter what I don't want that to happen. You know, Weus, I would rather to be with you than anyone else in the world. I would rather be with you than stuck away in Boston!"

Once that had sunk in, I said, "Now, Alice, I want you to get that kind of thinking out of your pretty head. You're going to Boston to study art, and it would kill your parents if you did anything else. I'm heading for Baltimore, like I said in my wire, to board a ship that's headed for Alaska."

"I could get an apartment in Baltimore," she mused. "Then after your ship leaves I could go up to Boston."

"You know you cannot do that."

"Oh, well, I was thinking out loud," she laughed.

"I want you to go to school, not chase around after me."

"Okay," she said offhandedly, "but *que sera sera.*"

In Seminole I nosed into a Sonic Drive-in. While Alice had rattled on, I had been working out a daring scenario. The question was, just how long could I keep her away from the ranch before her parents would call the Oklahoma Highway Patrol? Her parents had done an excellent job of keeping a watchful eye on her, and I knew for a fact that her father would not hesitate to call in the militia, if it came to that.

"I told Mother we were going to see a movie this afternoon," she whispered into my ear, as if she had read my mind. "So they won't expect me before five or six."

"Are you game for something wild?" I asked, pulling her close.

"The wilder the better!"

"I know a place we could go and be alone for a couple of hours. Do you want to do it?"

Her answer was to throw her arms around my neck and kiss me, long and wetly; and just before she pulled back I felt the tip of her tongue on his lips. Alice! Little Oklahoma girls weren't supposed to know about French kissing!

After Sonic burgers and fries, we left, looking for a telephone, and ended up at the Rexall Drug Store across the street from the Greyhound depot, whence I had called my brother earlier in the day.

Reliable Christine answered the phone.

"Let me talk to Luke, if he's around."

"Maybe I can get him on the radio. Is what you've got to say classified?"

"Naw, I just wanted to know if the company house down in the River Bend is empty, and if I can get into it."

"You're talking about the one across the creek from the Willow Bottom, on the farm? It's empty of people but still full of furniture, and the front door key's in the mailbox. Don't forget to lock it when you're—when you leave." She began laughing, pretending to cough.

"I won't, and thanks, Chris. Are you going to be all right? You ought to take something for that cough."

"Anytime, you wild man. Oh, what are you doing for transportation?"

"Glad you asked. Right now, I'm okay. But I'll need wheels tonight to take me to Ada.

*   *   *

The little cabin in the woods was actually a ten-year-old clapboard bungalow built by the Champlain Oil Company for my brother Dock and his new wife, Edith. At least he was the first occupant, since he happened to be the pumper for that area. As soon as the wells on our place slowed down to the point where it wasn't profitable to pump any longer, Dock had moved on to other oil leases.

It sat deep in the trees on the west side of our farm overlooking the Willow Bottom, which ran the entire length of a forty-acre stretch of post oak, blackjack, and hickory. The road from Konawa came in from the north across a cattle guard and passed the house in front a good two hundred yards down the hill. It made a sharp turn to the east about an eighth of a mile down and crossed the creek. From there it was only half a mile to our main house.

I parked the pickup below the house and went around and opened Alice's door. She was round-eyed with excitement.

"This is like being in a real forest, Weus! Don't you live down here someplace?"

"Not far from here, in fact," I nodded. "On a quiet night you can hear noises coming from our house. Come on, let's go inside this little shotgun hideout."

We walked up the steep path side-by-side, with Alice clinging to my hand (It was like leading a lamb to the slaughter, I thought). On all sides the birds of late summer were making a clatter, perhaps complaining about intruders in their peaceful world.

"Oh, listen, the birds are welcoming us! I've never seen so many in one place!"

Off in the distance came the plaintive call of a rain crow.

"That's so very beautiful," she purred, squeezing my hand.

We went up the steps to the porch and I found the key right where Christine said it would be, along with two acorns. I opened the screendoor and, holding it back, unlocked the main door and pushed it inward. Then I picked up my little prize as if she were a baby and carried her into the house, letting the screendoor slam behind me. She held onto my neck and kissed me on the ear.

"Remember two summers ago?" she laughed, as I carried her through the house. "Oh, God, right there in front of my parents!" She kicked with pleasure. "I will never forget that!"

"What I remember most was a lot of teasing," I said, "and stone aches later."

"I was only sixteen then," she said quickly. "I'll bet you haven't had any aches of any kind since you went to the West Coast."

"Hah. I've been too busy with other things. Girls take a lot of time and effort. And money, too, if you're on the West Coast."

I carried her into a bedroom and set her down. Without a word she began removing the dustcover. I helped her and we stored it in a closet.

"You wanted me," she said, smiling. "I could tell you really wanted me. But my parents were just sitting there watchin' us."

"Well!" I laughed. "How could you tell I wanted you? I almost passed out from wanting you and being so close and yet so far. And you teasing me with your foot."

"If you had succeeded, would you have kept in touch with me better?"

Alice did not have Jody's hourglass figure nor Darleen's sweet innocence, but those wide-set pale-blue eyes and that husky voice made her one of the most desirable girls I had ever met. And the memory of that summer weekend on Lake Washita, in southern Oklahoma, had haunted me for almost two years. With her parents watching us from a nearby hillside, we had frolicked an entire afternoon in the nude!

An hour later, when time was running short for us, Alice clung to me and confessed that she had given up ever seeing me again, all because she had teased me so heartlessly that summer weekend.

"Come on, Kid, I'll run you home."

"What are you planning to do between now and Saturday?"

"I've got a dozen people to visit, including my folks. Listen, we've got to plan this thing out. Your folks can't even suspect what we have in mind."

"They won't, silly." There was a lovely pink flush on Alice's face, and in her eyes there was a sparkle I hadn't seen there before.

"I hope your mother doesn't take a good look at you when you get home," he sighed. "Nor your father, either."

Alice laughed happily, "They will just simply think I'm falling in love with you, Weus."

"Oh, my lord, Alice!" I burst out, taking her into my arms. "If they think that, they'll suspect us of something!"

"I've been in love with you ever since Lake Washita." Her eyes had become dreamy and she hugged me tightly. Then, trying to be strong and firm, she whispered, "But we mustn't think about getting married just yet. You've got to finish your time in the Coast Guard, and I've got to finish college."

"Right," I said, relieved. What a bright girl she was. Much more reasonable than some others I knew. "You're a dream come true."

"Will I see you tomorrow?"

"I think I ought to spend a couple of days with my folks, don't you?"

"Yes, definitely. Besides, we'll be together all the way to Baltimore."

"Right. So I'll meet you when and where?"

"Well, I'm supposed to take off early Saturday morning. How about you meet me at the bus station in Seminole about ten? We'll have breakfast and make tracks."

"Are you sure we can get my seabag into that little *Fieri* of yours, along with all the stuff I know you'll be carrying?"

"Oh, yes, no problem. I'm traveling light this time. Why do you think I decided to Boston two weeks before school starts? I'm going on the goldangedest shopping spree in history. Daddy told me the kids there would be wearing stuff that isn't even sold in Oklahoma; so I'm going to observe the styles and buy six complete new outfits."

"Okay, sweetheart, let's get you home!"

I returned the key to the mailbox, took her by the hand, and led her down to the truck. We could hear my parents' cows over the hill to the east. It was milking time at the farm. A picture of my old man in worn overalls walking out toward the barn flashed into my mind. Mother would already be in the kitchen preparing supper.

             *   *   *

Luke's truck, once again fueled-up with "drip" gas, was parked at Garner's, as Christine had promised. I hopped out of Alice's sporty convertible and into it, shuddering from the culture shock. She waved without looking back, and I headed for Ada and my hotel room.

After dining in the hotel restaurant, I went straight to my room, and took a shower. Then I called my little porcelain doll on East 9th Street. She screamed and slammed the phone down. Ten minutes later she banged on my door.

"Oh, I was so hoping you would get back in town," she said. "I've been bored to death all day." She sat down on the bed and I could tell by the look on her face she had come to a very difficult decision. "Red, my parents will just die, but I want to sleep with you tonight."

I stopped in my tracks, staring at her.

"But you've got to promise me you won't do anything. We'll just sleep together."

"We're going to spend all night in that bed and I'm not to do anything? Darleen, be sensible! I can't do that!"

Her face was very white. "Then I'll just go on home."

"I can't believe you want me to do that."

"It's difficult for me, too."

I went into the bathroom and took my second shower of the hour, fuming and grumbling all the time. For two-bits, I told myself, I would go back in there and take her. That way I would have her from that moment on, and I would not have to bother with a marriage license.

When I returned to the bedroom, she was in bed, covered up to her chin with a blanket. I glanced around and saw her clothes, neatly folded and stacked on a chair. I pulled the blanket down, all of it except the part she was clutching, and got into bed.

"You proved I could trust you," she said, "that night in your brother's cabin in the woods. You are the best man I ever knew." She put her hand and touched my shoulder.

I slid my hand toward her under the blanket, suddenly encountering the sheet, into which she had rolled herself tightly!

My last words of the evening were, "I don't remember you rolling up in a sheet that other time."

"I'll take it off if you'll promise me."

The next morning I slid out of bed in pitch darkness, went to the bathroom, and dressed. When I checked back, before leaving, she was making a little popping noise in her breathing, not exactly a snoring but obviously a happy, contented sound. She had lived through the night still a virgin. Then I left, making certain the door was locked, and went down to the dining room for breakfast. It was a few minutes past six, and the place had just opened for business. An elderly man was sitting at a table waiting for his coffee to be delivered.

The final phase of my carefully constructed plan, all of which until now had gone up in smoke, was to see Jamie Lee without running into her folks or mine. I had seriously considered returning home and explaining to Mom and Jessica what was going on, but I shuddered at the thought of another ritualistic goodbye on Saturday. Of course, if anyone in the River Bend caught sight of me, I would have to check in at home.

Jamie, I knew, was an early riser; and unless I could make it down to her part of the country before she had completed her milking chores, she could be anyplace. The chances were good that she would be off with Jessica someplace. I thought how ironic it would be if she had spent the night with my sister.

By seven, when I turned off the highway onto the narrow, winding road to the River Bend, the sun was well above the horizon. I drove south, crossing Nigger Creek in a cloud of fine, white dust, and straightening out onto an even narrower road. At Fairview School I turned eastward into the brilliant sun, crossing the invisible line that separated the Upper Bend from the Lower. From this point on I could not let myself be seen.

A quarter of a mile from the Lee farm I parked the pickup and got out. I was counting on Jamie's alertness and curiosity to help me with my little scheme to keep my visit a secret. She was probably the only one in her family that would recognize the red pickup truck.

A dog began to bark somewhere below me, down near the winding creek bed that went past the Lee home. I headed in that direction, thinking it might be Jamie's collie. Then I heard voices, and dropping behind a thicket of wild blackberries, I heard a man's voice.

"It could be hunters. They come down here from town with their big guns and shoot ever'thing they see. I'm a good mind to go to the house and git my own gun and put some holes in the tires."

The voice, I realized, was that of Cecil Lee, Jamie's father.

"I wouldn't do that, Dad. It might be somebody we know."

"Not likely! Who do we know that's got a red pickup?"

"Well, doesn't Luke Hall have one?"

By this time the dog was standing not more than ten feet from me wagging her tail. I stood up, having no other choice, and called out to the girl and her father. They had been heading down the creek bed toward a cow pasture.

"Why, be danged if it aint one of them redheaded Hall boys!" shouted Cecil. He hurried over to me with his hand out. "That you, Red?"

I nodded, grinning, and we shook hands. Jamie finally walked up, refusing to look me in the face. She had taken her time reaching me, and from the expression on her face she was not at all happy to see me. Indeed, apparently, she was happier to see her own dog.

"How's the world been treatin' you, my boy?" asked Cecil. He put his hand on my shoulder affectionately. You joined the Navy ag'in."

"I'm just fine, Sir. How have you and your family been?"

"Oh, she's been just great, until about a minute ago," laughed Cecil. "She was brought up without'n any manners."

"What're you doin' in these parts, Marco Polo?" Jamie asked. "Slummin'?"

"Listen," said Cecil, "I'll git that cow. You two meet me at the barn."

When the father was out of earshot, Jamie said, "I don't know why you bother comin' around here at all. It's plain you don't care anything about me." She grimaced, backing away from my extended hand. "Please don't touch me. I'm not too happy with you right now."

"Jamie, behave yourself. If you only knew how much I do care for you."

"Well, you sure have a funny way showin' it! You don't write to me or call—"

"You don't have a phone."

"That's where you're wrong, Big Shot. If you weren't so busy with other matters, you'd know I've had a phone for six months."

"Why didn't you let me know?"

"Like a little puppy dog I'm supposed to send word what my number is? You must think you're something on a stick."

"Come here, Runt." I held out my arms to her.

"Not quite yet. I've got to milk the cows. You can stand and watch or go on about your business."

In the year and a half since I had last seen her, Jamie had grown taller, filled out in the breasts, and apparently lost all of her baby fat. She was still slender and as agile and quick as a young gazelle. I watched her stride off in her tight-fitting Levi jeans, feeling a fierce closeness to her that I felt for no one else. And although she was like family to me in many ways, no girl had ever made me feel the excitement and longing that she did.

In 1943, when I had left for the Pacific, she had been a long-legged girl of thirteen, more Jessica's friend than mine, a mere child. But at

Christmastime, 1945, when I was twenty and she was sixteen, one brief glimpse of her had convinced me that we had passed beyond playmates and good friends. Gone were the skinny-dipping at Little Sandy and the teasing and Indian wrestling on the Bermuda Grass Hill.

The collie and I followed along behind at a slower pace, reaching the barn well after she was settled on a stool at the back end of a cow.

I kneeled beside her for a time. On her beautiful Cherokee face I could read nothing. Finally, I said, quietly, "I feel something for you I've never felt for anyone else."

"I wonder what that something could be?" she said quickly, looking at me angrily. Suddenly, she lifted the teat she was grasping and squirted me in the face!

I tumbled over backward, kicking at her rapidly retreating butt. And by the time I got up she had put the cow between us. "You won't get away with that, Runt!"

"I reckon I will, because there's no way a big clumsy galoot like you can catch me!" She took off through the barn, dropping her bucket in my way.

She was quick on her feet and ran like a boy, but I caught her on the green hillside that overlooked the Lee farm, grasping her by the ankles and throwing her to the ground. And while Cecil and the rest of the family watched from the backyard at the house, I worked my way up her body.

"You're going to get it!" I hissed.

"Promises, promises!" she laughed, trying to kick me.

"If your folks weren't watching!"

I managed to pin her down and spread-eagle her arms above her head. Slowly, while she jerked her head from side to side, I lowered my face to hers; and when she finally gave out and our lips touched, a powerful bolt of electricity ran through my body! I pulled back from her, startled out of my wits.

"Jamie!" I whispered. "I swear to God, when we touched—"

"You're a late bloomer, Hall boy. I felt that jolt of lightning back before the war."

That forced a laugh out of me. "You were twelve when I left for the service, you liar!"

"It was a year or two before that."

"Is there someplace we can go?"

"Why, they'll just follow. What do you have in mind?"

We stood up and I put my arm around her tiny waist. Mrs. Lee and the two small children had gone into the house, but Mr. Lee was leaning against the corral gate chewing a straw and pretending not to look in our direction.

"How about the barn loft?" she teased. "Or my bedroom?"

I started down the hillside, pulling her after me.

"How about the creek bed? In that pickup? I know, our favorite fishing place down by Little Sandy."

"Quit kidding, will you? After you milk that cow, how about we drive around?"

"I've got a better idea. How about you milk the cow and we drive around a bit? You haven't forgotten how, have you?"

I found the bucket and took it to the well and rinsed the barn dust off it. When I settled on the little milking stool, she was sitting on the top panel of a nearby stall, ready to pick up where she had left off.

"We could shack up in Dock's cabin," she suggested. A long straw dangled from her mouth nonchalantly. "How long you got?"

"Today and tomorrow."

"That ought to be enough time." When I didn't fire back at her, she added, "That's all you're after, aint it?"

We got through the milking and I walked up to the kitchen and turned the milk over to Mrs. Lee, and we headed for the pickup. We went on up the hill to Lees' Corner and turned south on the section line road that paralleled the South Canadian River. I kept my eyes straight ahead and so did she. It wasn't until I made the turn onto our place that she said, "We goin' to the cabin?" It sounded like, " I knew it. We're going to shack up in the cabin." A few minutes later, having said not a word, I maneuvered the pickup down through the woods west of the main house and right on past the little company house. "Hey, you're passing it!" she teased. "There went your chance to score big with a little country girl, Alexander."

"Could you stay all night with Jessica tonight?" I asked, ignoring her.

"Sure. How about after the folks are in bed I—"

"Will you stop it, Jamie?" I said with a grin. "You're really asking for it."

"Well, you never did answer my question."

Suddenly, my right foot slammed down on the brake, stopping us just as the truck straddled the creek. I killed the engine and turned to face her. "Listen, I've sowed some wild oats. I admit that."

She stayed on her side of the truck with her back to the door, ignoring my outstretched arms. "That's the understatement of the day. An' I reckon you'll sow some more before it's over."

"I'm trying to tell you something—that I've never told anybody else."

Her fierce dark-brown eyes bore into mine.

"I can't explain it but something really strange happens to me every time I get close to you. And when I touch you, I go crazy!"

She nodded and blinked, once, looking very sad. A tear rolled down her cheek.

"I didn't know I could feel this way about—anyone," I stammered.

Suddenly, she leaped across the pickup into my arms with a pitiful little whimper, "Oh, you big ornery outfit! I thought you never would come to your senses!"

For a long time we kissed passionately, while the swift little creek splashed water on the side of the pickup. For us, during this time, the creek and the woods and the empty company cabin an eighth of a mile away did not exist. And when we again returned to the real world, a Jersey cow was standing at the open window on my side, chewing her cud contentedly and contemplating us.

"Haven't you ever seen anybody carry on like this?" I asked with a laugh. "Go on about your business."

Jamie buried her head in my ribs and sobbed happily. I started up the old truck and put it into gear.

"You could have had me, you know," she sighed. "And since you knew that, I guess that ought to say something about your scruples."

"It doesn't say anything about my scruples," I laughed. "But it says a whole lot about how I feel about you."

"Same thing."

Jessica met us out at the edge of Mom's lilac garden, having heard the pickup working its way up the hill from the Willow Bottom. And when I killed the engine, she opened Jamie's door and said, with a nod in my direction, "He's got a lot of explainin' to do, to both of us."

"Part of it has to do with his intentions toward me," said Jamie, getting out of the truck and putting her arms around Jessica's neck. They started off toward the house; and when Jessica glanced back at me over her shoulder, I saw fire in her eyes.

I followed some distance behind them, reluctant to face my parents. It was not going to be easy to explain why I was not on a bus headed east.

The CGC Storis

◆

When I saw the little red convertible flash around a corner half a block from the bus depot café, I stood up and walked out to the sidewalk, where my seabag was leaning against a telephone pole. I had said my goodbyes to the family and to southern Oklahoma; and when I looked into the laughing blue eyes of Alice Chastain, I knew I was headed into a very new and exciting experience.

It was a lovely day and obviously Alice was in a holiday mood. She was wearing a very skimpy yellow one-piece playsuit with straps, but nothing else; and she had the top down.

I wondered, *Had she changed after leaving home? What would her dear mother say about that outfit?* But I did not let myself think about what Mrs. Chastain would have said about Alice driving all the way to the East Coast with a sailor!

My seabag, once it was wedged in behind us, changed the superstructure of the *Fieri* considerably. I dropped into the bucket seat beside her and we were off.

"When we reach the City, I would like for you to drive!"

"Sure. Let's take turns."

By the time we zipped past the Seminole city limits it was impossible to carry on a conversation; so I slid down as far as I could in the seat and pulled my golfball cap down over my eyes. Alice was giddy about being off on her own in her new car, with a sailor boy. She was doing a very daring thing, and not a mile went by that she didn't punch or pinch me and sing out some silliness about being free of her chains.

Oklahoma City came and went and there was no stopping to change drivers. When we finally stopped for gasoline, without a word she dropped into the passenger's seat and went sound to sleep. I found a tiny silk cushion among her things and put it beneath her head, apparently without disturbing her.

In the western outskirts of Tulsa, Alice sat up straight and announced that she was hungry. I asked her what kind of food did she want, and she flashed me a smile and said, "Fast, with ketchup." I drove the length of Tulsa to the eastern outskirts before I spotted a large sign that proclaimed *Giant Hamburgers!* It was wedged between a large motel and a Texaco service station.

"We'll eat first then let's find a motel," she smiled nonchalantly. "What do you think?"

"Isn't it a little early? It's barely noon."

"I think we should rest awhile, don't you?"

I shrugged but said nothing, pretending to be occupied with parking.

"Let's make this a fun trip, Weus! Driving is awfully boring, if you let it be."

"I'm for that," I said, "but at this rate I'll never make it to the cutter in time. Maybe I ought to catch a bus."

Over hamburgers and French fries and lots of ketchup, her dancing blue eyes met mine and she said, "If you really want to go by bus, I can't stop you. But if you do you'll hate yourself later." After a pause, she added, "When's the latest you can report aboard without being in trouble?"

"Midnight, Saturday night."

"Don't you worry, we'll get there in time."

After the hamburgers and an embarrassing moment at the admittance counter of the motel next door, we rode an elevator up to our room on the eighth floor, pretending to be husband and wife. My adrenaline flow was about where it would have been during a *kamikaze* attack. Alice appeared to be as cool as a cucumber.

In the room she began to giggle and dance up and down, like a little girl. I frowned at her and she said, "Let's play around for just a little while, then we'll take a nap and be on our way!"

"I'm going downstairs and look for some protection."

"No rubbers, Wes. Let's do it bareback. I want nothing between us." She pulled herself up and wrapped her legs around my waist. "Besides, there aren't enough of those things in the world to get us to Baltimore."

I was thinking, *Can this be the same little Alice Chastain who teased me so unmercifully at Lake Washita? Alice the Innocent?*

"Alice, I cannot figure you out at all. Neither one of us can afford to let you get pregnant, little girl."

*   *   *

Route 66 took us through some of the biggest cities of the Corn Belt, and each one of these seemed to be having a state fair. And, of course, every state fair had fine breeds of horses that Alice had to admire. Reminding her that I had a deadline and that my record just didn't have any more room for another black mark seemed to do absolutely no good. Her stock-in-trade reply was:

"*Que sera sera*, Weus! Let's live dangerously!"

In Indianapolis, while we were searching for the Indiana State Fair, I said with a profound depth of meaning, "Alice, we're not going to make it in time." I repeated this in Columbus, Ohio, and Pittsburgh, Pennsylvania. The result was the same each time. Once I said, plaintively, "Do you know what is going to happen if I reach the ship after my leave expires, Sweetie?"

"Tell them you got held up by three state fairs."

"Alice, the Coast Guard does not care about such things."

"Well, then, they ought to. A few hours one way or the other won't make any difference, in my opinion. I think you just want to get away from me."

On Saturday we drove nonstop across Pennsylvania, arriving in Pittsburgh just three hours before midnight. Alice had been pouting because I had taken a firm stand against her settling down in Baltimore until my ship sailed.

As we entered the city, she turned and gave me a look that I had not seen on her face before. "You're due in at midnight tonight, right? That's the most ridiculous thing I ever heard of! Who is going to be awake at midnight to know one way or the other when you go aboard? Nobody will pay any attention, as long as it's still dark. Why should they?"

I patiently explained to her that the Coast Guard never slept, that the time I reported aboard was very important all the way to the Captain, and that one minute past midnight was A. O. L. Just one minute late and I would have to face a Captain's Mast; and for me, with my record, that would not be good."

"It's all so stupid! We're in Pittsburgh and, barring some kind of bazaar accident, we should be in Baltimore before daylight. You just sneak aboard your ship and pretend you've been there all the time."

"There is no way I can *sneak* aboard. Take my word for it."

Our last stop before we reached Baltimore was a small restaurant and clip joint in Gettysburg, Pennyslvania. Alice, becoming more nervous by the minute about soon being left alone, wasn't hungry. It was a first for her and said louder than her narrowed eyebrows how upset she was. I was for going on right away, but she had decided she wanted to shop for souvenirs. It was then that I realized with certainty that I was a dead pigeon.

Once we were back on the highway, she said, nonchalantly, "I want to find a motel, Sweetie. It's been ever so long!"

Actually, it had been, at most, about four hours.

"I need to go straight to the icebreaker, Alice."

She was driving, and the instant my words reached her ears she slammed her foot down hard on the accelerator. I sat straight-backed and stared dead ahead, disgusted beyond words. We began to pass every car on the highway, careening around some and narrowly missing every one of them.

"Alice! Stop the car! I want to drive!"

We were suddenly bearing down upon an eighteen-wheeler, with no place to go. She slammed on the brakes at the last possible second and we veered off to the right on two wheels! And when we came to a stop, we were on the shoulder of the highway looking down into a thirty-foot drop-off.

I got out and went around to the driver's side. Alice was staring straight ahead, with her hands locked to the steering wheel. I opened the door and, as gently as I could, removed her hands from the wheel.

"Slide over. I'm driving." I didn't recognize my own voice.

It was the first time I had spoken to her in that tone; and, without looking at me, she moved to the passenger's side.

"We're heading straight for the city of Baltimore, and when we get there I'm going to get out on a street corner next to a telephone booth or a taxi stand, and then you're going to go find you a place to bunk the rest of the night."

"I won't leave you any such place, Weus," she said, her voice a bit shaky. "I'll take you right up to your ship."

"We don't know where my ship is, and I can guarantee you it's not in the city of Baltimore. I'm going to look for someplace I can catch a taxi as soon as we reach Baltimore."

"Didn't you mention the Coast Guard Yard? You must think I'm stupid or something. We'll just stop somewhere and inquire where that is."

I soon had the Fieri wound up. Alice moved beside me, as close to me as she could get, all anger washed away with tears. And although she had nothing else to say, ever so often she would squeeze my left arm. Sometime around midnight we entered Baltimore, and after twice being insulted by pedestrians standing on street corners, we were given directions to the Coast Guard base.

For the hundredth time, I glanced at my wristwatch. It was one minute past midnight!

We drove right down to the docks. It was the worst mess of ships and warehouses and dock machinery I had seen since Puget Sound; and just as I began to explain to Alice that never in a million years would we find the icebreaker, there loomed ahead of us a white ship the size of a U. S. Navy destroyer! I stopped the car on the dock near the bow and we gave it the once over, with Alice snuggled against my shoulder. I was convinced that it was a cutter of some kind, because of its color, although I had never seen one built quite like it.

"That's it, Alice!" I sighed. "It's got to be the *Storis!*"

"What makes you so sure?"

Without replying, I drove the car down close to the gangplank. Although it was a very dark night, there was good lighting up and down the big pier.

"I am, of course, late," I said, more to myself than to her. "Not much, but late, nevertheless."

"Quit worrying. Nobody's going to say a word about it."

High above us at the other end of the gangplank I spotted a Coastie in undress blues, and I knew I was home.

"Hey, mate, is this the CGC *Storis?*" I yelled.

The sailor waved at me, "That it is!"

I leaped out of the *Fieri* and wrestled my seabag to the dock. Alice gathered up my cap, ditty bag, and other odds and ends and handed them to me. "Oh, Wes, let me stay around Baltimore for awhile!"

"You need to get up to Boston and do some shopping, remember?"

"I can do all that later. There's absolutely no rush."

"I want you to write to me as soon as you get an address, Honey. Now, let's don't part sad. Behave yourself like a good girl."

"God, you don't know how I hate for you to talk to me like that!"

"Will you do it?"

"Yes, if that's what you really want. Will you let me know how you're doing? Write me everything that happens to you."

"Of course. And you need to write to me as soon as possible so I'll have an address. We may be pulling out of here very soon."

I gathered her up in my arms, and with every word I spoke she kissed me hungrily on the lips. Her strong, lithe body was trembling as I pressed her close.

When I set her down, I said, laughing nervously, "Okay, I've got to log in. Every minute will count against me, baby."

"Oh, Weus, I hope they don't do anything to you—for not being here on time!"

"Well, it's just a bit late to be thinking about that now. I'll be looking forward to your letters Forget to write and I'll come up to Boston and give you a paddling."

"Yes! "she screamed. "I'd like that!"

*   *   *

Just maybe, I told myself as I ran up the gangplank, I could talk the watch into fudging a bit on the time. Maybe, as Alice had said again and again, it wouldn't make any difference on this ship. Every cutter I had served on seemed to have a different set of rules. Perhaps my West Coast record would not be held against me on the icebreaker.

The O. O. D. materialized at the gangplank to return my salute. He seemed amused. "What held you up, the traffic?"

"As a matter of fact, Sir," I said, nodding, relieved. Apparently, this officer did not think I had sinned all that much. "I did everything I could to make it on time."

"Well, hang around a minute and somebody'll take you down and show you a bunk. Chow call should be sounded in about twenty minutes, and at eight you'll have to report to muster."

"Yes, Sir!"

I wanted to get out of my dress blues and settle in before breakfast, but what I wanted and needed most, sleep, I wasn't about to get, not that day. For approximately two weeks I had been in Paradise. And as anyone but a half-wit knows, Paradise is a great sapper of energy. I was out on my feet. My drawn and haggard looks must have impressed the kid that guided me to the crew's quarters.

"I guess you tied a good one on last night," he said, grinning.

"Just point me toward the messhall."

"Back the way we came and on the right. Just follow the smells and the clatter."

I dragged myself back down the passageway and had no trouble locating the chowline. A dozen swabs had camped out at the big coffee urns, waiting for chow call; and when I fell in with them one nodded and seemed curious. I was in no mood to chat.

Finally, the PA system put a stop to the talk with a pre-recorded blast: "Now, hear this! Chow down for the Starboard Section!"

My hands were actually shaking with fatigue when I tried to fill a mug with coffee. And I found it difficult to hang onto my tray down the messline. After a quick glance around, I selected an empty table on the port side of the messhall and headed for it. Someone wearing pressed and faded dungarees and chewing on a black stogy angled across the open area toward the same empty table. It was unbelievable that anyone could tolerate a cigar so early in the morning. I took my place at the table and to my chagrin he sat down across from me. He nodded but I pretended not to notice.

Although the food was tasteless, I began to pick at it, aware that the swab across from me was glancing up every ten seconds. He had the looks of an old salt that had been there and done it. His cigar was lined up neatly with his knife and spoon, and between glances at me he was shoveling the chow down. Not surprisingly, he finished eating before I did.

Good riddance, I thought, expecting him to quietly pick up his cigar and go away. Instead, he looked me in the eye and let out a loud burp!

It was an obscene and deliberate burp, released not more than a foot from my face! He had picked up his tray and was rising from the table,

and as I stared into his grinning face I could see that he had no intentions of apologizing for that most blatant violation of table manners.

In that split second when our eyes met, I forgot about the predica-
ment I was already in and about my much-tarnished record and,
indeed, about everything except that burp and what I was going to do
about it.

With a quickness that must have startled the burper, I grabbed up my
tray and slammed it with considerable force against his chest! Indeed,
some of the chow landed in his face, while the rest dribbled down his
front and piled up on his tray!

He straightened up still holding onto his tray, and to my astonishment he was grinning! I had been prepared for just about anything but
that, and my first thought was that he was a total idiot. I brought my tray
up, to be used as a cudgel, just in case this was a ploy to throw me off.

"Nobody belches in my face at the chow table!" I said, hotly.

"Hey, now!" he laughed. "I'm sorry, Red!" He had lowered his tray
and was removing food from his face and neck. "I'll bet you're from way
out West someplace! Right?"

"What if I am?" I snapped, still braced for trouble. "Nobody that I
know does something like that at the table!"

Everyone in the messhall had come to attention and was watching,
certain that there was going to be a fight. One of the messcooks yelled,
"Give 'im hell, Red!"

The burper shook his head in amazement. "I guess you've never been
in Bahsten. Up where I come from it's a custom to burp after a meal,
unless the food is lousy. Apparently, you didn't think much of it."

I stared at him, disgusted. "Where are you from?"

"Bahsten." I frowned and he added, " You know, Bean Town.
Massachusetts. You wouldn't be the new sparks that's due in from the
West Coast, are you?"

I eyed him askance, wondering how he would know that, beginning
to feel very funny in the pit of my stomach.

"I'm Stuart Heller, Radioman Second Class."

"You're—?" I burst out, choking up. I took his outstretched hand, admitting that I was, in fact, the sparks from the West Coast. I nodded toward the mess on the table, managing a grin, "Sorry about that but in Oklahoma you would've been lynched for—what you did."

"Hah!" he laughed. "Oklahomer, is it? Believe it or not, that's where I thought you might be from. And you don't owe me an apology. Come on, let's clean this up and if you'll stick with me until I put on a change of dungarees, I'll show you the shack and introduce you to the gang." He retrieved his cigar from the pile of food, dislodging hashbrowns from it.

When the muster call sounded, Heller was introducing me to two radiomen, a salty old Chief by the name of Ed Rothman and a kid named Jeff Starns, who was a Radioman Third Class.

"You got in late?" asked the Chief, frowning. "Not good."

"Six hours," I admitted, sadly.

"Well, what they'll do right after muster is pipe you to the Skipper's cabin. And depending on your prior record I would guess he'll restrict you to the ship a couple of days."

"I'm afraid my record won't be of much help," I said, wondering how much the Chief knew about me. "Any chance he'll look the other way?"

"No chance at all."

Sure enough, immediately following muster I was piped to the Captain's quarters.

It had been my fervent hope that things would be different on the *Storis*. But obviously it was not meant to be. I thought of pretty little Alice, wondering why she just happened to be driving to the East Coast at the very time I was going, why indeed she had caused me to be A. O. L. It almost seemed deliberate, in retrospect. Was some minor deity on my case, seeing to it wherever I went I would be in trouble?

Oh, well, in just five months, one way or the other, I would kiss the Coast Guard goodbye. What did one more Captain's Mast matter?

The Skipper, whose name I had not heard mentioned, looked like an old Scandinavian seadog. He was wearing a full beard and sitting behind a mahogany desk, with my service record open before him. When I entered his tiny compartment, he stood up and glared at me for a time, saying nothing. And the longer he glared the more I became convinced my time on Earth was drawing to an end.

"So you're Hall?" He picked up my record and glanced at it.

"Yes, Sir."

"Did you set out to muddle this up?" He waved the thick sheaf of papers at me. "Or did it just happen?"

"It just happened, Sir."

"Yes, well," he mused, rubbing his jaw slowly. "It's a thorough job, however it happened. Maybe you're accident prone. Do you realize that your antics are well-known in faraway places, like loran stations in Newfoundland and icebreakers in the North Sea? Oh, yes! Why, you've amused me for sometime now. I don't know if you know this or not but we've got a grapevine in the Coast Guard that keeps us all informed of irregular behavior. I heard about you when I was up in the North Atlantic breaking ice. Tell me, Hall, what was your real motive for stealing that Jeep?"

I was silent for a time, but he was willing to wait for my reply. "I didn't actually steal it, Sir. I just borrowed it."

"Oh, you just borrowed it, you say!" He sat down, studying my face. "That's right, you took it back, didn't you, of your own free will?"

"Yes, Sir, I did. And it was in a lot better shape than when I took it."

"You were on restriction and standing a gangway watch, and you weren't authorized to drive any kind of vehicle, much less the O. O. D. Jeep. Whatever made you do it must have seemed very important to you at the time."

"Yes, Sir, it did. But I've turned over a new leaf since then."

At this he burst out laughing. "You've decided to turn over a new leaf. Was this before or after you reported in six hours over leave this morning?"

"No, Sir! I mean, Yes, Sir, but that was not intentional. You see, Sir, I was riding here with a friend from Oklahoma. And this friend wasn't nearly as anxious to get here as I was. I guess I just didn't allow enough travel time."

"Was this friend a girl?"

"Yes, Sir, no doubt about it. We were in her car, and we had to pass through three state capitals that were having fairs, and she loves horses."

"I think I'm getting the picture," he said, nodding. "I would like to just forget about the whole thing. But, of course, I can't. Got to be impartial. You know the rules. What I'm hoping is that you really have decided to turn over a new leaf, as you call it. I'm encouraged by some of the things I see in your record. Some of your superiors have written glowing reports of your abilities as a radio operator and your willingness to volunteer when the need arises." He returned my orders to a manila folder on the corner of his desk. "Think you can stay aboard the ship for a couple of days?"

"Yes, Sir, I sure can!"

"All right, you may go."

Back in the radioroom Rothman wanted a full report of what went on with the Skipper. I was a bit vague about my West Coast past but told him in some detail about my trip from Oklahoma and how the Skipper had reacted to that.

"Sounds good, Hall. I think the Old Man likes you. So he didn't mention what your punishment was going to be?"

"He just asked me if I thought I could stay aboard ship a couple of days."

Stuart Heller broke in, "I'll lay you odds he'll restrict you for our remaining time in port. Kiss liberty in old Baltimore goodbye, Red."

At that point the Communications Officer, Archibald B. How, stuck his head through the hatchway. I had had a look at him at muster and decided that he was just another Ivy League yachtsman out for a lark in the Coast Guard.

"Hall, I need to have a word with you. Chief, excuse us for a minute, will you?"

Rothman and Heller cleared out quickly, and I straightened to attention.

"At ease," he said, smiling. "You must have made an impression on the Captain. Anybody else with your record would've got three weeks' restriction. You got two days."

I breathed a sigh of relief. "Thank you, Sir!"

"Good," he said. "Well, welcome to the Com Department. We're going to be seeing a lot of each other, you know. Alaska's a long way from here."

"Yes, Sir."

The CGC Storis, underway from Baltimore to Juneau, Alaska (summer, 1948)

One Night in Norfolk

◆

Stuart Heller was my first up-close encounter with a Bostonian. And while we couldn't agree on a single thing and even had trouble understanding each other at times, we became practically inseparable on the *Storis*. He made no bones about how much he enjoyed my stories about Oklahoma, and he was more than a little amused at what he called my *Oklahomer* accent. Anyplace west of Syracuse, New York, I discovered, was the Far West to him; and Oklahoma was a mysterious place so far west he had no idea what it was like. For example, he was under the impression that the mode of transportation in all Western states was still the horse and buggy and that all the towns in Oklahomer had hitching posts on the main streets. And when I realized that he was not pretending, that he actually believed Oklahoma was one vast prairie without a single tree, I never failed to perpetuate and add to such ignorance.

Heller was incapable of leaving *R's* in words that needed them, and he was equally guilty of putting *R's* into words that did not need them. But to him it was I who spoke with an accent! All attempts on my part to right the situation were fruitless.

Each of the two afternoons that I was restricted to the ship I settled into my bunk and watched this swab prepare for liberty. He took a great deal of time with his toilet, more than any of my sisters had ever taken, showering and shaving and patting on after shave and combing and re-combing a dozen times. He already had a receding hairline at this point, but every single hair had to be in exactly the right place. But when he had completed this restoration and was finally outfitted in dress blues and black regulations shoes, he *looked* like a sailor on holiday. There was absolutely no doubt in one's mind that here was a swab that was ready for liberty!

I tried to visualize the kind of girl that would go out with this big opinionated, self-centered seadog. Despite the fact that his head was too big for his body and his shoulders were too small for his chest, he presented a good first impression when he dressed up and went into the public. And there was no doubt about his gift for blarney. He was a born talker and bullshitter. Even if he could find someone who would put up with him, I could not imagine him spending time wooing such a girl, saying sweet nothings to her. In the left corner of his rather generous mouth there was always a White Owl cigar. And without bothering to remove it, he rattled on nonstop in an annoying monotone, working in one Anglo-Saxon four-letter word after the other! He was particularly fond of *fuck* and *crap* as descriptive expletives. "*Fuck* you, Red. I don't know what the *crap* you did out on the West Coast, but you're gonna git a real *fucking* on this ship."

For two days I listened to him brag about a Bahsten girl named Diane, a true aristocrat with money, and, according to him, ready to tie the knot anytime. It made no sense to me at all that a beautiful, well-educated, cultured, loaded young lady would agree to marry my rough-talking, cigar-smoking, burping buddy.

"You've got to meet Diane," he told me the day before I was to get my first liberty. "Tomorrow afternoon she'll pick us up here and we'll treat you to a little tour about our nation's capitol. Ever been to D. C.?"

I admitted that had never been to that hallowed place and was all for it and couldn't wait to meet his wonderful girlfriend. By this time I was visualizing a female burper on the heavy side, which would confirm what I already knew, that my friend Stuart Heller was full of hyperbole and bullshit.

Dressed and ready, I was waiting in the radioroom the following afternoon when Stuart popped through the hatchway with the news that Diane had arrived, that indeed she had driven her Mazzaretti right down to the ship and was waiting for us.

He led the way and we went down to the dock. Sure enough, there was a new red Mazzaretti with Massachusetts license plates parked beside the gangplank. He rushed over and opened the door on the driver's side, leaving me to gawk.

"Come on, Red, I want you to meet Diane Strothmeyer."

The second great shock I was to receive at the hands of Stuart Heller occurred when I glanced at the lady behind the steering wheel of that car. And when she got out and extended her long, delicate fingers toward me, you could have knocked me down with a feather. Miss Strothmeyer looked even better, considerably better, than Heller had described to me. She was every inch a sophisticated lady, with the body of a New York model and the bearing of a royal princess! She was wearing a black, low-cut evening gown and a necklace of diamonds and sapphires, and there was no way under the sun she could be interested socially in Stuart Heller!

"Close your mouth, Red. I told you what she looked like!"

"So this is Red," she purred, extending her hand. "Stuart can't talk about anything else these days. I just had to meet you."

I finally found my tongue and said something about being pleased to meet her and that Stuart had likewise said a lot about her.

Stuart, acting as if I suddenly did not exist, then took her into his arms and kissed her voluptuous lips and led her around to the passenger's side. I got into the backseat and while Stuart was taking his time circling the car to driver's position, Diane confided in me that she was renting an apartment in town until Stuart's *boat* sailed, that she would then be returning to Boston. I suddenly felt like a real dunce for sending Alice away.

The D. C. trip, which I had assumed was going to be a tour of the nation's capitol, museums and historical landmarks and such like, turned out to be instead a whirlwind tour of nightclubs and dance halls. Stuart was quite the sophisticated gentleman and responsible host on this occasion, gracious to Diane and refusing to let me pay for anything. I had decided he was a beer drinker, but once again I was in for a surprise. Most of the gin-, rum-, and bourbon-based drinks he ordered for himself and Diane I had never heard of.

The tour ended sometime after midnight, with promises all around that we would have to do it again. Diane and I had become good friends, and as we were touching hands back on the dock at Coast Guard Yard she confided that she was captivated by my Oklahoma accent.

*   *   *

The following night I agreed to go into Baltimore with Stuart on the condition that we keep our drinking down to maybe two or three beers. No hard liquor and no tomcatting around. He reminded me that he was engaged, that if he wanted to tomcat around he would do it with Diane, and that after last night he was not interested in the hard stuff.

The evening began innocently enough in a small bar on the edge of Baltimore's red light district. But with the second beer Stuart decided that since this was our first liberty on our way to Alasker, we ought to toast the occasion with boilermakers. I reluctantly agreed on the condition that this toast would be the one and only intake of hard liquor of the evening.

Two boilermakers later, Stuart astonished me with, "Diane's in New York, so let's blow the lid off this town, Red. I know where we can get some women."

"I don't do that anymore," I said. "I'm engaged to four women already." After he stared at me in surprise for awhile, I said, "I guess I'll just head on back to the icebreaker." He chewed his cigar and glared, disgusted. "Unless you're willing to promise me one thing. No, two. No more hard liquor and no loose women."

"Fuck, I had you figgered different, Red. What about all of them stories about you steeling Jeeps and striking superior officers?" He waved at the bartender, "Two more, Jake!"

"There'll be no hanky-panky," I emphasized. "I'm through with all that kind of thing."

"Hah! And you call yourself a' Oklahomern?"

"I'm not an *Oklahomern* and never have been."

"I don't see anything wrong with checkin' out the broads."

"You can check out anything you like, but what I'm saying is that I don't want something to get in the way of this little sea voyage we're about to take. I'm anxious to get back to the West Coast, and if I mess up I just might get transferred to some local scow."

Stuart had lighted up a new White Owl and was doing a good job of stinking up the little bar. After my little speech, he eyed me for a time, rolling the stogy around in his mouth and sniffing at it from time to time. "The shit I've heard about you was just shit, Red."

"Depends on what you heard."

"The brawling and the stealing and the trips to the hospital with the claps and the brig time in laundryrooms."

"That's right, it was all just something somebody made up."

"Hah! And I thought you might turn out to be a good liberty buddy. Come on, let's go over to Second Street."

Outside I staggered around some, enjoying the fresh air, while Stuart hailed a cab. His rationalization was that since we wouldn't be spending any money for a long time we could well afford to splurge a bit. He talked nonstop while I nursed one of his White Owls, got sick at my stomach, and suddenly realized, as the scenery began to flash by, that we were inside a fast-moving vehicle.

It was a cloudy, drippy evening and Second Street turned out to be a sleazy, rundown artery of south Baltimore that had apparently lost all of its lights and street signs. We paid the cabby, who seemed to be in a hurry to be on his way. I doubted seriously that we were on Second Street, but Stuart swore it was and proceeded to lead me to the front door of a building that appeared to be deserted.

"Compared to Boston," he confided, pausing and glancing back at me, "this town looks like shit. And that's the best thing about it, its looks. Come on, the *Eagle's Nest* here has a floor show."

I stood back, surveying the hole-in-the-wall to which he was referring, a small, battered storefront with a door but no windows; and above the door was an ancient wrought-iron eagle sitting on what looked like a roll of wire. It looked worse than *Ted and Roy's* in east Oakland. Stuart had not waited for me, but I caught up just inside as he was beelining it for a booth. I was relieved to see that there were no freelance women in the place. What I did see scattered about the room at little tables and in booths were perhaps a dozen sailors, all in dress blue uniforms. The white shield on the Coasties' right sleeves set them off from the Navy swabs.

I followed Stuart to a table in a dark corner and about ten minutes later the waiter, a sour-faced middle aged man with a hairline even farther back than Stuart's, drifted over and wiped once between us.

"Hey," said Stuart puffing smoke in his face, "got a boilermaker?"

Before the waiter could say anything, I said, "Give us two draft beers and two shots of bourbon."

The bartender grimaced and left and Stuart said, "Jake's in a playful mood tonight."

When the drinks came, I lifted one of the shots. "On the West Coast this is done by downing the bourbon and chasing it with beer."

"Shit, that aint a boilermaker." Stuart carefully lifted his shot glass and dropped it into the bear. It settled to the bottom." The trick is to drop it straight, so it won't turn over."

I grimaced and gulped my shot down, then turned up the glass of beer and finished it.

Stuart removed his cigar from his mouth and downed his drink, taking the shot glass in his mouth.

I signaled to the bartender, whose scowl had changed to a quizzical look. And when he made it over to us, he said, "You boys tryin' to git drunk?"

Stuart was tearing a bit but seemed happy, and after I downed the second shot and chased it with another glass of beer I was feeling considerably better, also.

"What happened to that solemn oath you took?" I demanded.

"Hah, what about yourself?"

"Where's that floor show you promised?" I asked. "Or did you have some other place in mind?"

"It'll be here," he frowned. "It's only seven o'clock for Chrissake."

The place began to fill up and the waiter-bartender, whose name turned out to be Harvil, was beginning to have his hands full. On one of his trips to our table he confessed that his girl had quit that very day, leaving him short-handed. The thought made him so sad he sat down and had a beer with us, and then put it on our tab.

After another boilermaker, a tall civilian with a weatherbeaten face and hungry, piercing eyes came in with a guitar strapped over one shoulder.

"Wha'd I tell you?" demanded Stuart. "There's the floor show."

"That's no floor show," I said. "That's a Texan with a guitar, and I'll bet you he can't even play that thing."

Stuart stared at me. "But I'll bet you sure as hell can, Oklahomer."

"Everybody in my family can play a guitar." This was almost true.

Stuart got unsteadily to his feet and headed for the bar. I watched him, wondering what he had in mind, if anything. The jukebox in the back was going at it; and the thought, half-formed, suddenly occurred to me that the volume had been turned up to compensate for the noise that the overflow crowd was making. And, of course, the crowd had retaliated by getting still louder. I was working on this rather complicated thought when I saw Stuart climbing upon the bar.

It was dark and cloudy in the place, but I could tell that the climber was Stuart by the big black cigar in his mouth. He knocked a few glasses over and sent a pitcher of beer crashing to the floor before he rose, most unsteadily, about halfway down on the bar. Beneath him the bartender was waving frantically, and his mouth was flapping up and down; but I couldn't make out what he was saying.

Suddenly, Stuart's voice cut through the bedlam, drowning out even the jukebox, "All right, people! Listen up! Quiet down, goddamnit! This evening we have a special treat for you!"

Quite suddenly he had the attention of everybody in the bar, including the bartender, whose mouth had frozen at half-flap.

"Tex, give me that guitar!" Stuart wavered on the bar, reaching for the instrument. It took a bit of tugging, but he managed to wrench the guitar from its owner and stand up.

"Our special guest this evening—" (He turned and pointed toward me) "—over there in that booth—"

Alarmed, I half-rose from my chair and began waving and shaking my head. This merely attracted more attention to me; and Stuart, of course, kept pointing until everyone in the room was staring at me.

"I know he looks like a down-and-out sailor, but that's because he's traveling *incognito*, which I'm sure many of you can understand." Stuart winked down at an old man who was sitting at a table with a young woman. "He's on his way from Miami Beach to Boston, where he's scheduled to appear before an audience of thousands!"

Several in the audience began to yell, "Who the hell is he?"

"Ladies and gentlemen, appearing tonight only at Baltimore's *Eagle's Nest Lounge*, I give you none other than *the* incomparable ex-Coast Guardsman, Arthur Lee Godfrey!"

"Git off my bar, you goddamn drunken sailor!" screamed the bartender. "That's not Godfrey!"

I suddenly found myself being ushered across the room and hoisted up beside Stuart; and before I fully realized what was happening I was seated on the bar with the guitar, and the crowd was calling out songs for me to pluck and sing.

"You can play that thing, can't you?" asked Stuart, grinning broadly. "Because if you can't, old partner, we're in deep shit!"

"The next time you volunteer me for something, Heller, I'm going to personally brain you!" I moaned, pretending to check the tuning of the instrument.

In no time at all it became quite clear to the majority of the revelers that I was not at all Arthur Godfrey and, even worse, that I could not play the guitar. Everybody did not agree with this harsh assessment, however, and this became amply clear when fights began to break out beneath me. The ones taking up for me were, for the most part, a bit too drunk to be considered serious judges of guitar music or those who plucked on guitars. I felt hands tugging at my legs, which were dangling over the bar; and, as I climbed to my feet beside Stuart, the entire bar-room erupted.

The bartender had, of course, called the police; and the noise of the fighting, which eventually spilled into the street, had attracted the Shore Patrol, who arrived on the scene just as Stuart and I dived into the men's head. When we finally emerged in an alley, I made the announcement to any and all who might be listening that I was going home to the cutter.

"Hell, the evening's young," said Stuart. "I know another real good bar—"

          *   *   *

Every wake-up day was potentially our last there at Curtis Bay; and as the crew of the CGC *Storis* waited for the word from Coast Guard Yard, excitement mounted. Each conversation began or ended on this subject, and scuttlebutt was rampant aboard the ship.

On September 26, a foggy, miserable Monday, I decided to check out the recreation facilities on the big Coast Guard base, having been

informed that all liberty had been canceled. According to the scuttlebutt, there was a special attraction in the Reck Hall, some new invention
that would revolutionize communications.

"It's a device something like a radar," said Stuart, "which the English
developed during the war and we took one step further. This thing is
wireless and *shows moving pictures of real people and places!*"

"Yeah, sure," I said. "Live pictures, huh?"

"They're calling it television, and you not only hear what's being said
but you see the people that're saying it. Come on, I'll go over with you."

The recreation room turned out to be as big as a high school gym-
nasium; and, mounted on one of the columns that supported the overhead, was a metal box with a glass window in front. It looked like a
radar set, only the window was square and considerably smaller.

In the large open area before the television set a group of about fifty
swabs had gathered to gawk at the one-foot-square black-and-white
picture. It was a picture that fluttered and blinked and, to my amazement, there were tiny people and automobiles and even animals moving about on that screen! The snow on the picture turned out to be
interference.

"What will they think of next?" I marveled.

"Is that all you've got to say? Man, that's a fuckin' miracle!"

At that moment a PA speaker opened up, "Now, hear this! All personnel of the CGC *Storis* report immediately to your duty stations!"

I hit Stuart on the shoulder and yelled, "This is it!"

"Alasker, here we come!"

*　　　　　*　　　　　*

The first leg of our voyage turned out to be a shakedown cruise to
Norfolk, Virginia. There the *Storis* underwent extensive tests to see if it
could make the twenty-thousand-mile trek to Juneau, Alaska. Every
morning for two weeks we left the harbor and returned to our mooring

about sundown. And until every motor and mechanical device aboard had been triple-checked, there was no talk of shore leave for the crew. But on the eve of our departure for parts unknown, shore leave was announced over the PA system. All hands not on restriction or assigned some kind of a watch could go ashore, but liberty would be terminated at zero-two-hundred the following morning.

Stuart was visibly elated at the prospects of a night in a new town. His pitch to me was that it just might be our last liberty port for a very long time. We owed it to ourselves to *check out the broads.*

"I don't need anymore broads," I assured him. "And I understand it is not a pretty sight downtown for servicemen."

"Well," admitted Stuart, "there are about twenty servicemen to every civilian in Norfolk. But you and I are not ordinary servicemen. Right, Oklahomer?"

"Stuart, where do you get your statistics?"

"Ask anybody."

After some consternation and a bit of perturbation, I agreed to go in for one beer, maybe two. I just was not interested in boozing and chasing skirts. Also, I was way behind with my letter-writing. I had not heard from Jamie since Baltimore, and that was clouding my sky. I had told her to write me General Delivery, Colon, Panama, but for all I knew it could be a month before I would reach that place.

"One or two beahs, for Pete's sake!" grumbled Stuart.

"There will be absolutely no funny stuff. After about one or two beers I'm headed back for the ship."

"Ah, come on, Red!" groaned Stuart, lighting up a White Owl. He did not appear to be upset at all, and for a time he puffed away and looked me over. Then he said, "Okay, we'll go in, find a decent tavern, have a couple of drinks, and come on back to the ship." There was no pain at all in his voice, and that should have alerted me.

"No boilermakers and no false claims about what I can do and can't do. No Arthur Godfrey shinola and no broads."

"Hell no. We'll look but we won't touch."

At the bus stop near the base we were told there would be a fifteen-minute wait. Stuart led the way and we strolled over to a battered old white car with the word *Cab* painted on the driver's door. He leaned through the window and carried on for a time, none of which could I hear.

When he straightened up, he said, "Git in, Red. He knows right where to take us." With that he led the way to the backseat.

"What did you say to him?" I asked, suspiciously. For all I knew, he might have asked the guy to take us to a whorehouse.

"I asked him if he knew where the party was in this town."

The driver, toothless and apparently drunk, dropped us in front of a veritable palace of glittering neon and fancy signs. It was big and it looked expensive, and uniformed bouncers were all over the place.

"What's the name of this place?" I asked, looking for a readable sign. "Did you attempt to read the name out front?"

Stuart, elbowing his way toward the bar, which stretched out of sight around a corner to the right, shook his head and continued to puff on his White Owl. The place was wall-to-wall servicemen, but after five minutes I hadn't caught sight of a single Coastie.

"The women're all upstairs," said Stuart, waving at a bartender. "Look at that." He pointed his cigar toward a wide circular stairway. "See that goon with the billy club there at the foot of the stairs? He's letting certain people go up."

"Yeah, certain people with money."

"We've got money. What say we check it out?"

"What's up there that's not down here?" I complained.

"Come on, let's go see." As we made our way across the crowded room, he added, "That's where the real party is. This down here is for peons."

I followed, protesting, reminding him of his promise and that I did not want to get involved with a skirt.

"This is our last night before Panamer."

The big goon at the bottom of the stairs was standing in front of a silk rope that was attached to the banisters on either side of the stairway. Stuart reached him first.

"Do yall have a pass?" this giant of a man asked pleasantly.

"What kind of pass?" asked Stuart.

"This heah is a private club, suh. Yall will need a pass."

"What does membership cost?" Stuart peeled a twenty from his thick roll of bills.

The goon glanced at the twenty and cleared his throat. Stuart peeled off another and held the two out.

"That'll do nicely, suh. Someone'll he'p you up there."

Shaking my head distastefully, I handed over two twenties and fell in behind Stuart. Upstairs we found ourselves in a large, deeply-carpeted hexagonal room full of overstuffed furniture. It was obviously a lounge area. On three of the walls, I noticed, were numbered doors. We joined half a dozen other Navy sailors in this area, and shortly a woman came out and took two of the swabs with her down the hallway.

"Stuart, I want no part of this," I said with determination. "I'll wait here for you." Then I grumbled, more to myself than to him, "To think that I paid two sawbucks just to come up here."

"You've already paid for full membership, Oklahomer. Think of it as a last fling before a big ocean voyage."

A short, dumpy woman huffed into view, carrying a tray of drinks. We had our choice of bourbon-and-soda or bourbon-on-the-rocks, neither of which suited my taste. Stuart, shrugging, commented, "What the hell? It's free booze."

"Not actually," I said, lifting one of the tall glasses from the tray.

Then an extremely tall, serious-faced woman, whose body was permanently bent forward at the hips, was standing above us. "Follow me, pleazz." To Stuart she said, "You'll be in Ten. We'll put Red in Twelve."

"Don't we have a choice?" complained Stuart, blowing cigar smoke in her face.

"We don't parade our girls out for everybody to look at them, if that's what you mean," snapped the woman. "Yours will be Number Ten."

"That's not a very good number," he said doubtfully. "I'd like to take a peek at Number Twelve. Maybe we'd like to exchange."

"We don't do that here."

"Oh, but we do," insisted Stuart. And with that he headed for Twelve.

The tall woman and I followed, complaining, both of us curious about what Stuart had in mind. He flung back the door and entered, encountering immediately a light-yellow-skinned woman, who eyed him disapprovingly, with hands on hips. He puffed contentedly on his cigar and studied her from head to foot.

She was wearing nothing but a light-yellow slip and a heavy frown.

"Huh," said Stuart, backing up and closing the door in the woman's face. "Not my type." He flung open the door to Ten. This time a very white woman with dark rings beneath her eyes smiled at him from the center of the room. "Now, you're talkin'."

She smiled and said, "Hi, yall," weakly.

"I'll take this one," said Stuart. "How about it, Oklahomer? Can you be put up with that *high yaller?*"

At this point I was thinking seriously of leaving in a hurry.

"Hummph!" snorted the tall, angular woman, disapprovingly. But she pushed me inside Twelve and slammed the door shut with finality.

The yellow woman was standing just inside the room smoking a cigarette. When I stumbled inside, she turned a perfectly expressionless face upon me and sat down near a small nightstand.

"Where you from, sailor?"

"The Coast Guard."

She laughed, staring at me. "God, you're young. Ever been in a place like this before?" She got up and moved the straps of her slip over her shoulders and let the garment fall to the floor.

I had turned away from her and was pretending to look for a place to sit.

"You've got fifteen minutes, sailor." She sounded bored.

"I hope you don't mind," I said, looking at her, "but I've got no intention of doing anything with you. I just agreed to come along with my buddy."

At this the woman turned and ogled at me. I glanced quickly at her, reluctant to focus upon her nakedness. She was not a pretty sight, standing there in nothing but crotch-high nylon hose, her weight on one leg. Very used goods.

She turned back to her small lavatory. "Sailor, you've already paid for fifteen minutes of anything you want. Do I turn you off?" She bent at the waist and removed the nylon hose, and I noticed that it was hooked to a strap around her waist. Then she walked over to me with her hands out. "Come on, don't waste your money like this."

"I agreed to come along with my friend because we're getting ready to go on a long voyage," I said, studying the walls of the sad little room. My eyes settled on a framed picture of an ancient water mill.

"About a month ago I—met someone."

"Someone that you fell in love with."

"Yes."

"Say no more. Mind if I smoke?"

From next door came the sound of a body falling into the wall. That was followed immediately by the noise of bodies thrashing about on the floor. A heavy vase or pitcher crashed into a wall.

"Sounds like Pearl's in trouble," said the yellow woman. "Maybe we'd better check."

Pearl had begun to scream threats and curses.

The yellow woman, once again in the slip, rushed out into the lounge area. I followed and there we were joined by the tall woman and two young men in bellhop uniforms. We lined up in front of Number Ten.

"Open that door!" the tall woman shouted.

One of her attendants flung the door back, revealing a scene that etched itself indelibly upon my mind: Stuart, naked except for his golfball cap, was chasing the terrified occupant of the room around the bed, which had been moved into the center of the room! He was puffing mightily on his cigar; and just as the tall matron-in-charge screamed at him to stop or else, he tackled the woman, taking her to the floor with a crash that must have shaken the chandeliers downstairs!

"Git out!" screamed the tall woman. "Or so help me I'll call the police!"

Stuart glanced toward the door and spotted me. He had assumed a riding position on the chalk-white woman's back and seemed about to spur her. "Hey, Oklahomer!"

"Git offen me, you big ape!"

Stuart, who weighed at least two hundred pounds without his cigar, continued to bounce around on the woman, grinning stupidly.

"God damn it, git that beast off her!" shouted the matron to her attendants, who had not jumped right in as she had evidently intended. "Pin him down until the police can git here!"

"Stuart, are you ready to go?" I shouted, grabbing one of the attendants by the back of the neck. "Or do you want to end up in the brig?"

"He's not goin' anyplace!" announced the other attendant, lunging into the room.

"Hey, I'm not ready to go!" bellowed Stuart, holding out his arm for the diving attendant. "I paid for thirty minutes!"

The yellow woman had reached him and was yanking at his shoulder and shouting, "You had fifteen and your time's up!"

At that point, the kid I was wrestling with broke free and I dived after him.

Stuart, hunching forward vigorously on the very white woman, pretending to be a cowboy, suddenly had the other attendant on his back. The three of them sprawled out in the center of the room.

"I'm leaving, Stuart!" I announced. "It was good knowing you!"

"Wait just a goddamned moment!" protested Stuart, trying to put an end to his attendant's whacking and clawing. Finally accomplishing that with a punch in the nose, he struggled to his feet. "Oklahomer, let's get to hell out of here!"

The tall, angular woman had departed noisily, ostensibly on her way to get the police; and the white woman, bellowing like an enraged Brahma bull, had turned over, leaped to her feet, and was trying to kick Stuart's legs. However, he was aware of her and each time she kicked, he moved one step away from her, trying to get his cigar lighted.

"God damn, what's wrong with you, woman?" he said, frowning. Then he straight-armed her with the flat of his hand, knocking her down. "I never saw a woman that loved pain the way you do."

"Get your clothes and let's go!" I pleaded, already outside the room.

"Okay, you're probably right. But I paid hard cash—"

I was becoming more nervous by the second, having sobered considerably in the last minute or so. I headed down the hallway toward the wide circular staircase. Before descending, I glanced back to check on Stuart's progress, in time to see the yellow woman take a swing at him, lose her balance and go down. Stuart had his cigar going and was hopping about with one leg inside his trousers.

"Catch you later, Stuart!"

"I'm with you, Red! Just give me a minute!"

Stuart came stumbling out of the room, carrying his blouse and shoes under one arm. A disheveled attendant was right behind him, and I could tell by his flared nostrils and the murderous look in his eyes he was a *kamikaze* about to strike.

"Look out behind you, Stuart!" I yelled, just in time.

He bellowed, "Well, shit! What's wrong with you people?" Then he caught the attendant by the front of his jacket and slung him down the hallway toward me. "Finish him off, Oklahomer, while I git dressed!"

I gave the fellow a serious whack or two and headed down the stairway. I was met by a very curious crowd of onlookers in the reception area, and in the vanguard was the enormous bouncer, who had positioned himself in the center of the stairs on the bottom step.

It was plain to see he had no intention to negotiate.

"Oh, shit," said Stuart, coming up behind me. "Now, what do you suppose it would take to get that big sucker to move to one side?"

Without a word, I loosened the knot on my neckerchief, zipped it off, and hefted it, centering my thirty-seven dimes. Understandably, Stuart was paying no attention to me.

The bouncer watched us and waited, confident, willing to let us descend to him. I was trailing my little surprise down around my right shoe, and I as we neared him I noticed with relief that he was planning to take Stuart first. He made his move and I brought the half-pound of dimes up, did a turn around my head for momentum, and let fire. The hollow clacking sound my little collection of dimes made on his big empty skull was followed immediately by his agonized cry of pain. With his arms high in the air, he crashed backward like a giant Sequoia, taking down a wide swath of spectators, thus opening up a pathway for us toward the front entrance. I brought the dimes around again, just in case, almost catching Stuart in the nose.

"Maybe some of the things I heard about you are true, after all, Red," said Stuart. "Shall we quit this place?"

The crowd, made up mostly of U. S. Navy sailors, began to cheer us on. Some of them called out, "Way to go, Coast Guard!"

No Shore Patrols had showed up, but in the distance we could hear the squeal of a siren.

"Wait a minute," said Stuart, "my left shoe—"

By this time I had my neckerchief back in place, and I did not pause or even so much as look back on my way out through the wide front doors to a waiting cab.

Stuart, his cigar bent into an L-shape and crushed just a bit on the end, came hobbling behind me on one foot and scooting the other, trying to get his shoe on. He climbed into the cab beside me and closed the door. "Got a light?"

There were a number of sirens heading our way by this time, and one of them was not far off.

"Could we possible get this thing underway?" I asked, nudging the cabby. "I don't want to spend the night in the brig."

"Sure. Just give me a' address, mate."

"Know anyplace where sailors can have a drink in peace?" asked Stuart. To me he said, "The night's still young."

"Take us to the Navy base!" I said, getting a little loud. "And drop us off next to the Coast Guard cutter there."

"You got it. Hang on," said the cabby.

To Stuart I snarled, "Don't they teach you how to treat ladies in *Bahsten?*"

"Hah. That was no lady. Take my word for it."

Panama

———◆———

Mail Call had become the high point of my day until we left Norfolk, for without fail there were two or three and sometimes half a dozen fat letters from my girlfriends. Jamie, who wrote less than any of the others, was something of a philosopher with a pen. Her letters invariably transported me back to the Bend quite completely, forced me to see and smell the homely places where we had played and hunted and fished as kids. With a single stroke of her subtle pen she often brought a lump to my throat and a tear to my eye.

There were frequent letters from Jody, Darleen, and Alice, as well as my little sister, Jessica, enough to keep me awake nights writing replies.

But at zero-four-hundred hours on October 4, 1948, all of this quite suddenly ceased for me. The Chief Boatswain's Mate aboard the CGC *Storis,* who turned out to be none other than Ole Olson, came through the quarters wrapping his billy club against metal bunk racks and yelling the news that we were getting underway for Panama and points beyond. Someone flipped on a light and there he was, standing over me grinning. "Reveille! It's D-Day-minus-nothin'! Rise and shine! Drop your cocks and grab your socks!"

"Where did you say we're going?" I joked.

"Where are we goin'? We're goin' to Panama, my boy, where the women are plentiful and beautiful and the men are few and far between!"

"Yeah, yeah!" laughed Starns, above me. "When we get down there it'll be a different story!"

"Well, I was down there in '42," said Ole. "Now, how could things change all that much in just six years?"

As always it was good to get out of that dark and smelly crew's quarters, and on this day it was particularly delightful to go up on deck and take in the fresh air from the Atlantic. A lively breeze was coming in from the east, which told me that it would be choppy going once we had cleared the harbor. But that was all right, too, I thought, because finally we were on our way to Alaska.

Immediately following chow the ship went into its sea routine, with most of the men aboard assigned to four-hour watches. Practically all topside work was suspended, creating, it seemed to me, an almost holiday spirit. And since there were four of us in the radio shack besides the Chief, each of us had been assigned a four-on and twelve-off schedule. How much better could it get? Any more time off and we would become bored!

For a full day we paralleled the East Coast, with an enormous flock of seagulls for company. Then at the southernmost point of the Keys, on a south-southwest heading, we entered the Gulf of Mexico. The sea around us, as far as the eye could see, was a shimmering and unbroken table top of molten silver; and where it ended and the sky began no one could say. All day we drifted toward the Yucatan in this surrealistic world, with not even a gooney bird to give us a point of reference.

The ship, in a very short time, became our *cosmos*. We stood our watches, went below for chow, bitched and bragged our way to the quarters for sack time. For two entire days the radioroom became the eyes and the ears that linked our little world with the much bigger one of Norfolk and Key West and Panama City. With visibility hardly more than a thousand yards most of the time, the bridge watches could only stand around and worry about the ship plowing into something.

One day looked exactly another, and all things Stateside were put on hold. From our radios came nothing but static and momentary crashes of QRM, and after a week even letter-writing seemed a waste of time. I for one had run out of anything to put down on paper. There was a very limited number of ways of telling a girl you loved her and wished to be with her.

Long, slow, lazy days followed, with nothing but the gray, unchanging surface of the sea and the gray, unchanging sky above. There was absolutely no point of reference in all that vast emptiness to remind us that we were part of a bigger scheme of things. We were indeed a little world drifting in space. And after a time it was difficult to think that anything else existed.

Sometime after we had made our last voice contact with Stateside Coast Guard (We had no idea at the time it was our very last), we switched to the big Collins transmitter and the Hallicrafters receiver and began looking for CW contacts. But the regulation Coast Guard radio frequencies were relegated to the VHF and UHF bands, and except during the very early hours of the morning there was little hope of making a radio contact of any kind beyond line-of-sight.

Although we had no traffic to pass to anyone (nor did we anticipate any incoming messages), we wanted to maintain some kind of communications link with the mainland. Once each four-hour watch the radioman on duty would warm up the transmitter and ask for a signal report from a Coast Guard station in Florida or Louisiana. To my delight, unlike the tight rein I was used to in the Twelfth District, there were no restrictions on the CGC *Storis* concerning plain language or even the piping of music into the messdeck. Except during bad weather when the atmospheric conditions prohibited it, we were able to tune in shortwave broadcasts, which provided us with music, news, and sporting events.

Then one morning on the four-to-eight watch Stuart made the first contact with Coco Solo Naval Base, at the Panama Canal! He was asked what our E. T. A. was. Stuart, usually a calm professional at his radio post, let out a yell that brought Ensign Archibald How on the run.

"When will we reach Panama, Sir?"

"The twentieth! The morning of the twentieth!" was the reply.

Only two days away! *Terra firma* once again! And to make the metamorphosis complete (Our cosmos had turned back into a mere *ship*), the gray, awful clouds evaporated and a lovely blue sky appeared!

And, of course, all I could think of was the great pile of mail I would get in Panama, especially the thick, wonderful letters from Jamie Lee!

To Stuart, who was once again his old calm self and showing no signs that he had heard the great news, I confided that I had given my forwarding address as Colon, Panama. "In care of General Delivery," I said, proudly.

"Fuck, Red, you can't go into Colon. That's off-limits to American servicemen."

"What!" I shouted. "Are you sure?"

"Ask Olson, if you don't believe me."

"Well, one way or the other I'm going to get my mail."

For a week the heat had been almost unbearable aboard the ship, and the farther south we went the worse it got. The ventilation system had gone out almost immediately after we left Norfolk, and all attempts to repair it had been futile. Below decks was a steaming cauldron, especially during the daytime.

As we were nearing Panama, however, at a time when the heat and humidity had driven us all topside, a gentle but refreshing breeze sprang up from the southwest.

On the morning of our arrival at the Coco Solo Naval Base, from the PA system came the astonishing news that all hands were to muster on the quarterdeck in dress whites! There followed a great scramble all over the ship, for only the old salts had anticipated such a thing. To me the excitement of having arrived in Panama, at this very famous old Naval base, more than outweighed any discomfort I might suffer in the one-hundred-and-ten-degree heat attired in a heavy dress white blouse and trousers! For a time, that is.

The slight and unpredictable breeze from the southwest flopped our long collars about our necks (We must have been a sorry sight for the two dozen or so spectators on the dock), but it did little to lessen the discomfort from the heat. And for an eternity, it seemed, we waited patiently for the order to retire to a shade. It came only after someone, a yeoman I think, collapsed and had to be carried away to the Sick Bay.

Once we were moored and all watches had been secured, our attention quite naturally turned to shore leave. It seemed unnecessarily cruel to me that the brass had not bothered to have a quartermaster announce which division or divisions would be given liberty. But there in the intense heat of topside we waited for the posting of the liberty list outside the Ship's Office.

Stuart Heller, always in there competing, reached the coveted list first (among the radio gang); and when he made it back to where I was standing near a lifeline, the look on his face jolted me into silence.

"Guess what I get instead of liberty?" he asked me.

"The *guillotine*," suggested Starns, smothering a snicker. He pronounced it *gill-o-teen*.

Ignoring the remark, Stuart looked at me and said, "I've been volunteered by our esteemed Chief to do Shore Patrol duty in Cristobal." After staring at me for a time, he added, "You're on the list for tomorrow." To Starns he snarled, "They aint about to trust you with a firearm."

"I think that's a bit of okay," I said. "A good way to get acquainted with the place fast." When Stuart turned and glared at me, I added, "At least you're going ashore."

I was determined to make an attempt to get my mail, despite what Stuart had said about Colon being off limits to American servicemen. While I was preparing to leave the ship, Ole Olson showed up in the crew's quarters looking for me. He had run into Heller and knew what I was planning.

"They don't speak any English over there, Red," he said, grinning. "If they've got any mail for you, how're you gonna talk them out of it?" When I hesitated, he slapped me on the back, "I got to admit you was thankin' ahead, but Colon's off-limits to American servicemen. The MP's and the SP's won't permit you to go over there."

"I haven't heard from my girl in a long time," I said, stubbornly.

"Wal, I can't do nothin' 'bout that. But you shore as hell better stay 'way from Colon. You hear?"

I nodded, absentmindedly. "Thanks, Boats, I understand."

"Yeah, well, I hope to hell you do."

*   *   *

The vehicle that picked up the *Storis* liberty party was an olive drab, Navy-issue personnel carrier, and there was no fee for the ride in to the bus stop in Cristobal. All of the liberty hounds got off there, and I bee-lined it for the souvenir shops and clip joints, still mulling over what Olson had told me.

Remembering that he or one of the other old salts aboard the ship had said something about Colon being separated from Cristobal only by a street, I decided to go look for that demarcation line, pretending to be a curious tourist. Evidently, the two cities were really one, divided more or less down the middle, the one occupied and run by native Panamanians and the other a tourist town for Americans. I wanted to ask directions but decided that might arouse suspicions.

As I walked farther and farther into town, I began to suspect that the line separating the two towns might become obvious by the absence of U. S. servicemen on the Colon side. And sure enough, eventually, I came to a street crowded with sailors and soldiers on one side and civilians on the other. MP's and SP's were cruising up and down the Cristobal side regularly, I noticed.

Waiting my chance, I fell in with a crowd of brightly-dressed men and women that were crossing the street; and within two minutes I was down a side street and well inside the city of Colon! The absence of Americans, especially servicemen, livened up my adrenaline somewhat, for with each step into the forbidden city I was going becoming more and more of a spectacle!

I was well aware that I would accomplish nothing unless I could locate the post office. This caused me to begin stopping at shops and inquiring at cash registers. For a time all this accomplished were raised eyebrows and startled looks; but at last a young lady smiled and said in English, "Sailor, do you realize that you should not be in Colon?"

"I am aware of that," I said nervously, "but I've got to find the post office! Please, can you help me?"

"Well, that's easy. Take a right at the next street and you will find it in the middle of the block." She was pointing away from the American side.

With my heart zipping along excitedly, I left and in no time found the *Oficio de Posto*. There I fell in line before a window that looked very much like a bank teller's cage back in the States. Around me no English was being spoken. Finally, after what seemed a very long time, I was standing before a bright-looking young lady, who was peering at me in alarm from behind her cage.

"*¿Si, señor?*"

I had had plenty of time to rehearse what I was going to say. And having mustered up all the *español* I could remember from that one semester of college Spanish with Professor Myrtle Drain, back in Oklahoma, I blurted out:

"*¿Tiene Usted una carta por Wesley Hall?*"

The girl stared at me with her mouth wide, batting her pretty eyes and smiling. "*Si.* I believe we do have mail for a someone by that name! Quite a stack of it, to be exact!" She turned to some open mail slots behind her and quickly returned with a pile of letters! "These are from a sweetheart, no?"

"Yes, ma'am."

"Then you should call them *cartitas*, señor."

*   *   *

Back on the ship everyone who saw the stack of letters stared at me in astonishment. How had I managed to get mail in Colon, of all places? Ole Olson just shook his head and laughed. "That takes the cake, Red! How you got them letters out of Colon without being caught is a mystery to me. Every time I've gone over there, I've ended up in the brig!"

Stuart, when he returned from his duties as a Shore Patrol, eyed me suspiciously. "You went into Mexican town, found the post office, and asked for your mail," he said matter-of-factly.

"That I did."

"What'd you say to the mail clerk?"

I repeated my triumphant line of Spanish, this time with a great deal more confidence.

"Yah, yah," said Stuart, rolling his eyes and puffing on his White Owl. "The hell you say."

Despite his words and his tone, I was certain my Bahsten friend was impressed, not only because of the Spanish but because of my daring raid into the off-limits city.

"So you can specka da Spanish, no?" he said, studying me, obviously trying to decide whether he might be able to capitalize on this talent at some later date.

"*Oui, monsieur.*"

"Get outta here!"

We strolled the length of the cutter to the bow, during which time Stuart told me about his SP duty in Cristobal. Two Coasties had been assigned to work a four-hour shift with two MP's, relieving the local Navy boys. He had been one of the lucky *volunteers* for the job, for which, he said, he would not soon forget Mister Archibald How, our

Com Officer. Why he had decided it was the ensign and not our CPO who had done the volunteering I was never to know.

When word began to circulate among the crew that I had gone into Colon and picked up my mail, directly violating the law, while Stuart was patrolling the city, my buddy began catching a great deal of ribbing. A number of the crew were in the quarters, along with Ole Olson and another CPO, when the two of us showed up there after morning chow. Among other things Stuart was accused of turning his head and looking the other way while the law was being broken.

"While you was down there patrolling the street, ole Red was sneaking across into Colon!" somebody called out, bringing a great deal of applause. "Both of you boys could be in trouble over this!"

"Shit, I knew what he was doing!" said Stuart. "In fact, I saw to it the MP's left him alone!"

"You taking credit for Red's misdemeanor?"

"By the way, Red," put in Stuart, trying to change the subject, "you've got SP duty tomorrow night."

Olson put his hand on my shoulder. "That SP duty really is volunteer work, Red, so don't let 'em kid you into doin' it if you don't want to."

"Then why did I spend the evening so disposed?" asked Stuart.

"You got snookered, I guess," said Ole, winking at one the other CPO.

"That's okay," I said. "I think I'd like to try it. Sounds like fun."

"Okay, if you say so. But volunteerin' aint the way to go, huh, fellows?" said the boatswain's mate.

There was a chorus of affirmatives.

Somebody said, "Yeah, an' if old Heller tries anything, you'll be there to throw *him* in the jug, right Red?"

"I'll help him out the same way he helped me," I said quickly. This pleased everybody and brought a round of applause.

That night most of the crew stayed topside to sleep because it was steamy hot and stuffy below. But about midnight here came Chief Olson with the news that we had to go below. Orders of the O. O. D.

"I hate like hell to tell you this, boys, but whether you sleep up here or not aint up to me. You-know-who just roused me out of the sack to get you off the deck."

"Damn it, Boats, we can't sleep down there in the crew's quarters!" complained Collier, a yeoman. "The officers have air conditioning or they wouldn't be able to do it."

"Nope, they're just made of firmer stuff," said Olson with a chuckle.

"I'll bet I can tell you who the O. O. D. is," said Heller.

"You're right," nodded Olson. "It's that ensign of yours."

We reluctantly crawled off to our bunks; and there we lay, stark naked, trying to get some shuteye. It was difficult to breathe, and, for me at least, impossible to sleep.

About one o'clock, shortly after I had drifted into a place somewhere just short of the Land of Nod, Carlos Markos, the self-styled *Wild Wop from Waukegan, Wisconsin,* came in off liberty and flopped into the bunk immediately beneath me. I was vaguely aware that someone had been stumbling around and falling into my bunk; and a few minutes later I began to realize that a great stench had permeated the area. I stood this for a time but finally the Wild Wop's breath lifted me out of my sack and sent me lurching toward the ladder! Markos was, as everybody knew, a devoted wine drinker and a great fancier of Italian food; and on this night he had evidently consumed a great deal of garlic, washing it down with a cheap Italian wine! The combination was just too much for me in that dead compartment—which had smelled like a sewer even before Marcos had entered it!

This was a first for me. After riding a small wooden vessel from New Caledonia to the Philippines to the Marianas and then back to the States without ever having been seasick, I was about to *feed the fish!* I made it topside and dived for the starboard lifeline, dry-heaving all the way. Then, one by one, the others in the crew's quarters joined me, until eventually only Carlos Markos was left below.

While this sad and defeated bunch was thusly occupied along the lifeline, Ole Olson showed up. After one look at us, he tossed his hands in the air and declared, "What the hell?" When nobody paid him any attention, he called out, "Okay, go ahead and sack out on deck!"

Having been unable to feed the fish anything, I turned to thank Olson, too weak to say a word. I wanted to tell him I would be eternally in his debt. But no words would come out of my mouth.

"Somebody oughta kill that sorry bastud!" growled a once-strong and healthy quartermaster.

"Which one?" demanded Heller. "You talkin' about the Dago or the O. O. D.?"

"Hey, you men there! Get below to your quarters!"

It was, of course, Mr. How, from his lofty perch on the bridge railing. He was dressed in a full khaki uniform, with his long sleeves buttoned at the wrists!

"Look at that," growled Heller, disgusted.

I stopped and glanced up at Ensign How. "Sir, would you check our quarters out? There's evidently a gas leak of some kind down there!"

Immediately, the officer was down the ladder from the bridge. "A gas leak? What's your name?"

"Hall, Sir."

"Okay, Hall, follow me!"

As we were leaving, somebody mumbled, "Your ass is mud, Red."

But within two minutes I was back on deck with the news that the ensign had indeed detected the gas, even before he reached the quarters, and had given his permission for us to sleep topside!

"Well, I'll be goddamned," said Olson, slapping me on the bare shoulder. "If you don't beat all!"

*   *   *

The next afternoon a white Navy Jeep showed up at the gangplank of the *Storis*. Beneath the windshield the letters *SP* had been painted in

large red letters, and from the front fenders pennants with the words
Shore Patrol waved snappily in the breeze. In undress whites, I piled
aboard, nodding to the driver. He was dressed similarly but wearing a
Navy Colt .45 strapped around his waist. Stuart stood beside the gangplank smoking a White Owl and flipping the ashes into the strip of
water that separated the cutter from the dock.

"Give 'em hell, Red!"

"You behave yourself this evening, Stu. Stay out of my jurisdiction."

"Roger!"

"No hanky-panky."

"Just a couple of drinks and a glance or two at the broads."

"I'll jail your ass if you get out of line."

"Shit, you couldn't jail Starns."

The driver whipped the Jeep around on the dock and we headed out.
Without another word, he floorboarded it all the way to downtown
Cristobal, finally coming to a halt at the City Police Station, where half
a dozen SP and MP Jeeps were already parked. "Come on," he said, "I'll
point you in the right direction."

Inside, I was introduced to a Navy lieutenant, who told me to get a
cup of coffee and wait to one side for a couple of minutes. "I'll pair you
up with somebody," he said, looking around. "Didn't the *Storis* send two
of you?"

I shook my head. "I was the only volunteer, I guess."

"Okay, no sweat."

The place was full of law enforcement officers, civilian and military,
most of whom were congregating around a long table loaded with
donuts, cookies, and coffee. Evidently, they were waiting around to
relieve units then out in the battle zone.

About the time I had a cup of java in hand, here came the lieutenant.
Behind him was a Navy sailor and two MP's. "Red," he said, "You'll go
along with these men." He introduced everybody, handing me an SP

armband. "They'll fill you in on the details." He turned to the young sailor, "Simpson, how about you give him the scoop."

The four of us left the building in pairs and circled about the parking lot, looking for the Jeep that had been assigned to us. Simpson fell in beside me. "You must be on that icebreaker that came in yesterday."

I nodded but said nothing.

"Man, that's got to be some kind of duty!" When I didn't respond, he added, "That's the cleanest ship I ever saw."

"Spit and polish," I said with a nod. "Maybe you'd better fill me in on this *duty*."

He laughed and we climbed into the backseat of the Jeep the two MP's had settled upon. "Well, it's quite simple. We cruise around until we spot excitement, such as a lynch mob, a burning building, dead people. If we decide the partiers are having too much fun, we break it up and take the instigators to headquarters and have some coffee and donuts. Then, if they sober up right well, we release them and head out again."

"That's it?" I asked, doubtfully. "Will we have much business during the evening?"

"It'll pick up as the evening goes on. Don't worry, we won't get bored!"

One of the MP's turned around as we were leaving the parking lot and said to me, "Better strap on one of those forty-fives. And there should be a stick and a holster back there."

I had noticed a pile of equipment lying in the floorboard, apparently part of the stuff checked out by the girenes. I picked up a belt and strapped it around my waist. Then I fitted the pistol into the holster and snapped the club to my belt.

"I hope there will be no reason to use these things," I said with a nervous laugh.

"Let me tell you something," warned the driver, still looking over his shoulder, "don't ever hesitate to do what you know you've got to do. You never know when some nut is going to take it into his head to brain you. A moment's hesitation is all they need sometime."

"Yeah," said the other MP, "speak softly but use that sick if you have to. We, my friend, are the law in these parts, which makes us different from all the other servicemen. You're not a sailor tonight—and nobody will think of you as a sailor. To the drinkers and partiers you'll be the enemy, bad news from the word *go*."

Evidently, the MP at the steering wheel knew where he was going. He headed the Jeep in a beeline for the edge of town, then made a right and went two blocks before wheeling back toward the center of town. In this fashion, skipping every other street, we toured the city, being careful to avoid crossing over into Colon. The MP on the passenger's side was in constant touch with headquarters via a walkie-talkie, which kept us informed about the trouble spots in town and which ones we were to check out.

"We don't bother with civilians, right?" I asked.

"Not if we can help it," said the driver. "But sometimes they give us no choice in the matter."

"If civilians are fighting civilians and destroying property—?"

"We put a stop to it and hold the culprits for the local police."

From seven o'clock on, as it turned out, we did little cruising. By the time we were disentangled from one fracas, the radio would be announcing another in our vicinity! Things went from interesting to scary fast. Between about seven-thirty and nine we hauled six angry sailors, two mean and dangerous soldiers, and a chagrined prostitute to the police station. And the only reason we did not transport more law-breakers to the *hoosegow*, as Simpkins called the brig, was because there wasn't enough room in our vehicle!

At the end of a long break, after we had had six fast cups of coffee, word came in that a big brawl had broken out at *Rosie's Hacienda*, reputed to be the nastiest, meanest place in town. As we skinned around corners and flattened out on straight-aways, the radio informed us that all branches of the Armed Services seemed to be involved, including the Coast Guard!

"Oh, man," I said, "that will more than likely be where my buddy is."

Simpson looked curious. "What makes you think this buddy of yours will be involved?"

"Involved? Who said anything about *involved*? If Coasties are in this fight, Stuart Heller more than likely started it. He just naturally gravitates to the hottest spots in town."

We were the first constabulary unit to arrive on the scene, which by this time included a sizable chunk of the sidewalk in front of *Rosie's* and was fast spreading across the street. The MP's, both well over six-feet tall and wearing white combat helmets and black field boots, leaped out of the Jeep and headed for the confusion. Simpson stood up, cinched up his forty-five and billy club and climbed carefully out of the Jeep. "Follow me, Red!" One of the MP's began frantically blowing his whistle, and the other began harvesting bodies. I would see his club moving in an arc, like a scythe, hear a deadening thud, and down somebody would go. Once, I saw a man khaki standing on his head.

The noise center of the fight was still inside the tavern, but there was a great deal of screaming and cursing going on outside on the sidewalk and street. And, of course, as soon as the whistle cut loose, several of the more squeamish souls began yelling, "Police!" at the top of their voices. And the crowd that had assembled to watch the blood-letting began to retreat into doorways.

I wanted to inform the MP's that in *case* they spotted a barrel-chested, cigar-smoking Coastie in there someplace to turn him over to me. But even if I had had the opportunity, I knew it would have done no good. These boys were professional military policemen, and I knew that they would give no quarter, regardless of who was involved.

On our way in, we separated several knots of angry sailors and soldiers, and banged a few heads doing it. A tall corporal in the Army Engineers came at Simpson with a beer bottle and received for his trouble a mouthful of seasoned oak from one of the MP's, who turned on me and bawled out, "Act alive, sailor, or they'll kill you!"

The crowd inside *Rosie's* was milling about, shoving and kicking each other. And two or three swirling masses made up of both sailors and soldiers were trying seriously to murder each other. Apparently, this was a war between the Army and the Navy. But, of course, to soldiers a sailor suit was a Navy sailor suit, whether it had an innocent little white shield on the lower right sleeve or not.

Relieved that I had not seen Stuart on the street or in the main lounge area, I laughed at the thought that he might be somewhere in the sprawl of rooms in the back. *Shades of Norfolk,* I thought and dismissed the idea. I fell in with Simpkins, who had forged ahead of me, *feeling good* that my buddy was somewhere else on this occasion. We were trailing somewhat behind the MP's and, during the fifteen minutes or so that it took us and two other Jeep loads of MP's and SP's to reach them and bring order out of chaos, I saw neither hide nor hair nor White Owl of Stuart Heller.

Olson and three of his deckhands had finally been separated from six soldiers and were being restrained by the MP's. As soon as I could break away from other problems, I angled over and asked the boatswain's mate if he had seen Heller.

"Hah! Have I *seen* him? He was the one that started this whole mess, Red! That boy will bear watchin'!"

"Well, where is he, then?"

"How the hell would I know? Probably in one of them back rooms with a woman!"

The other parts of the premises were being cleared out methodically; so I dashed toward the back, hoping I wouldn't be too late. A narrow hallway ran down the center of the back portion of the large building, and on either side were doors that opened into small rooms, which were evidently being rented on an hourly basis. I was in the vanguard of an invasion force that consisted of two SP's and at least four MP's, who were flinging the doors open and turning on lights.

Halfway down the hall I began hearing a mighty commotion going on in one of the rooms. Apparently, someone was about to burst out through the flimsy door into the hallway. The whole wall, at one point, seemed about to fall outward! Just as I reached for the door knob, it was jerked violently away from me, disappearing through the door itself. Which then swung inward slowly on its own!

Attempting to come through the door was a very large, pink woman, whose progress was being impeded by something or someone hanging onto her pink silk underskirt. She was bawling like an enraged Spanish fighting bull and threatening to dismember whatever it was hanging onto her. Then I got a look at what that something was. My cigar-smoking friend was stretched out on the floor with both hands locked onto the woman's skirt! And he was wearing nothing but a flattened White Owl cigar and a stupid grin!

"Let her go, Stuart!" I advised loudly. "Or I'll break some bones!"

He released his hold on the garment and I scrunched against the door facing to keep from being turned into a grease smear by the escaping woman. In a flash that enormous naked blur dashed off down the hall, just ahead of the MP's, who began yelling, "Stop her!"

My problem, I decided, was to get Stuart dressed and out of there before the whole force of MP's and SP's came rushing in upon us. Simpson showed up and helped find some of Stuart's gear.

"Is this the one?" he asked. "Your Coastie friend?"

"That's him."

Stuart had stood up and was leaning against the door in a slightly hunched position chewing on his cigar. It was obvious that he was in no particular hurry to depart the premises.

Another SP came speeding down the hallway. "You need any help, Red?" Then he stopped dead in his tracks and stared at Stuart and the destruction in the room. "My God!"

"Nah, we can handle it here," I said. "But, thanks, buddy."

North Toward Home

━━━━━━━━━━━━━━━━ ◆ ━━━━━━━━━━━━━━━━

One week (It seemed much longer) after arriving at the Coco Solo Naval Base, the CGC *Storis* made preparations for going through the Panama Canal. It was a bright, hot October day, and all hands were on deck. Some, like me, were there to see the famous canal; but most of the crew had abandoned the boiling cauldron below decks in hopes there would be a breeze once we were out in the open water.

By eight o'clock the only shade on the ship was a patch about two feet wide and thirty feet long in front of the pilothouse and the bridge; and by then we were practically dead in the water, waiting our turn to go through the locks. There had been no identifiable breeze on our way from the base.

Dressed in dungaree cut-offs and a tie-dyed T-shirt, I was moving about on the bow with my camera, which was the size of a package of cigarettes and took pictures no larger than my thumbnail. Stuart Heller, with a big ugly stogie clamped firmly between his teeth, stood nonchalantly beside me looking, not in the direction of the Canal like everybody else, but at something off the port bow. As usual, he was dressed in clean, faded dungarees and a pair of white tennis shoes.

"Do you think it's this bad on the other side, in the Pacific?" he asked. "I don't remember it ever being this hot."

"Then you haven't crossed the Mojave Desert in a Model A Ford," I said, aiming my camera at a section of green grass and trees on the upper side of the locks. An enormous oil tanker was blocking our view of the locks themselves. "It gets so hot on that stretch of highway between Needles and Barstow it kills Gila monsters."

"Shit, it can do that right here," said Stuart, flicking ashes in front of my camera just as I snapped a picture.

Between us and the tanker was a yippy boat and something else that I couldn't make out. And within an hour after we lined up, two ships had topped the horizon behind us.

"I wish I had a dollar for every time a ship goes through this place," said Stuart.

"That's probably about what Uncle Sam charges foreigners for the privilege," I said.

"We're the foreigners down here. And one of these days Panamer is going to kick our ass out and really start charging us and ever'body else for goin' through."

"Now, that would be something to watch," I scoffed. "It'd be like you and me trying to take over this ship."

"Hell, that could be done, especially if we were the rightful owners already."

"This place wasn't anything but a swamp until Teddy Roosevelt built this canal. And nobody is ever going to take it away from us."

Finally, the tanker, maneuvered by two tugs, went into the first lock. I took a picture of it, proud as hell.

"Now, that ought to be something to frame," commented Stuart. "Why don't you take a picture with somebody in it?"

"Make fun if you want to," I said, "but some of these days I'll get a kick out of looking at these pictures with my grandkids."

"Shit, your grandkids? If you ever have any, they won't be legal."

"I showed you a picture of the gal I'm going to marry, didn't I?" I stuffed my camera inside a pocket of my shorts and took a letter out of another.

"Now, let's see, you showed it to me when you first got it, once in the radioroom immediately following, twice in the crew's quarters, and a dozen or so times in the messdeck."

From the envelope I extracted a number of pictures and began to shuffle through them. "She's actually better looking in the flesh."

"With those overalls on you can't make out much of her figure," complained Stuart, taking one of the pictures and examining it.

"She's precisely right in all departments."

"Be more specific."

"Think of the best you've ever seen. If you raise that to the tenth power, you'll be headed in the right direction."

"You've seen everything these overalls are coverin' up?"

"Since she was a baby I've watched all of her attributes enlarge and become precisely right."

"Be specific, goddamnit."

"Don't use foul language in front of her."

At that point our conversation was interrupted by the arrival of the two tugs. One lined up on the starboard and the other went around to the port. From the latter emerged a man in a black uniform.

"Somebody's comin' aboard," said Stuart. "Looks like brass. Now's when you ought to be takin' pictures."

"Look at the scrambled eggs. He's our pilot."

Suddenly, the ship's engines went dead; and as the officer mounted the ladder to the bridge. Stuart said, "Right, he's taking over."

"That's a good thing. We might've done irreparable damage to the locks if old Tomlinson had stayed at the helm." (Ted Tomlinson was a quartermaster famous for *snafus*.)

Later that day I commented to Stuart that the inland lakes, which stretched (more or less) end-to-end from the canal to the Pacific, had been a real surprise to me. "I guess I just always thought the Panama Canal was a canal all the way from the Atlantic to the Pacific."

"Yeah. If it wasn't for the damned mosquitoes and heat this would be a helluva place. It's like a beautiful woman. You look at it from a distance and you think it's a gift from God, but up close it turns out to be mean and ugly as hell. You know what they say."

"You can't judge a book by its cover."

"The fuckin' one gets aint worth the fuckin' one gets."

"That's not what they say," I groaned. "Where'd you hear that, for Pete's sake?" I headed toward the radioroom.

"Watch out for old Ed. He'll git you with one of his practical jokes."

"You know," I said, stopping, "One of these days, we're going to have to teach that dude a lesson."

"I'm ready. That last trick he pulled on us came close to killin' me." As I turned to leave, he added, "You ought to be able to catch a little shuteye this watch."

"We've already lost Coco Solo?"

"We've lost everything. I couldn't even tune in an Armed Forces shortwave station."

"Well, on three sides of us are mountains and on the other side is about ten thousand miles of ocean."

*   *   *

With the Pacific had come a refreshingly cool, brisk wind that brought instant relief from the stifling heat and humidity. And, by the time my watch ended at midnight, it had begun to clear away some of the accumulated stink of Panama and the mildew of the past three weeks. I paused in the open passageway outside the radio shack to enjoy the almost chilly wind that was coming from the northwest; and suddenly I was remembering a similar balmy night in the Pacific, back during the war with the Japs. For a brief moment I was there, body and soul, in that time and place, just off Sansapore, New Guinea. My ship was a little wooden subchaser, the *SC-995*; and I was, then as now, coming off an eight-to-twelve watch and had paused to take in the night air. Suddenly, I felt a tightening in my loins, as the old fear came back.

We had been averaging about two *Divine Winds* a day.

Then I realized that my nose had picked up a faint something in the wind, something tropical and sweetly prolific. But then it was gone, along with the trip back in time.

At eight that morning, with only a couple of hours of sleep, I was back in the radio shack. Willie Starns, having just come off the four-to-eight, was allowed to sleep in until twelve; but Stuart and I, out of old habit and the fear of being assigned some kind of work detail, were hanging out in the shack.

Chief Ed Rothman, who prided himself on having a mind that was always one jump ahead of everybody else's, had worked out a watch schedule that gave his men some relief at very little sacrifice to himself. One day he would take the eight-to-twelve and the next he would take the twelve-to-four, that way his three radio ops didn't have to stand the same watches every day. Of course, during those hours he had to be somewhere besides his bunk anyway; and the man he was bumping up to the next watch was forced to be in the radioroom.

About half the time Ed would begin his watch and then, since there were always two qualified operators in the room with him, he would give some lame excuse and duck out, never to be seen again during that watch. We knew he was heading for the Chiefs' Quarters to catch some sack time.

From the west coast of Panama to Lower California there was nothing to do on the radio watches except sleep, drink coffee, read old issues of *QST* magazine, log in NO SIGS every fifteen minutes, clean and trim toenails, and work out scenarios about getting back at the Chief.

One late night I tuned in an Armed Forces Radio Station that was playing Beethoven. It must have been coming from the other side of the globe because I was actually picking it up from two directions. And since one of the signals was taking the high road and the other was taking the low, the end result was a fascinating *waviness* in the music. To me it was an improvement over the way it was supposed to sound. When it ended, finally, I began humming my own version of Beethoven's *Fifth*, making it sound as if it were coming from deep space.

At this point, Stuart showed up with coffee.

"Man, I think you need help. Here, try some of this."

I began whistling softly the opening of the Fifth, trying to achieve the waviness effect.

"Listen, I couldn't sleep. I got to thinking we ought to work out some kind of counter offensive against old Ed. Have you heard the latest?"

"What?"

"You know that dream I have ever so often? The one where I talk in my sleep? That sonofabitch somehow got it on tape and played it in the Chiefs' Mess. And, sure as hell, he plans to put it on the PA system one of these days."

"Did you say anything incriminating? I remember you sometimes talk about him. Do you know for sure he was the one that did it?"

"Who else would think of something like that and have the time and wherewithal to do it? It was him all right."

"He likes to fool around with tape recorders," I agreed, nodding. "Let us not forget that little stunt he played on me."

"Oh, when he taped our conversations and then cut and spliced all that shit to make it sound like you said the Old Man was a queer and ought to be thrown to the sharks. Yeah, that was something else. He must've planted tape recorders here and in the quarters to get all that."

"And he even went to the trouble to steer us onto certain subjects, until he had everything he needed."

"I about shit when he plugged that tape into the PA system and played it at full volume for the entire crew and officers. I'll bet the Old Man about shit his pants!"

"Well, yeah, and Archibald How had to tell him and the entire ward-room whose voice it was on that tape. I think the Old Man still dislikes me for that. Even after the Ed got on the PA and said it was a practical joke."

"I knew all along it was Rothman that did it because of the elaborateness of the whole thing. Nobody else on this ship would have gone to that much trouble."

"He needs to be taught a good lesson."

"Got any ideas?" asked Stuart. "How about catching him asleep and castratin' the bastard?"

"No telltale scars or blood," I said, shaking my head. "But I have been toying with something that just might be more long-lasting than deballing him. You know how he loves to sit around and hammer away on that code oscillator of his? He thinks he's something of a hotshot at CW, and I've noticed that he subconsciously taps out code even when he doesn't have a key with him. It could be that he's just a bit *dit-happy,* huh? Maybe we could see just how close he is to the edge."

"Shit, I think you're onto something!"

"Yes!" I said, whacking the desk. "And I've spent a couple of mid-watches working out a possible *modus operandi.*"

*   *   *

The first thing we did was tape-record a great deal of high speed CW news press that was, by this stage of our voyage, coming in loud and clear on the shortwave radio. It was being sent by a teletype machine and so fast it would challenge even the salty old Chief to read it; and, although most of it was S5, Q5, some of it was marred by waves of static.

Next, we checked on the Chief's sack schedule and began carefully observing his daily routine. He was, as we both knew very well, quite predictable. While he was on watch, we inserted a small speaker just inside the air vent near his bunk and carefully ran the connecting wires up through the system into the jumble of cables in the radio shack overhead. One late evening, when he was asleep and snoring content-edly in his bunk, we completed the wiring job to the tape recorder in the radioroom.

It took us a week to complete this project and another couple of days to check the lash-up for bugs. But we were in no hurry. During the course of our delvings into the Chief's lifestyle, we had confirmed a number of damning things about him. For example, he was spending ninety percent of his time either in his bunk or in the Chiefs' Quarters playing cards, and he seldom bothered to go to the Chiefs' Mess for chow, having worked out an agreement with the cook to have his food delivered to him at chow time.

Eventually, everything was ready for a trial run. The tape recorder was in place and the volume had been turned so low it was impossi-ble to *read* the CW copy. It was possible, with a great deal of concen-tration, to catch a word here and there, just enough to suspect that the *ditty-dah-dahs* really were Morse Code and not the crackle of the air conditioning system, which was working again (now that we no longer needed it).

The tape was a long one. When it had pretty well run its course, one of us would turn the volume off and re-wind it. The plan was to run at least two hours of this stuff each time the Chief hit the sack. How long we would need to keep this up was anybody's guess; but our plan was to keep it up until he was hauled off to the Sick Bay strapped in a strait-jacket, or until the ship entered San Francisco Bay, whichever came first.

The morning following the first taping session Stuart and I were relaxing in the radioroom with fresh mugs of coffee when the Chief dropped in. Stuart was on his way to breakfast and I was about to assume the eight-to-twelve watch. The Chief, we noted with consider-able satisfaction, was a bit bleary-eyed.

"Hey, Chief," I said, casually. "Heard any good ones lately?"

Instantly his tired old eyes swung in my direction. "Heard any *what?*" he growled.

"Good stories."

"Oh. Not actually." He tapped Stuart on the shoulder and waited impatiently for him to get out of his swivel rocker. The two exchanged places and the Chief cleared his throat. "Tell me something, do either one of you ever think you hear CW in your sleep?"

"Are you kidding?" said Stuart, scowling. "I sure as hell I never do." He began sidling toward the door. "You hearing *dit-dahs* in your sleep these days, Chief?"

"Hell, no. What makes you say that?"

"Well," chuckled Stuart, "why did you ask that question?"

The ship's bell began gonging, signaling the end of the four-to-eight watch.

"Guess I'll get some chow and hit the sack," said Stuart, departing through the open hatchway.

I busied myself at the starboard radio position, and the Chief settled into his chair, his brow furrowed. Finally, he said, "I don't think I got any sleep at all last night. The goddamned air conditioning was makin' too much racket."

Each day after that the Chief made some comment about people that hear code when there is no code. Stuart and I let him do the talking, agreeing from time to time, but adding little. Starns, as usual, had not a clue that anything was going on.

One day Rothman popped into the shack with the news that he had actually *read* some of the code, that it was the real thing, not just his imagination. Or at least he was pretty damned sure it wasn't. Something funny was going on, he was certain. After a time, during which he glared from one of us to the other, he got up and left the shack. Stuart went over to the hatch and glanced down the passageway, to make sure he was gone.

"Let's feed him some stuff at a slightly higher volume. Give him something he can get his teeth into."

"How about we find out the call sign of the ship he's spent the most time on and send him a little code that will *make sense*."

"Oklahomer, you're hot!"

I had no trouble finding out that Ed had spent a big chunk of time back years ago on a buoy tender, and with this information we contrived what turned out to be an S O S message from that ship. And when it was ready, Stuart suggested that I send it, since my CW *fist* would be more difficult for the Chief to identify.

I went along, with the remark that at least my *fist* would be readable.

Stuart brought out the tape recorder and I began sending the message with a brass key, dropping *NRUD* here and there, which was the call sign of Ed's old buoy tender home. And when I was finished, we listened to it critically, adjusted the volume, and put the tape recorder back in its place in the radio shack overhead.

"That ought to give the old bastard something to think about," said Stuart.

"It's a lowdown dirty trick," I agreed, happily. "I think it's just about the ticket."

"Yup. Especially since the old *NRUD* went to her grave about twenty years ago!"

The next morning right after breakfast Stuart and I settled in the radio shack with our coffee and waited. The tape recorder had been turned on during my midwatch, and I had half-expected some reaction during that time. But all had gone quietly, and Starns had just a few minutes before assured us that Rothman had not showed his head during his four-to-eight.

When the ship's bell sounded the half hour, I suggested that perhaps the Chief had jumped over the side.

"I'll bet the old bastard's up to something," said Stuart.

"I think I'll go check on him."

But before I could get out of my chair there he was in the door, his face flushed and his breathing sounding like that of a dying horse.

"I swear I heard the old *Dolphin* sending out an *S O S* last night!" he burst out. "I'm certain of it!"

"What dolphin was that, Chief?" I asked, winking at Stuart behind the Chief's back. "You reckon dolphins actually send out code of some kind? I read somewhere—"

"Goddamnit, I was talkin' about the CGC *Dolphin*, a buoy tender I was on one time!"

"Oh," I said, frowning, "did you alert the bridge? Shouldn't we be going to her rescue?"

"You heard your old ship calling *SOS?*" exclaimed Stuart. "I thought the *Dolphin* went down in a bad storm off Cape Hatteras several years ago."

"Git to hell out of my chair!" yelled the Chief, lunging at Stuart.

"You seem to be running a bit late today," I suggested, as the two exchanged places.

"I've been rippin' hell out of my mattress, trying to find a source for that goddamned CW! At first, I figured maybe you bastards had started sendin' code down through the ventilation system, but I checked with Hancock in the engineroom and he told me the shack is on a different hook-up. Then I figured it had to be something planted in my mattress, so I checked for wires. But I was so goddamned mad I just tore my fuckin' mattress all to hell for nothin'! Nobody else in the compartment seemed to be able to hear the code but me!"

"Chief," said Stuart, looking glum. "This sounds bad."

"I swear to hell somebody's—!"

"Chief," said Stuart, "we've got a practicing head-shrink on board. Want I should call for an appointment?"

"You sonsabitches are responsible for this, sure as hell!" Rothman swiveled back and forth, glaring first at one of us and then the other. "I know it and I'll damn well prove it!"

"Just maybe, Chief," I suggested, drawing a long face, "you've begun to crack. It happens to the best of them. I knew a radio operator on an

Indian cutter once that slashed his wrists and jumped overboard during the dark of night. *Dit-happy* was the prognosis."

"Can the shit," said the Chief. "I'm not half as dit-happy as you two turds are."

Later that day Stuart erased the tape, and I made a new message, using the brass key and sending it in easily readable Morse Code. It went like this: "The Old Man is a dirty sonofabitch who ought to be fed to the sharks!" I repeated this until I had about fifteen minutes of tape.

"Now, let's turn up the volume just high enough for him to be sure to get the message!" Stuart said with a grin, chewing happily on his dead cigar.

"Do you think we need all the repeats?" I asked. "Wouldn't just once be enough?"

"Maybe we won't need all of it, but I'm pretty sure he'll lie there in his bunk and fume for a good while, and maybe he'll look some more for the speaker. We want him to do quite a bit of that."

Since I was scheduled for the midwatch that night, it was decided that the first playing of the new tape should take place then. Stuart wanted to be present; so around two I sent a kid on bridge watch down to get him. And when he came up he had two cups of coffee and some stale donuts that the cook had put out. We were riding high with our initial success, but we needed a final whammy.

A clincher, that would send old Rothman to a shrink.

"I went by and checked," said Stuart. "He's dead on his ass, trying to make up for lost time I guess. Turn it on."

"I'll bet he wondered why there was no code, for a change," I said. "Here goes nothing."

"He's going to shit," said Stuart, nodding.

I turned the tape recorder on and swiveled back with my hands behind my head.

The ship's clock bonged twice.

"I'll give him fifteen minutes," said Stuart, moving things around on the operating position, just to have something to do. "Twenty at the outside."

For fifteen minutes we sipped our coffee and waited, keeping an eye on the chronometer. I tuned across the shortwave bands looking for an AFR station. Then, at twenty past, I tried once again to raise the States. San Diego could not be that far away.

On the button, as the ship's clock gonged once, announcing two-thirty, there came a great slamming and banging from below, followed by a mighty bellowing from inside the passageway! It continued, getting louder; and, as we sat up at attention, I hissed, "Here he comes!"

"God damn!" cried Stuart. "He's cracked!"

We could easily trace Rothman's progress by the slams and bangs against bulkheads and railings, and by the volume of his cursing!

"He's at the ladder just below us!" reported Stuart. "Do you suppose the old boy's armed?"

"One thing for sure, he's dangerous!"

At that point Rothman's upper body burst through the hatchway, and there he hung, leaning just inside the shack, supported by his clutching hands. He glared at the two of us through bloodshot eyes, gasping for breath. When he was able, he cried out:

"I've got you, goddamn you! I knew it was you all along, you miserable, underhanded bastards!" He stumbled into the shack. "You are on report, both of you!"

Convinced by this time that he meant no bodily harm to us, I lifted first one foot and then the other and placed them on the typewriter in front of me. Stuart had not moved. He was seated in the Chief's favorite chair, and for a moment the two stared at each other.

"What's wrong, Chief? You *all right?*" asked Stuart.

"I caught you, goddamn you!"

His fists were doubled and he was beginning to do a little jig in the center of the radio shack. Then I noticed a fine white froth in the corners of his mouth!

"What will you put in that report, Chief?" I asked, not unkindly. "I'm curious to know."

"You're on report, by God! I'll show you! I'll—!"

"Are you going to say that I said the Old Man is a sonofabitch and ought to be tossed to the fish?"

"Now, you see? It *was* you!" He lined up on me, hammering the air with his clenched fists. He dropped into a fighting crouch.

Then suddenly old Rothman stiffened and his eyes bugged out a bit. As we watched, he slumped to the deck, assumed a fetal posture, and began to shake.

At that moment a voice from Speaker One announced, loud and clear, "That is a roger. San Diego Coast Guard out."

Stuart removed his cigar and said, "When it rains it pours. Better let the bridge know we're back in the civilized world while I notify Sick Bay about *this.*" He nodded toward Rothman.

Davy's Locker

◆

After checking in with the San Diego Coast Guard Radio, I tuned the ship's big Collins VHF transmitter to a very familiar frequency and called NMC, Coast Guard Radio, San Francisco. Since the distance was still too great for voice operation, I hauled out the brass key and started sending CW, asking for a signal check.

Suddenly, the silence of the radio shack was broken by a powerful carrier wave, so powerful I had to back off the volume. At first I was so rattled I had difficulty concentrating on the Morse Code that was flooding the place. Then, with heart pounding, I realized it was old NMC, in Frisco Town! I broke in and acknowledged, giving my ship's call.

From Frisco came: NRUS DE NMC DO NOT RECOGNIZE CALL SIGN BUT FIST SOUNDS VERY FAMILIAR HI HI INT RD K

Without giving it a thought, I hastened back with a bit of plain language of my own: "You've got RD all right. Don't you hooligans have a log book of the cutters in the Service?" Then it hit me that the Coastie in San Francisco had communicated with me in *plain language!* Who at NMC had the balls to do something like that? For a small cutter someplace to revert to plain language was one thing, but for the headquarters station to do it—! That was just not done, except maybe by a character named Collins!"

I had been so excited about making the contact with my old stomping grounds I had paid no attention to the style of the sending. But in retrospect, considering the sloppiness and the frequent glitches, it could be no one else but Collins, who had served with me on the CGC *Roger B. Taney!*

My reply was short and to the point: NMC DE NRUS HI HI JC YOU REBEL GOODTIME CHARLEY K.

From Collins, "What are you trying to pull? I looked NRUS up in the book, and there's no such animal on the West Coast. And I know damned well you're not on an icebreaker in the North Atlantic. Why don't you just admit you're on that little nothing *Alert* up around Crescent City someplace?"

"You go right on believing that, JC, but in about two minutes I'm going to have a priority message for you. Can you monitor this frequency?"

"I'm going no place for about three hours."

I reached for the voicetube. "Bridge!"

"Bridge, aye. What's up?"

"Tell the O. O. D. I'm in touch with Frisco, and ask him if he wishes to make our whereabouts known."

"Hang on."

        *   *   *

Three hectic, wonderful days later the *Storis* steamed into San Francisco Bay, with a full halyard of pennants. It was truly like a homecoming to me. All I could do was hang onto a lifeline and grin!

The crew on the icebreaker was, of course, a tired and scroungy lot. Every man not on watch was lined up along the lifelines to take a gander at the fabled Bay. Not only was this one of the world's greatest liberty ports, it was our first port-of-call in over a month!

As we neared Government Island, most of us moved to the port side to view the drab barracks buildings and the two cutters tied up at the dock, the CGC *Chautauqua* and the CGC *Taney.* We were greeted by what appeared to be the full complements of both cutters, and on the dock a large number of the Ship's Company from the Base were on hand to wave and shout insults.

Having turned the radioroom over to Starns, Stuart and I joined the spectators on deck just as a commotion occurred on the stern of the *Chautauqua.*

"I think they're yelling at you, Red," said Stuart. "Were you ever on one of those Indian cutters?"

"I was this one and the Escanaba, as well as the big dude up ahead," I said, and pointing toward the *Taney,* I added, "Remember the Jeep incident?"

Somebody on the stern of the *Chautauqua* caught my attention, "Hey, Red! I thought you was on the *Alert* in Eureka!" Then a swab on the *Taney* countered with, "I thought he was in Eureka on the *Bramble!*"

"I hope you're on speakin' terms with the hard cases on these cutters," said Stuart. "We don't need no complications ashore tonight."

We moored astern of the *Chautauqua,* and when the gangplank was in place I told Stuart to hang on, that I was going to catch up on the scuttlebutt on the Chat.

"Yeah, well, don't take more'n about five minutes because as soon as I'm ready for liberty I'm headin' out."

"It takes more than an hour and five minutes for you to get ready," I said with a laugh. "Don't forget I'm your guide in this port."

*   *   *   *   *

Stuart Heller, who had bragged on a regular basis that no liberty port in the world could compete with *Bahsten,* took to the Bay Area like a duck takes to a mud puddle. He couldn't get over the party attitude of San Franciscans and the limitless possibilities of the Bay cities. On our way to Fisherman's Wharf on our first liberty he blew cigar smoke in my face and said, "Goddamn, Red, if this aint Bahsten, Baltermore, and D. C., all rolled into one! You was a crazy bastid for ever leavin'!"

"It's better than Norfolk," I said, nodding. "There are no signs on the lawns here that say, *Sailors and Dogs Keep Off.*"

That night I introduced Stuart to Goodrich, who was still on the CGC *Chautauqua* and went on liberty with us. I was going to introduce him to Archer, but when we checked in at Pier Forty-Three-and-a-Half the cook on the Coast Guard tug told us he had transferred to the CGC *Yacona* and was in Eureka, California. I jumped all over Gooch for not keeping up with our curly-haired boatswain's mate friend and saving us a trip all the way to Fisherman's Wharf.

We had two rounds of drinks at the *Harbor View Lounge* and headed for Chinatown, landing at a gay bar called the *Paper Doll.* Of course, Gooch and I did not bother to mention what kind of a place it was to Stuart. This turned out to be our mistake of the evening.

We were ushered to a table close to the stage, and it was obvious from the outset that Stuart was impressed with the floor show, four very attractive and extremely well-built dancing girls. He couldn't keep his eyes off them; and once, when they were mooning the audience, their way of saluting, he leaped upon the stage and stuffed a five-dollar bill beneath the G-string of one of the girls. As soon as they finished their number, the four of them slipped on skimpy little outfits and joined us for drinks, plugging in between us and jostling us, as pretty girls will sometimes do to sailors. The trouble started when Stuart ran his hand beneath the very short skirt of the girl he had tipped and made the discovery that *she was a he,* and very well slung at that.

The night ended with a hasty retreat, on our part, back across the Bay Bridge and, sometime around midnight, a walk across the Government Island bridge.

The day word was passed that the *Storis* would be shoving off for Seattle at dawn the next morning, Stuart and I, in undress blues, visited *Ted and Roy's,* the little hooligan bar in East Oakland, for a few quiet beers.

The place was packed and there was electricity in the air. But we had made a solemn pact that we were not going to touch hard liquor.

"Let's do a boilermaker, for *auld lang syne*," said Stuart before we had finished our first beer. "This is a swingin' place!"

"No way, Hosay. After this beer I'm heading back to the ship. But you do whatever you wish."

"I swear!" groaned Stuart. "The farther you get from that little country girl the worse you get. By the time we reach Alasker you'll be a teetotaler. Well, don't wait up for me."

"All right, I'll have just one with you. But that's it."

*　　　*　　　*

The northern California coast had become as familiar to me as San Francisco Bay, and I liked every foot of it. From the Big Sur and Pebble Beach to Sand Point, on the Oregon state line, I knew ever cove and inlet. Now, as the *Storis* steamed north, I hung out topside like a homesick kid and drank in the scenery, with only an occasional visit to the messdeck for coffee. Stuart and the others who had lined up to see us off had long ago hit the sacks to dream of liberty in Seattle.

As we cruised past Humboldt Bay the evening of the first day out from Frisco, I tried to imagine Archer sitting at the long bar in the *Triangle* listening to Rosa Rita sing Portuguese songs. It was funny how things had turned out for me and my two hometown buddies. I had begun my Coastie career there in Eureka, and now Curly was finishing his there. Of course, for all I knew, he might shipover, become a twenty-year man. Provided he could fake another eye examination.

Finally, as the green forests of Oregon loomed off our starboard bow, I went below for some sack time. I had spent most of that day on deck, in rain gear, pondering some heavy questions. One of which was, did I really want to get out of the Coast Guard?

The scuttlebutt began to circulate that our mail had been routed on to Juneau! However, I had had the forethought to send Jamie the Seattle Coast Guard P. O. box number, which I just happened to remember from that character-building trip on the *Chautauqua*. Something good had come out of that terrible trip aboard the subchaser, after all.

"This is gettin' to be disgustin'," Stuart growled, glaring at me. "I haven't heard from Diane or any of my family since we left Baltimore, and as far I know we haven't stopped a single time that you haven't received mail from that little Indian princess of yours."

"Mail comes to them that use their noggins," I said.

"Let me read one of your letters."

"That will be the day."

The PA system blared, "Liberty for the Port Section!"

"Well, I guess that's me," said Stuart.

"You're supposed to be in the Starboard Section, mate. How did you work that?"

"Liberty generally comes to them that know somebody in the Office. Come on, get your duds on. I'm supposed to meet Boats in the messdeck."

Sure enough, when we finally made it to the messdeck, Ole Olson was drinking coffee with two CPO's.

"Old Red," he said to me with a grin. "Take a load off an' tell us about Seattle."

"Chief, you've been here more than I have," I said.

He shook his head, "Only once, back in '42. This was my jumping off place for the South Pacific. Now, the way I hear it you've been by here recently. Where's the hottest place in town?"

"He means in the Red Light District," said Stuart, nudging me. "Not a motion picture show or art gallery."

"Actually, I don't have the slightest idea where the *hottest place* is, but I can point you toward the so-called Red Light District."

"You two want company tonight?" asked the big boatswain's point-blank, looking at me and then at Stuart.

Stuart said quickly, "We might need him, Red."

"No, we won't *need* him, Stuart," I warned, "but, Boats, we'd like for you to go along with us anyway. All we're going to do is have a few quiet drinks and Stuart here is planning to glance casually at civilians of the female persuasion. Nothing more."

"I'm with you on that," agreed Olson, looking pleased. "No rough stuff till we git to Alaska."

I nodded, looking hard at Stuart, waiting for some sign that the matter was settled. The thought occurred to me that this big, good-natured Swede just might have a settling effect upon Stuart. That night in Cristobal excepted, Ole had surely proved that he was a peacemaker and a gentleman.

The three of us took the bus in, accompanied by about thirty other liberty hounds, all of whom were anxious to *see the sights and sample some of the local stuff.* I for one was hoping we could shake the others right away. As it turned out, Ole and Stuart had the same notion. When the bus stopped, we skipped the nearest pub and went to the second. However, to our chagrin a number of the uninitiated were right behind us.

"This will not do," said Stuart, glancing at me. "I'm not going to spend my evening with this ugly bunch of hooligans."

"They are our shipmates," I kidded, "don't be hateful to them."

We all lined up, twelve abreast at the long bar; and the bright, expectant faces of our shipmates said plainer than words that they were looking forward to a good time—with us.

"They remind me of a pack of hounds," said Stuart, not attempting to save any feelings. He leaned over and down the bar, glaring at them. "Hey, the next time we zig I want you fucks to zag. Do you get my drift?"

A ripple of grumbling went down the bar.

"But we don't know anything about Seattle," complained one of Ole's deckhands. "We figured you guys would know where to go here in Seattle."

"You stay right here and have fun," said Ole, not unkindly. "Do some exploring on your own after we've moved on, follow your natural instincts. It's more fun that way."

"Yeah," said Stuart. "We don't want to see any of your ugly faces again tonight." To Ole and me he said, lowering his voice, "Come on, finish your drinks and let's find another joint." He hopped off his stool and headed for the door. The Chief downed the rest of his beer and fell in behind him, leaving me to pick up the tab for the three of us. At the door Stuart waited, standing to one side while Ole and I filed through and watching the sad sacks at the bar to make sure his order was being carried out.

"As long as they're all bunched up, they'll never find anything," commented Ole to me, sounding a bit worried, like an old mother hen. "Three's a maximum number for hunting skirts." Then he glanced at me and grinned. "Of course, I was thinking of them, not us. You're not interested in skirts these days."

"Hey," I scoffed, "let's don't carry that too far."

Ten minutes later, after passing half a dozen taverns, we shouldered up to a high bar in big place on Coeur d'Leon Street. I glanced around, casing the joint, deciding that we could have done worse. The music was a bit loud and the place was full of blue collars and their dates, but I spotted an empty booth along one wall that looked big and spacious. I exchanged glances with Ole and Stuart and headed for it.

No sooner were we settled in and sipping on beers than I realized that something was wrong. A tall, sad-faced man with a crooked nose at the nearest table was staring at Olson. Apparently, Boats had bumped him on his way to the booth. From his rough civilian clothes, including a turtleneck sweater, I decided he was a merchant sailor or a dock worker. There were three other men at his table, all rough-looking characters.

"Goddamned Navy," I heard the man say.

I glanced at Ole, who was paying no attention to anything but his draft beer. Stuart, likewise, had no idea anything was going on nextdoor.

I lifted my beer and drank. What the heck, I told myself, maybe this slug will cool off if we ignore him.

But it was not to be. Suddenly, Sad Face was standing and saying in a loud voice in our direction, "If the goddamned Navy swabs would stay out of this town, it might be fit for decent folks."

Ole poked me in the short ribs and snickered. "I do believe that swab is trying to rile you, Red Dog."

"Not me, I'm no Navy swab."

"I know that and you know that," said Ole, still grinning. He slid out of the booth and stood up, facing Sad Face and his three friends. "What's your problem, mate?" Olson's voice was so soft I could just barely make out what he had said.

I glanced at Stuart and shook my head, wishing I had stayed aboard ship.

"You sonofabitch!" shouted Sad Face, leaping to his feet. His chair crashed backward into the next table.

The bartender, without saying a word, headed for the telephone at the end of the bar. Stuart and I got out of the booth in a hurry and lined up with Ole.

I felt strangely indifferent to the whole thing, like a bystander, and actually gave some momentary thought to departing, the first chance I got. An angry face, belonging to one of the men at the table, was suddenly obscuring my view, his mouth flapping. I struck out, thinking, *Why is this jerk mad at me?* I was vaguely aware that Olson was swapping punches with Sad Face. Stuart was no longer by my side. Maybe he had done what I had thought of doing.

In a split second the evening had been fairly launched. And whose fault was it? Ole's, of course, but I had seen him do nothing that would have provoked a fight. Maybe it was, after all, just the sight of our uniforms. Maybe the hooligan was just looking for a fight.

At the bar someone yelled, "The police is on the way!"

In the mad stampede that followed, I found myself sliding through the door to the street. Stuart, unruffled, appeared beside me. We backed off to the middle of the street, keeping an ear out for the sound of a siren. Ole Olson suddenly shot through the door and headed toward us.

"Follow me, mates. I just remembered a swingin' place where sailors of all kinds are welcome, but riffraff aint. If it's still open."

"Maybe we ought to call it a night," I suggested.

"We will, real soon, Red, real soon. But first let's see if ole *Davy's Locker* is still the swingin' place it used to be."

We headed down the street, led by Ole, and before we reached the first intersection we heard the distant wailing of a siren. The big boatswain's mate began complaining that it was about time we settled in and did some serious drinking. We were letting other things get in our way.

Half a block from our destination, Olson pointed it out, a big black building with not a single window facing the street. One neon sign, in flowing (cursive) red, took up most of the false front, proclaiming nervously, "Davy's Locker."

The front door to this place was so massive and heavy Olson had to strain to get it open. Stuart filed through first, stopped abruptly, and I stumbled into him. Outside, the street was almost pitch dark, and would have been had it not been for the big red jittery sign; but inside it was even darker. Over the bar were tiny pinpoints of red light spaced about four feet apart, and around the gymnasium-like lounge were other pinpoints of green and blue and yellow lights, positioned well apart on the walls and at some of the tables.

"I don't think I can see how to drink in here," observed Stuart. "Somebody lead me to a table."

"Now, don't you fret," said Ole. "In no time at all you will be adjusted to this place. And the thing I remember most is what wonderful surprises keep coming out of the shadows in here."

"Yeah," I scoffed, "I can imagine all kinds of surprises."

"Order something at the bar and I'll go find us a booth."

Stuart and I did as we were told, agreeing that Boats was on an impossible mission. For one thing, we could see no sign of a booth; and, for another, the place was so crowded it was going to be difficult finding a chair or a stool. After we had put down two *Olympia Lights*, I suggested that we go looking for Ole.

He had been right about adjusting to the darkness. We saw him, finally, at a booth talking to four very large men in new Maritime Marine uniforms. As we drew close, it became clear that he was urging these partiers to vacate their corner table for him and *his party*. His argument was that he and his friends had been at sea a very long time and therefore deserved the booth more than they did. And, besides, he reminded them, this was a *Navy* bar, not a Merchant Marine bar.

Why the four men had let Ole advance his argument so far I could not imagine. They were with four attractive young women, who were becoming impatient for his departure.

"And you can leave your nice lady friends where they are," said Ole in his softest, most obliging voice. "They'll be all right with us."

Stuart shifted his White Owl to the side of his face, nudging me.

The men at the table had risen and were staring at the big Swede, with side glances now at Stuart and me. When Ole paused in his monologue, one of them blurted:

"Obviously, Mack, you're—!"

Olson took a quick step forward and hit the man in the face; and even though he was in close he struck with such force the big man flew into the booth, taking down two of the women.

Suddenly, amidst the screaming of the women and the bellowing of the merchant sailors, fights began to break out all over the big lounge. Everybody was shoving and swinging, and it was all I could do to defend my face! I yelled at Stuart but my voice was lost in the bedlam. Near the door, I thought I caught a glimpse of the White Owl and yelled, "Come on, Stuart, let's find Olson and drag him back to the ship!"

Then Stuart was in my face yelling, "You take the one with the bottle, and I'll take the one that's trying to escape through the front door!"

Looking around for somebody with a bottle, I saw Ole punching a Navy sailor. A civilian, apparently eager to get in on the fun, made the bad judgment of bringing a half-filled bottle of Pabst Blue Ribbon down across Ole's head. If the man had used the thick edge of the bottom, he might have had some success; but as it was the weapon shattered into a thousand pieces around Ole's head and therefore did little more than get his attention. With one short jab, he sent the man flying backward into the crowd.

I began trying to get Ole's attention. Finally, he looked at me and yelled, "Come on, Red, let's join the ladies!"

But the ladies, all four of them, had somehow escaped. How they had managed it was a mystery to me, because the entire lounge had become a battleground. It occurred to me that their going, however it was accomplished, was probably a godsend.

"They just left, Ole!" I screamed. "Come on, I think we can catch them outside!"

Without hesitation, Olson fell in behind me and me managed to get through the door to the street. Stuart joined us on the sidewalk, just as the police came swooping in. With billy clubs in hand, they entered *Davy's Locker.*

Ole had forgot all about the women and agreed that it was time to hit the sack. And on the bus back to the ship, he put his arms around our respective necks and purred, "I want to tell you boys something. Both of you. I think you'll do to ride the river with."

"What river are we talking about?" asked Stuart, suspiciously.

"We appreciate that sentiment, Boats," I said, "but I for one question whether it would be advisable for the three of us to attempt a river together. Any river."

"That you will, that you will!" said the Boats, irrelevantly.

Juneau

———————◆———————

The CGC *Storis* entered the warm Japanese Current outside Puget Sound, heeling slightly as it nosed about to a more northerly heading. All sign of life had disappeared from topside, but there at the port lifeline Stuart and I stood beneath the dark figures moving about on the bridge. From deep inside Stuart Heller's hood came an occasional puff of cigar smoke, foul and out of place in that crisp, virgin air. For sometime we stood there taking in the rugged Washington coast.

"We'll make it to Ketchikan day after tomorrow morning," I said, for openers. I felt good in the impregnable foul-weather jacket and my old golfball cap, with its brim turned down over my ears.

"What makes you think so, Einstein? I've got a twenty that says it'll be at least four days."

"I don't want to take your money."

"I insist," he said, removing his wallet and showing me a twenty-dollar bill. "There's no way we can make it by day after tomorrow."

"Okay, if you insist."

"Have you made this trip before? Come on, let's see if the messcooks have made some fresh coffee."

We went below to the messdeck and found an almost-empty coffee urn. No one had been near the thing all day. Stuart removed two mugs from the rack and handed me one. Leaning over the serving counter and peering inside the galley, he shouted, "Hey, how about some god-damned coffee?"

Suddenly, the cook himself appeared and glared at the two of us. "Drink that up and you'll git more!"

"Yeah, yeah," said Stuart. "Thanks a whole hell of a lot."

We took the mud to a table and sat down.

"I should never bet with you, Red," said Stuart, looking glum.

"You've got that right, Stuart, you shouldn't. I don't make sucker bets."

"You got a goddamned map out and measured the distance from Seattle to Ketchikan, figured our speed, allowed for currents and winds, and came up with day after tomorrow."

"That's right I did. You want to give me the twenty now or when we tie up at the Juneau dock?"

"No, you didn't go to all that trouble. Nobody would do all that to win a goddamn bet. Not even you."

"You've already lost twenty. Want to make it forty?"

"We could always run into a rock or something," he said, grimacing. "I hear this Inside Passage is full of crags and boulders."

The ship's bell began to give it hell, counting out eight hundred hours; and without saying anything I got up and returned my mug to the serving counter. On my way out of the messdeck, I lifted one finger at Stuart in farewell.

"I'll see you at noon," he said, filling the air above him with cigar smoke. His way of lifting a middle finger to the cook.

I had to laugh at the thought of what was going to take place in about a minute, when the cook picked up a whiff of White Owl smoke.

Two mornings later when I went out on deck early, the shock of what I saw caused me to stop in my tracks! I was on the starboard side at 'midships and my view to the port was blocked by the superstructure of the ship, but to the right about six hundred yards away was a white-blanketed but still very rugged coastline. Looking toward the bow, I could see that the cutter was moving down the center of a waterway lined on both sides by snow-covered mountains that came right down to the water's edge.

It was a white world with a brilliant strip of very blue water cutting through it, and up head perhaps a couple of miles I could see buildings and smoke coming from chimneys! I burst out laughing. It had to be Ketchikan! Stuart was suddenly behind me, hunkered inside his peacoat collar.

"I was just up on the bridge," he snarled, "and sure as hell that is the little tourist Mecca known as Ketchikan."

"I'd like the twenty in cash," I said. "No IOU's."

"Tell you what. How about I buy the drinks the first night in Juneau? You'll make money on the deal."

"Nothing doing. I'm thinking of becoming a teetotaler. So fork over."

"Can it wait till we go below? I don't carry cash around in my dungarees."

As we approached the little picture postcard town, word was passed that we would tie up overnight and be on our way early the next morning. All hands were free to go ashore.

"That's the first time I ever heard of such a thing," I said. "Nobody at all to keep our home safe?"

"Yeah, who's gonna man the gangplank?" added Stuart. "I can't get across that ten feet of water without help."

Without bothering to change into uniforms, the two of us waited at 'midships for the gangplank to be put into place and were the first ashore. On the dock and all the way to the main street of the town, townspeople were lined up to shake our hands and welcome us to Ketchikan. They hadn't seen a tourist since August, they told us, and didn't expect any until the following spring.

"Let's find a saloon," said Stuart. "Everybody's down at the ship; so maybe we'll be able to help ourselves."

"Too early for me," I said. "I just want to look around and breathe some of this great air!" I noisily sucked in a lung full of air.

"It's the same air that's on the ship."

"Not so. This air ashore is enough to make a person drunk! We brought most of that air on the ship from Baltimore. And some of the hot air came all the way from Boston."

We walked along the street, drifted into a few shops, and not once did we see anyone to take our money for items we wanted to buy. Apparently, everyone, as Stuart had said, was down welcoming the crew of the *Storis* to town. I selected some picture postcards, leaving coins on the counter. Stuart found some White Owls, which he stuffed inside his peacoat quickly.

"That'll be a buck-twenty," I said, pointing toward the cigar box whence he had removed the cigars.

"The hell you say! What'd you do, figure in the tax, too?"

"Yep. Hand it over."

On our way back toward the ship, we began meeting the returning townspeople.

"Would you boys like a do-nut?" asked a lady standing in the door of a bakery. "Here, take a sack full back to your shipmates!"

I thanked her and tried to pay, but she blushed and told me it was on the house.

"We don't ever get to see people from the States up here this time of year," she confided. "Please take the do-nuts."

Another lady took us through her shop looking for a special souvenir for each, although we had not mentioned wanting anything. "I want you to remember us," she smiled. "It's so good to see American sailors, especially Coast Guardsmen!"

In front of a small tavern, we paused and Stuart said, "You don't suppose the drinks here are free, too?"

At that moment a man stuck his head through the open doorway. "I'll be open about four, sailors. First drink is on the house."

"Well," I said with a grin, "I guess you got your answer."

*　　　　　*　　　　　*

After Ketchikan the ship seemed to float along in a wonderland of snow, ice, and jagged outcroppings. It was impossible for me to stand on deck and resist the inebriating effect of the air and the bright, sharp images of things. All sights and sounds and smells seemed to take on a purer quality in this frozen northland. The sky was bluer than any I had ever seen, and the water looked as though it had been artificially dyed a brilliant blue.

I strolled about the ship, tipsy from just breathing in the fresh, clean air, reminded of Emily Dickinson's poem about the little tippler, who was an *inebriate of dew.*

"You're turning to mush," observed Stuart, when I quoted a few lines of the poem to him. "Next thing I know you'll be looking for a church to join."

"Nature is my church," I said. "I go there every day."

Stuart looked off, grimacing and puffing on his cigar.

"Let's change the subject. I say we'll make to the dock at Juneau before evening chow today. But I don't want your money."

"Hah!" Stuart blasted. "I'll make my twenty back on this!"

"Speaking of that twenty—"

We climbed the ladder to the passageway that led to the radio shack; and in the shack we found Chief Rothman talking to the bridge. He was saying, "Yes, Sir. I will, Sir. Thank you, Sir." Since his trip to an analyst in San Francisco, he had become a changed man. He looked around at me. "Red, you'll take the first watch after we get to Juneau. We'll be doing six-on and eighteen-off on two dead circuits! What do you think about them apples?"

"What time do we get in?" asked Stuart.

"The bridge is saying sixteen hundred hours, just before chow. We'll git to eat tied up at our own dock, for a change."

"Is that today or tomorrow?" asked Stuart, frowning.

I put out a hand, palmside up. "Do you want to give me the forty right now?"

"God damn it, Chief! Are you sure about our ETA?" complained Stuart. "That can't be right!"

"No doubt about it. We're on the home stretch now."

After a pause and a couple of hard looks at me, Stuart said, "We might still run into something."

And so it was, about sundown, some two hours after evening chow, we tied up at our permanent mooring, a quarter of a mile from downtown Juneau. Around us on all sides were towering, snow-covered mountains; and to me there was a soul-satisfying feeling that we had at last reached home. No more waking in the mornings to that slightly off-balanced feeling and seeing nothing through the portholes but endless miles of water.

It had been a long, tiring journey, a veritable odyssey as it were, one that none of us would ever forget. And as the engines were stilled, it seemed as if the entire ship gave a great sigh of relief, as she settled in next to her mooring.

I went to the radioroom and relieved Starns, who was anxious to explore the city of Juneau. And once Stuart and the Chief had dropped by on their way ashore, I settled at the typewriter and wrote a *billet-doux* of such charm and tenderness that, try as I would, I could not improve upon it. Finally, convinced that I had said exactly what I wanted to say, I made two copies of the original and addressed envelopes to Jody Summers, Alice Chastain, and Darleen Caulfield.

And then, with a great sigh of satisfaction, I settled in to write a long and very detailed letter to one Jamie Lee, in which I said, among other things:

"Dear sweet beautiful lady of my dreams, how lucky I am to have your love! When I think of how chance and coincidence plays such a dominating role in people's lives, I can only marvel that we found each other before it was too late. Stay always the same as you are right now. Don't go into the world, as I did, risking temptations of all kinds. For although you might escape unharmed, you will not escape unchanged.

"Someday, when I am finished with all this, I will be with you. Until then I will have to be content with fantasies. I will see you as you go about your morning chores and when you take your dog and go for a walk to see Jessica. And when you visit our secret rendezvous, my spirit will be there with you.

"From that moment you offered yourself to me in the hay I have known that you are the one. There can be no other for me, so take very good care of yourself and write to me often.

"With all my love, now and forever, Red."

    *   *   *

The *Storis*, which had eight solid feet of concrete in the bow for making mincemeat out of ice-jams, had been sent to Alaska not so much as an icebreaker as an air-sea rescue ship and as a means of transportation for the Provost Marshal of the Territory. Who just happened to be the skipper of the *Storis*, newly appointed. Our ship, we were informed, was to be the base from which the top law enforcement officer of the Territory would operate. The Skipper would act as the judge and the jury of all crimes committed by and against the Eskimos of Alaska, as well as the soul arbiter of any other crime that in some way affected the United States Government.

This, of course, included crimes committed on the remote islands of the Aleutian Chain and in distant Eskimo villages. Every six months the *Storis* would make its round of those places accessible by the sea where crimes had been committed.

The second evening after our arrival in Juneau, Stuart, a self-proclaimed tour guide of the city after one liberty, invited me to leave off with letter-writing long enough to sample the hot buttered rum of a nearby pub. A recent snowstorm had reduced the road into town to a single pathway, up which the two of us walked single file.

Perhaps an eighth of a mile from the ship we caught sight of a blinking red neon light up ahead that was just peeping over a pile of snow.

"The *Triangle Tavern*," said Stuart. "Old-world charm. You'll like it. They don't do better hot-buttered rums in Bahsten."

"Seems I've heard that name before," I said. "You don't suppose it's a chain." When he stopped and looked back at me, I shrugged and said, "Sounds good to me. Do you suppose I can drink forty-dollars worth of that hot-buttered rum all in one sitting?"

Once again he stopped and turned. "Listen, Red, I'm not carryin' that kind of money."

"How much money you carrying?"

"Thirty-six bucks."

"All right, hand over thirty now. I can wait until payday for the other ten."

"Who's goin' to pay for the drinks? Mine, I mean."

When we shoved open the heavy oak door and entered, taking a great deal of snow in with us, Eddie Arnold was crooning *Give Me One Dozen Roses* on the jukebox. The only person in the place was a short, stocky, balding bartender with a happy smile on his face.

"Sid, I want you to meet a former friend of mine. I think his name's Hall. He's recently of Broken Bow, Oklahomer."

The bartender reached across the bar to shake my hand, "Danged good to make your acquaintance, Red!"

I took his hand. "Don't pay any attention to him, Sid. This foul-smelling pile of Bahsten beans owes me forty bucks. Doubled that would be eighty, and he's willing to spend it all here tonight."

Sid was as happy as a birthday child. "I'll just get busy on a couple of buttered rums." He turned away chuckling, "I can see right now old Juneau's about to come alive!"

*   *   *

A few days later I talked Stuart into walking into town with me to do some shopping. I needed some film and stationery, and he was always in need of White Owls. It was a bright, still morning and, since my purpose had nothing to do with pubs and drinking, it was a miracle he agreed to go with me.

Snow was piled high in town, as it had been in Ketchikan. But in the territorial capital one layer had followed another until at least three feet of hard-packed and very slippery snow covered all surfaces; and, although a narrow path had been beaten down in the center of the sidewalks, the mountains of white stuff completely blocked from view the other side of the street. At each corner it was necessary to proceed with extreme caution to avoid colliding with someone approaching from the right or the left.

Prices on certain items, I found, were very high. A hamburger, for example, was fifty cents, which was at least twice as high as in the States. Food of any kind and perishables like vegetables and fruit were especially dear. A waitress at the snack bar of a drugstore informed me that although Alaska grew enough vegetables in the Matinuska Valley to feed the entire Territory, the cost of transporting them to Juneau was so great it was actually cheaper to buy from Seattle!

Once again stocked up on cigars, Stuart was ready to explore the town for additional taverns. I, on the other hand, wanted to shoot some of the film I had bought. So at a street corner near the only drugstore in town, we split up.

"If you don't watch it, Red, you're going to develop into an old maid," complained Stuart. "What's happened to my old Norfolk and Panamer buddy?"

"I'll meet you back at the *Triangle* in say two hours."

Stuart nodded happily and clomped off.

It had turned blustery by the time I made it back to the little tavern on the edge of town. Two Coasties from the bridge gang were sitting at the bar, and as I joined them Heller came in, beating snow from his heavy overshoes and windbreaker.

Sid hustled up two buttered rums, beaming his pleasure.

"Here's to one hell of a storm," said Stuart, lifting his mug.

As if in response to his toast, there came the piercing blast of the ship's whistle, which even at an eighth of a mile away was so loud it brought all four of us at the bar to attention. It continued, unbroken, a signal that we were to double-time it back, that the ship was going out!

"But on a night like this!" protested the friendly bartender. "You guys realize it's gonna be forty degrees below zero out in the Passage?"

As we took our last gulps of hot-buttered rum and ran through the door into the snow, the ship's whistle paused and then cut loose again. Then, to our surprise, just as we took off down the pathway, a Jeep came plowing through the snow and stopped for us!

"It's a real emergency!" shouted Ted Johnson, a quartermaster on the ship and the driver of the Jeep. "And you four are holding up the ship's departure!"

"Well, pardon the shit out of us," said Stuart. "How the hell was we to know?"

As it turned out, our mission on this terrible night was to go to Haines, a distance of about seventy-five miles, to *rescue* Governor Gruening and his party. They had flown in from Washington, D. C., and found themselves grounded at White Horse, Yukon Territory. The *Storis* was going to pick them up at the nearest port city, Haines, and take them the rest of the way to Juneau!

"Fifty men and a dozen officers are going to risk life and limb, not to mention a million-dollar icebreaker, in weather that's life-threatening to an Eskimo, just to speed up the homeward journey of a few politicians!" complained Stuart.

"You should squawk," I joked. "Think of all the money you saved by this. I'm keeping track of what you owe me."

"Shit, you'll never give up till I'm out that entire forty bucks."

A few minutes later in the radioroom of the *Storis* Chief Rothman delivered a little speech. "In the report of this night's work we'll no doubt get credit for *saving* the lives of several important people. You two go down to the quarterdeck and get your foul-weather gear. Better do it right away, before it's all picked over."

The quarterdeck was piled high with crates of foul-weather gear, and the Supply Officer himself was overseeing the distribution of heavy coats that reached to our heels and were equipped with fur-lined hoods. One storekeeper was issuing face masks and heavy boots, and another was checking off names.

Chief Olson came by as I was examining one of the face masks. I waved it at him and said, "Don't you think this is overkill, Boats?"

"Have you ever been out in forty-below weather, Red?" he asked. "It doesn't feel any colder than ten-below, but it freezes your flesh instantly. And if you breathe it, your lungs'll never be the same again."

As the ship was getting underway, word was passed that no one was to expose himself on deck without the protection of the hooded overcoats and the face-masks.

It was the darkest night I had ever experienced, and I was anxious to get outside the radioroom in the fresh air. And since I wasn't standing a watch, as soon the ship cleared the harbor, I buttoned and snapped myself up and stepped out onto the starboard wing of the bridge. Not one square centimeter of my body was exposed to the deadly air; and although what I was breathing felt very cold to my lungs, I might as well have been inside a capsule looking through a window.

At first I could see nothing at all, including the bridge railings and the very ladder I had just ascended! But slowly the dim outline of the ship's superstructure began to be faintly visible. Then, with a great deal of imagination, I realized I could just make out the rising and falling bow. In time I began to think I could see the vague shadows of land masses around us, but one moment it was there and the next it wasn't. We were, of course, relying entirely upon the radar!

"That you, Red?" asked Ted Johnson, at my right shoulder.

By what magic this tall drink of water had been able to recognize me I had no idea. I grunted and said something about the difficulty we were going to have locating Haines in that pitch blackness.

Finally, deciding that it was useless to worry about something over which I had no influence, much less control, I slapped Johnson on the shoulder and returned to the warm and cozy radioroom.

"How about some coffee?" I asked Stuart and Rothman, both of whom were on watch. They nodded quickly and I ducked back outside and headed for the messdeck, feeling my way along the railings. Starns was sitting at one of the long tables with two yeoman when I entered. When he saw me taking down three mugs from the big rack beside the coffee urn, he hastened over.

"Need any help?"

"Sure," I said, "but you'll have to put on all your gear."

"Naw, I won't need it just to run up to the shack."

"What are you going to do, hold your breath? Take my word for it, that air will destroy your lungs."

"It's not *that* cold!" he continued. "You know how the Coast Guard is about safety precautions. Besides, I read a Jack London story once about a man that traveled a long distance in minus-forty-degree temperatures, and he had nothin' on his face."

"Maybe that was just a story," I said." Maybe Jack London meant to write *minus-twenty* degrees. If I remember correctly, the man died as a result of the cold."

Starns laughed and headed out with two mugs of coffee. Making sure my face mask was on tight, I followed with two additional mugs. Sure enough, even before I reached the ladder here came the kid, with two empty mugs. He stumbled into me, coughing pitifully.

I paused, started to go back, then thinking better of it, went on up the ladder with the coffee and sandwiches. It was no easy climb up to the radioroom, since the ship was rolling and pitching. When I made it back to the messdeck a few minutes later for another mug of coffee, I was told that Starns had one to Sick Bay.

⋆　　　　　　　　⋆　　　　　　　　⋆

To my astonishment, we made it to Haines without a hitch. It was one A. M., local time, when we docked at a frozen pier that someone said was Haines. I was back on the starboard wing of the bridge on a break from the midwatch when four bundles of fur moved cautiously down the pier and boarded the ship. They were immediately whisked up to Officers' Country, and the ship lost no time reversing engines and moving away from the long arm of the pier.

We arrived back in Juneau about mid-morning, tired and testy, especially the deck gang and the grease monkeys. Stuart was threatening to send a dispatch to Washington, D. C., about the whole thing; but I pointed out to him that doing such a thing would more than likely terminate his tour of duty in the U. S. Coast Guard. That trip to Haines had been an experience that none of us would never forget, I added, so why not forget about making a fuss?

"You know, Red, you'll never get out of this hooligan outfit. You love everything about it. Doesn't he, Starns?"

The kid, just back from Sick Bay nodded, painfully, pointing toward his throat.

"You're wrong," I said. "I've got less than three months to go now, and I can't wait to collect my severance pay and shake the dust of the Coast Guard forever. I'm going to marry my girl and go back to college."

"I've got twenty bucks you'll ship over. No, make it forty."

"That's a sucker bet, Stuart. I don't want to take your money."

He pulled out his wallet and showed me the corners of two sawbucks. "This is where I'll recoup a goodly part of my losses."

"You want in on this, Starns?" I asked. "Don't forget, I have never lost a bet to this swab."

Starns got out his wallet and showed me the empty insides, again pointing toward his throat.

"I'll advance you credit."

Cautiously, he began to nod, looking at Stuart. Then in a strained whisper he said, "You'll probably go ahead and get out just to win the bet."

One morning in mid-December, immediately following chow, I was summoned to the XO's office. The scuttlebutt among the bridge gang was that I was going to be advised not to attempt to reënlist. One variation of this gossip was that if I did request another tour of duty I would be refused on the grounds that I had not lived up to the high standards required of career Coast Guardsmen.

Just as the announcement was piped to the radio shack, Chief Rothman showed up, closely followed by Starns.

"Chief, why would the Exec want to see me?" I asked. "I haven't been on liberty in a week. "

"Search me. Maybe to give you a medal or something, for not fuckin' up lately."

"Ha, ha," I said, deadpan.

"Maybe ole Archibald How has come up with somethin' on you," said Stuart. "He spends most of his time trying to get somethin' on me."

I stood up, straightened myself, buttoned the sleeves of my dungarees, and headed out. Despite the scuttlebutt, I was convinced that the Old Man wanted me to shipover. Mr. How also seemed to like me, something that Stuart could not understand. The ensign was on his case all the time, but not once had he snapped or snarled at me.

At the Exec's stateroom door, I tapped three times, lightly. It was opened by a mess attendant. I entered and came to attention before Lt. Comdr. Branden, who was seated at his desk. I gave my name and rating.

"Hall," he said, studying a sheet of paper, "I've been looking over your record of service." There was a slight arching of one eyebrow, as he lowered it, peering at me. "It seems to me that you have kept quite busy in the short time you've been in the Service. I might even say that it's been rather remarkable that you could have covered so much ground in just under two years. Do you agree?"

"Yes, Sir."

"Is everything going all right for you in the Communications Department?"

"Oh, yes, Sir."

"Good. Do you like your work, in the radioroom?"

"Very much, Sir."

"Have you thought about reënlisting? Your term is just about up, you know."

"No, Sir." Then I hastily added, "I mean, yes, Sir, I know my time is just about up. But I haven't given any thought to reënlisting. I plan to return to college, Sir."

The commander studied my face for a time, nodding thoughtfully. "Hasn't the Coast Guard treated you rather well, considering?"

"I've been treated fine, Sir, aboard the *Storis*."

"It's commendable that you wish to finish college, Hall," he said, nodding. "But let me suggest that you give some serious consideration to a second hitch in the Service. The Communications Officer and Chief Rothman have said good things about your work since you came aboard. And it is my opinion, as well as the Captain's, that it would be a mistake for you to return to civilian life at this time."

"Yes, Sir."

"If you return to college, what do you plan to do afterward? You tried civilian life once and it didn't work for you. Stay in the Coast Guard and you have my word you'll be advanced quickly to First Class."

His words stunned me, to say the least. I *had his word*? I had never heard an officer make such a statement.

"*Advanced*, Sir? To First Class?"

"As soon as is possible," he said, nodding. "I'll personally guarantee you Radioman First Class within the required minimum time."

Within the required minimum time. These words rang through my head. The commander had completely protected his butt. Yet, on his face I could see written the assurance that I would jump at such an offer.

"Thank you, Sir. But I intend to return to school."

"Once you become Radioman First Class you'll be looking at Chief! Within a matter of a very few years you could be wearing a Chief's cap and be Radioman-in-Charge aboard the *Storis!*"

Now, I was seeing something else on the XO's face. I wasn't certain what it was.

We stared at each other. I had the distinct feeling that he had been given a task for which he had very little enthusiasm. Perhaps the Skipper had instructed him to recruit me, butter me up. My head was reeling with the implications of this interview. And regardless of how it turned out, I considered it a compliment that the XO had gone out of his way to ask me to stay in the Service.

"Well, Hall, you've still got a little time. Give it some serious thought."

"Yes, Sir! And thank you, Sir."

The CGC Storis, breaking ice (Courtesy of Fred's Place)

The Hooligan

———— ◆ ————

The crew of the CGC *Storis* had settled into an inviable routine. Most of the time the ship remained tied up at its own private dock, and the crew spent the mornings cleaning and painting and doing chores that were required to keep the ship seaworthy. After noon chow, almost the entire crew was free to go on liberty or do whatever they pleased as long as they stayed within whistle-distance of the ship.

One short blast of the whistle was the signal to stay alert for a possible departure; two meant return to the ship within the hour; and three long blasts meant return double-time it to the ship.

Occasionally, the *Storis* would be called upon to break ice in one of the countless coves and inlets up and down the Passage, the purpose invariably being to free some stranded fishing boat. The huge, specially-designed engines, operated alternately, were capable of making the ship do a hop-and-jump across the ice, slamming the heavy bow first to the right and then to the left. And while this action put an end to most coffee-drinking in the messdeck, it was our ticket to all of the coves in that part of the world.

As the ship entered a frozen cove from the turbulent ocean, there the lonely fishing boat would be, sticking out of the great table of white ice like an obscene deformity, completely unable to move in any direction. Generally, it would be without power, and the men aboard would be half-frozen. As we moved in close to the fishing boat, the depth of the ice would increase, causing the icebreaker to buck ever higher and higher. Aboard the icebreaker, we would grit our teeth and wait for the bucking to stop. Those on the frozen bridge would observe the endless expanse of brilliant white surface, calculating the time it would take to wham and bang a passageway to the stranded men.

The surface of the inlet would be as flat as an airfield and sturdy enough to drive an Army tank across.

To me the whole procedure, from the initial hustle and bustle at the dock and the urgent preparation to cast off all lines to the dash out into the Passage and finally the actual sighting of the poor souls in the little hidden cove—was better than a John Wayne movie. In addition to the drama and suspense involved in the ultimate rescue of the victims, our own collective necks were on the line. These dashes into the dark (Invariably, we were needed late at night and in the worst weather imaginable) were for real, not someone's idea of what was real.

It was one thing, I told myself, to observe the cruel and dangerous world of ice from the comfort of the icebreaker, which was in its element in this place, but quite another to be stranded in a tiny boat without warmth from any source. So my heart always went out to the stranded victims.

I never tired of watching the final approach and seeing the excited and happy faces of those we rescued, who would thank us a thousand times for coming *just in the nick of time*, hugging the steaming mugs of coffee handed to them once they were aboard. After the icebreaker had completely circled the boat and was back in its cleared path, the deck gang would attach a tow line to the bow of the fishing boat, and the cutter would then return to the unfrozen (and almost invariably quite choppy) waters of the Passage.

Instead of dreading the calls for our services, most of the crew actually came to enjoy the break from the regular routine. Juneau, as a liberty port for lonely sailors, left something to be desired. There were no unattached women, no houses of prostitution, and very few taverns.

And once the possibilities of the little town were exhausted, there was little to look forward to within commuting distance. Douglas, a fishing village not far away could be reached by ferry; but it was too far to go on foot, and Juneau had only one taxicab! And, after Herculean efforts to reach this Mecca, there was only one functioning bar and, from time to time, one woman, the Eskimo spouse of the bar owner!

About the time the little group of radiomen and quartermasters from the *Storis*, of which I was one, tired of spending our evenings at the *Triangle*, Ted Johnson discovered that the local high school had a basketball team.

Starns developed a bad case of ulcers and was returned to the States His replacement turned out to be Bill Townes, a kindred soul from Beaumont, Texas. Unlike every Texan I ever knew, Bill was quiet natured, soft spoken and unassuming. And since he liked to play basketball, he naturally became a part of the gang that included Stuart, Ted Johnson, me, and an Irish cutup named Chuck O'Neal.

Townes and O'Neal had one important thing in common with Johnson and me: They had played varsity basketball in high school.

The four of us, with the blessings of the XO, fell into the habit of spending our evenings there watching the local team play visiting schools. All of the competition had to fly in from great distances, places like Anchorage, Ketchikan, Fairbanks, Cordova, and White Horse; so the out-of-town teams always arrived with a great deal of fanfare. Most of the time, there were unscheduled games between the Juneau High School *Wildcats* and independent teams, like the one we organized.

We called ourselves *The Hooligans*, and we could never settle upon a mascot.

Stuart was not interested in competitive sports, but for the lack of something better to do he did occasionally go with us to the gym.

       *   *   *

It was at one of the conference games, a very important event in
Juneau, that I ran into an old Coastie buddy from my *Roger B. Taney*
days. The former Radioman First Class Dudley Sears materialized
before me in a U. S. Army uniform! I was on the sidelines with Townes
and Johnson and suddenly a big hand whammed down on my shoulder
from above.

"Red, I know I shouldn't be surprised to see you up here in Alaska—
but I am just the same!"

I whirled around, trying unsuccessfully to place the voice. There
standing on the second row of the bleachers was old Sears, now an
Army sergeant! He appeared to be by himself.

"Sears? You shipped over to the Army?"

"Hey, don't make it sound like I committed a crime! They made me
an offer I couldn't refuse." He stuck out his hand. "And you're on that
big icebreaker down at the docks!"

I was dazed. To think that a former CPO in the Coast Guard,
reduced to the permanent rank of First Class Radioman after the war,
had chosen the Army! We shook hands and I introduced him to
Johnson and Townes.

"But I'm really not all that surprised to see you at a basketball game!"
he laughed. "Remember telling me all that stuff about your basketball
career?"

He was referring to one particular evening we had spent on the bow
of the *Taney* while on Weather Patrol, during which I had told him in
great detail about qualifying for varsity basketball in three different
high schools.

"Sorry about that, Chief—I mean Sarge! But what are you doing in
the Army? I mean what made you become a turncoat?"

"Well, as you know, I had *had* it right up to here, in what you used to
call the *Hooligan Navy!*" He grinned, pointing to his chin. "Man, in that
outfit once the brass get something on you your goose is cooked from
then on. It's like a goddamned country club, with the officers knowing

each other and exchanging information to each other about the *peons* who keep the machines oiled and the wheels turning. But you ought to know that better than I would! Nobody ever got a rawer deal than you."

"Right now," I laughed, "things are going pretty good for me. My time's about up and, who knows, I may just ship over." After I lined up Townes and Johnson, the only members of my group present, and introduced them to him, I asked, "What are you actually doing up here? What's your specialty?"

"I, my boy, am the Chief Message Handler in this area for the U. S. Army Signal Corps. Don't laugh, because it's a very responsible job."

"I'm impressed, I'm impressed!" I said, looking around at Townes and Johnson. "This guy has done all right for himself!"

Sears hastily raised a hand for attention. "Well, I lost a rank in the shift from the Coast Guard to the Army. But the money's about the same as before and there's no comparison between my present job and standing four-on and eight-off on the *Taney.*" He grabbed my shoulders and faced me: "Listen, Red, I want you to meet Virginia, my little hen-huzzy! As soon as the game's over, let's cut out, okay? I want to show you my home, too. Bring your friends along, okay?"

I glanced at Townes and Johnson and they nodded.

Johnson sang out, "Yeah, heck yes!"

Townes' reply was, "How often does a lonely sailor get invited to a soldier's home in remote Alaska?"

As the game ended, Sears grabbed my arm and headed for an exit, beckoning to the other two. I had never seen him so lively and excited. Obviously, he was quite proud of his new wife and his new home.

"How can you afford a house and a wife?" I wanted to know.

"You'd be surprised," he said, ushering across the frozen parking lot to his brand-new Ford sedan. "Believe it or not, but everybody in Juneau, with the possible exception of some of the Eskimos, has a car of some kind. And on a Saturday afternoon in the summer time, we have traffic jams downtown!"

"Come on!" scoffed Johnson, who had settled into the back seat with Townes. "Somebody told me there was only five miles of highway attached to this town."

"That's about it!" laughed Sears.

Within five minutes we had slipped and slid our way to a street of small tract homes. All had narrow driveways, ice-covered, at the end of which were tiny one-car garages. Sears parked the car at the curb of one of these bungalows and turned the motor off.

"This is it!" he laughed. "Looks a little barren right now, but don't let all this ice and snow fool you. In the spring and summer this is one beautiful little homestead. And just wait till you meet Jenny!"

By this time I had decided that the woman we were about to meet had to be a combination of Miss America and Joan of Arc!

While we were standing on the slippery front yard surveying the house and grounds, Townes wanted to know how Sears had come by all this. He sounded genuinely curious.

"If hamburgers are fifty cents apiece, this must have cost a mint!"

"It's not bad," admitted Sears, pleased. "Maybe a little expensive. But every bit of it was worth the money. Wait till you meet the wifey."

Virginia was suddenly standing in the front door yelling at Sears to get his ass inside before he froze it off. She said nothing at all to us as we filed inside, but we were soon to learn that she was not at all unhappy to see us.

Immediately, even before we had a good look at her, we learned two things about Sears' wife, that she was an *outspoken woman* and that she had a real gift with language.

"What the hell you draggin' people in here this time of night for, Dud?" she demanded, good-naturedly. "Am I blind or are them Coast Guard uniforms?" She grabbed my right arm and stared at the shield. "Yep, this one's a hooligan, all right!"

Sears nodded at me and said to Virginia, "Remember hearing me go on about a guy named Red, on the *Taney?* Well, Honey, I want you to meet the one and only Red."

"I guess I ought to remember!" laughed Virginia. "Wasn't he the fart that gave you the migraine headaches and finally drove you out of the Coasties?"

"Now, Jenny, cut out the kiddin'! Red might take you seriously."

"Shut the door, Arkansawer!" she shouted at Townes, who was lingering in the little entrance hall. "Before the house loses all its heat! Besides, I want to get a close look at you! Which one of these handsome young fellers gets to go to bed with me first?"

"She's a great kidder, fellas," laughed Sears, blushing. "Don't pay any attention to her."

She had to be about ten years older than Sears, I decided, once I got a good look at her face. Which would put her close to forty, I calculated. And it was plain to see that she had been down some rough roads.

She let go of Townes and lined up on me, in the center of the livingroom. I noticed that she was barefooted and sockless. Without shame or apology, she stared straight into my eyes, having to tilt her head only slightly—which, I calculated, made her just about six feet tall! And, to add to her attractions, she was wearing close-fitting jeans!

At that point, I began to notice her figure. It was suddenly quite clear to me why Sears was convinced he had a thing of rare beauty, why he had been blind to any possible age difference between them or, indeed, any shortcomings the woman might have. She was built like a youthful Raquel Welch, only on a much grander scale!

I swallowed and glanced at Ted Johnson, who was standing beside me taking in the attributes, his Adam's Apple going up and down. And before I could stop myself I laughed out loud! Married perhaps two months, Johnson was gawking at Jenny's half-exposed breasts, which, unhampered by any kind of restraint, seemed about to burst out of her shirt!

"Aint she an eye full?" asked Sears.

"Gawd," gulped Ted, nodding. "I mean, uh, you really did find—uh—!"

"Yeah," agreed soft-spoken Bill Townes, moving closer.

"Yall stop gaping and talkin' about me like I wasn't even here!" laughed Jenny. "Ever' woman's got basically the same things." After a pause for that to soak in, she snickered, "I just happen to have developed 'em a little more'n some."

It suddenly occurred to me with a shock that we were discussing this woman's body and that she was participating in the discussion without shame! Where, I wondered, could this possibly go?

"Yeah," said Bill, his breathing audible now, "but you got more than your share!"

"Aint you boys had any since you been in town?"

At this I stopped breathing, astonished that she had said that. A woman just did not discuss the sex needs of her husband's friends and acquaintances—at least not in his presence!

Jenny had been moving constantly since we had entered the house, pivoting about, nudging us with her hips, slapping us on the backs and the buttocks. Suddenly, as she turned to go toward the kitchen, four pairs of eyes became fixed upon her over-generous, inverted-heart-shaped bottom, as it rapidly disappeared through the swinging door! In her wake there was only the sound of Bill's heavy breathing.

"How do you keep other men away from her?" sighed Ted, shaking his head incredulously. There was no humor in his voice.

"Aw, you fellas are just weakened from such a prolonged abstinence. Has the cook run out of saltpeter?"

"I'll bet you don't let her out of the house," suggested Bill.

Perhaps an hour later, after several bourbon-and-coke highballs, I found himself alone with Jenny in the kitchen. She had asked me to help her with a fresh round of drinks; and, once we were alone in the kitchen, she seemed to fill the place with her hips, arms, shoulders, breasts. Every time I moved, it seemed, I touched some part of her.

"Dud tells me you've got a girl you're real sweet on in the States," she said, rubbing one of her breasts against my elbow. Up close she didn't look all that bad, I realized. And everything about her except her face looked young and healthy. "You poor dear, it must be hard coming way up here and leavin' your little sweetie back home."

"It is that," I said, trying to move back a bit.

"Listen, I know how it gets *with a man*, when he can't get any. Dud is always bowling on Thursday nights, so why don't you drop by and tell me all about yourself and your love life?"

My heart had stopped beating, along with my breathing.

"Do you think you can you make it, honey?" Without waiting for an answer, she picked up the tray of drinks and carried them out to the livingroom.

Later, as the three of us prepared to leave, Sears stopped us at the front door and said, "It's coming up Christmas pretty soon, fellas. How about having dinner with us on Christmas Eve? Right, Jenny?"

"I'd be madder'n hell if they didn't."

*　　　　*　　　　*

A few nights later in the crew's quarters Townes, from the bunk above me, said, "Hey, Red, that Jenny's some woman, huh?"

"*Some woman* doesn't even begin to describe her," I said with a laugh. "Although there is such a thing as too much of a good thing."

"Did she—invite you to drop in on her?"

Startled, I leaned out of my bunk and looked up at him. "What do you mean? She and Sears both asked us to visit again."

"Yeah, I know, but Ted was invited to drop by on Tuesday nights and I was invited for Saturday nights. So we figured you must've got an invite for some other night. Which was it, Thursday?"

For a time I just lay there, laughing uncontrollably. When I could, I said, "Sears is so proud of her."

"Old Sears knows all about what she's doin'."

"What!" I leaned out of my bunk again. "Come on, Bill. That's not true!"

"Oh, yeah? Ted took her up on her offer night before last, and when they got past the amenities, she told him she'd need a twenty. *For wear-and-tear* was the way she put it. He gave her a twenty, they consummated the business, and when Ted was headed for the door she told him not to worry about Dud, that he knew exactly when to come home."

That took the wind out of me for a time. Finally, I said, "You mean Ted actually took her up on it? He's a newlywed."

"Red, there are not many men in this world that could turn that woman down! Ted's walking around in a daze, acting like he's drugged. All he'll say is, "Gawd!"

"So you're going over on Saturday night?"

"You're damned right. And I'm going to stay all night! Sears has gone down to the States for a week."

*   *   *

On December 15, I received my second summons to the Exec's stateroom. Lt. Comdr. Branden met me himself at the door with a big smile on his face.

"Thought you might like a Christmas present, Hall."

"I don't understand, Sir."

Since my initial encounter with the commander, I had done a lot of thinking about my situation back home, which included my relationship with Jamie, the iffiness of college and throwing in with civilians, and to the Exec's offer. If I went home for good, I would quite logically get married, if not to Jamie then to Darleen, Jody, or Alice. In other words, *I would have to settle down*, a thought that never failed to give me the cold chills. Also, I would have to get a steady job, buy a house, borrow money, worry about the economy. Children would then begin to appear, and, by that time, *freedom* would be only a word in the dictionary.

Lt. Comdr. Branden turned and went to his desk and picked up a sheet of paper. "This just came from District Headquarters, young man! Relax and have a chair." He appeared to be reading what was on the paper. "Have you given my proposition some thought?"

"Yes, Sir, I have."

The smile was back. He waved the paper at me. "In exactly one year you'll be eligible to apply for Radioman First Class."

I wanted to ask if I could see that in writing. But all I could get out was, "Thank you, Sir."

"Furthermore, if you're serious about shipping over, I think I can arrange a thirty-day leave so that you can go see that girlfriend of yours. How would you like that?"

"Yes, Sir, I would like that." Did he think I was stupid? Everybody received at least thirty days leave upon reënlisting. "But, Sir, I was thinking I might go home for a couple of months and then maybe join up again sometime next spring."

*   *   *

Later that day I ran into Sgt. Sears in downtown Juneau. I had walked into town to find gifts for my four girlfriends and kid sister and had just realized that I would need to send wires to them and my parents that I would soon be arriving home. I was entering the drug store when Sears' happy voice called out, "Hey, Red, wait up!"

Although Townes and Johnson had relayed a number of messages to me from Sears and Jenny, I had not replied to any of them.

"Hey, old buddy, I've missed the hell out of you! Where've you been?"

"Busy," I said, grinning. "How have things been with you and your wife?"

"Jenny, man! That's her name! Aren't we on better terms than that? She talks about you a lot and wants you to drop by and visit us. Listen, we're expecting you for dinner on Christmas Eve, all right? You and Bill and Ted. We'll party like hell!"

"I'll try," I said. "Say, could you tell me how I could send a wire to the States? I've looked all over for Western Union."

"You're lookin' at Western Union, man! Come with me."

I felt off-balance walking beside Sears. Here was a man I had totally misread, and I felt certain there was still a great deal more to know about him. If a man will sell the services of his wife, what will he not do? We went two blocks down the street and, with Sears leading and talking all the time, made a right and entered a stone building with a big U. S. Army sign outside.

"You want to send a telegram to the little sweetie back home?"

"Well, actually, I'd like to wire flowers—to three girls."

"My God! Three?" After a good laugh, he added, "That can be arranged. My staff does that all the time."

As we entered a large room filled with bustling people in civilian clothes, the anxious and convincing voice of Eddie Arnold filled the place: "Give me one dozen roses—and send them to the one I love!"

"Martha, will you take care of this young fellow?" Sears called out. "Don't forget, Red!" With that the sergeant lifted a section of the long counter and joined the civilians. "See you on Christmas Eve!"

Martha moved down the counter and took a position in front of me. She handed me a yellow pad and a pencil, smiling. "Hello there, sailor. Are you missing someone?"

"Yes, I am," I said, smiling. "Is it possible for me to send a dozen yellow roses to three addresses in the States?"

"Do they all live in the same town, does that town have a florist, and do you have an account with that florist?"

"Maybe I will just send three telegrams."

"Yes, of course." She handed me a pad of blank telegram forms.

Back at the ship I ran onto Stuart Heller in the radioroom listening to Vaughn Monroe. Without a word I removed two twenty-dollar bills from my wallet and handed them to him.

"What's this for?" he asked with raised eyebrows.

"Figure it out for yourself."

He took the money and pocketed it. "Well, that was one sucker bet all right, but for once I wasn't the sucker! What changed your mind?"

"Think about it. I've got four girlfriends back home, every one of whom is beautiful and thinks I'm going to marry her. If I get out of the Service, I'll be on the lam for bigamy within a month."

"Does that mean the trip to Douglas is on for tonight? Olson wants to go along with us to keep down trouble."

"I'll go on one condition."

"What condition?"

"That we drink nothing but hard liquor and check out all the women."

"Does Douglas have any women?"

THE END

About the Author

◆

Wesley Hall, now retired from teaching, lives in Holly Springs, Mississippi, with his wife, Sharon. Surrounded by an almost impenetrable forest of hardwoods on a ten-acre estate just outside town, they grow wine grapes and lavender and all shapes and sizes of sunflowers (and whatever else reminds them of Provence).

Printed in the United States
869500002B